THE YELLOW ADMIRAL

The sails of a square-rigged ship, hung out to dry in a calm.

1 Flying jib
2 Jib
3 Fore topmast staysail
4 Fore staysail
5 Foresail, or course
6 Fore topsail
7 Fore topgallant
8 Mainstaysail
9 Maintopmast staysail
10 Middle staysail
11 Main topgallant staysail

12 Mainsail, or course
13 Maintopsail
14 Main topgallant
15 Mizzen staysail
16 Mizzen topmast staysail
17 Mizzen topgallant staysail
18 Mizzen sail
19 Spanker
20 Mizzen topsail
21 Mizzen topgallant

Illustration source: Serres, Liber Nauticus.
Courtesy of The Science and Technology Research Center,
The New York Public Library, Astor, Lenox, and Tilden Foundations

THE YELLOW
ADMIRAL

Patrick O'Brian

W•W•Norton & Company
New York   London

For information about permission to reproduce selections from this book,
write to Permissions, W. W. Norton & Company, Inc., 500 Fifth Avenue,
New York, NY 10110.

Library of Congress Cataloging-in-Publication Data

O'Brian, Patrick, 1914—
    The yellow admiral / Patrick O'Brian.
        p.   cm.
    ISBN 0-393-04044-5
    1. Great Britain—History, Naval—19th century—Fiction.
    2. Maturin, Stephen (Fictitious character)—Fiction. 3.
    Aubrey, Jack (Fictitious character)—Fiction.   I. Title
PR6029.B55Y45   1996
823'.914—dc20   96-24149 CIP

ISBN 0-393-31704-8 pbk.

W.W. Norton & Company, Inc., 500 Fifth Avenue, New York, NY 10110
http://www.wwnorton.com
W.W. Norton & Company Ltd., 10 Coptic Street, London WC1A 1PU

1 2 3 4 5 6 7 8 9 0

FOR MARY, WITH LOVE

THE YELLOW ADMIRAL

Chapter One

Sir Joseph Blaine, a heavy, yellow-faced man in a suit of grey clothes and a flannel waistcoat, walked down St James's Street, across the park, and so to the Admiralty, which he entered from behind, opening the private door with a key and making his way to the large, shabby room in which he had his official being.

He looked over the papers on his desk, nodded, and touched the bell. 'If Mr Needham is in the way, pray show him up,' he said to the answering clerk. He half rose as Needham appeared and waved him to a comfortable chair on the other side of the desk. 'Having finished with poor Delaney,' he said, 'we now come to another gentleman of whom we have no news: Stephen Maturin. Dr Stephen Maturin, perhaps our most valuable adviser on Spanish affairs.'

'I do not think I have heard his name.'

'I do not suppose you have: yet you and your people have quite certainly found his cipher at the foot of many a cogent report. When he is going up and down in the world on our behalf, as he so often does . . .' Sir Joseph stifled an 'or did' and carried on, 'he almost invariably sails with Captain Aubrey, whose name is no doubt familiar.'

'Oh, certainly,' said Needham, who wished to make a good impression on this formidable figure, but whose talents did not really lie in that direction. 'The gentleman who was so unfortunate at the Guildhall trial.' This reference to Captain Aubrey's stand in the pillory did not seem to be well received and to remedy the situation Needham added a knowing 'Son to the notorious General Aubrey.'

'If you wish,' said Sir Joseph coldly. 'Yet he might also

be described as the officer who, commanding a fourteen-gun brig, took a thirty-two-gun Spanish xebec-frigate and carried her into Mahon in the year one; who cut out the French frigate *Diane* in a boat-attack on the heavily guarded port of Saint-Martin; and who, most recently, returning with his squadron from a most active cruise against slavery in the Gulf of Guinea, utterly frustrated the French descent on the south of Ireland, driving a line-of-battle ship on the rocks, to saying nothing of . . . Yes, Mr Carling?' – this to a secretary.

'The pardons, sir, engrossed at last,' said Carling, laying them on Sir Joseph's desk. 'Those you asked for particularly are on top.' He made his usual ghost-like exit.

Sir Joseph glanced at their effective date, well before Maturin's departure for Spain, nodded and went on, 'To revert to Dr Maturin, for whom we here are particularly concerned, and on behalf of whom we should value any assistance your people can give us – one of these,' – holding up a parchment – 'refers to him. You probably know more about the late Duke of Habachtsthal than I do, the kind of men he privately mixed with, and the creatures he employed for some of his activities.'

'We have a very great deal of material. And the creatures, as you so justly call them, were the immediate cause of his self-murder.'

'Yes.' Blaine paused, and said, 'I will not make a long story of it, with circumstantial details, but only observe that he had conceived a hatred for Maturin, who had been the death of two of the friends in question, putting an end to their traitorous practices; and the creatures Habachtsthal employed about his revenge found out that before the Irish rising of ninety-eight he had been a friend of Lord Edward Fitzgerald, that he had committed some indiscretions in favour of Irish independence, and that with the help of hired Dublin informers and fresh evidence he might yet be taken up on a capital charge. Furthermore, he had brought back two transported convicts from Botany Bay before their time and without leave. Ordinarily I should have dealt with this situation much as you dealt with William Hervey's case; but with such high-placed and influential enmity, I dared not move for fear of making things even worse. Instead, I advised him to withdraw privately to Spain, together with his protégés and his fortune, which was liable to forfeiture on such a charge. This he did, adding his little daughter to the company. Not his wife, who happened to be in Ireland – I believe there were certain difficulties, since accommodated. All this, you understand, was before the cruise in the Gulf . . .'

'Dr Maturin took part in the expedition?'

'Certainly. Not only was it his duty as the *Bellona*'s surgeon but he is passionately opposed to slavery.' Needham pursed his lips and shrugged. 'He is also an eminent naturalist, one of our best authorities on comparative anatomy.' In more liberal company Sir Joseph might have spoken of the paper on pottos, with particular reference to their anomalous phalanges, that Dr Maturin had read to the Royal Society and the sensation it had caused among those capable both of hearing what he said and of appreciating the full import of what they heard: in the present circumstances he carried straight on. This meeting was wholly necessary from departmental and political points of view, and the files available to Needham might be of great and immediate value in spite of the man's limited intelligence; yet the interview was in no way congenial and Sir Joseph could not wish it prolonged. 'A few days before the returning squadron reached Bantry Bay, Habachtsthal killed himself: opposition no longer existed and I at once took the necessary steps, obtaining immediate consent for the pardon. I sent over an express telling him that all was well and that he might gather his family and wealth as soon as he chose. He came back to England, accompanied by his wife, and they both set off by the shortest route, Mrs Maturin being subject to the seasickness, with the intention of posting down to the Groyne to make arrangements for the transfer of his fortune – all in gold, by the way – to this country and then of picking up the protégés and the child at Avila.'

3

'Where is Avila?'

'In Old Castile. Eight days after he left we had information from one of our best agents that he had been denounced to the Spanish government as the prime mover in the Peruvian conspiracy – in the Peruvian attempt at declaring themselves independent of Spain.'

'Was there any truth in the denunciation?'

'Yes, there was.'

'Oh,' cried Needham, deeply impressed. And then, 'It very nearly succeeded, according to our information.'

'Very nearly indeed. A matter of a few hours and we should have been home, home hands down, but for a silly, busy, prating, enthusiastic fool, a prisoner of war who escaped from Aubrey's ship and ran up and down in Lima calling out that Maturin was a British agent – that the revolution was paid for by English gold. At the last moment the cry was taken up by the French mission, sent there on the same errand but with inadequate funds, and they made such a noise that the leading general cried off and Maturin had to leave the country. This wretched Dutourd reached Spain a little while ago – and they asked us for an explanation.'

'You denied everything, of course?'

Sir Joseph bowed. 'But it was clear they did not believe us. They clapped an embargo on his money in Corunna and they meant to seize him when he went to collect it. I sent warnings by three several agents and telegraphed Plymouth for the fastest cutter to take a message to our man in Corunna itself. We had a few reports of his passage, chiefly from military intelligence, the last being a dubious account of a wealthy pair with an escort travelling through Aragon in a coach and four: then nothing. Nothing whatsoever: all traces lost. And the Aragon report was geographically improbable, since it would have been right off his route. Then again, although Maturin is a wealthy man, an uncommonly wealthy man, he never gives that appearance, being habitually threadbare and always inconspicuous. Your people have some contacts in Spain that we do not as yet possess, and if they can throw any light whatsoever on the subject, we should be most grateful.'

'I shall of course do everything in my power.'

'Many thanks. He has been much on my mind. A pearl of an agent – totally unmercenary – polyglot – a natural philosopher with innumerable contacts among the learned abroad – a man with a profession that introduced him everywhere – a physician is welcome everywhere – and a Catholic, which is such a recommendation in the greater part of the world.'

'A Roman and trustworthy?' asked Needham, with another worldly look.

'Yes, sir,' said Blaine, touching a private bell under the desk with his foot. 'And in the very first place I should have said that he utterly abhors all tyranny – Buonaparte's above any.'

The door opened. Carling glided in, and bending respectfully over Sir Joseph he said, 'I do beg your pardon, sir, but the First Lord particularly desires a word.'

'Is it urgent?'

'I am afraid so, Sir Joseph.'

'Mr Needham, sir, I must crave your indulgence,' said Blaine, rising with something of an effort. 'But fortunately we have reached a natural term in our most interesting and valuable conversation. May I hope to hear from you in due course?'

'Certainly, sir: without fail. Tomorrow at the latest.'

Stephen was still in Sir Joseph's mind as he walked back to his house in Shepherd Market – a walk much insisted upon by Dr Maturin, who distrusted both the colour of Blaine's face and the eminently palpable state of his liver. Stephen was one of the few men Sir Joseph cordially liked; it was true that they had many tastes in common – music, entomology, the Royal Society, excellent wine, and they both *hated* Napoleon – but there was also that particular sympathy and mutual respect which transformed such . . . he hesitated for the word – shared interests, inclinations, traits, characteristics – into something of another order entirely. At the corner of St James's Street the usual crossing-sweeper was waiting to see him across Piccadilly with a waving broom: 'Thank you, Charles,' he said, handing him his weekly fourpence. On the other side, by the White Horse, a man was carefully extracting a woman from a carriage, a very handsome woman indeed; and as Blaine walked along Half Moon Street he found that he was reflecting on Stephen's marriage. Stephen had married a woman more handsome by far, the kind of woman Blaine loved to gaze upon – the kind he would have loved to marry had he met her and had he possessed the courage, the presence, and the fortune. How Maturin, who possessed even less presence and at that time no fortune whatsoever, had presumed so far he could not tell ... yet again and again she had made him bitterly unhappy, he said inwardly; and as his feet carried him towards his own doorstep the words 'Handsome is as handsome does' crossed his mind, although he was very fond of Diana, and greatly admired her spirit.

Musing, he walked with his head bowed. The three well-worn steps came within his field of vision; he was conscious of a slight form standing at his door itself, and then of Stephen's face smiling down at him. 'Oh, oh!' he cried in a voice more like that of a startled ewe than of the Director of Naval Intelligence. 'Stephen, your name was in my mouth. You are as welcome as the first Red Admiral in spring. How do you do, my dear sir? How do you do? Walk in, if you please, and tell me how you do.'

Stephen walked in, shepherded with a surprising amount of fuss – surprising in so reserved and phlegmatic a man as Sir Joseph – along that familiar corridor to the even more familiar, comfortable, book-lined, Turkey-carpeted room in which they had so often sat. A cheerful fire was already burning, and Sir Joseph at once stirred it to a still livelier blaze. Turning, he shook Stephen's hand again. 'What may I offer you?' he asked. 'A dish of tea? No, you despise tea. Coffee? A glass of Sillery? No? I will not be importunate.

You look wonderfully well, if I may be so personal. Wonderfully well. And I had been seeing you in a Spanish prison, pale, unshaved, thin, ragged, verminous.' He felt the force of Stephen's pale, questioning eye and went on, 'That reptile Dutourd reached Spain and denounced you. Gonzalez, who knew something of your activities in Catalonia, believed him, sequestered your treasure in Corunna and gave orders that you were to be taken up the moment you came to gather it. This I learned from Wall and other wholly reliable sources a week after you had left. You cannot imagine the efforts I made to warn you or the quantities of coca-leaves I devoured to keep my wits active . . . and now to see you sitting there, apparently perfectly well and quite unmoved, almost makes me feel ill-used, indignant. Though in parenthesis I must thank you yet again for those blessed leaves: I have a reliable supply from an apothecary in Greek Street. May I offer you a quid?'

'You are very good, but were I to indulge, the insensibility about my pharynx would persist until early supper-time, a meal I particularly wish to enjoy. And then I wish to sleep tonight.'

A pause, and Blaine said, 'I will not be so indiscreet as to ask whether you had other and earlier sources of information.'

'I had not,' said Stephen, whose mind was yet to grasp the full extent and all the implications of Sir Joseph's news. 'Faith, I had not. My safety, our safety, depended, under Providence, Saint Patrick, Stephen the Protomartyr, and Saint Brendan, solely upon my own ineptitude, my own gross ineptitude: I might even say inefficiency. Will I tell you about it?'

'If you would be so good,' said Blaine, moving his chair closer.

'It does me no credit at all, at all: but since you have been to such pains I owe you an account, however bald and inadequate. We landed on a sweet calm day, and Diana having recovered from what slight remains of the sea-sickness still hung about her, we took coach and travelled

7

westward along the coast. There was a good inn at Laredo, where we ate some hundreds of new-run infant eels two inches long and took our ease; and when we were arranging our baggage for the next stage in a fine new carriage that was to take us all the way, Diana, a far better traveller than I – a more orderly mind where packing is concerned – suggested that I should make sure that everything was in place for our arrival at Corunna. Proper clothes for waiting on the governor, hair-powder, my best wig, and above all the elaborately signed and countersigned acknowledgement that the Bank of the Holy Ghost and of Commerce had received the specified number of chests containing the stated weight of gold and would deliver it up on the production of this document. Everything was in place – satin breeches, red-heeled shoes, powder, silver-hilted sword – everything but this infernal piece of paper. I blush to own it,' said Maturin, his sallow face in fact changing colour as a pinkness rose from his lower cheeks to his forehead, disappearing under his wig, a physical bob, 'I am ashamed to say it, but I could not find the wretched thing.'

Against all his principles Blaine cried out, 'You will never tell me you lost the bank's receipt for all that gold, Stephen? *Lost it?* I beg your pardon . . .'

Stephen shook his head. 'I turned over innumerable other sheets – ornithological notes I had brought for a friend, the Archdeacon of Gijon, and many, many others – turned them again, formed them into heaps, sorted the heaps – Joseph, the tongue of angels could not tell you the degree of frustration. And I had not the face to attempt the impossible task of persuading the Holy Ghost and Commerce to yield that treasure on my mere unsupported word.'

'No, indeed,' said Blaine, deeply shocked.

'The Dear knows, and *you* know, that it was in fact all for the best,' said Stephen, 'yet I was very near cursing the day. But, however, I did not quite do so, because in the course of the night an inner voice said, as distinctly as the small beast in the Revelation of Saint John the Divine, "Poor worm: think on Latham", and my mind was at ease

8

directly – I slept until sunrise, waking with the name Latham still in my ears.'

'Latham of the *Synopsis*?'

'Just so. Immediately before leaving I had leafed through a magnificently-bound copy of the *Synopsis*, the recent gift of –' he was about to say 'of Prince William' but changed it to 'a grateful patient' and went on '– a sadly muddled piece of work, I am afraid; though as laborious as Adanson.'

'I have no patience with Latham,' said Sir Joseph.

'I shall love him as long as I live, indifferent ornithologist though he be; for I knew with a total (and I may add subsequently justified) conviction that my receipt was between the pages of his *General Synopsis of Birds*. In the morning, therefore, I saw the mishap as an uncommonly well disguised blessing: not quite so much of a blessing as I now know from what you tell me; but a blessing still and all, and a great one. As you know, Diana and her daughter had not seen one another for some time – there had been certain difficulties . . .'

Sir Joseph bowed. He was perfectly aware that the child had been thought dumb, mentally deficient, impervious; and that Diana, unable to bear it, had gone away, leaving Brigid in the care of Clarissa Oakes. But an inclination of his head, a general murmur seemed the best form of response.

'And although the child is now living in this world and speaking with perfect fluency it occurred to me that the meeting would be far better, far easier, if everyone were in a coach, bounced together, seeing new things, unknown wonders, strange inns however bad, curious meals, fresh ways of dressing, always something to remark upon, to cry out at. Furthermore, I had always wanted to show both of them my Catalonia, and to consult Dr Llers of Barcelona, that eminent physician; though however he could improve the present Brigid I cannot tell. So since for immediate needs I had plenty of money without going to Corunna that wet and dismal town the back of my hand to it and all the thieves it harbours I sent a well-mounted courier away to Segovia, where Clarissa Oakes – you remember Clarissa Oakes, my dear?'

'Indeed I do, and the invaluable information she gave us: oh Heavens, yes. And in any case her formal pardon reached my desk today, together with yours and Padeen's.'

Stephen smiled and went on, 'To Segovia where Clarissa Oakes and Brigid were staying with my Alarcón cousins by way of a holiday. There we picked them up and I do assure you, Joseph, that I have never made a better-inspired move in my life. Clarissa and Diana had always agreed very well, and after a little shyness Brigid joined in, so that the coachful could have been heard talking and laughing a furlong off, particularly as Brigid so very often leaned out to call up to Padeen behind, desiring him to look at the brindled cow, at the great yoke of oxen, at the three children on one ass. Such weather we had, and such wonders we saw! I showed them the great colony of fulvous vultures beyond Llops and a distant bear on the slope of the Maladetta, bee-eaters by the hundred in the sandy banks of the Llobregat, and my own place under the Albères, where I brought Jack Aubrey out of France in '03. And there I found something that may please you. You know, of course, that in the micaceous schist of those parts the arbutus is a usual sight and that therefore Charaxes jasius, the Two-Tailed Pasha, is not so rare as he is elsewhere in Europe. It was the sight of one sailing by that brought you to mind.'

'Sailing by. Yes, indeed. On the few occasions I have seen him I have run with all my might, net outstretched; but all to no avail. And purchased specimens, though very well for comparison and study, are by no means the same thing. You might as well buy your quails and partridges from a game-dealer.'

'I was more fortunate. Behind Recasens, in what I might call my own back-yard, I watched one emerging from his chrysalis: I placed a bell-jar over him, let him spread his wings, assume his full glory, and then by night carried him in, cut him short with a painless waft, and so put him up for you.' Stephen brought a soft packet from his bosom, unwrapped it, and passed a small glass case.

After the briefest moment Blaine's happy, eager look changed. He said, 'You would never make game of me, Stephen? Not on such a subject?'

'Pray look closer. Pray turn him upside down. Pray compare him with those you have.'

Moving slowly, and with backward glances, Sir Joseph moved over to his cabinet, drawer after drawer of beautifully mounted insects. He held his present over the relevant specimens, and slowly, in a voice of wonder, he said, 'By God. It is a *melanistic* Charaxes: a perfect, wholly melanistic Charaxes jasius.' He turned the orthodox butterflies and his new acquisition over and over, holding them to the light and murmuring about the exact repetition of the pattern and the exact reversal. 'I never knew it occurred in Charaxes, Stephen – no books, no collection has ever recorded it. Oh Stephen, what a treasure! No wonder you clapped a bell-jar over him. God bless you, my dear friend. You could not have made me happier. I shall write a paper on him for the *Proceedings* – such a paper!' He went slowly back to his chair, privately turning the case in various directions and his face rosy with contentment.

But the recording part of his mind was still intent upon Stephen's account of this idyllic ramble through a variety of landscapes, all more or less torn by recent or even actual warfare. 'How I wish I had a better memory for geography,' he said. 'If we were at the Admiralty I could follow on a map; but as it is I cannot understand how you escaped from the raiding parties or foragers of either side, and from the notice of both military intelligence and our people.'

'It is almost impossible to explain without a chart, since we rarely steered the same course for more than two watches.' Dr Maturin, as a ship's surgeon, was rather fond of using nautical expressions, correct nautical expressions on occasion; and this he repeated with a certain emphasis before going on 'That is to say, we wandered in an unmethodical, even a whimsical fashion, guided by youthful recollections, by the prospect of a noble forest, by side-roads leading to the houses of remote friends or cousins: but when we have an enormous atlas before us I will do my best to retrace our journey. For the now, let me only observe that our path from Laredo to Segovia was far, far south of such dangerous parts as the neighbourhood of Santander or Pampeluna. To be sure, there were the signs of war in many a field, many a devastated village or shattered bridge; and it is true that there was a little trouble from English, Spanish and Portuguese stragglers on occasion, while once we saw a troop of French hussars pursued into the darkness of the upper Ebro by a numerous band of dragoons.'

'Were the ladies distressed?'

'Not that I observed.'

'No, on reflection. No, to be sure,' said Blaine, who had seen Diana driving a four-in-hand along the Stockbridge road and outgalloping the Salisbury Flyer itself, to the cheers of the passengers aboard, and who knew that Clarissa had been sent to Botany Bay for blowing a man's head off with a double-barrelled fowling-piece.

'But when we struck north into Catalonia I was among friends, protected by a network of intelligence. So having consulted dear Dr Llers, we viewed the estuary or rather the estuaries of the Ebro – such myriads of flamingoes, Joseph, with two spoonbills and a glossy ibis, all in the course of a single picnic – and so took ship from Valencia to Gibraltar, where we changed to the packet: as brilliant a voyage as could be imagined. Diana did not feel even the least uneasiness, and now we are all at the Grapes together, with Mrs Broad and the black children I brought from the South Sea, Sarah and Emily. Will you not come and sup with us? You would enjoy the little girls. They are so pleasant together – they play puss in the corner and hunt the slipper.'

'Ah? Indeed? Unhappily,' said Sir Joseph, 'unhappily I am engaged to supper at Black's.'

'Then let us walk along together. At this time of day it is the best place in London to find a hackney-coach setting down.'

'By all means,' said Blaine, 'but I believe I shall throw a very light greatcoat over my shoulders. There is a certain bite in the evening air.' He rang for his man-servant. It was his housekeeper however who answered and a little vexed he asked, 'But where is Treacher? I rang for Treacher.'

'He is not back yet, Sir Joseph.'

'Well, never mind. Pray fetch me my very light greatcoat. I am going to have supper at the club.'

'But Sir Joseph, the sweetbreads and asparagus . . .' she began: then checked herself.

They walked along very companionably, talking mostly about beetles, their almost infinite variety; and passing a house in Arlington Street Blaine said, 'That was where Hammersley lived, a very great collector. Did you ever meet him?'

'I believe not.'

'Yet he too was a member. We have had several far-travelled, learned members, eminent entomologists. I wish we had more. And speaking of Black's, have you seen Captain Aubrey?'

'I ran into him as he was leaving the club, and there was just time for him to tell me that all was well at home – that he still had the *Bellona*, now on the Brest blockade – that he had kept my place aboard her – that they were living at Woolcombe, as handier for Torbay or Plymouth, and should be happy to see us all for as long as ever we chose to give them the pleasure – vast great house – whole wings empty. He had just been up for the naval estimates – must run not to miss the coach – and so vanished, cleaving the throng.'

Blaine shook his head. 'Will you not walk in and take at least a glass of sherry before your puss in the corner? Some added fortitude, Dutch courage, is essentially called for, where the ceaseless din of children is concerned.'

'I will not,' said Stephen, 'though I thank you kindly. It is already late for girls of that age, and we must be up early for the journey into the west.'

'Are you away so soon?'

'A little before the dawn itself.'

'Shall I not see you again?'

'Oh surely. I come up next week for the meeting of the Royal and to see about the lease of our house in Half Moon Street. In the present state of affairs we cannot possibly afford to keep it up: but just now we mean to go down to the Aubreys and stay with them until a suitable little place can be found in the country: and of course I must rejoin my ship. We are selling or trying to sell that gaunt cold ill-omened Barham, which will put us in funds again; and in the meantime I shall borrow a few thousand from Jack Aubrey.'

Blaine gave him a quick look; and a few paces on, when they were almost at the door of the club, with members going in and out like bees, he took Stephen's elbow, halted him by the railings and in a low voice he said, 'Do beg your friend to be quiet in the House, Stephen. On naval estimates he addressed the Ministry as though they were a parcel of defaulters, and now that he has most unhappily overcome his diffidence as a new member he does so in a voice calculated to reach the main topmast-head in a hurricane. His friends do so wish he were not in Parliament; or if he feels he has to be a member (and indeed there are great potential advantages) that he would rarely attend and then sit mute, voting as he is told. I dread the moment he gives his voice against the Ministry, in his dashing, headstrong way. He is very often in town, with a jobbing captain aboard his ship, doing her no good, nor her reputation. Stephen, do take him to sea and keep him there.'

They were now at the steps leading into Black's. Down them hurried a tall thin member, pursued by the cry of 'Your Grace, your Grace.'

His Grace turned, and with an anxious look he asked, 'Have I done something wrong?'

'Your Grace has taken Mr Wilson's umbrella,' said the head-porter, walking down to recover it; and now a positive company of members came streaming in from a cockpit over the way, making conversation impossible.

'Until next week,' cried Stephen.

'A safe and prosperous journey, and my dear love to the ladies,' replied Sir Joseph, kissing his hand.

Captain Aubrey (Commodore no longer, since the appointment lapsed with the dissolution of his squadron, and the temporary title with it) and his wife sat at the break-fast-table, looking out over the broad grey courtyard of Woolcombe House to the veiled woods and the sky, a some-what lighter grey but quite as melancholy.

They sat in silence, waiting for the newspaper and the post, but a companionable silence; and as Jack's gaze moved indoors it paused on Sophie before travelling on to the coffee-pot. She was a tall, gentle, particularly sweet-looking woman, thirty-odd, and Jack's rather stern face softened. 'How well she is bearing up under all this,' he reflected. 'She may not have quite Diana's dash, but she has plenty of bottom. Plenty of bottom: a rare plucked 'un.'

'All this' was a spate of litigation arising from Jack's cruise against slave-traders in the Gulf of Guinea. When he and his captains were confronted with a stinking vessel crammed with black men and women chained on a low slave-deck in that tropical heat they did not always pay the very closest attention to the papers that were produced, above all since the first ten alleged protections had proved to be forgeries. Yet genuine protection did exist: Portuguese slavers for example could still legally trade south of the Line, and if one was found in the northern hemisphere, obviously head-ing for Cuba, it was difficult to prove that the ship's master had not been compelled by stress of weather to put his nose over the equator, or that he did not intend to steer for Brazil tomorrow, particularly as a cloud of witnesses would swear to the fact. Navigational error, shortage of stores, and the like, could always be brought forward with a fair appearance of truth. Then again there were all sorts of legal devices by which the true ownership of the vessel could be disguised or concealed – companies holding on behalf of other com-panies and so on four deep, with the true responsibility for the cargo growing more dubious at each remove: nor was there any shortage of legal talent to make the most of a wealthy ship-owner's case.

The day was as still as a day could well be, extremely damp and so silent that the dew could be heard dripping right along the front of the house, which an earlier Jack Aubrey, in the fashion of his day, had built facing north: right along the front and on either of the somewhat later wings, even to the very end of that on the east, whose ultimate drip fell on a cistern whose leaden voice was part of the Captain's very earliest memories.

To these, in time, was added the sound of hoofs, the high-pitched hoofs of a mule approaching: then an old man's creaking voice and a boy's shrill pipe. This was George Aubrey, the Captain's son; and presently he appeared outside the window, smiling, a little cheerful fat boy with his father's bright yellow hair, blue eyes and high colour.

Although he did not encourage them to breakfast with him when he was on shore, Jack was fond of his children and with an answering smile he walked over to the window. 'Good morning, sir,' cried George, handing in *The Times*, 'Harding showed me a wariangle in the hedge by Simmon's Lea.'

'Good morning to you, George,' said Jack, taking the paper. 'I am amazingly glad about the wariangle. He showed me one too, just before I went to sea. Remember all the details you can manage, and tell me at dinner.'

Back in his chair he opened the pages eagerly, for this was the day when the flag-promotion would be announced, and he turned straight to the Gazette. There were the familiar names, the whole list of admirals (that glorious rank) from the most junior rear-admirals of the blue, just promoted from the most senior names on the post-captains' list, onwards: all of them moving steadily up through the ranks and squadrons – rear-admirals of the blue, then of the white, then of the red; vice-admirals and then full admirals of the same, and finally the sailor's apotheosis, admiral of the fleet. The last nine stages of increasing splendour were devoid of suspense, progress being wholly automatic, depending on seniority – no merit, no royal favour even, could advance a man a shadow of an inch, and Nelson died a vice-admiral of the white – yet Jack read out many of the admirals they knew or liked or admired.

'Sir Joe will hoist the red at his mizen. He will like that: I shall drink him joy of it at dinner. I should like it too. Lord, if I were ever to hoist my own flag, I should keep it to be buried in.' He carried on, picking out friends in the squadrons red white and blue; but just before he reached the really interesting part, the dividing-line, the crucial boundary between the top of the post-captains' list and the rear-admirals of the blue, Sophie, still much put out by that unfortunate reference to a shroud, said, 'I am glad about dear Sir Joe, and Lady Le Poer will be delighted: yet after all, surely it is no surprise, any more than moving up the dance? And what do you mean, *if you were ever to hoist your flag*? You are quite near the top of the list, and no one can deny you the right to one.' She spoke with the particular emphasis, even vehemence, of those who wish to establish the truth of their words; although as a sailor's wife she knew perfectly well that the Navy List contained twenty-eight superannuated rear-admirals and (even worse) thirty-two superannuated post-captains.

'Of course,' said Jack. 'That is the usual way: you go up and up, like Jacob on his ladder. But with something so important it would be courting ill-luck to speak of any certainty about it. You must not tempt fate. If I were Stephen, I should cross myself whenever I had to mention flag-rank. God bless us all. No. They do not usually superannuate post-captains unless they are very old and sick, or very mad and froward, or unless they have often refused service: though I *have* known it done. No. On the whole, and speaking quite impersonally, you understand, it could be said that men at the head of the post-captains' list may assert a right to a flag at the next promotion of admirals. But that don't mean they have a right to hoist it, let alone to any employment. What happens if they do not like the cut of your jib is that they make you a rear-admiral "without distinction of squadron". You have a rear-admiral's half-pay: you have the nominal rank. But you are neither red, white nor blue; neither fish, flesh, fowl, nor good red herring; and when sailors call you *admiral* the decent ones look away – the others smile. In the cant phrase you have been yellowed.'

'But that could never happen to you, Jack,' she cried. 'Not with your fighting record. And you have never refused *any* service, however disagreeable.'

'I hope you are right, my dear,' said Jack, searching down the column. 'Yet I am afraid it has happened to Captain Willis. John Thornton is not here either, but I think he has accepted a place as commissioner, which puts him out of the running. Craddock is missing too.'

She came and looked over his shoulder. 'So he is, poor soul: though I never liked him. But there is no mention of "without distinction of squadron": and I have never seen it either, in any Gazette.'

'No. They do not make it public. You just get a letter saying that Their Lordships do not have it in contemplation and so on. And I am afraid more and more people are going to get that damned uncomfortable letter. Unless Napoleon wins yet another of those shattering unexpected victories by land all over again, it looks as though this war was pretty nearly over, with the French cleared right out of Spain and Wellington already well into France.'

'Oh, how I hope so,' said Sophie.

'So do I, of course, a very good thing, to be sure. No more carnage. But can you imagine the cut-throat struggle for commands in a Navy reduced to three wherries and a gig? Armageddon would be nothing to it. No, no. Rather than make things even worse and overcrowd the flag-officers' list they will superannuate right, left and centre, and the Devil take the . . .'

They both turned their heads, listening: hoofs again, far off, and sea-going cries: 'Give way, there. Luff and touch her. Thus, thus, very well thus. Easy, as she goes. Easy. *Easy*, God damn and blast your eyes. This ain't the fucking Derby stakes.'

Whenever Captain Aubrey was ashore for any length of time, as for that part of the parliamentary session devoted to the naval estimates, he naturally brought his coxswain, his steward and one or two followers with him. The first, Barrett Bonden, was a tough, powerful, very able seaman; the virtues of the second, Preserved Killick, were less evident – he was a passable seaman and a brilliant silver-polisher, but as a personal servant he left much to be desired: indeed almost everything. Jack brought them because it was customary for a post-captain to have a minimum of retinue, and Captain Aubrey had the greatest respect for naval customs; yet they were beings so wholly nautical that they were of very little use to him by land. In the present instance, for example, they were barely capable of inducing a staid old mare, well past mark of mouth and thoroughly accustomed to the road, to carry them and the gig to the post-office for the Woolcombe letters without overturning into a ditch or two, or even, in her agitation of mind, losing the way.

The voice died away as the mare, quickening her pace, headed for the familiar stables behind the house. Jack and Sophie sat waiting. The post had been a matter of dreadful importance ever since the first action for wrongful seizure opened with a broadside of writs, each more injuriously phrased and menacing than the last.

In a properly-run household it was the butler's duty, indeed his privilege, to carry in the family's letters, taking them out of the leather bag in which the postmaster at Wool-hampton had placed them, considering them back and front, and arranging them on a salver. Woolcombe was still a properly-run house, though terribly threatened and managing on the strictest minimum; but its due order was shaken every time the Captain's coxswain appeared. He had an unshakable view of his own prerogatives; and since Mnason, the regular, hereditary butler, knew that the broken-nosed coxswain had knocked out or otherwise disabled all challengers for the championship of the Mediterranean fleet, he confined himself to verbal complaints and Bonden carried the salver in, smoothing his hair and buttoning his jacket to do so in style.

Jack Aubrey had certain rules, somewhat tainted with superstition, and one of these obliged him to take the nearest letter. Sophie knew no such laws and she instantly reached over for a cover addressed in a well-known hand and bearing an Ulster post-mark: it was from her sister Frances, a young, pretty and more or less penniless widow who had turned her big house into a girls' school, where, with the help of their former governess she was educating the Aubrey twins, Charlotte and Fanny, among a score or so of others. She enclosed two fairly creditable letters from them, written on hot-pressed pink paper. Sophie, a deeply affectionate soul, read them twice, and with such pleasure that a tear dimmed her eye. She then put them in her lap and picked another from the array, a singularly wretched choice that brought tears of quite another kind: or almost brought them, for by now she had had a good deal of practice at mastering the actual flow.

Each put down a letter. Each looked at the other. 'What news, my dear?' asked Jack. Her back was to the light and he did not see how distressed she was. 'Good news from Frankie and the girls,' she said, and he heard the tremble, 'but Cluttons say that with the times so bad and the cost of removing all the inscriptions so high, they are afraid they cannot offer more than the melting-pot price for the Jamaica service.' Jack nodded, but said nothing. 'What was yours?' she went on, for they dealt with these things on an equal footing, with no concealment on either side, almost no concessions.

'It was from Lawrence,' he said. 'Leave to appeal has been refused.'

She digested this. It was the wreck of all their cherished, accumulated hopes as far as that particular case was concerned. 'We shall have to sell Ashgrove,' she said after a pause. 'The creditors will not wait.'

Jack cast her a loving glance. What she said was true; the only evident solution, since Woolcombe was entailed; yet it was scarcely one that he could have proposed. Ashgrove was her own, and could neither be sold nor mortgaged by him, very much her own, and even legally so, by settlement – a rambling house they had planned together, piece by piece, but of course carried out almost entirely by her, with Jack being so long at sea. Although quite by itself in its own woods it was a wonderfully convenient house for a naval officer, within sight of Portsmouth, and at present it was let to an admiral who had done very well out of prize-money and who had thrown out many a hint about buying it.

'May I see the girls' letters?' he asked. And when he had read them he said, 'I am afraid you miss them cruelly, but it is really much better that they should be with Frankie. There is nothing worse for children than a house with law-suits hanging over it – threats they do not really understand – universe crumbling – parents nearly always sad or cross – perpetually anxious.' He spoke from intimate knowledge, since it was his father's litigious propensities even more than his other faults of character that had made Jack's mother's short life so unhappy and that had at times so oppressed his naturally cheerful boyhood that even now this house cast a gloom upon his spirits – he was never cordially happy there except in the parts behind, the stable courts, the walled garden and the far garden with its grotto. 'But I think George is still too young to feel it. And in any case we do not quarrel.'

'No, my dear,' she said, looking at him kindly. 'But he *is* lonely, poor lamb. Shall we look through the rest? Perhaps we are both missing heirs.'

No sudden fortune, but Jack's face lit with much the same light as he turned the last letter of his undistinguished pile. 'Why, this is Stephen,' he exclaimed, breaking the seal. 'By God, they will be here today! Stephen, Diana, Clarissa Oakes, Brigid, Padeen, the whole shooting-match. What joy! Listen, sweetheart. "My dear Jack, may I indeed inflict myself, all my women, and a numerous band of followers upon you indefinitely? Diana (who sends her love) says it is a monstrous imposition, above all with no notice; but I reassure her, saying it was an understood thing between us – we had met at Black's – you had stressed the empty immensities of your palatial home. And I would not wound you for the world, as I must by taking hired lodgings until a suitable house can be found . . ." My dear, what's amiss? Ain't you delighted?'

'Oh, indeed I am. I love Stephen. I am fond of my cousin . . . I am as delighted as a woman can be, who has nothing ready for a single guest, let alone a regiment, including that Mrs Oakes – nothing whatsoever – you were to have yesterday's beefsteak pudding again for dinner, and there is nothing else in the house. We shall have to put them in the east wing – there is room enough there, God knows – but it has not been turned out, it has not been *touched* since Michaelmas.' She started up, gathering her wits and saying, 'I shall never be ready in time,' hurried from the room.

She was not what she called ready when the coach and four, driven in great style by Diana, rolled in a smooth curve across the courtyard and pulled up exactly at the foot of the steps, discharging an improbable number of people; but she was at the open, welcoming door, pale but properly dressed, conscious that the main rooms of the east wing were as spotless as the decks of a man-of-war (and cleaned in much the same hearty fashion), that an unspeakably well-timed gift of venison ensured their dinner, and that the reprieved Jamaica service, the West India merchants' expression of thanks to Captain Aubrey for ridding them of privateers, would lay it out in splendour.

She received them prettily, kissing Diana and Brigid, dropping that Mrs Oakes quite a deep curtsy and hoping that she saw her well, and then leading them into the blue parlour to drink tea while their baggage was carried away and whilst Jack, Stephen, an aged groom and a stable-boy put the splendid coach and its team of bays in stable and coach-house.

'Why, Diana,' called Jack in his strong voice, coming in

and brushing the oat-dust from his coat, 'where did you get your magnificent cattle?'

'I borrowed them from my cousin Cholmondeley,' said she. 'We met him in Bath, glum as a gib cat, with a gouty toe that nailed him to his chair – said the horses were bursting for want of exercise – it made him low in his spirits. So I offered to drive them down here. He will send his coachman to take them back on Thursday.'

'He must have an amazing opinion of your powers,' said Jack. 'I once asked him to lend me a perfectly ordinary dog-cart with a perfectly ordinary animal to pull it, just for an hour or so, and he would not.'

'Jack,' said Diana, smiling, 'a thousand repartees come to mind, each wittier than the last, but I shall not utter a single one. This is a very striking case of magnanimity in a poor weak woman who rarely thinks of any repartee until it is far too late to produce it.'

'Admiral Rodham says that for ship-handling Jack has not his equal in the entire service,' said Sophie.

Diana looked down without even a hidden smile; and in the silence that followed Stephen watched George and Brigid. The little boy walked round and round her, gazing: sometimes she smiled at him; but sometimes she turned away her head. Eventually he came right up to her, offered her the best part of a biscuit and said, 'Should not you like to see my dormouse? He is a prodigious fine dormouse, and will let you touch him.'

'Oh, if you please,' she said, jumping up at once.

'Stephen, Diana, dear Mrs Oakes,' said Jack, 'I do not believe you have any of you been here before. Should you like to see the house? The library is rather good, and the justice-room; though I am afraid much of the rest was modernized a few years ago.'

'Oh, my dear,' cried Sophie, aware of the horrors stuffed into both, and they totally unswept, 'the light is quite gone, and you really cannot see the panelling when the light is quite gone. Besides, dinner is almost ready, and you must certainly change that disreputable old rat-catcher's coat.'

Chapter Two

In general Stephen Maturin was a poor sleeper, and since his youth he had turned to a number of allies against the intolerable boredom – and sometimes far, far worse than boredom, he having a most vulnerable heart – of insomnia: poppy and mandragora being the most obvious, seconded by the inspissated juice of aconite or of henbane, by datura stramonium, creeping skerit, leopard's bane. But here in the soporific atmosphere of Dorset even three cups of coffee after dinner had not been able to keep him awake: he had nodded over his cards to such an extent that by general agreement Sophie took over his hand and he crept off to bed. Here he awoke at dawn in a state of rosy ease and perfect relaxation, infinitely refreshed. In this blessed posture he lay for some time, luxuriating, collecting himself and the recent past and listening both to Diana's even breath and to a moderate chorus of birds, all pleased to see the day.

Presently life stirred in his bosom: with infinite precaution he collected the clothes he had strewn about the floor, and carrying his shoes he took them to the closet.

'Why, Stephen, there you are,' called Jack from the breakfast-room, hearing him on the stairs. 'Good morning to you. What an early worm you are to be sure. I trust you slept? You was quite fagged out.'

'Wonderfully, I thank you: wonderfully: I do not remember getting into bed, and when I woke I could hardly tell where I was, at all. What a pure joy it is, the awareness of having slept.'

'I am sure of it,' said Jack, for whom this was an everyday occurrence. He poured him a cup of coffee and went on, 'What do you say to taking out a gun and seeing whether we can knock over a rabbit or two? And there might be a snipe in the plashy bottom.'

'With all my heart.'

'We can breakfast properly when we come back. But before the women get up let us first have a quick look into the library and the justice-room. I am rather proud of them, and *you* will not mind a little dust. Or squalor.'

The library was indeed a noble room, running almost the whole width of the first floor, with five bays to the south and an east window; though the early light had scarcely yet strength enough to show more than shadowy ranges of book-cases, all of a kind, panelling, and countless dim spines behind glass, long tables in the middle, wing-chairs by the fireplace, and some rolled-up sacking bundles, Sophie's shame. 'My great-grandfather the judge was a prodigious reader,' said Jack, 'and so was his great-grandfather – it skips generations, sometimes, like stamina in horses. You must spend a day or two in here, if it comes on to rain.'

'So must Clarissa Oakes. She has been fairly starved for books.'

'I had no idea she was a learned lady.'

'Sure, she has nothing of the bluestocking; but she reads Latin as easily as French, and Greek with no more difficulty than most of us. And she dearly loves a book-room.'

'Do you suppose she would teach George amo amas amat?'

'She is a very good-natured woman, in spite of her apparent reserve.'

'I shall get Sophie to ask her. But for the moment we must jump down to the justice-room and away, or the rabbits will all have gone to ground. I am sorry about this staircase,' he said as they went down. 'I had hoped to make it as it was when I was a boy – I did have the panelling put back in my mother's room – but before the men could get to work on this, funds ran out. Here' – opening a door – 'is the justice-room.'

'It is not a term I know,' said Stephen, looking at the bare, formal arrangement of a large table set across, with some chairs and benches facing it, the walls clothed in the soberest linenfold oak: no pictures. 'What happens here?'

'This is where we deal with the manor's legal proceedings, court baron, court leet, and so on. And when I am sitting as a justice of the peace, that is my chair behind the table, with the high back. Sitting as a magistrate, if you follow me.'

'Long, long ago you once told me that you had it in mind to preach a sermon to the ship's company, there being no chaplain aboard: but even that did not so astonish me as now hearing that you are a judge, my dear; one of the righteous.'

'Oh,' said Jack, carelessly, 'the Aubreys have always been justices of the county, time out of mind. It had nothing at all to do with the righteousness. Mind your step in the doorway: there is a damned awkward plank. No. I regard it as an infernal nuisance, and it has caused a deal of trouble with my preserving neighbours, because I will not come down heavy on poachers – I often knew them as boys. This is the way to the gun-room. Here is a fourteen-gauge Manton that might suit you.'

They walked along a passage to the back of the house, coming out in the stable-yard, where Harding was waiting with a dog. 'Should you like me to come along, sir?' he asked.

'No,' said Jack, 'you wait here for Master George and take him along for the paper. But Bess can come.'

The rough, more-or-less spaniel bitch heard the words and bounded across, quivering with zeal and gazing into Jack's face to see which way they were to go.

They went in fact through those back regions where Jack had been so happy as a boy – stables, tack-room, double coach-house, the fine red-brick wall against which he had played single-handed fives for so many hours, the grape-house, the kitchen garden – where they sat in the grotto for a while and Stephen examined his gun. 'Sure, this is the elegant fowling-piece of the world,' he said, 'and beautifully balanced.'

'Joe Manton was thoroughly pleased with it. He said the stock had the prettiest grain he had ever seen. And Stephen, take notice of the touch-hole, will you? It is platina, which never corrodes or chokes – no others shoot so sharply.'

'Upon my soul, Jack, you do yourself proud. I have never had a Manton gun at all, let alone one with a platina touch-hole, rich as Beelzebub though I was.'

'Ain't you rich now, Stephen?' he asked with never a hint of vulgar curiosity; only with a very deep concern.

'I am not. I carried my fortune to Spain, as you know; and there it has been seized. They had wind of my doings in Peru. But I am in no way desperate, Jack. I have my pay – much in arrears, I may observe – as a naval surgeon; and we mean to get rid of that ill-omened place at Barham and take a little small cottage somewhere in these parts. No. I am not desperate at all: it is just that I am in no way to indulge in a platina touch-hole to my gun.'

'Then we are in the same boat, brother. I had scarcely been home a month before writs started coming in – actions for wrongful seizure, forcible detainer and the like, based on my taking slavers who by one damned quibble or another could claim protection. Most were dismissed out of hand, but two or three were argued before the court and although that dear good man Lawrence did all he could, I was cast in damages. Stephen, you would never believe the amount of damages when it comes to shipping and cargo. I have been refused leave to appeal on the most recent, and there are at least two more pending. Lawrence spoke to the Admiralty counsel, a member of the same inn, who told him that my instructions had been perfectly clear: they forbade me to interfere with any protected vessel, and if in spite of that I did so, I must bear the consequences. For my own part, I spoke to the First Sea Lord – I had always regarded him as a friend – but he was pretty cold and distant, as high as Pontius Pilate, and he gave exactly the same answer, except that he said I must *pay* the consequences. Well, I can *not* pay them, if any of the other cases goes against me. Even as things are, we can only just scrape by if Sophie sells Ashgrove: this place and the whole Woolcombe estate are entailed.' Stephen shook his head, looking so wretchedly low that Jack went on, 'But like you, I am not at all desperate. I too have my service pay, and so long as I am a member they can't arrest me. Lord, Stephen, we have been very much worse off. Shall we see if we can find any rabbits?'

The moment that he stirred from his damp seat the spaniel sprang up and whimpered with eagerness, cast to and fro among the seedling asters, and vanished behind a row of myrtle: here she could be heard marking, at a stand, but she was a silent bitch and uttered nothing but an urgent whine.

'That will be the gate leading to the common,' said Jack. 'I wanted you to see it in any event, a lovely piece of country.' They walked quickly through, and there on the path some thirty yards beyond there was a white scut bobbing along. Jack whipped up his gun; the rabbit made a somersault; the spaniel raced out and brought it back, breathing deep with satisfaction.

'So this is the common,' said Stephen, looking over a broad expanse of rough pasture, fern-brake, scattered trees, with here and there a pool; the whole agreeably undulating, autumn-coloured, with a fine great sky over it, adorned with the whitest sailing clouds. 'An elegant common too, so it is; but my ideas are all confused. I had supposed your father and his friends had enclosed it, to your great distress, when we were on the far side of the world.'

'Certainly they inclosed *Woolhampton* common and it *did* grieve me. But this is another piece of common land called Simmon's Lea – it was always my favourite – and now they want to inclose it too. Over my dead body! Such fun I had here when I was a boy: mostly alone but sometimes with young fellows from the farms or the village – netting, ferreting, drawing the mere, poaching on Mr Baldwin's land, leading his keepers a rare old dance, wild-fowling in a hard winter – Heneage Dundas used to come down sometimes. And when the Blackstone came over in this part of the country we would always find a fox in the furze. Did you notice that old chap in the stable-yard?'

'Certainly.'

'That was Harding, a real country-man, born and bred in

the parish – there are a score of Hardings here. He began as a kennel-boy with the Blackstone, where his father was huntsman; then he whipped-in for another pack, but having a nasty fall he took to being an under-keeper beyond Wimborne, and then after a spell as a water-bailiff he came to us as keeper, oh, well before I was born. I can't remember a time without him. I am no expert on birds, as you are very well aware, but what little I do know I learnt from him. This very path leads to a place where he showed me a nightjar's egg, lying there on the ground. Have you ever seen a nightjar's egg, Stephen?'

'I have; but it was brought to me. I have never found one.'

'Then I do not have to tell you how beautiful they are. Then as for fishing and setting snares and finding a hare, and shooting for that matter, he – oh, well shot, Stephen.'

The spaniel brought the rabbit back. Stephen praised the gun, as pretty a gun as he had ever seen. 'Do you preserve, at all, Jack?' he asked as they went on.

'Oh no. I just take a gun out from time to time, more for the walk than anything else: I love this common. If a shot offers, well and good, but I have no notion of breeding birds up in order to knock them down again. And a shot does offer most days, because many of my neighbours do preserve, and do breed up pheasants by wholesale, so when they have one of these big shoots, with driven birds, a good many come on to our land. Some of these people resent it, and one mean-spirited sodomite says that my reason for opposing the enclosure is that I like getting high-reared game for nothing. There is a lot of ill-feeling . . . and that fellow,' said Jack, cocking his head to bring his good eye to bear in what was now a habitual gesture, 'that fellow on the pony, coming into sight behind those willows, is a perfect example. A sailor, I am sorry to say, and a scrub.'

'That sounds a contradiction in terms.'

'You are truly good to say so, Stephen; but when you consider . . . However, this fellow Griffiths is not so much as a sailor, neither. You will remember him in Valletta and

Gib as a commander – he had the *Espiègle* and then the *Argus* – a big black-haired red-faced domineering cove, younger than me but with much more influence – a member for Carton and Stranraer's heir, his nephew – and he was made post in the same month. But after a cruise or two in the *Terpsichore*, when he had an ugly mutiny on his hands, he refused commands that would have taken him to the West Indies. He prefers farming, high farming; he has a deal of land over towards Paston. He was the prime mover in enclosing Woolhampton Common – by the way, we say either Woolcombe or Woolhampton here: it's all one – and now he wants to do the same to Simmon's Lea. He and his friends want everything laid out like military camp, with straight lines and right angles. High yields and high rents, of course, and the game-laws enforced to the letter Z. I may malign him, but just as he seems not to know the odds between a ship kept in apparent good order by Botany Bay methods and one which is in really good order, seamanlike order, because officers and men know their duty and do it without being driven, so he don't know the difference between a well-run estate and a place not far removed from a penal settlement, where people are turned off for a trifle, and a suspicion of poaching is a man's ruin. Tenants at will, of course, whenever a lease falls in . . . he is veering this way. I shall just move my hat to him, and ask him how he does. We are still on speaking-terms, after all.' They walked on in silence for a while and then Jack moved well off the path to give the pony room, called out 'Good day, sir. How do you do?' – touching his hat as he spoke.

Griffiths returned the greeting without a smile, looking very closely at Stephen, who, for his part, saw one of those heavy, dissatisfied men, much more inclined to ill-humour than to any hint of gaiety – if indeed gaiety had not deserted them entirely, together with their youth. Victims of the power of giving orders? Of a disordered liver? Or both no doubt, together with a froward spleen and pancreas.

'It was Burton, I think,' he said some minutes later, 'who observed that there were men who sucked nothing but poison from books. And who has not met youths and even maidens with ludicrous ideas of *what is the thing* for persons of spirit, and with permanently distorted notions of conduct that is acceptable and conduct that is not? Yet may not authors be even more poisonous?'

'In the Navy there are usually people to bring a puppy to his senses,' said Jack. 'Though I must confess . . .'

The confession was lost. They had reached the plashy bottom, and a snipe got up with its usual cry, corkscrewing away at a tremendous pace. Jack fired and missed: the dog looked at him with contempt. 'It serves me right,' he said as he reloaded, 'I had almost said the service was not perfect.'

'There would be more water here in the winter, sure?' asked Stephen.

'Oh yes, much more: almost a little lake.'

'It is very much like what we call a turlough in Ireland,' said Stephen. 'Sometimes far from barren,' and he gave Bess a discreet but significant look, nodded towards a dense patch of reeds. She ran questing forward and within two minutes she flushed a brace of teal, and they rising straight up from their confined piece of water. Stephen hit the right-hand bird: Jack missed the other.

'I should never have spoken at all,' he said, quite out of countenance – Bess had brought the little duck to Stephen's hand. 'You can never get into trouble by holding your God-damn tongue.'

'It was the gun entirely,' said Stephen. 'The sweetest little gun – comes up so quick, and, as you say, shoots wonderfully sharp.'

Jack only shook his head; and presently, partly to gain knowledge and partly to put his friend at a moral advantage, Stephen said, 'Pray tell me about inclosures, Jack, will you now? I have often heard of them, with some saying they will save the country from starving and others saying that it is all stuff – a mere job or a series of jobs to get the land into rich men's hands and keep the labourers' wages down; and that anyhow, with the war so nearly over – these are only reported words, Jack: not my own, God forbid – with the

31

war so nearly over, imported wheat will soon be coming in again, so there is no need to upset the old order.'

'As for the broader issues,' said Jack, ' – what is that bird?'

'A bar-tailed godwit, I believe.'

'I am not qualified to speak. I leave that to people like Arthur Young or dear Sir Joe; but certainly earlier on and where really suitable land was concerned inclosing the huge old common fields did by all accounts increase the country's supplies of corn. But I was at sea – or we were both in one prison or another – most of the time and I have no more right to get up in the House and prate about inclosures in general than nine-tenths of the members have a right to talk about naval matters. Yet where these two particular commons are concerned, I *do* know what I am talking about, and I am absolutely opposed to the change. And that is what I shall tell the committee loud and clear.'

'What kind of a committee?'

'Why, a parliamentary committee, in course.'

'Oh, indeed? Pray, Jack, let us start at the beginning. Who set about inclosing? Where does the power lie, the authority? What says the law?'

'As for the law, God help us: every manor is a law to itself, and the courts always say *consuetudo loci est observanda*.' He looked at Stephen and repeated '*Consuetudo loci est observanda*' rather louder, before saying, 'But I don't suppose you need to have that translated,' with a sigh. 'And the consuetudos differ amazingly, and always have, from one manor to another. Even in Woolcombe Common and Simmon's Lea, which almost touch, the commons of piscary and of estovers are quite unlike, and here in Simmon's Lea there is no common of turbary at all. Then there are all sorts of other rights, like bite of grass and fire-bote, hey-bote and house-bote, underwood, sweepage and so on, different from parish to parish but all strictly ruled by custom time out of mind and giving a man a place in the village and making it more like a right ship's company. Mark you, Stephen, I am talking about the lord's waste, not the common field nor the pasture, but the *waste* – what is ordinarily called the common

32

nowadays. Most of the plough-land and grazing here was inclosed long ago, though there is still some of both attached to Simmon's Lea.' He broke off as a heron flew high over them, travelling straight with a steady, massive beat. 'They used to nest, a score of them and more, in the trees on the far side of the mere,' he said. 'But one year the water-bailiffs and some of the keepers pulled down all their great unwieldy platforms when they were breeding, and they never came back. Old Harding was one of them. He could never abide anything that competed with us in killing, whether it swam, flew or ran – fish, flesh; fowl or good red herring – and you, Stephen, you would have wept to see his barn door with hawks, falcon, owls, two ospreys and even an enormous great eagle with a white tail spread out wide, and weasels, stoats and the odd marten all nailed up – and he sold the otters' skins. But that was when he was an active keeper and I was a boy; now he don't go out, and the vermin thrive. Though I can't say I notice much odds as far as the shooting is concerned. Ware riot, you vile bitch,' he cried, for Bess, roaming as they talked, had put up an explosive pheasant, well out of reach.

'I have rarely seen a dog look so ashamed,' said Stephen. 'She droops in all her members.'

'And well she may,' said Jack. 'Rambling about like a mad lunatic in that indecent way. If she were younger, I should beat her. That, by the way, must have been one of Griffiths' birds, a ring-neck. Well, now, an inclosure usually starts with those who have most right in the common agreeing that it should be divided up into separate parts, into single freeholds proportionate to their rights. I do not mean all those concerned, but a good many. Then, with the blessing of the parson, the patron of the living, and as many of the gentlemen, yeomen and freeholders as are of their opinion or whom they can persuade, they appoint proper people to measure and chart everything. When this is done they present a petition to the House, begging leave to bring in a private bill, so that parliament may authorize the sharing out – so that it may become law.'

'On the face of it, that seems fair enough. After all, the country is run on those lines: the majority is always right, and those who do not like it may lump it – an expression I heard in the mouth of an officer leading a press-gang, when one of the captives expostulated with him.'

'It *would* be perfectly fair, if it were like a jury or even a vestry, where every man has a voice, and where all the others know him and value his opinion according to his reputation in the village. But in this case the majority is determined not by counting heads but by counting shares: that is to say the value of the holdings. Griffiths, a fairly rich newcomer, has perhaps ten thousand pounds' worth. Harding and all his relations in the farms and cottages may have come by holdings worth two or three hundred in the last two or three hundred years. So what will their vote amount to? And then there are three or four other big men apart from Griffiths. My own cousin Brampton, at Westport, longs to round out three of his farms, where the common runs deep into the estate. Well, now, when we were sweltering in the Gulf of Guinea, and while you, my poor Stephen, were not only sweltering but also turning as yellow as a guinea, they got together their precious petition, with a majority of shares supporting it – I need not tell you how easy it is for a man with a fair-sized estate to persuade cottagers who earn much of their living on that estate to put their signature or marks to a paper that takes away their share in a common – and after a long pause while it was being put into proper order and the bill drafted, Griffiths presented it to the House. It was read twice in the usual gabble, no one paying the least attention, and it was referred to a committee, the parliamentary committee that I was telling you about. If that committee reports favourably the bill will be read a third time, almost certainly without debate, and passed as a matter of course and commissioners will come down and start the sharing out. But if I can prevent it, the committee will *not* report favourably.'

'How shall you prevent it?'

'If my shares in the common are not enough to do away

with their majority, they will at least reduce it to precious little; and then I should lay handsome odds, say eleven to three, that the weight of my position will swing the balance – will turn the scale.'

'Sure, a post-captain in the Royal Navy is a most imposing creature; but is not Captain Griffiths of the same rank and somewhat greater seniority?'

'Certainly. But he is not lord of the manor and I am.'

'Heavens, Jack, I had no notion of it, no notion at all. So they still exist? The office or perhaps I should say the eminence I had heard of, but supposed it to belong to the distant past, when lords exercised the droit de seigneur with the utmost rigour, and the high justice and the low, with a private pair of gallows. So they still exist? I am amazed, amazed.'

Even now, after all these years, the extent of Stephen's ignorance by land as well as by sea, of course, could astonish Captain Aubrey. He looked affectionately down, and in the simplest words explained the nature of his function. 'It amounts to little nowadays, after all the modern passion for paring down and changing for the sake of change: the lord of the manor has few rights left apart from what the manor courts leave him, and the occasional escheat; but logically or not he does retain a certain standing, and it is rare for a committee to go against his opposition. And then again, he does have some powers coming down from earlier times: I may not be able to lie with the commoners' brides on their wedding night, but I do open the fair in the Dripping Pan – by the charter it cannot start without I am there, or at least my deputy – and I do kick the first football of the season and bowl the first ball when cricket comes round, unless I am at sea.'

They had been rising steadily through his account of lordship of a manor and now, from the top of a grassy bank he waved down to a shallow amphitheatre – it was too large to be called a dell – with a fine sward kept trim by sheep and rabbits and now by a small, remote flock of snow-white geese tended by a girl. 'You would not think so to look at it now,' he said, 'but on Old Lammas Day you can hardly get along for stalls and tents – Aunt Sally, the great rat of Tartary, two or three bearded ladies, boxing-booths, where our lads get finely battered by knowing old bruisers from Plymouth – such fun. And this is where we have our football in the winter and cricket in the summer, as well as leaping and foot races. In good years we field an eleven that can beat teams of fifteen and even seventeen from most of the nearby villages. Down there, a little south of east, do you see – no, to the *left* – there is the lane the fair people come up on the days before Old Lammas. It will take us a little out of our way, but I should like to take you down and across; there is something in the south pasture that may please you; and' – looking at his watch – 'we have plenty of time before Welland comes to see me.'

As they dropped, Bess started a hare that ran straight from them, going awkwardly down the slope with the dog so close that neither man chose to fire. Ten yards almost touching and then the hare, now out of range, jigged to the right, changed to her natural uphill pace and fairly raced away, a pleasure to behold, Jack hallooing after her, echoed by the shrill voice of the goose-girl, and Bess bounding like a cricket-ball, but with no effect, hopelessly outrun. The hare vanished over the high bank. Bess returned, gasping, and soon after they reached the lane.

'You can still see the mark of their carts, in spite of the rain,' observed Jack. 'And before the last heavy fall you could just make out the print of a camel, a camel, a camel with two bunches that carried the tent belonging to one of the bearded ladies, a present from the Arabian queen, she said.'

'There is something magic about a fair,' said Stephen. 'The smell of trampled grass, the flaring lights . . . you still have wheatears, I see.'

'Yes, but they will soon be gone, and we with them.' A wood-pigeon, flying straight and high, crossed over. 'Your bird,' said Jack.

'Not at all,' said Stephen.

Jack fired. The bird came down in a long swift glide, its wings still spread. 'I am glad to have hit something, however,' he said. 'That is one of the droits de seigneur, you know. In theory only the lord of the manor can shoot, though he can always give his friends a deputation.'

They talked about preserving game, poaching, keepers, and deer for half a mile, and then, when another lane branched off, winding through deep furze on either side, they followed it and so reached a white line of post and rail. Jack said, 'This is the limit of the common. Beyond the fence our south pasture begins, demesne land. You have only seen a small corner of Simmon's Lea – another day I hope to show you the mere and beyond – but it gives you an idea . . .'

'A wonderfully pleasant idea, a delightful landscape indeed; and in the autumn, the late autumn, you will have all the northern duck down here, to say nothing of waders, and with any luck some geese.'

'Certainly, and perhaps some whooper swans. But I really meant an idea of what these unhappy commoners are signing away. You may say they do not value the beauty . . .'

'I say nothing of the kind: would scorn it.'

'But they do value the grazing, the fuel, the litter for their beasts, the thatch and the hundred little things the common can provide: to say nothing of the fish, particularly eels, the rabbits, the odd hare and a few of Griffiths' pheasants. Harding does not see them, so long as it is villagers, and on a decent scale.'

For some time they had been hearing an odd continuous sound that Stephen could not identify until they came to the gate itself; while Jack was opening it Stephen looked back along a straight piece of the lane, and there he saw a woman leading an ass harnessed to a sledge piled high with furze; she was wearing a man's old, very old coat and gloves and it was evident that she had cut it herself. Jack held the gate for her, calling out, 'Mrs Harris, how do you do?'

'And yourself, Captain Jack?' she replied in an equally powerful voice, though hoarser. 'And your good lady? I will not stop, sir – I fairly dreaded that old gate – for the ass is so eternal sullen I should never get him to move again, if I let up to open it.' Indeed the ass's momentum slackened in the gateway; but with a singularly vile oath she urged him on and through.

'We are going to look at Binning's meadow,' called Jack after her, as they turned away to the left.

'You will see the mare right comely,' she replied.

'Jack,' said Stephen, 'I have been contemplating on your words about the nature of the majority, your strangely violent, radical, and even – forgive me – democratic words, which, with their treasonable implication of "one man, one vote", might be interpreted as an attack on the sacred rights of property; and I should like to know how you reconcile them with your support of a Tory ministry in the House.'

'Oh, as for that,' said Jack, 'I have no difficulty at all. It is entirely a matter of scale and circumstance. Everyone knows that on a large scale democracy is pernicious nonsense – a country or even a county cannot be run by a self-seeking parcel of tub-thumping politicians working on popular emotion, rousing the mob. Even at Brooks's, which is a hotbed of democracy, the place is in fact run by the managers and those that don't like it may either do the other thing or join Boodle's; while as for a man-of-war, it is either an autocracy or it is nothing, nothing at all – mere nonsense. You saw what happened to the poor French navy at the beginning of the Revolutionary War . . .'

'Dear Jack, I do not suppose literal democracy in a ship of the line nor even in a little small row-boat. I know too much of the sea,' added Stephen, not without complacency.

'. . . while at the other end of the scale, although "one man, one vote" certainly smells of brimstone and the gallows, everyone has always accepted it in a jury trying a man for his life. An inclosure belongs to this scale: it too decides men's lives. I had not realized how thoroughly it does so until I came back from sea and found that Griffiths and some of his friends had persuaded my father to join with them in inclosing Woolcombe Common: he was desperate for money at the time. Woolcombe was never so glorious a place as Simmon's Lea, but I like it very well – surprising numbers of partridge and woodcock in the season – and when I saw it all cleared, flattened, drained, fenced and exploited to the last half-bushel of wheat, with many of the small encroachments ploughed up and the cottages destroyed, and the remaining commoners, with half of their living and all their joy quite gone, reduced to anxious cap-in-hand casual labourers, it hurt my heart, Stephen, I do assure you. I was brought up rough when I was a little chap, after my mother's death, sometimes at the village school, sometimes running wild; and I knew these men intimately as boys, and now to see them at the mercy of landlords, farmers, and God help us parish officers for poor relief, hurts me so that I can scarcely bring myself to go there again. And I am determined the same thing shall not happen to Simmon's Lea, if ever I can prevent it. The old ways had disadvantages, of course, but here – and I speak only of what I know – it was a *human* life, and the people knew its ways and customs through and through.'

'I am of your way of thinking entirely, my dear,' said Stephen. He had rarely seen Jack so deeply moved and he said nothing for a furlong, when Jack cried, 'There he is! There is your wariangle! Harding showed him to George only yesterday. I hoped we should see him.'

'A very fine fowl indeed,' said Stephen. 'I have rarely seen so fine a specimen. Some people call him a butcher-bird. He has horrible ways. But who are we to be prating?'

The lane turned again, showing the house far to the left and another meadow – fine clover and grass – on the right, with a thatched shelter in the middle and a horse grazing by it in the company of a goat. He followed Jack's gaze, cried, 'Oh, oh,' in an undertone, and then rather louder, 'Lalla, Lalla, acuisle.'

Even before he called the mare had raised her head and brought her ears to bear, her nostrils flaring: now she moved towards them, and as surmises became certainty she whinnied, broke into a fine canter and cleared the rail as neatly as a deer, wheeled to Stephen's side, blew upon him and put her head firmly on his shoulder, her face against his cheek, uttering a quick little panting whimper. The goat stood staring from the shelter. They all walked slowly towards the house, Lalla keeping close to Stephen's side and looking into his face from time to time. She was one of a stud of Arabians that Diana had formed and then dispersed during one of Stephen's interminable absences at sea, and she was the only one he had been able to recover, the most affectionate and intelligent horse he had known.

'I did not know you had her here,' he said.

'Why, yes,' said Jack. 'We have let Ashgrove, as I think I told you; and Admiral Rodham, though a capital seaman, can be guaranteed to spoil a horse's mouth and temper in a month, or even less.' Then feeling that something more was due to so intimate a friend, he went on, 'We left soon after the first case was decided against me. I live at free quarters here of course, with a good deal in the way of victuals coming from the farm, while the Admiral pays a handsome rent, and his retinue looks after the garden. An admiral has a pretty numerous retinue, Stephen.'

'I am sure of it,' said Stephen, who was acquainted with admirals' views on the number of servants required to keep up the dignities of a flag, but who at the same time wondered about the probable effects of the retinue's zeal. 'Come, Lalla, my dear, do not slobber, I beg.' The little mare, nuzzling his collar, was making an already shabby coat unwearable. She looked at him affectionately, and then suddenly away, right aft, her ears erect. It was her usual companion, the nameless goat, an unclaimed stray from some remote village, mincing delicately along behind them, distrustful of the men and the dog. Lalla whinnied again, encouraging her, and they all walked along together, larks rising on either hand.

'May I revert to the sharing of the common?' asked Stephen. 'Surely the commoners have compensation for the loss of their rights?'

'In theory they do,' said Jack, 'and where the commissioners have any bowels of compassion they do in fact get something – almost invariably if they can produce legal proof of their claim. In that case they are given an allotment in freehold. With a fair-sized common like this a man with two shares might get as much as say three quarters of an acre by his cottage. Yet three quarters of an acre will not keep a cow, half a dozen sheep and a small flock of geese, whereas the free range of a common will. But an allotment as good as that is rare; quite often the land is in several pieces, sometimes far apart, and there may well be a provision in the act that each piece must be enclosed and sometimes drained. A poor man cannot afford it, so he sells his holding for five pounds or so, and then for the whole of his living he has to rely on wages, if he can get them – he is in the farmer's hands.'

By the smell it was clear that the goat had joined them. 'May I break off for a moment and tell you an anecdote of an Austrian medical man I knew in Catalonia?'

'I should be happy to hear it,' said Jack.

'There was an English soldier, a Captain Smith, with me, and we were walking to the village to drink horchata when we met Dr von Liebig. I asked him to join us. Ordinarily he and I spoke Latin, his English being as indifferent as my German, but now Liebig had to use Smith's language, and as he drank his horchata he told us that coming down the hill he met a ghost, a ghost with a beard. "A ghost in broad daylight?" cried Smith. "Yes. He was quite pale in the sun. A man was leading him with a string." I wish I could convey something of the very beautiful contrast between Smith's amazed solemnity, merging into deep suspicion, and Liebig's cheerful face, casual tone and evident pleasure in his ice-cold drink.'

'Ghost. Pale, bearded ghost: it must have been very rich indeed,' said Jack with relish. 'Did your soldier smoke it, in time?'

'Never. Not until I told him, afterwards; and then he was angry. Jack, I beg pardon. This is the end of my parenthesis. Pray go back to your inclosure; a sad subject, I am afraid.'

'Upon the whole, I think it is. There may be some good conscientious landowners who inclose, paying real attention to the commoners and making sure they are no worse off than they were – as far as that is possible. Men who appoint commissioners who have instructions not to take advantage of the cottagers' ignorance, their lack of papers justifying their ancestors' encroachments on the waste and the building of a cottage: men who do not put clauses in the bill insisting upon fencing, hedging, draining, paying part of the expense of the whole operation and that of fencing the tithe-owner's piece. There may be some such men, but Griffiths and his friends are not of that nature. They want all they can get and be damned to the means; and what they and the bigger farmers *hate* is the possibility of the labourers growing saucy, as they call it, asking for higher wages – for a wage that keeps up with the price of corn – refusing to work if they do not get it, and falling back on what they can wring from the common. No common, no sauciness.'

Here the lane grew so narrow that they were obliged to walk in file, Jack, Stephen, Lalla and the goat, and conversation languished. When at length they reached plough on the right hand and open pasture on the left Stephen said, 'One of the advantages of life at sea, for men of our condition, is freedom of speech. In the cabin or on the balcony behind, we can say what we wish, when we wish. And if you come to reflect, this is a very rare state of affairs in ordinary circumstances, by land. There are almost always reasons for discretion – servants, loved ones, visitors, innocent but receptive ears or the possibility of their presence. In much the same way good sullen reading is rare in a house, unless one is blessed with an impregnable and sound-proof room of one's own: interruptions, restless unnecessary movements, doors opening and closing, apologies, even whisperings, God forbid, and meal-times. For the right deep swimming in a book, give me the sea: I read Josephus through between Freetown and the Fastnet rock last voyage: the howling of the mariners, the motion of the sea and the elements (except perhaps in their utmost extremity) are nothing, compared with domestic incursions. Since then, mere newspapers, gazettes, periodical publications, all light frothy fare apart from the *Proceedings*, have imperceptibly drunk the whole of my time and energy. Now, Jack, pray tell me about this Admiral Lord Stranraer, whom you have mentioned so often.'

'Well, as you know, he commands the squadron on the Brest blockade, our squadron. He is an agricultural sailor, like his nephew Griffiths: there are a good many of them, stuffed with high-farming theory, and sometimes owning large estates: but unlike Griffiths he is a pretty good seaman. A taut commander, with a rough side to his tongue. He is a little man, apt to bark and indeed to bite on occasion.'

'A Scotch title, would it be?'

'No, English; from Dutch William's time. The family name is Koop. He is a Whig, but a moderate Whig, voting sometimes against the ministry, but sometimes – and on important divisions with – which means that he is much courted. Yet he is still enough of a Whig to dislike me for my father's sake. You may remember that before he took to Radical ways, my father was a passionate Tory, and at one election he flogged the man who stood for Hinton in the Whig interest. It made a great noise at the time. Yet on the other hand he does not object to Griffiths' way of always voting with Government on those rare occasions he attends the House: he is member for Carton, a pocket-borough like mine, though with even fewer electors. The Admiral also dislikes me for taking parliamentary leave, which means a jobbing captain has to take my place; and he will dislike me even more, when he learns that I mean to upset this inclosure scheme, which he very strongly advised in the first place, coming down quite often and predicting vast capabilities for the common. He is very much in favour of throwing farms together, doing away with the fifty or a hundred acre men entirely and having huge great places with good roads, modern buildings and prodigious yields – God knows how many bushels to the acre.'

'There seem to be many of these as it were clans in the

service, quite apart from the obvious political divisions. There are men like you, who are devoted to celestial navigation and who favour others of their kind; and those who delight in surveying anything that can be surveyed however wet, remote and uncomfortable; but I believe this is the first time I have encountered a band of sea-going farmers. I look forward to meeting the Admiral.'

'Yes, and there are chains of kindness and connection. Lord Keith was very good to me, for example, when I was young, and I will do anything I can for his mids or his officers' sons. It runs clean through the service, particularly with the old naval families, like the Herveys. The same applies to particular regions. You find ships where the whole quarterdeck is Scotch, and many of the people. I knew one sloop whose captain hailed from the Isle of Man, and close on every hand had three legs. But as for the Admiral, you will see him soon enough: we must be aboard within the fortnight. I shall just have time to run up to the House for the committee meeting, deliver my thunderbolt, and then post down to Torbay, where Heneage Dundas will touch before the change of the moon, landing Jenkins –'

'Who him?'

'My jobbing captain, my temporary replacement,' said Jack, and from his tone and the set of his face Stephen gathered that he did not think highly of the man. 'With the wind in the south and even south-south-east I have been expecting a signal these last three days.'

Once again Lalla brought her ears to bear on the bushes to the left, within sight of the house but well this side of the park. From them burst a little boy, George, closely pursued by a little girl, Brigid.

'Oh sir,' cried George, 'there is an express from Plymouth. And Cousin Diana is coming.'

'Oh Papa,' cried Brigid, 'there is a man on a steaming horse, and he destroyed with the thirst, bearing a letter so he is, an express letter. Mama carries it in her hand itself, driving the great coach. We came through the shrubbery and then through the whins.' By this time she was with them, and moderating her voice a little, she held up her face to be kissed.

'We saw you through the spy-glass,' said George, 'and since Cousin Diana already had the horses to, she said she should come by the drift: it would save your poor legs.'

'I can hear them, I can hear them. Mother of God, I can hear them. Oh Papa dear, and may I go up on top with Padeen?' She plucked urgently at his coat, distracting him from a remote and broad-winged bird, conceivably an osprey, right in the sun's eye. 'If Mama agrees,' he said. 'She is the master and commander of the coach.'

Lalla was a somewhat nervous, touchy creature, but now she offered an example of that wonderful patience that even the most unpromising animals will often show to the young. George, whom she knew perfectly well, had heaved himself on to her back by halter and mane, with a hand from his father, and now Brigid, who had only met her yesterday, did much the same, but less skilfully. Lalla gazed at her, standing firm until she was more or less seated, and then paced gently along.

The lane marking the edge of the pasture came out on a much broader affair called the drift, along which all Woolhampton's cattle travelled to be marked and registered on the second Wednesday after Michaelmas: here stood the elegant coach with its four matching bays, the leader's head held by Padeen, Diana on the box.

'I have a letter for you, Jack,' she cried, waving it. 'An express from Plymouth.'

'Thank you, Diana,' he replied. 'Should you like me to help you wheel the coach?'

'Lord, no,' said Diana. 'But take care of Lalla. She is apt to lose her head with horses about, even geldings.' Then to Brigid, 'Child, come and take this letter to your cousin.'

'Are you my cousin, sir?' asked the child as Diana turned the horses in her usual brilliant manner. 'I am *so* glad.'

The coach spilled its cargo in the forecourt, and Jack called to Sophie, standing there on the steps, 'It is from

Heneage, my dear. He has lost his bowsprit, foretopmast and I dare say a good many headrails. He is leaving *Berenice* at Dock and coaching up here with Philip and perhaps a couple of hands: they will reach us on Thursday, God willing. It was handsome to give so much notice.'

'Oh, very handsome indeed,' cried Sophie faintly.

'Do you know Heneage Dundas?' he asked Diana, as he handed her down.

'A sailor? Lord Melville's son? I have met him. Was not his father in charge of the Navy?'

'He *was*, and a very fine First Lord too. But now it is Heneage's elder brother who has succeeded and who is also First Lord.'

'Sophie, Clarissa,' called Diana, 'should you not like to take an airing? I am going to stretch the horses for a couple of hours: they are in great need of exercise. We might go as far as Lyme.'

'My dear,' cried Sophie with great conviction, 'I really *cannot*.'

'Are you taking Brigid?' asked Clarissa.

'Oh yes: of course. And George, if he would like it.'

'Then I will come too, if I may have five minutes.'

The Thursday that brought Captain Dundas and Philip and that was also expected to bring Mr Cholmondeley's coachman to deprive Diana of her supreme delight, in fact brought the owner himself with two friends, in a post-chaise. He arrived shortly after the others while the drawing-room was still in something of a turmoil with introductions, enquiries after the journey, the health of friends, the likelihood of a French sortie from Brest (most improbable), and Stephen noticed how well Sophie, a retiring provincial lady, coped with the situation – better, indeed, than Cholmondeley, a wealthy and obviously fashionable man. He apologized profusely for this intrusion and protested that he should not stay five minutes; his only errand was to beg Mrs Maturin to keep his coach and horses for a while, if she could bear it. He was on his way to Bristol, there to take ship for Ireland on an urgent piece of legal business that had been delayed too long and that could be delayed no longer lest it go by default; and he was most unwilling that the team should be left idle in their indifferent London stable – no air, no light. He then had the exceedingly awkward task of asking Jack whether he might see Woolcombe's head groom, to arrange for the feeding and the care of his cattle: this having been civilly but very firmly declined, he turned to his not inconsiderable social powers, cheerful, fairly amusing and not small enough to be mere prattle. He and his friends had many acquaintances in common with Captain Dundas and Diana and news of them filled the dangerous gaps that threatened to appear before he stood up and with eloquent gratitude took his leave of Sophie and all the company – a particularly civil farewell to Dr Maturin.

He had not in fact stayed long (though it seemed longer) and the men had little more than the impression of a well-bred man, a fairly agreeable rattle, something of a coxcomb; but it had been long enough for the ladies present to be convinced that he admired Diana extremely.

When he and his friends were gone the place seemed pleasantly empty and free. What small awkwardness there might have been with Heneage and Philip now vanished entirely – they belonged to the home side – and from dinner-time onwards the household settled down enjoying these last days ashore as much as ever they could. In this they were reasonably successful, in spite of the crises threatening Jack Aubrey's future. He and Dundas had a great deal of naval talk to exchange quite apart from the very highly-detailed account of how, in a dense fog off Prawle Point a lost and blundering East Indiaman had come smack across the *Berenice*'s stem with her courses set and all the forces of the tide at three bells in the graveyard watch, shattering her head and bowsprit in the cruellest manner, so that *Berenice*'s foretopmast came by the board and there was a butt sprung low beneath the starboard cathead – 'a perfect jet of water, like a God-damned Iceland geyser'.

Much of their talk, which was really not fit for mixed

company because of its profoundly nautical character, was conducted as they walked over the common with guns or sat in hides either side of the mere, according to the direction of the wind; duck had grown more plentiful, mallard for the most part but also the occasional teal. They always invited Stephen for the dawn and evening flighting, but he rarely went: although he would eagerly shoot specimens and of course bring birds home for the pot when they were called for, he was not fond of killing; and since young Philip took care of Brigid and George entirely, he lapsed back into that contented solitude of an only child, going his own way, in silence, without reference to anyone at all. It was a natural way of life and it suited him very well. Sometimes he went driving with Diana, but although he greatly admired her skill – the four bays were likely to be the best-drilled, best behaved, best-paced team in the county quite soon – her concentration on speed distressed him. Natterjacks were common in no part of the world – he had seen comparatively few – and now in one drive he had been swept past four. Shrews were another of his present studies, and Diana could not be brought to like them very much, having learnt as a child that every time you touched or even saw a shrewmouse you aged a full year; and then, as everybody knew, they gave you the most excruciating rheumatism and made in-calf heifers abort.

He had hoped to interest Brigid if not in shrews then at least in what flowers were still abroad and the more usual birds; but in this he was disappointed, since both children were wholly taken up with admiring Philip, Jack Aubrey's half-brother, the just legitimized son of the late General Aubrey by a dairy-maid at Woolcombe House, at present a long-legged midshipman in Captain Dundas' ship. He was indeed a very likeable young fellow, fresh-full of youth and good-nature, and he was very kind to the little creatures, showing them how to lay aloft in the coach-house with hay-wain ropes for shrouds, made fast to the topmast beams, whirling them to extraordinary heights on swings, teaching them the rudiments of fives, and carrying them to all manner of curious places in the attics (bats by the hundred), cellars and elsewhere, for he had been born at Woolcombe and he knew the house and its even older buildings through and through.

Sometimes, if Philip would come too, they drove out with Diana, and on shopping days Sophie joined them, but only as far as the village, or Dorchester at the utmost. She was not a cowardly woman – fortitude and courage in plenty, on occasion – but she disliked driving fast; and childhood falls, hard-mouthed froward ponies and inept, sometimes cruel masters had made her reluctant to ride; and on the whole she disliked horses. Clarissa was Diana's most usual companion, apart from the necessary groom and boy.

Stephen took his disappointment philosophically. After all, he had himself reached nearly seven years of age before he paid really serious attention to voles; and shrews, in spite of the fine crimson teeth that some possessed, had certain unfortunate characteristics: not quite the best mammal to begin with. There was time and to spare for shrews; and in any event Catalonia, where he hoped she would spend much of her time once peace was restored, was much, much richer in species. While as for botany, that would necessarily come with the return of spring.

He therefore wandered alone, much as he had done when he was a boy, peering into the water-shrew's domain (the streams on the common held scores) and making a rough inventory of the resident birds: he also read a good deal in Woolcombe's noble but utterly neglected library, where a first folio Shakespeare stood next to Baker's *Chronicle* and a whole series of *The Malefactor's Bloody Register* mingled with Blackstone's *Commentaries*. Yet some of his time he spent at the Hand and Racquet or the Aubrey Arms on the little triangular green, watching the slow, regular sequence of agricultural life and sipping a pot of audit ale. He was taken very much for granted, it being known that he was Captain Jack's surgeon, and people would sometimes come for a whispered consultation. They treated him kindly, as a person known to be on their side, like the Captain himself, and they did not conceal their opinions when he was there. He was esteemed not only for his connexions and his pills, but for dividing his custom, trifling though it was, between these two houses and for avoiding the Goat and Compasses, a more pretentious place run by one of Griffiths' partisans; and although in each house he heard or was directly told quite different things the general burden was the same – intense opposition to the inclosures, hatred of Griffiths and his gamekeepers, who were represented as hired bullies, and of his new intruding tenants, settled on what had been Woolcombe Common, together with a great affection for Captain Aubrey, but a very anxious doubt about his ability to do anything to prevent the destruction of their whole way of life.

All this was confirmed by his slow perambulations of the common and the village with old Harding, who told him the exact nature and tenure of each small holding and cottage (often merely customary, tolerated by indulgence long, long since, but with no formal, written grant) together with its rights on the common. Neither Harding nor Stephen had sentimental, misty views of rural poverty: they both knew too much about the squalor, dirt, idleness, petty thieving, cruelty, frequent drunkenness and not uncommon incest that could occur to have any idyllic notion of a poor person's life in the country. 'But,' said Harding, 'it is what we are used to; and with all its plagues it is better than being on the parish or having to go round to the farmer's back door begging for a day's work and being turned away. No, it ain't all beer and skittles but with the common a man is at least half his own man. And without the common he's the farmer's dog. That's why we are so main fond of Captain Jack.'

They were indeed. At all times they were kind and civil, but as the day for the committee's meeting in London came nearer, so they grew more articulate. 'Bless you, Squire: you will never let them do us down.' General cries of 'Good old Captain Jack!' 'No inclosures!' and 'Down with Black Whiskers' accompanied his progress through Woolcombe, and those villagers who were now Captain Griffiths' tenants moved quickly out of the way: jostling and harsh words were not unknown, even among cousins – in fact the village was full of ill-feeling and potential violence.

This was particularly marked one day when Stephen was sitting outside the Hand and Racquet, sorting a handkerchief-full of mushrooms he had gathered. He heard the greetings and blessings some way along Mill Street and before he saw Captain Aubrey and heard him say, 'Thankee, William; but where the Devil is my coxswain? Where is Bonden?'

'Why, sir,' said William, hesitant, rather frightened, looking about his friends in the vain hope that they might tell. 'Why, sir, he has gone into the Goat. Which one of Captain Dundas's men wanted to look at the pretty barmaid.'

He had gone in, sure enough. Now he came out, together with Dundas' men, violently propelled by a hostile band, with Griffiths' head gamekeeper foremost.

'What the devil is this?' roared Captain Aubrey. 'Belay there. D'ye hear me, there? If you want a proper mill, have a proper mill, not a God-damned pothouse brawl.'

The gamekeeper was in too scarlet a passion to answer coherently but his long thin neighbour, Griffiths' clerk, said, 'By all means, sir. Whenever you choose. Wednesday evening in the Dripping Pan, for a ten-pound purse, if your man will stand?'

Bonden nodded contemptuously. 'Very well,' said Jack. 'Now get you home. Not another word, or I shall commit you for a breach of the peace.'

Chapter Three

The sun, distinctly later now, rose over Simmon's Lea, and penetrating into the lanes it lit up Ahab, the Woolcombe mule, with George on the double sack that served for a saddle, Harding on the left side, with the halter in his hand, and Brigid on the right, trotting along and uttering a very rapid series of observations that tumbled over one another like the babbling of a swallow. George was carrying not only the paper, as was his duty, but also the Woolcombe post-bag, as he explained when they came to the breakfast-room window.

'Good morning, Mama,' he began, beaming through the window, 'Good morning, Cousin Diana, good morning, sir, good morning, sir, good morning sir,' to each of those within. 'We overtook Bonden and Killick just before Willet's rickyard. The gig had somehow run into Willet's slough, and they were puzzled to get it out.'

'I told them that my Mama would have it on the road in a moment,' cried Brigid, on tip-toe.

'So we have brought the letters too' – holding up the bag.

'I carried them part of the way, but they happened to drop. Oh please may we come in? We are so hungry and cold.'

'Certainly not,' said Stephen. 'Go round to the kitchen and beg Mrs Pearce to give you a piece of bread and a bowl of milk.'

It was usual at Woolcombe to read one's letters at table, and Jack opened the bag with an anxious heart, dreading to see a lawyer's seal or an official mark of any sort. There was nothing of that kind for him or for any of the women, but he did notice the black Admiralty wax on one of the covers he handed to Dundas.

'It is just a friendly note from my brother,' said Dundas after a moment, 'saying that if he had known I was to stay ashore so long he would have asked me over for a day or two with the partridges at Fenton, but he dares say that it would be too late now: the Admiral is sure to summon us the minute *Berenice* can swim, and you perhaps earlier still. I do wish he would give me a decent ship: the *Berenice* is so old and frail she crumples like a paper nautilus. What is the point of having a brother First Lord, without he gives you a decent ship?'

No one could discover the answer to this, but Sophie said it was a shame, Diana thought downright shabby, and Clarissa, coming in rather late, made a generally sympathizing murmur.

After a while Jack said, 'So long as the Admiral don't summon me before Friday, when the committee sits, he may do as he damn well pleases: and give me a duck-punt for a tender, too.' This was an oblique reference to the *Bellona*'s true tender, the *Ringle*, an American schooner of the kind called a Baltimore clipper, Jack's private property, much coveted by the Admiral for her fast sailing and her outstanding weatherly qualities.

After breakfast Stephen went to see Bonden in his quarters over the coach-house. He was sitting with his hands in a basin and he explained that he was pickling his fists against Wednesday's fight. 'Not that I can ever get them real horny-leathery by then,' he said, 'but it is better than going in raw-handed, like a fine lady, or a dairy-maid, soft with the butter and cream.'

'What is your liquor?' asked Stephen.

'Well, sir, vinegar, very strong tea and spirits of wine, but we put in a little tar-bark and dragon's blood as well. And barber's styptic, of course.'

'Little do I know of prize-fighting, though I have always had a curiosity to see a right match; but I had supposed that nowadays gloves were used.'

'Why, so they are, sir, for light sparring and teaching gentlemen the noble art, as they say; but for a serious boxing-match, for a genuine prize-fight, it is always the bare mauleys, oh dear me, yes.' He turned his fists in the basin, quite amused.

'Will you tell me the first principles, now?'

'Anan, sir?'

'I mean, just how a prize-fight is conducted – the rules – the customs.'

'Well, first you have to have two men willing and proper to fight – that is to say a fairly well-matched pair – and someone to put up a purse for the winner. And then you have to find a right place, meadow or heath, where there is plenty of room and no busy-body magistrate likely to come down on you for unlawful assembly or breach of the peace. With all that settled you either mark out a ring with posts and ropes or you leave it to the members of the fancy: they link their arms and stand in a circle. I prefer the ring myself, because if you are knocked down or flung down under the feet of the other man's friends you may get a very ugly kick, or worse.'

'Is it a brutal sport, then?'

'Why, truly it is not for young ladies. But no gouging, kicking or biting is allowed, nor no hitting beneath the belt or striking a man when he is down. To be sure, that still leaves a good deal of room for rum capers, such as getting your man's head in chancery, as we call it – pinned under your left arm – and hammering away with the other fist till he can neither see nor stand. Another great thing is grappling close and then throwing your man down with a trip and falling whop on to him as hard as ever you can, accidentally-done-a-purpose, if you understand me, sir. Oh, and I was forgetting. Another of the capers used to be to catch your man by the hair and batter him something cruel with his head held down: which was reckoned fair. That is why most bruisers are cropped short nowadays and I shall tie my pig-tail up uncommon tight in a bandage. Which Killick will make it right fast again after every round.'

'You would not consider being cropped yourself, I suppose? I do not like to think of that fellow seizing you by the queue and whirling you about to your destruction.'

'What?' cried Bonden, jerking the long heavy plait on the table. 'Cut off the best tail in the barky? A ten-year tail that I can sit on, without a lie? And then think of that cove in the Bible, and his bad luck when he was cropped. Oh sir.'

'Well, you must be the judge. But tell me, how does it all begin?'

'The two men come into the ring with their seconds and bottle-holders; the referee introduces them, like "Gentlemen, this is Joe Bloggs of Wapping, and this here is the Myrtle Bough of Hammersmith. They are to fight for a prize of – whatever it is – and may the best man win." Then the friends of each chap whistle and cheer and call out, and sometimes the two shake hands before the referee sends them back to the corners where their seconds sit, reminds them of the rules and the agreed time between the rounds – half a minute usually though some call for three quarters – scratches the mark in the middle of the ring and says "Come on when I say *start the mill* and fight away until one of you can't come up to the scratch before time is called."'

'I do not quite gather the force of the words *time* and *round*. Is the contest set to last for a certain period – for so many glasses, as it were?'

'Oh no, sir: it can go on till Kingdom Come if both men have the strength and pluck. It only comes to an end when one cannot come up to the scratch after a round, whatever his second may do to revive him, either because he is dead, which sometimes happens, or because he is too stunned and mazed to stand, or because an arm is broke, and that happens too, or because he don't choose to be punished any longer.'

'Pray let us come back to this concept of a round, which puzzles me yet.'

'Which I must have explained it badly, because it is as simple as kiss my hand. A round is when one man is knocked down, or thrown down, or flings himself down in missing his blow – I mean that is the *end* of the round, and it may have lasted a great while or only a minute. Then they must go back to their corners and come up to the scratch when the time-keeper calls time.'

'I see, I see: so it is as indefinite as a game of cricket, where a truly dogged batsman can tire down the sun. But tell me, what is the usual length of a bout?'

'Why, sir, if it were another gent as asked,' said Bonden, with his singularly winning gap-toothed smile, 'I should say, as long as a piece of marline. But being it is your honour, I will answer that three or four rounds or say a quarter of an hour is usually enough for young fellows new to the game, fellows with some pluck but with little wind and no science; but with right bruisers, fighting for a handsome prize or from a grudge against the other cove or both, right game bruisers, with plenty of bottom, it can last a great while. Even in just Navy fighting, I saw Jack Thorold of the *Lion* and Will Summers of the old *Repulse* knock one another about for forty-three rounds in just over an hour; and talking of myself, it took me sixty-eight rounds and an hour and twenty-six minutes to beat Jo Thwaites for who should be champion of the Mediterranean.'

'Barrett Bonden, you astonish me. I had supposed it was a five or ten minutes affair, like a bout with the small-sword.'

'It does seem a long time; but the London fancy are used to even longer battles. Gully fought the Game Chicken for two hours and twenty minutes – the sixth round alone lasted a quarter of an hour – and Jem Belcher and Dutch Sam went on near as long before their seconds agreed to call it a draw. Both men were still game, but they could barely stand, neither could see, and their mothers would not have recognized them.'

'Oh Papa,' cried Brigid, shrill as a bat in her anguish. 'Come quick! Come quick! George is bleeding terribly.' She broke into her still somewhat easier Irish, panting as they ran, and explained that she had only given him a little small push to show how prize-fighters did it, and now he was bleeding like a holy martyr. 'O, if George should die, the sorrow and woe, O, the black grief of the world . . .'

'Why, child,' said Diana, meeting them, 'never be so distressed. You only tapped his claret. It is all over now. I have mopped him up and put his shirt to soak – always remember, my dear, cold water is the only thing for blood – and he is eating sillabub in the kitchen. If you run very fast, you may get some too. Stephen, my dear, Jack is in a great rage. He has been waiting almost five minutes to take you to see the mere. I was coming to fetch you.'

'God love you, sweetheart,' cried Stephen, kissing her, 'I had forgotten it entirely.'

On their way out to the great mere, where an osprey had been seen that summer and where hard winter might bring down the odd great northern diver, they saw Captain Griffiths riding along his former track and peering about. He wheeled his horse on catching sight of them emerging from the bushes. 'Damn it all,' said Jack. 'We shall have to speak to the fellow again.'

'Good morning, Aubrey,' said Griffiths, touching his hat to Stephen, who responded. 'Have you any news from the squadron?'

'Not a word.'

'That is surprising, with the wind so strong and steady in the south-west, hardly varying a point. You could run up from Ushant in a day . . . However, I hear there is to be a fight between your coxswain and my head-keeper on Wednesday. Shall you be there?'

'It depends.'

'I am afraid I shall not: I have to go up to town for the committee. Shall you attend?'

'Conceivably.'

'In spite of our majority? Well . . .' shaking his head. 'But to go back to this match: I take the liveliest interest in it, and I will back my man for any sum you may wish to name, giving seven to five.'

'You are very good, sir,' said Jack, 'but on this occasion I do not choose to bet.'

'As you please, as you please. I dare say you know best.

But' – turning his horse again – 'faint heart never won fair lady, they say.'

They were by the mere again on Wednesday, on the far side, farther than Dundas cared to walk until the wigeon should start coming in, and as Jack set about repairing a hide on the edge of the reed-bed, repairing it so that it should be almost indistinguishable from the other reeds, as Harding had showed him so many years ago, he said, 'That fellow was prating about faint hearts the other day. I cannot tell you how faint mine is at present, when I consider: one unlucky fall on the part of one single unhappy horse, a post-chaise losing a wheel, a friend being out of the way, and my ride to London gets me there after the fair – I do not get there for Friday's committee. I am keeping very quiet today, so as to ride with a clear mind and a firm, untroubled hand. I have not even been to look at the Dripping Pan. I have kept perfectly calm. Yet I don't know how it is . . .' He paused for quite a while and then in the tone of one quoting an aphorism he went on, 'The heart has its reasons that the . . . that the . . .'

'Kidneys?' suggested Stephen.

'That the kidneys know not.' Jack frowned. 'No. Hell and death, that's not it. But anyhow the heart has its reasons, you understand.'

'It is a singularly complex organ, I am told.'

'And I am uneasy about a whole variety of things. Tell me, Stephen, did you think there was anything odd about the way that fellow talked?'

'It seemed to me that he was a little more obviously false than before; and I was quite struck by his insistence on the steadiness of the wind from the blockading squadron. If I do not mistake, the relations between you and Captain Griffiths hardly warrant his riding out to ask you for news?'

'No, indeed. The barest civilities, that is all. No invitations on either side, ever since I came home and said I was dead against their scheme of inclosure and should *not* sign but should heartily oppose their petition.'

'Has this affected our admiral, Lord Stranraer? I mean, as far as you are concerned?'

'I cannot tell. I hardly knew him before the *Bellona* was sent to join his command. But as I told you, he was perfectly ready to dislike me from the start, as a Tory, as a naval member of Parliament, and as my father's son.'

'Another question, Jack: does a great deal of money depend upon this scheme?'

'I have not gone into it thoroughly, yet I should say that in time there is. They would have to spend a very considerable amount in hedging, ditching, draining and above all clearing, but some of the common, farmed by men with capital, would make famous wheat and root land; and with canals cut through the wet, low-lying waste it would be capital pasture in a few years' time. Eventually I believe the whole operation would pay the promoters hands down. They would make a great deal.'

'The kind of money that would push men on to extreme measures?'

'I think much more than money is involved: for one thing there is the very high station of a man with some thousands of acres laid out in fair-sized fields with hedge and ditch, ideal country for hunting, and for shooting too, if you care for that kind of shooting. And above all, country inhabited by a few big tenant-farmers anxious about their leases and by a crowd of respectful villagers who have to do what they are told and accept what they are given or go on the parish. A man in that position is as much of an autocrat as the captain of a man-of-war without the loneliness, the responsibility, the violence of the enemy and the dangers of the sea. Then again there is the pleasure of having your own way against opposition. And it is but fair to add that they think, or have been persuaded to think, that it is all for the country's good.'

'From Lord Stranraer's reputation, would you say he was a man whose love of his country, of high station, and incidentally of a considerable addition to his fortune, might induce him to bend the ordinary course of morality so that good might result?'

'I should not assert it. I know very little of him. His reputation in the service is that of a good seaman and a strict disciplinarian, but I do not think he is much liked. He has had little opportunity of showing his courage, yet as far as I know it has never been doubted. Before the recent spring-tide of prize-money that came to him as a flag-officer – you know, Stephen, do you not, that even now, after Mulgrave's reforms, an admiral still pockets a third of his captains' prize-money, though he may be sitting in port a thousand miles away from the battle? So if he has several lucky, active, enterprising frigate-captains under his orders he can very soon grow rich.'

'Iniquitous, iniquitous. Yet you may see it in a different light when you hoist your flag.'

Jack cast him a haggard look, but went on, 'Before that, he was by no means well to do; and even now he still keeps a very modest table.' He considered for a moment. 'No. From the cut of his not very attractive jib, I should never have said he was a man to do good that evil might come of it; yet to tell you the truth, Stephen, the older I get, the less I trust in my own judgment. I have been wrong so often.'

Stephen said, 'Even I have made errors,' shaking his head dolefully; but Jack's attention was elsewhere. He stood tall and straight, a hand behind one much-battered ear. 'Do you hear?' he asked. 'They are beating in the posts to make the ring in the Dripping Pan.'

When Woolcombe's early dinner was over the men only sat long enough for one single glass of port: then Jack said to his brother, 'Philip, will you make our excuses in the drawing-room?' But before the boy had answered he went on, 'No, damn it. I will go myself.

'Ladies,' said he, 'I must beg you to forgive us. Stephen and Heneage are grown so prodigious impatient I can no longer restrain them – it is not consonant with my duty as a host to restrain them. They say it would be disrespectful to the noble art not to see the first exchange; and anyhow the Doctor should be there to revive either of the dead.'

'From the way they bolted their food,' said Diana, then

the door had closed behind him, 'I wonder that we were allowed to finish our dinner at all.'

'Yet at least we can drink our coffee in peace,' said Sophie, 'but first I must change my gown. If I do not get this wine-stain out directly, it will never go: and then I can darn a stocking with a clear conscience.'

'How they do love a mill,' said Diana when she came down again. 'The Colonel Villiers I stayed with in Ireland when Stephen was away – you remember him when he came over, Clarissa?'

'Certainly I do. A splendid old gentleman: so very kind.'

'So he was, but very frail too. Yet even so he and an equally ancient friend from Indian days drove close on forty miles to see a fight between two well-known bruisers, Ikey Pig and Dumb Burke. They came back as merry as grigs, and almost speechless with shouting.'

'Forty miles is a great way . . .' began Sophie.

'Beg pardon, ma'am,' said the cook, a short, thick woman, of much greater importance now that Sophie was her own housekeeper. 'Which the kitchen pump won't fetch; and without water how can I boil the Captain's puddings? Let alone Master Philip's, who fancies a roly-poly today.'

'Why won't it fetch, Mrs Pearce,' asked Sophie in alarm. 'Surely the well cannot possibly be dry yet?'

'Which the pin is broke,' said Mrs Pearce, folding her arms.

'How did it come to be broken?'

'I never was a teller of tales, ma'am; but perhaps *someone* has been swinging on the handle, though told it was wicked.'

'Oh, I see,' said Sophie. 'Well, you must get a man to put in another pin.'

'God love you, ma'am,' said Mrs Pearce, 'there ain't a man left in the house, nor yet in the garden nor the yard. Even poor old Harding has crept off, bunions and all, agog to see this horrible murdering-match.'

'Oh come, it cannot be as bad as all that,' cried Sophie.

'Ma'am, I do assure you it is: or worse. That gamekeeper fellow, Black Evans as they call him, served out our poor

61

Hetty's William so cruel over some paltry rabbits that he has never been the same man since; and his wife says he never will be. They say the Beelzebub creature was fit to be matched with Tom Cribb himself but he was barred for fighting foul and gouging out the other party's eye. Right eye. Henry, the blacksmith's young man, had a turn-up with him, oh dear me . . .' Mrs Pearce had been in the house before Sophie was born; she was a valuable soul, a good cook, but voluble, voluble, and it was long before Sophie could check the bloody narrative and persuade her to use the dairy pump until the men should come back to replace the broken pin. 'Very good, ma'am,' she said: but pausing with the door-knob in her hand she added, 'Which I only hope Mr Bonden ain't brought home senseless on a bloody hurdle, like poor Hal.'

The door closed at last. Sophie picked up her stocking and presently the thread of her discourse. 'Yes, to be sure,' she said, 'forty miles is a great way. But when I think of the distance Jack has to go this very night and all tomorrow . . . Oh, how I wish it were over.'

'He will be in the post-chaise much of the time,' said Diana. 'And although it may not be a feather-bed – I abominate a feather-bed, by the way: I love to have something really firm under my bottom –'

'Oh, Di,' cried Sophie, blushing extremely and throwing an anxious glance at Clarissa, who, to her relief, betrayed no emotion of any kind. Clarissa was a clever needle-woman, intent on her work; and her past was of such a nature that rather free or even licentious words made no impression on her at all.

'– and a man who can sleep aboard a small man-of-war beating into a gale can certainly sleep in a chaise. Anyway, it will not take anything like as long as that. I remember Captain Bettesworth telling me that when he had the *Curieux*, carrying dispatches, he anchored at Plymouth on the morning of July 7 and reached the Admiralty at eleven on the night of the eighth. And Plymouth is nearly eighty miles west of us. Do not grieve about Jack, my dear. On a turnpike road you can do wonders in a post-chaise nowadays. A post-chaise . . .' She paused, for at this moment a chaise and four rolled into the courtyard with a fine clatter of hooves and harness. A tall young man in naval uniform leapt out, a letter in his hand. 'My God,' cried Diana, 'it is Paddy Callaghan of the tender.'

'What tender?'

'Why, *Bellona*'s tender, of course, booby. The *Ringle*.'

'Oh Lord,' said Sophie in a low tone of horror, 'and here I am with no cap. And this squalid old yellow dress. Pray keep him in conversation for five minutes, and I will be down looking more or less like a Christian.'

'Never mind about that,' said Diana. 'I know what he is about. I will deal with him there in the courtyard.'

She ran out, along the hall, reaching the door before the servant. 'Good evening, Mr Callaghan,' she called. 'What good wind blows you here?'

'And a very good evening to you, ma'am. A fine double-reef south-wester, so it was,' said the young man, his large simple face (not unlike a ham) beaming up at her as she stood there at the top of the steps. 'How delightful to see you, and I trust the Doctor is well? But I have brought orders for Captain Aubrey' – holding up the packet ' – and brought them as swift as a bird. This is the first time I have ever been in a four-horse chaise. Captain Jenkins insisted so that *Ringle* might just catch her tide; there is precious little time to go. She is waiting at single anchor in West Bay.'

'Alas, my poor Mr Callaghan, Captain Aubrey is away in London on important Government business.' She came down the steps and went on, 'But if you will give me the letter I promise he shall have it as soon as he returns. Forgive me if I seem inhospitable, but I really think you ought to hurry straight back to West Bay so that the tender may rejoin the ship at once, without missing this selfsame tide. There is not a moment to lose.'

The young man, a master's mate, looked confounded, worried, deeply uncertain; she took the packet from his hand, urged him back into the chaise and called, 'Take a wide sweep, postillion, and you are out in one. Mr Callaghan, my best compliments to Captain Jenkins, if you please.'

She stood on the steps, holding the envelope, as the chaise swung out of the gateway.

'Diana,' said Sophie from just inside the hall, speaking in a low, shocked voice, 'how could you speak so? You know he is at the Dripping Pan.'

'Come into the drawing-room, sweetheart,' said Diana; and there, with the door shut behind them, she went on, 'The tender came with orders for Jack to rejoin his ship immediately. It would have broken his heart to miss this committee meeting and lose the common.'

'But he will never forgive us for lying.'

'No, dear,' said Diana. 'Now the first thing we must do is to send a message telling him not to come home but to go straight on to Wooton and take his chaise from there.'

'There is no one to send,' said Sophie. 'None of the maids could possibly be sent, with that rough crowd. There is a whole tribe of gypsies; and both the Aubrey Arms and the Goat have been wheeling barrels of beer out there since early dawn.'

'I will go,' said Clarissa. 'I do not stand out as much as either of you would do, and when I get to the edge of the crowd I can call one of our people to go and ask the Doctor to come. I shall put on ankle-boots and an old tippet.'

The others looked at her for a moment. 'Do please take Grim,' said Sophie at last, anxious and ashamed.

'Yes: but he must wear his choke-collar,' said Diana who had seen the stable mastiff discourage a stranger. 'I shall put it on to him while you get ready.' She spoke with a fairly easy conscience: in this house and this village Clarissa was seen as a dependant; her presence at the Dripping Pan would be far less remarked; her scheme was better than any other, and though Diana was not proud of herself she honoured Clarissa for it.

'You will not be afraid of all those rough men?' asked Sophie, when Clarissa came down.

'No. As far as I have seen, apart from mere brute strength

they are no more formidable than we are. Less so, indeed, since most have that dog-does-not-bite-bitch rule deeply engrained, while nothing of that kind applies to us.'

Mere brute strength was Stephen's first impression of the prize-fight. The referee, a knowing publican from Bridport and a former pugilist, called the men to the middle of the roped-off square: they were both stripped to close-fitting knee-length linen drawers and to pumps, and they stood on either side of him, Bonden still tanned from his seafaring and slightly taller than the other, his pigtail turned tight about his head (the bandage had been disallowed, as too much like a protection), Evans broader, heavier, his flesh corpse-pale except where it was covered by a great mat of black hair. Neither had had much time to train, but both were in reasonable shape – big, powerful men. The referee named them to cheers from either side, and having spoken the ritual words in a hoarse shout he dismissed each to his corner, scratched a mark on the green level turf, retired beyond the ropes and called, 'Now start the mill, gents; and may the best man win.' Amid the cheers and counter-cheers of all those assembled – most of the men and boys from at least seven villages and their surrounding farms – the two men came up to the scratch.

There was no motion towards shaking hands. They eyed one another intently for a moment, with a few slight feints of head and stance, and at exactly the same moment exchanged a series of heavy blows to head and body, most warded off on either side, and then closed, each trying the other's weight and strength.

'This is more like wrestling than anything else,' said Stephen: he, Jack, Dundas and Philip were sitting on the rising slope behind Bonden's corner. 'See, that ill-looking hairy fellow has seized Bonden's arm.'

'He is trying for a cross-buttock,' said Jack.

He was indeed – a deadly throw – but unsuccessfully, for with a sudden twist and heave Bonden flung Evans forward, flat on his face.

'Drop on him. Fall heavy. Kick him in the balls,' bellowed the Woolcombe House supporters on either side of Jack and far up the hill behind him; but Bonden only nodded and smiled, and walked back to his corner, where he sat on his bottle-holder's knee – Tom Farley, a former shipmate, who had come with Captain Dundas – while his second, Preserved Killick, sponged the blood from his face: an unimportant glancing blow that had nevertheless opened his eyebrow. He was breathing rather quick, but he looked cheerful and composed and when the umpire called time he sprang up as lively as his friends could wish, met Evans at the scratch and instantly struck him over his guard, left and right to forehead and ear, blows that were borne with apparent indifference though they staggered him and drew a surprising flow of blood. Once again Evans closed and once again there was a long obscure struggle for mastery until Bonden, breaking away at last, leapt back and then sprang forward, leading with his left at full stretch – a punch that would have ended the match had it gone home. But surprisingly fast for so heavy a man, Evans shifted six inches to the left and Bonden, slipping on the green grass, came down, to hoots of derision from the far side of the Dripping Pan, where the keeper's friends and Captain Griffiths' more subservient tenants sat with the hereditary opponents of Woolcombe, the men who lived in the villages of Holt, Woolcombe Major and Steeple Munstead.

It was not until the third and above all the fourth and fifth round that Stephen began to see that much more than mere brute strength was involved, very much more. Both men had been hit and hurt; their blood was up; each had taken the other's measure; and although Bonden moved quicker and had more science, Evans's blows, above all his body blows, were heavier by far. At one point they stood toe to toe in the middle of the ring, hammering one another with extraordinary rapidity and force, but he perceived that almost all the blows he could follow were diverted by the guard: indeed, in spite of the apparent confusion of arms and fists the whole was not unlike a fencing-match with its almost instant anticipation of attack, recoil, parry and lightning counter-strokes.

He sat there, watching them circle, manoeuvre, come in with a storm of blows, close and strive locked together, or break apart for a fresh attack: he watched them under the clear light of a high, veiled sky, fighting there to the roar of the opposing sides – they might have been in the arena of a small provincial Roman town – and he too was as tense as any as he urged his old friend and shipmate to go in and win, shouting for him in a voice he could barely hear for the huge din on either side.

Two long rounds close on ten minutes each, and the next, all ended in a knock-down blow, the first two in Bonden's favour; but neither was a genuine stunner, though Evans's bottle-holder had to help him back to his corner after the second. The third came after a confused mêlée in which Evans closed, tripping Bonden and throwing him backwards, most deliberately falling on him and, amid a great howl of reprobation, planting his knees where they would do most harm. To the shrieks and yells of *Foul* the two umpires looked at one another and at the referee, who agreed with one of them that the match should go on, though he shook his head as he said so. Killick and Farley brought Bonden back to his corner, revived him as well as they could, and when time was called he came up to the scratch quite briskly.

By this point both men were much marked: Evans's face and ears were mostly blood and his left eye was nearly closed; but Bonden, though showing less, had been severely punished during the in-fighting and from his attitude and breathing Stephen thought that two or three ribs might be sprung. Their lack of training told on them too and as though by tacit agreement they closed early in the next round, not so much hitting as trying for the cross-buttock and the decisive throw: or at least for a certain respite and breathing-space – they had been fighting for forty minutes now (Stephen, watching them gasp in their corners between rounds, was astonished that they could have lasted so long), and in their untrained state both were nearly exhausted, while Bonden's knuckles were split to the bone.

During this slow, laborious, grunting dance the blood from his open forehead blurred Bonden's sight and he let himself be manoeuvred to the far side, almost on the ropes of a neutral corner, where Evans's bulk hid him from the umpires and the referees. Here he felt a sudden change in the tension of the clasping arms, a different grunt, and the wicked knee came furious up between his legs. He shot back before it reached its mark, leaving Evans with dangling hands, and hit him two terrible blows, somewhat short since he was on the ropes, but full in the unguarded face. He felt the teeth go, heard an animal shriek of pain and rage and he was heaved back against the ropes by a great hairy sweating weight. In the brutish grapple his head was thrust under the top rope; the lashing of his hair parted and as he forced his way back into the ring to end the fight Evans seized his pigtail in both hands and with his last remaining strength hurled him against the corner post, himself falling as he did so.

In the silence that followed the enormous din the seconds carried their men away: but whereas Evans's friends could just prop him, staggering, half-conscious, half-blind to the mark when time was called, Killick and Farley could not.

Bonden lay flat on his back, his face to the placid sky; and Stephen, kneeling over him, said, 'Do not fear, Jack. There is a concussion, sure, but there is no fracture. The coma may last some hours or even days, but then, with the blessing you will have your coxswain again. Killick, now, will you find a hurdle? We must carry him home and put him in the dark.'

Behind them fighting had broken out between the Woolcombe men, who swore the throw was foul, and the now anxious minority of the gamekeeper's friends and their supporters. But Killick and a shepherd had brought the hurdle, and the sad little train walked off towards Woolcombe House, disregarding the battle.

'Was it fair, at all?' asked Stephen in a low voice, when they had gone a little way.

'Well, just, *just*, I believe,' said Dundas. 'Gentleman Jackson held Mendoza by the hair when he beat him in '97 and . . . surely that is Mrs Oakes coming along the path with the stable dog?'

It was indeed: and a variety of signs – her somewhat hesitant attitude, the improbability of her choice of a walk, and many more scarcely to be defined – awoke all the intelligence-agent in Maturin. Profiting from the hurdle-bearers' necessary slowness he hurried forward: Clarissa had a total confidence in him and told him exactly what was afoot, taking no more than ten words to do so. 'Will I deal with it?' he asked. She nodded and he rejoined the party. 'Jack,' he cried at some distance, 'I grieve to say that there has been a sad misunderstanding and the chaise you are sharing with Mr Judd has been ordered for *Wooton*: it stands there at this moment, and he begs you will join him directly.'

Jack was not always very quick in taking the point of Stephen's longer, more elaborate and even wholly mythical anecdotes, but he knew his friend intimately well – he could interpret a certain fixity of look better than most men – he had a vague recollection of Mr Judd as one of the deeper old files of Whitehall, and without hesitation he replied, 'Hell and death: I must go at once.' And to Clarissa, 'Thank you so much for coming. Please give my dear love to Sophie and tell her I am very sorry if the blunder was my fault, as I dare say it was.'

'I will see you a furlong on your way,' said Stephen. 'No more, because of my patient.'

In the course of this furlong he told his news and Jack cried, 'God bless Diana: and Mrs Oakes, that fine woman. I am sure Sophie would have thought of it in time – she don't want spirit, no, nor yet bottom – but perhaps not quite quick enough. It had to be taken on the half-volley. Bless them. I would not have missed that committee for the world; and as for the blockade during three or four days, why at this stage of the war, my withers are unwrung.' A pause. 'Yet I do wish to God I were going up without this damned unlucky omen. It really does cast a prodigious damp on a man's spirit. The keeper was dead beat: there was not another round in him. And even if he had come up to the mark Bonden only had to give him a shove to floor him for good.'

Stephen knew of old that it was useless to call out against the weakness of mere superstition: no sailor he had ever known, even the most eminent, even a full admiral in all the glory of gold lace, had ever been moved an inch by reason, however eloquent. He therefore came to a halt, said, 'Fare thee well, dear Jack, and may all the luck in the world go with thee. I must follow my patient.'

'You do not fear for him, Stephen?' asked Jack, looking earnestly into his face.

'I do not. God bless, now.'

'One last thing. Do you suppose they meant to nobble me?'

'That is an expression I do not know.'

'Of course not. I beg pardon. It is a cant word I first heard when I was breeding horses at Ashgrove: the riff-raff hanging about racing-stables and Newmarket and so on use it to mean interfering with a horse so he don't run well, and you can safely bet on him losing. There was a nobbler called Dawson hanged for it not long since. What I should have said was: do you think Griffiths and his uncle, our commanding officer, worked out this order to rejoin so as to prevent me from attending the committee?'

'It would not surprise me in Griffiths; but since I have never set eyes on Lord Stranraer I cannot form any opinion of him at all.'

'To be sure. It was a foolish question. But I hope you will see him on Sunday. I mean to come back on Friday, post down to Torbay on Saturday, and there we are sure to find some vessel belonging to the squadron that will carry us out, perhaps by Sunday. They always put in to Torbay, you know.'

'Until Friday, then: and God and St Patrick go with you.'

* * *

There are few more versatile saints than Patrick, and he managed the parliamentary business and the return journey supremely well until the very last lap, when one of the horses lost a shoe just outside Trugget's Hatch, a village that would have been in clear sight of Woolcombe had a hill not stood between them. There they waited at the King's Head and Eight Bells, and while the smith was blowing up his forge Jack sat in the bar, where he called for a pot of ale.

'Well, squire,' said the landlord, setting it down and wiping the table, 'might I be so bold . . .' He knew Jack well; he had a sister married to a commoner on Simmon's Lea; he was by only one remove an interested party; yet he hesitated until he saw Captain Aubrey's beaming face emerge from the tankard, with an unmistakable look of satisfied desire. '. . . so bold as to ask whether everything was to your liking?'

'Mr Andrews, I could not have wished for better. The petition for inclosure was rejected both for inadequate majority and above all for the lord of the manor's direct and firmly-stated opposition. So the common is safe and we can go on in the way we are used to.'

The landlord laughed aloud with pleasure, and having dried his hand on his breeches he held it out. 'Give you joy of your victory, sir. That will wipe Black Whiskers' eye: the lads went through his pheasant coverts the night after that dirty God-damned match, and I dare say that when they hear of this they will stir up his deer. Oh, sir, may I tell Tom, my sister Hawkins's son? She will be so relieved. She was cruel anxious – worn thin and pale – not a scrap of paper to show the place is theirs, though there are Hawkinses in the churchyard by the score.' His voice could be heard moving towards the back of the house: 'Tom! Tom! Tom! Get on your nag and tell your mam she's safe at last. The Captain did the buggers in the eye.'

Tom's nag was no Flying Childers, but running in its own curious nameless pace, belly very near to the ground, feet twinkling, it did reach Woolhampton well before the Trugget's Hatch smith had fitted and fastened the shoe, so that when Jack's chaise reached Woolhampton both sides of the street were lined with cheering villagers, many of whom wished to shake his hand, while others told him they had already known it would end like this; but most were content with bawling, 'Good old Captain Jack' or 'Huzzay, huzzay, huzzay'. And when it reached Woolcombe House, there was his entire family, the entire household, arranged on the broad steps, like the tableau closing a Drury Lane play with a happy ending, except that no legitimate theatre would ever have countenanced so squalid a pair of children as Brigid and George – the little girl had inherited her parents' fearless attitude towards horses and she had been showing her cousin how to muck out the stable in which the splendid borrowed team spent what time they could spare from carrying Mrs Maturin about the countryside. Having kissed the women all round Jack shook Bonden's bandaged hand and in a low voice fit for one so battered he said, 'Well, Bonden, I hope I see you tolerably comfortable? I scarcely thought to find you on your feet so soon, after that cruel foul play.'

'Which the Captain says he trusts you are pretty well,' said Killick in a tone that he judged suitable for one so recently comatose. 'And no pain.'

With so much notice Bonden hung his head and muttered something that Killick translated as, 'He says the other sod – the other party – copped it worse, and is despaired of.'

They all moved into the hall, and from the hall to the front morning room, where Padeen detached the children and led them away towards the pump; yet even so Jack's account of his triumph in London was not as open and candid as it would have been with fewer people present. Nor was Sophie's production of the orders to rejoin his ship 'which came after you had left,' as she put it, blushing as she did so.

Yet bridled as his words were obliged to be, Jack spoke pretty freely, and with growing relish. The orders he dismissed with, 'Yes, my dear, I heard about them. I shall post down to Torbay with Stephen tomorrow, if he can manage it, or the day after.'

'Never mind about posting,' said Diana. 'I will drive you down in Cholmondeley's machine: and if General Harte is as good as his word, with his extra pair, I shall drive you down in a coach and six. There's glory for you! I have always wanted to drive a coach and six on an English turnpike.'

'Have you not driven one before?' cried Sophie in alarm.

'Certainly I have: but in India. And once or twice in Ireland – Ned Taaffe's machine,' she added, nodding to Stephen.

'We should be very happy,' said Jack, bowing. 'But now let me tell you about the committee. First, as you know, Captain Griffiths is a newcomer in these parts. He has no great acquaintance in the neighbourhood; he does not know the connexions between the older families or the long-standing friendships, intermarriages and so on, and both he and the parliamentary lawyer he employed were unaware of the fact that Harry Turnbull is my cousin – indeed, my cousin twice over, since he married Lucy Brett. And then he is not a member of any decent club and he don't know the importance of that connexion either.' Both Jack and Stephen were members of the Royal Society Club, which did their heads great credit; but they were also members of Black's, which spoke well for their power of discernment, for although the place was not quite so learned, it was somehow more companionable and, incidentally, much more to the point in the worldly line. 'I met Frank Crawshay in the coffee-room, the member for Westport: he said he was sitting on the committee – I gather the members had been chosen for their propensity to vote blindfold for the Ministry, and it was known that I had abstained when the naval estimates came up – a black mark – and he let me know in a very tactful and what you might call alluvial fashion that his boy was down for election and he should be very grateful for my name in the candidates' book. And he told me there were some other Blackses on the committee as well as Cousin Harry. Just as well, thought I, for Harry was in a horrid rage, having lost more money than he cared for to Colonel Waley – was barely civil – would not lend me a shirt – should be damned if he would lend me a shirt – scarcely had a shirt to his name – barely a single shirt to his back. You know how cross Harry Turnbull can be: he must have fought more often than any man in the country – a very dangerous shot and very apt to take offence. So when I walked into the committee-room and saw him still looking furious and contrary and bloody-minded, I felt quite uneasy: and though smiles from Crawshay and two other Blackses comforted me a little I did not really have much hope until the lawyer started proceedings. His low soapy tone did not suit Harry, who kept telling him to speak up, to speak like a Christian for God's sake, and not mumble. When he was young, people never mumbled, he said: you could hear every word. If anyone had mumbled, he would have been kicked out of the room. Then came the petition itself: it was handed to the chairman – Harry, of course – and he began to read out the names of the petitioners and their station: Griffiths, some of his friends, some of the richer farmers. Then he cried, "But where's the parson? Where's the patron?"

'"The rector has been travelling for his health these last five years, sir: he is said to be in Madeira now, but he does not answer letters; and the curate cannot speak in his name."

'"Well, where's the patron of the living? And where's the lord of the manor? The same person, I suppose. Why is his name not here?"

'Griffiths went red and muttered something to his lawyer. I stood up and said, "I am the patron of the living, sir, and the lord of the manor. My name is not there because I am very strongly opposed to the inclosure and to the petition."

'Harry glared about him, scribbled sums on a piece of paper, and then said to Griffiths, "God's my life, sir. You have the effrontery to present this with just the barest majority by value, when you know perfectly well that three quarters or four fifths is the usual figure. And to make things worse, far, far worse, you do so against the will of the lord of the manor, your natural superior. I have never heard of such a thing. I wonder at it, sir. I wonder at it.''

All this time Killick and Mnason the butler had been standing outside the door. Their mutual hostility had kept them away from it to begin with, but intense curiosity and the useful formula 'We might either of us be sent for' had brought them to a truce and their ears were very close to the wood at this very point, when Mrs Pearce thrust indignantly between them and burst into the room. 'Ma'am,' she cried, holding up a noble fish, 'I could not get the men to hear, I could not send a maid, and I have to know this directly minute. If I am to cook this here for dinner it must go on at once, *at once*. Which it came a quarter of an hour ago by the chiming clock. Twenty-six pound four ounces, without a lie.'

They gazed upon it with admiration, a silvery, quivering-fresh, clean-run salmon: and on its side it bore a card *For our Captain with love from all at the Aubrey Arms.*

That night, which should have been equally triumphant, was not: misunderstanding, mistiming, and mere weariness played their not uncommon part and for once Jack Aubrey got up in a bad temper of mind. He cut his chin while he was shaving and when he came back into the bedroom he heard Sophie, her head muffled under her shift, uttering a discontented remark whose beginning he had not heard but which, as her head emerged, finished with '. . . that Mrs Oakes.'

Jack checked his immediate answer, but having tied his neckcloth he said, 'You often say "that Mrs Oakes" in a tone that makes me think you imagine something improper about our having been shipmates. Even if I had been Heliogabalus or Colonel Chartres there could not possibly have been anything improper. She came aboard without my knowledge under the protection of one of my midshipmen: I at once insisted upon their being married – I even gave a piece of that crimson silk I bought you in Java for her to be married in. I may have been something of a rake when I was young, but I give you my sacred word that I have *never* played the fool at sea and I should never, never at any time look at the wife of one of my officers. So I beg we may hear no more of "that Mrs Oakes".'

Sophie blushed as crimson as her Java silk, hung her head, and made no reply, the extreme awkwardness being resolved by the breakfast gong beaten in a frenzy by George and Brigid, still in their nightshirts.

Diana, late for most things, was prompt for this. Having breakfasted by candle-light they made an early start in the half-day, the stars still to be seen due west, with Venus declining. 'Let go,' called Diana from the box, and the coach rolled smoothly away, followed by a chaise carrying Killick and Bonden, who was in no state to travel outside a coach, and leaving such a melancholy group waving on the steps, some indeed in tears.

The men had drawn lots to decide which should sit next to Diana for the first stage: it had fallen on Dundas, so Stephen and Jack were inside, with the head groom and a boy up behind. Jack remained silent for a while. He and Sophie disagreed fairly often, though perhaps less than most married people, but never had they done so on parting. It was true that this was not much of a parting – leave from the Brest blockade was reasonably frequent and letters passed to and fro – and it was true that Sophie's attitude towards Clarissa Oakes (a guest, after all) had irritated him extremely, all the more so since he had at one time been strongly tempted to lead Clarissa far astray – he was not a man to whom chastity came easy – and had had to impose a most rigorous self-command: but he was sorry he had spoken. Eventually he said, 'Old Harding is of opinion that the salmon had been ordered by Griffiths, and that it came by coach, being left at the Arms – according to village gossip he had ordered dinner for a score – for none of our streams ever yielded a fish like that. But I do hope our people are not coming it too high.'

'The young fellows took some of his deer last night, and his keepers were out in force. I heard shots.'

'The Devil you did?' cried Jack, and he would have gone on but that the coach was now in the village street and that many of the over-excited youths were still about. They started cheering, and waving, and the horses began to caper. Fortunately General Harte had thought better of his promise to provide an extra pair, but even so Dundas was tempted to take the reins. The determined expression on Diana's face – most vividly alive – and the language in which she recalled the horses to their duty checked him, however; and presently the team were steadily climbing the hill before Maiden Oscott.

'I wish they may not be coming it too high,' said Jack. 'Stealing deer may be fun, but it is a very grave matter indeed when you come before a court, above all if you were disguised in any way – and Billy Iles, who ran by the coach just now, had a sort of skirt on and the remains of black round his face – or above all if you were armed. You heard shots . . . That Griffiths is a rancorous sort of cove – weak – you should have seen him quail before Harry Turnbull – and cruel. And there was that damned unlucky omen.' He jerked his head towards the chaise with poor Bonden in it, and sank into an uneasy train of thought while the coach climbed up and up, the horses well into their collars, warming now.

Near the top he looked back for a last sight of Woolcombe, spread out far, far below, with both broad commons, the villages and the great mere, silver now with the coming day. 'Oh my God,' he cried, for there, over beyond Woolcombe, stacks were ablaze, a great pall of smoke drifting westwards, the bottom lit red. He let down the glass, leant out and called to the groom behind, 'Is that Hordsworth's rickyard, John?'

'It is on Captain Griffiths' land, sir. The new piece he took in to round the home farm.'

They were over the crest: nothing could be seen on the far side of the hill. Indeed they were well over and on the flat stretch of road before the much steeper descent to Maiden Oscott and the stream; and both Stephen and Jack heard Diana encourage the horses. There was a dog-cart ahead, drawn by a likely-looking chestnut mare and driven by a young man with a girl beside him.

'Give him a halloo to pull over, will you, Dundas?' said Diana, and he let out a fine nautical roar.

The girl nudged the young man, who looked round, flicked the mare with his whip and crouched forward, urging her on.

Gradually the coach overhauled the dog-cart, Diana tense and concentrated, in complete control of the horses: but there was a left-handed corner ahead and not two hundred yards to go. 'Pull over, sir. Pull over directly,' called Dundas with all the authority of twenty years at sea. His vehemence, coupled with the pleas of the pale-faced girl, induced the young man to rein in, with his off wheel on the grassy verge; the coach swept by, followed by a look of pure hatred.

'There was a good two foot to spare, so there was,' said Stephen, relaxing.

'It is very well,' said Jack. 'Very well. But I dread the Oscott bridge. Does Diana know it, Stephen?'

'Sure, she has been driving about the countryside day and night: it is her liveliest joy. But tell me, where is young Philip?'

'Oh, he stayed at home to worship Mrs Oakes. Did you not remark his moon-struck gaze? No, of course you were sitting next to him. Still, you might have seen him pick up her napkin and press it to his lips. But this bridge is a most damnably awkward one. You come down a wicked steep hill in the middle of the village, and there right in front of you there is the bridge, hard on your left, a blind corner at an angle of ninety or even a hundred degrees, before you are aware of it. You have to turn terribly sharp – a damned narrow bridge with a low stone wall on either side and unless you judge it just so you hit the corner and you are in the river twenty feet below – deep water – with the coach on top. Don't you think you might mention it to her?'

'I do not. She is a very fine whip, you know.'

'Then perhaps I should,' said Jack.

Stephen bowed, and after a moment Jack lowered the glass again, leant out, and in a conciliating tone he called, 'Coz, oh coz.'

The coach slowed perceptibly. 'What now?' replied Diana.

'It is only that I thought, being a native as it were, that I thought perhaps I should tell you about the very dangerous bridge at Maiden Oscott. But perhaps you know it?'

'Jack Aubrey,' she said, 'if you do not like the way I drive this coach, take the bloody reins yourself, and be damned to you.'

'Not at all, not at all,' cried Jack. 'It was only that I thought . . .'

The horses resumed their fine round pace: Jack sank back. 'Perhaps I have vexed her,' he said, 'though I spoke both meek and civil.'

'Perhaps you have,' said Stephen.

The downward slope grew steeper, and even steeper. The first houses appeared and very soon they were in the street itself, Dundas hallooing to clear dogs, cats, asses and children out of the way and the horses going rather faster than Diana would have allowed at another time. She had the tension of the reins just so: her hands were in close touch with the horses' mouths and her keen gaze was fixed on the left-hand leading corner of the wall that crossed the bridge, a wall scarred by innumerable vehicles in the last four hundred years. With a last glance down at the hub of her near forewheel, she changed the pressure on the reins, clucked to the leaders and swung the coach square on to the narrow bridge, avoiding the stone by half an inch and trotting superbly across to the other side.

Where the Maiden Oscott road, having risen again and fallen again, joined the Exeter turnpike she pulled up at a famous coaching-inn by a delightful stream, and while the others held the horses' heads she climbed nimbly down. Jack gave her a hand from the lower step and said, 'I do ask your pardon, Diana.'

'Never mind it, Jack,' she said with a brilliant smile – she was in excellent looks, with the fine fresh air and the excitement – 'I have been frightened too, aboard your ships. Now be a good fellow and call for a room, coffee, toast, and perhaps bacon and eggs, if they have nothing better – Lord, I could do with a decent second breakfast. But for the moment I must retire.'

Jack had given orders for the horses to be watered and walked up and down before their moderate bite, and he was rejoining his friends in front of the inn when he heard his name called. It was William Dolby, followed by Harry Lovage, both old friends (Lovage was called Old Lechery), crossing the road from the stream, both carrying fishing-rods, and both looking thoroughly happy – indeed it was a delightful morning, a delightful scene – the water flowing in its smooth green banks, the scent of a late aftermath drifting across, and the air full of swallows.

'Look what we have caught,' cried Dolby, opening his bag. 'Such trouts you might dream of, the glorious day!'

'My best was still larger,' said Lovage. 'You must breakfast with us. The two fishes ain't in it, nor the five loaves. Dick' – this to a waiter – 'lay for us all in the Dolphin parlour, will you?'

They moved slowly across the forecourt, admiring the fish, talking of claret and mallard and the mayfly hatch, and Lovage said, 'There will be plenty for supper; and if there ain't we shall make up on the evening rise. Fish suppers make a man skip like a flea, ha, ha, ha. We have Nelly Clapham with us, and her young sister Sue, such a cheerful, jolly . . .' He stopped abruptly, looking appalled, for there in the porch, pausing to join them, was Diana: very clearly not a lady of pleasure.

They broke off to receive her – introductions – and Stephen said, 'My dear, these gentlemen have invited us to breakfast with them on some of the noblest trouts that ever yet were seen. But it may well be that you are tired after your drive, and would as soon sit quietly with a little thin gruel and perhaps a very small cup of chocolate. I cannot recommend cream or sugar.'

'Never in life. I should be very happy to breakfast on

these gentlemen's catch, in the company of their friends, whom I met on the stairs. They seemed good-natured young ladies – and they were singing, oh so sweetly.'

It was a successful breakfast. The young ladies, finding that Diana gave herself neither airs nor graces, soon got over their shyness; the trout were excellent; the conversation free and cheerful; and at the end Nelly, having run upstairs for a small guitar, gave them a song, cheered to the echo by many people in other parts of the inn, and by a beaming, barely recognizable Killick at the window, while Dolby begged Diana and her party to stay to dinner – there would be a famous hare soup, and blackcock from Somerset.

'Thank you, sir,' she replied. 'I would with all my heart, but I have promised to deliver these gentlemen to Torbay, and deliver them I shall, in spite of a certain timidity on the part of some of the crew.'

Chapter Four

This she did quite early the next morning, they having spent the night at a coaching-inn some way inland, for the fishing-villages on the coast itself were somewhat barbarous, and she brought them over the northern hills at the turn of the forenoon tide.

The present blockade of Brest was being carried out by a much smaller squadron than that commanded by Cornwallis in the heroic days of 1803, yet even so Torbay was filled with shipping – sloops, cutters, liberty-boats and victuallers inshore and several larger men-of-war, ships of the line and frigates in the offing, the whole diversified by ships on passage and the scores of red-sailed Brixham trawlers coming round Berry Head, close-hauled on the freshening north-east breeze, for the south-wester had died in the course of the night.

Diana reined in on the brow of the hill, and as they sat there, gazing down through the cool clear air, smiling as they did so, an elderly two-decker lying beyond the Thatcher rock hoisted the Blue Peter and fired a gun, galvanizing the three of her boats that were ashore.

'That must be the old *Mars*,' said Dundas. 'Woolton has her now.'

'What a glorious moment to get under way: breeze and tide just as they might have been prayed for,' said Jack. 'Harry Woolton is a fine brisk fellow, and if he can pick his boats off the Berry he will be in with Ushant by breakfast tomorrow. Oh Lord, how I hope I may catch one of her people. Dear Diana, Cousin Diana, pray be a good creature for once and run us down into the village – don't spare the horses and never mind our necks, so I get alongside that yawl before they shove off.'

'Do, my dear, if you please,' said Stephen. 'It is our certain duty to be aboard without the loss of a minute.'

But the road down wound intolerably, and even the most skilful, most intrepid whip could not clear a passage through the dense, sullen regiment of dull-red bullocks that flowed slowly but steadily from a small side-lane, stopping and staring, deaf to cries, entreaties and threats. By the time the sweating, exasperated horses had brought the coach to the strand at last all *Mars'* boats were skimming over the main towards the headland, there to intercept their ship in her course; and no amount of hailing, however passionate, would bring them back. Nor was there any report of another ship going for Ushant before Thursday, if that.

'I beg your pardon, sir,' said Stephen, taking off his hat to a grave elderly man in black who had a solen shell in one hand and who was watching an immature gannet with close attention, unconscious of the loud and often ribald conversation of the liberty-men and their shipmates. 'I beg your pardon, sir, but I am a stranger in this place, and should be extremely grateful for the direction of a respectable inn that would shelter my wife and horses while my friends and I, sea-officers, seek for some vessel outward-bound.'

The grave gentleman did not at once apprehend the question, but when it had been repeated he said, 'Why, sir, I am sorry to say that as far as I know there is no such place in this village, if village it may be called. At the Feathers, to be sure, she would not be insulted with the company of – of trollops; yet the Feathers has no stable-yard, no coach-house, being little more than an eating-house, or tavern: a genteel tavern, however, capable of providing a lady with a pot of chocolate. But,' he went on after a slight hesitation, 'have I not the pleasure of speaking to Dr Maturin?'

'Indeed, sir, that is my name,' said Stephen, not quite pleased at being recognized so easily; and through his mind darted the reflection 'Intelligence-agents should have turnip faces, indistinguishable one from another; their height should be the common height; their complexion sallow; their conversation prosy, commonplace, unmemorable.'

'I had the happiness of hearing your discourse on Ornithorhynchus paradoxus at the Royal Society – such eloquence, such pregnant reflections! I was taken by my cousin Courteney.'

Stephen bowed. He was acquainted with Hardwicke Courteney, who though only a mathematician when he was elected had come to a reasonably intimate acquaintance with bats, with west-European bats.

'My name is Hope, sir,' said the other, loud enough to be heard over the strong voices of Jack and Dundas asking a young officer in a gig some two hundred yards offshore 'whether *Acasta* were going to sail tomorrow or not till Bloody Thursday?' 'And' (more gently, with a distinct shade of embarrassment), 'perhaps I may propose a solution . . . my cousin Courteney has a large decayed house not a furlong from here. It has no furniture – indeed it is almost entirely empty apart from the bats in the upper chambers – but it has noble stabling and a most spacious yard. May I suggest that while Mrs Maturin sits in the decent comfort of the Feathers, the coach and horses should take their ease in Cousin Courteney's inclosure? I have a rustic youth who looks after me while I count and register the bats – I camp in any odd corner – and he will certainly find hay, water, oats, whatever is necessary.'

'You are very good indeed, sir,' cried Stephen, shaking Mr Hope by the hand, 'and I should be most uncommon happy to accept your generous offer. Allow me to introduce you to my wife.' They made their way slowly through the throng towards the coach, and as they went Stephen said, 'If my friends do not find a suitable conveyance today, perhaps we might count bats together.'

With the horses cared for and Diana installed with Stephen in the Feathers' St Vincent parlour (the Feathers himself had served in the glorious action, losing a leg below the knee) and Bonden in the snug with the sea-chests, Jack and Dundas set off again, with Killick in tow to question his innumerable acquaintance among the seamen, thick along the highwater mark or lying in the dunes behind.

The seamen, upon the whole, were a very decent set of men and Jack felt happy among them and at home – many he had served with and barely once did he forget a name – yet once again it surprised, even astonished him that such a decent set, with so much hard-won knowledge, should have so primitive a notion of what was fun, and that they should attract such an obviously false set of hangers-on, such a forbidding crew of doxies, so very often short, thick and swarthy, sometimes so obviously diseased.

Still, both he and Heneage had known this long before their voices broke, when they were mere first-class volunteers, not even midshipmen, and they were not much moved by the spectacle, repeated again and again as they went along from respectable taverns to boozing-kens to billiard rooms to places that were not quite open brothels so early in the day. They were looking primarily for a captain who might be on the wing for Ushant and the squadron; but any officer, commissioned, warrant or petty who could give news was welcome – or of course old shipmates now serving out there. It was a homely quest, variegated and pleasant in its way, thrusting land-borne cares into the background; and they learnt a great deal about the present way of life, the most recent news, out there off the Black Rocks and what was called Siberia.

Yet familiar and congenial though this was – a kind of inverted homecoming, with the smell of sea and tide-wrack in their nostrils – it seemed as though their quest, so hopefully, so confidently begun, must end in disappointment and a dreary search for lodgings. A wider, much wider stretch of sand was showing now: the breeze was still steady in the true north-east, but the lovely tide alas was at half ebb as they reached the last place of all, a more reputable eating-house than most.

'It is scarcely worth going in,' said Dundas. 'We have

seen all the serving officers ashore, and this is no place for the penniless mid.'

Yet there was a penniless mid, or at least a master's mate: young James Callaghan, laughing and talking, his large red face crimson with mirth, and he was entertaining a young person as cheerful as himself but of a more reasonable colour – a fresh, pretty, well-rounded girl, not a trollop at all.

Captain Aubrey's tall shadow fell over them; they looked up; and in a moment their colours changed, the young woman's to an elegant rosy pink, Callaghan's to that of purser's cheese.

Jack was a humane creature, upon the whole, and he checked the question 'What are you doing here?' – the only possible answer being 'Neglecting my duty, sir; and disobeying orders in order to lead out a wench (or some more civil equivalent)' and substituted 'Mr Callaghan, where is the tender?' Callaghan had of course leapt up, upsetting his chair, and he was almost launched into an explanation of his being here because Miss Webber could not be asked out in her home town when a glimmer of sense returned to him and he said, 'Brixham, sir: all hands aboard under Mr Despencer, at single anchor in the fairway.'

'Then when you and your guest have finished your meal,' said Jack, with a bow to Miss Webber, 'be so good as to bring the tender round. We are at the Feathers. You need not press yourself unduly, so we catch the tail of the tide.'

The tail of the tide swept Captain Aubrey, his surgeon, steward and coxswain round Berry Head, and they shaped their course for Ushant, all the *Ringle*'s hands attentive and zealous, as meek as mice, they being to some degree implicated in Callaghan's crime. In spite of their zeal the *Ringle* could not show her best pace with the breeze so very far aft; yet even so, by the time Jack and Stephen turned in she was making rather better than thirteen knots.

The sea-change was already working strongly. Stephen was no greater mariner, but even his mind and person found the long easy yielding of a hanging cot more natural than a motionless bed by land; and although neither had more than a nine-inch plank between him and eternity (indeed, not so much) while at the same time both were exposed to the perils of the sea and the violence of the enemy, a kind of blessed relief came over them, as though the intricacies of conducting first a tender and then a large and crowded man-of-war to a rock-strewn and hostile coast, notorious for its foul weather, perpetual south-western gales and wicked tides, were little or nothing compared with those of life on shore, of domestic life on shore.

'I do hope Diana don't savage Heneage on the way back,' said Jack. 'You might not think it, but he is a very sensitive cove, and he feels harsh words extremely. I remember when his father called him a vile concupiscent waste-thrift whore-monger he brooded over it a whole evening.'

'She is not much given to moral judgment,' said Stephen. 'What she really dislikes is a bore, man or woman; and a want of style.'

'No. I mean if he were to criticize her driving, or to suggest – even in a very round-about and subtle diplomatic manner, you know – that he might do better.'

'Oh, he is wiser than that, sure. After all he knows she can put a dog-cart through the eye of a needle.'

'I hope you are right,' said Jack. 'But she gave me a cruel bite when I happened, just happened, to throw out a remark about the bridge.'

'I heard the remark. It was artificial, composed, *tactful*, and it would have vexed an angel, let alone a woman with four spirited horses between her fingers, and the sun hot on the back of her neck. And in any event, Dundas cannot claim a cousin's freedom of speech. Jack, I wish I had a memory for verse. If I had I should tell you a poem out of that dear man Geoffrey Chaucer, the way women in general have one consuming desire, the desire for command. A very true reflection, you are to observe. And he made some tolerably severe remarks on marriage, the sorrow and woe there is in marriage.' He paused for some kind of response: all that

could be made out through the all-pervading ship-sounds
and the run of water along the side was the steady breathing
of a man lying on his back, a breathing that would presently
take on flesh and become a great reverberating snore. With
scarcely a thought Stephen reached for his balls of wax,
kneaded them for a short while, thrust them into his ears
with a prayer for the night and sank easily into a recollection
of his late voyage in this vessel, with Brigid in the bows,
entranced by the scent of the sea. He did not wake with the
change of the watch nor barely with the coming of the light,
when he lay perfectly relaxed, perfectly comfortable, until
the cabin door gently opened and a midshipman came in.
He tiptoed to Jack's cot and said, 'Mr Whewell's compliments, sir, and the squadron is in sight.'

Jack growled and turned on his side. 'Mr Whewell's compliments, sir,' said the boy rather louder, smiling at Stephen,
'and the squadron is in sight. Topsails-up in the east-
south-east.'

'Thank you, Mr Wetherby,' said Jack, now broad awake.
'Have the idlers been called?'

'Not yet, sir: perhaps five minutes to go.'

'Thank you, Mr Wetherby,' said Jack again, dismissing
him. 'I thought as much,' he observed with satisfaction.
'I rarely miss the reluctant creeping about of those poor
unfortunate creatures.'

After a pause Stephen said, 'Jack, I have heard the term
idlers for ever; but in your private ear alone I will confess
that I do not know its exact signification.'

A penetrating glance showed Jack Aubrey that however
wildly improbable it might seem he was not in fact being
made game of and he replied, 'Why, do you see, it means
those who are not required to make part of a night-watch
unless all hands are called. Another word for them is day-
men, because they are on duty all day. But for fear they
should grow proud, and give themselves airs, they are roused
out rather before the sun and made to help clean the decks.
Your loblolly-boy is an idler: so is the butcher, and the
cooper and a whole lot of people like that ... tell me,

Stephen, what will you do for a loblolly-boy now that you have left Padeen behind?'

'The Dear knows. I shall look through the new draught in case we now have a paragon aboard the *Bellona*, a wholly reliable man that will give exact doses as regularly as my watch strikes the hour.' He held it up, waited for the few moments until it uttered its little silvery note: six o'clock, and as though by magic a clash of buckets broke out overhead, a splash of water, the creak of pumps and the steady grinding of holystones, together with the usual orders, cries, and even oaths as the decks were restored to a barely-lost perfection. Stephen knew that even in a vessel as small as the *Ringle* the hullabaloo would go on for the best part of an hour, and rising on his elbow he spoke somewhat louder, '. . . a man that will not cod the hands with dog-Latin or half-understood medical terms, a kind modest truthful creature. Where is such a treasure to be found, for all love?'

'Could you not call Padeen back?'

'I could not. As you know very well, he became addicted to one of my tinctures – it is worse than the drink, so it is, far worse – and I dare not leave him a daily temptation. And then again I promised him a few acres in the County Clare, enough for a small but decent living, if he would look after Brigid and Clarissa in Spain. But will he go there? Sure he is with child to go there. He knows just how the few fields lie, and the little small house – but a slate-roofed house, Jack, which is a very near approach to glory with us. Yet will he go there? He will not. What if there should be owls? Or good people under the hill where he has the right to cut turf? Or if he should find himself alone and frightened? I tell him the priest would find him a decent wife or any of the countless go-betweens, so busy in Gort or Kilmacduagh. Indeed, the whole thing is very like marriage: he would and he would not. Two men have I known that conducted a proper, regular courtship, urging their suit: both killed themselves the day they were to go to church. And no doubt there are and have been many like them.'

'Do you know of any young women who have done the same?'

'I do not. But I do know of three and have heard of more that ran away on their wedding night.'

'So have I.'

'There is a great deal to be said for a country education, where a girl may see a cow led to the bull as a matter of course, the filly to the stallion, and where a phallus is an acknowledged object – a matter of some curiosity perhaps but certainly nothing wholly unexpected, possibly wholly unexpected and even apprehended as a horrid malformation, an unnatural growth.'

'I scarcely think a country education always . . .' began Captain Aubrey, but he was cut short by a singularly violent and reverberating crash as two idlers, carrying a large matted block of stone, loaded with shot and intended for the perfect cleansing of the planks just overhead, dropped the entirety. This was followed by a great deal of howling, agonized howling, and Stephen ran up on deck in his nightshirt – a crushed foot for sure.

By the time he had dressed the mangled limb and administered his usual thirty-five drops of laudanum the sun was up, Jack was washed and shaved, his fine clubbed queue of yellow hair was new-tied behind his nape and himself seated before the breakfast-table in a small cabin smelling gloriously of toast, coffee and kippered herring.

'Forgive me, Stephen,' he cried, 'I am afraid I did not wait. Greed overcame me.'

'You say that almost every morning, brother; and I am afraid it is true,' said Stephen. 'But I pray that you may yet be saved from gule, that most brutish and most unamiable of the seven deadly sins. But come, Jack' – looking at him attentively – 'you are fresh-trimmed, neat as a bridegroom, almost handsome, in your fine coat and golden epaulettes. What's afoot?'

'You have not been on deck, I find. The squadron is hull-up already, and pretty soon *Bellona*'s number will break at the admiral's mizen topmast together with the signal *captain repair aboard flag.*'

'Be so good as to pass what is left of the toast; and naturally the coffee-pot.'

'And,' went on Jack in a low voice, 'if I know anything of your doings on a foreign shore, he or at least his secretary will ask to see you. Stephen, would it not be prudent to shave, and shift your coat and breeches?'

'Jack,' said Stephen. 'I have it in contemplation to grow a beard and put an end to these ill-timed fleers for good and all. In time of war the Roman emperors always wore beards. And as for this coat' – looking at his sleeve – 'it will do very well for many years yet.'

'At least let Killick give it a brush. There is lint on the front; and I fear *that* may be blood. You would never wish to put the barky to shame aboard the *Charlotte*.'

'Perhaps I should have put on my apron,' said Stephen, dabbing at the blood with his napkin. 'But there is no possibility whatsoever of finding a new coat until my sea-chest is unpacked.'

In the natural course of events Killick heard all this, and before Stephen had fully answered Jack's enquiries after Evan Lloyd, cook's mate, whose foot had been crushed by the bear – a conversation very much at cross-purposes until at last it became apparent that Stephen had never yet gathered that a bear, at sea, was only a holystone writ large – Preserved Killick was standing there with a prim expression on his face and a respectable blue uniform coat (virtually unworn) over his arm. 'Which it was almost on top,' he said. 'And you will have to get out of those there old breeches. The *Bellona* don't want no more of them there London cries. Monmouth Street cries, for shame.'

Stephen hung his head, keeping himself in countenance to some slight degree by pouring coffee. Not long before this, when the *Bellona*'s yawl had been taking him ashore in Bantry Bay, dressed it must be admitted in a way that did neither himself nor the service much credit, one of the *Royal Oak*'s cutters, with a ribald crew commanded by a drunken midshipman, called out 'What ho, *Bellona*! Any old clo'? Any old rags, bottles, bones, rabbit skins?' in the manner of the London street traders; and to the infinite grief of the ship the cry had become popular in west Cork. Killick and his shipmates prayed that it would not be imported into the blockading squadron; and in this they were supported by the whole wardroom and by the midshipmen's berth. And indeed Captain Aubrey, who almost always checked Killick's wilder flights, remained silent on this occasion.

It was therefore with a fairly respectable surgeon that Jack walked the quarterdeck after breakfast. 'There, do you see,' he said, nodding over the starboard quarter at a tall dark rugged mass of granite with white water all round its cliffs, 'that is Ushant, of course, as you know very well; but I do not believe you have ever seen it from the east, from the landward side: not that you can see the land for the moment, but you soon will, when the early mists have cleared. At present we are sailing through the Fromveur Passage, keeping well out in forty-fathom water – it shoals horribly as you go east towards that island on the larboard beam: Molène, a capital place for lobsters on a calm day. Once we are a little farther south and once we have skirted the Green Rock and reached those wicked old Black Rocks four miles further on, you will be able to look over some very ugly, dangerous water indeed right into the Goulet de Brest, a long channel into the harbour, into the inner and outer roads, rather like the entrance to Mahon: they cannot get out with the wind in the south-west, as it so often is; but on the other hand it batters us most cruelly when it blows hard, while they lie at their ease perfectly sheltered. And then again, if we are blown right off, to Cawsand, say, or Torbay, and the wind comes round to north or even north-east, out they come, knock our mer-chantmen and convoys to pieces while we are beating up, tack upon tack, like so many Jack-Puddings.' Jack spoke eloquently and at length of the hardships of the Brest block-ade, and although Stephen listened with a decent attention he also watched the squadron, or at least all the squadron then present inshore, as they stood towards the *Ringle*, close-hauled to the kindly breeze.

'They are going to wear in succession,' said Jack, breaking off; and hardly had he spoken before the leading ship, the *Ramillies*, fell off the wind in a long smooth curve, bringing it full aft and so on to her larboard beam, followed at exact intervals by her second astern – '*Bellona*,' cried Stephen, recognizing his old home as she came broadside on, 'the dear ship: good luck to her.' 'Amen,' said Jack; and as the third followed '*Queen Charlotte*, the flag: white ensign at the fore, since Lord Stranraer is a vice-admiral of the white, do you see? Now *Zealous*. All seventy-fours except the *Charlotte*, 104, of course. And here are two of his frigates: *Naiad* and *Doris*. No doubt they are standing in for the little *Alexandria*. She is only a twelve pounder but she sails almost as well as dear *Surprise*, and with this wind she has probably sent her boats in to see what the Frenchmen are doing in the harbour. If so, the gunboats in Camaret Bay may come out. When the haze over the land has cleared. We shall see.'

But before anything could be seen at all the deep sound of gunfire reached them, the rolling fire of heavy cannon, briskly plied. 'That will be the Grand Minou,' said Jack. 'Forty-two-pounders.' And after a moment of tense listening – not a murmur aboard, not a sound but that of the rigging and the following sea, the *Ringle* right before the wind – 'There she looms.'

Dim on the tender's larboard bow and directly in the path of the squadron a pallor showed through the landward haze, a pallor that quickly resolved itself into the sails of the *Alexandria*.

'Ha, ha,' said Jack. 'She is clean out of range; and she has picked up her boats. How those foolish creatures blaze away: fourteen pounds of powder wasted every shot – a stone, no less. No doubt they hope it will be taken for zeal.'

'Sir, sir, our number, sir, if you please: and the signal *Captain repair aboard flag*', cried Callaghan.

'Thank you, Mr Callaghan,' said Jack. 'Let us bear down on the *Bellona* with all the sail we can spread. Mr

Wetherby, pray take a glass aloft and see what the frigate is saying.'

A few moments later the midshipman's shrill, somewhat breathless voice began to pipe away, at first hesitantly, and then, as the distance lessened, more surely, calling down the frigate's signals, while Callaghan, having said, 'Reading from last Tuesday's plan, sir,' translated them: 'A first rate, wearing a rear-admiral's flag: a line-of-battle ship with sixteen ports, bearing a broad pennant: a line-of-battle ship: doubtful – probably a seventy-four: a frigate, yards and topmasts struck: a hulk: another: a corvette: a brig without topmasts: two frigates ready for sea, everything aloft . . .'

'Are we not to go to the Admiral?' asked Stephen in a low voice, when the list had ended and the tender was passing well east of the *Queen Charlotte*.

'Yes, but by way of the *Bellona* and so in my own barge,' said Jack, smiling at his simplicity; and in the same undertone he went on, 'I shall watch my step this time, I can tell you. When the Almighty hears my news he will love me even less than he did before; and with such a damned unlucky omen I may expect some wicked squalls. I shall look out for them.'

'To what omen do you refer, brother?' asked Stephen.

'Why, to poor Bonden's being beat, of course. What could be more unlucky? And you say you are not quite happy about his head.'

'Shame upon you and fie, for a poor weak superstitious creature. What connection can there be between the two matters?'

'Well, the heart has its reasons . . .' Jack began, but then with a confused memory of kidneys troubling his mind he dropped the heart and went on, 'I may be no great scholar, but I do know that Julius Caesar put off an attack because he saw a damned great black bird flying from an unlucky quarter. And Julius Caesar was no weak, simple, womanly creature. It's all one, you know. But tell me, will poor Bonden be fit to see us across?'

'I believe so, with the blessing,' said Stephen. 'May I have ten minutes?'

Jack turned his glass on the *Bellona*, where they were already well on the way to getting the barge over the side – an arduous business, perfectly unnecessary as far as carrying Mr Aubrey to the flagship was concerned, but of the first importance to Captain Aubrey, to the custom of the sea, to the pride of the Bellonas, in their ship and to their concern for their commander's dignity. They were nearly all thoroughly established seamen – often hereditary seamen – and they liked things done proper, particularly in this case, for well over half had served with Jack before, either in the last commission or in other ships entirely: he was a taut captain but very well liked, a capital seaman, much given to battle and above all exceptionally lucky in prize-money (his present legal difficulties affected only himself, not the hands in any way at all, nor the officers). 'Yes, I think so,' he said, and gave orders to gather the fore-sheet aft, gently lessening the tender's pace.

Hurrying below, Stephen found Bonden half in and half out of his formal rig as captain's coxswain. 'Good day, now, Barrett Bonden,' he said. 'Take off that neckcloth; come here under the skylight and let me see your wound. How do you feel within yourself?'

'Tolerably, sir, tolerable, I thank you kindly,' said Bonden, sitting on the stool and submitting his poor head to have the bandages removed. Stephen gazed down at the scalp, quite hairless now, and at the still-angry wound: he pondered, weighing the possibilities. 'That was a cruel unlucky throw,' he said.

'It was indeed, sir. I fair cherished that tail, the finest in the fleet.' Bonden felt behind his neck, where the plait had hung so thick. 'Fair cherished it. But I came home by weeping cross, as they say. It gave me one more wrinkle in my arse, however: which is to the good, no doubt.'

'Do you feel capable of taking the barge across to the flag, Barrett Bonden?'

'Of course I do, sir. What, let the Captain wait upon the Admiral without his coxswain? Never in life.'

'Then I will dress the place again, and you may cover it

with your wig,' said Stephen, nodding towards a shaggy pale yellow object run up aboard from well-combed tow: and while he was busy with his ointment and bandage he said, 'Will you tell me about the wrinkles in your arse?'

The relations between Bonden and Stephen, always close since their first voyage together, when Stephen had taught the coxswain to read quite fluently, had grown closer during this course of treatment and now Bonden spoke with a greater freedom, often using the rakish and even licentious cant expressions of his youth in the London streets and of his prize-fighting days – a familiarity that thoroughly displeased Killick, who thought the terms low, ignorant, disrespectful.

'Why, sir, in Seven Dials everyone knows that each time you learn something new, your arse takes on another wrinkle: well, in the Dripping Pan I learnt that it is better to be as bald as a coot than risk such a fall and such a cruel loss. That's what I learnt, and it was worth the wrinkle.'

Stephen finished the dressing. The tender hooked on to the *Bellona*'s larboard afterchains just as the bosun's pipe guided the barge evenly down to the water on the leeward side and the bargemen – blue jackets, duck trousers, broad-brimmed ribboned hats – ran down into it, joined by Bonden.

Jenkins, the jobbing captain, left the ship with little ceremony after a few minutes of conversation with Jack: Mr Harding, the *Bellona*'s first lieutenant, reported a signal for the Doctor, and Jack, having first urged Stephen to venture the descent before him, ran down and took his seat in the stern-sheets.

Five minutes later the long slim twelve-oared boat reached the flagship's starboard mainchains, and this time Jack was received with all the honours due to a post-captain, the bosun and his mate winding their calls, white-gloved side-boys running down to offer entering-ropes, the *Charlotte*'s Marines presenting arms as he came aboard, and, the moment he had saluted the quarterdeck, her captain, John Morton, advanced to welcome him, to ask him how he did, and to lead him to the Admiral.

Stephen's coming aboard, though less ceremonious, was also less discreditable than some of his old shipmates had feared. Even before Captain Aubrey was out of sight Bonden murmured, 'Right away, Bob: on the roll,' to young Robert Cobbald, a wiry, nimble young man rowing stroke, who stepped across the void, gave Stephen a hand, swung him up a few steps, writhed behind and so ran him up to the entering-port without disgrace.

The *Charlotte*'s lieutenant of the watch and her surgeon greeted him, and to the latter, after the usual civilities, Stephen said, 'Mr Sherman, I rejoice to see you again. I have been reading your paper on the larvae of calliphora with the utmost interest; and apart from that I have a case upon which I should like your opinion.'

'Come with me, dear colleague, and let us drink a glass of madeira while I tell you about my treatment.' He led Stephen to the wardroom, but on seeing some officers playing backgammon he withdrew, saying, 'Perhaps my cabin, such as it is, would be better. There is so much childish prejudice against what are vulgarly known as maggots, even among the educated, that the people in there would look upon us with dislike during my explanation: they might even protest.'

'Pray how do you introduce your larvae into the wound?' asked Stephen when they were sitting in the little cabin. 'I know that Larrey began by simply leaving it open, having first ensured the presence of blow-flies by hanging decayed meat in the ward: but this of course was by land.'

'I encourage my assistants to keep a fair stock,' said Sherman. 'We usually isolate the eggs or the very small larvae, and in appropriate cases we sew them into the wound, leaving a little ventilation, naturally. The result in a really ugly suppurating lacerated wound is sometimes extraordinarily gratifying: I have known gangrenous legs that any surgeon would have amputated without a second thought become perfectly clean and perfectly whole after little more than a month. How I wish I had a few cases to show you: but I am afraid we have seen no action for a great while.'

'Do you experience much resistance to the treatment – reluctance to submit?'

'Tact is called for: even an economy with literal truth and ugly names. But where the hands are concerned we can always fall back on discipline. However, you were speaking of a case that does not quite satisfy you?'

'To be sure. A profound stertorous coma, resolved after some days: no apparent fracture of the skull, but recently I have seemed to detect a slight crepitation: and there is a change in behaviour and vocabulary that strikes one who knows the patient well. At times I feel there may be a certain aberration, and I should be grateful for the opinion of one who has studied the naval mind so much longer than I have done – of the author of the *Mental Health of Seamen*.'

In the great cabin the Admiral half-rose from his desk, gave Jack a hand and said, 'Well, Aubrey, here you are at last. Good morning to you.'

'Good morning to you, my lord. I trust I see you well?'

'Oh, as for that . . .' said the Admiral. 'Sit down, Aubrey, and tell me how you come to be so infernally late.'

'Why, sir, I regret it extremely, but by the time your orders reached Woolcombe I had already left on my way to London. I did not receive them until I came back, when I set out directly, boarding the tender in Torbay.'

The Admiral gave him a long, considering look. 'You was going to the House, I collect?'

'Yes, sir. I had to attend a committee deciding on a petition for the inclosure of a common.'

'Simmon's Lea? The common in which my nephew Griffiths is interested? It seems to me very suitable for inclosure. I told him so. I advised him to proceed.'

'So I understand, my lord: but I am afraid there was a great deal of opposition on the part of the commoners and – with all respects to you, sir – on my part as lord of the manor. In short, the petitioners' majority was considered insufficient and the petition was dismissed.'

'I see, I see,' said the Admiral, looking wicked. He made

two abortive starts, but then in a controlled voice he said, 'To return to service matters, I must tell you that your frequent absences on parliamentary leave has had a most injurious effect upon *Bellona*'s discipline and general efficiency. She was never, at the best of times a particularly well disciplined or efficient ship; but when I was drilling the squadron in the mouth of Douarnenez Bay on Friday, while you were amusing yourself in town, she very nearly fell aboard of me in a very simple manoeuvre – had to be fended off, with half a dozen voices on her fo'csle and quarterdeck bawling out contradictory orders. You know as well as I do that Captain Jenkins is no more of a seaman than his grandmother, even when he is sober, but I had expected more of your officers. After all, you chose many of them – they were your personal choice, having served under you as reefers or the like. No one would ever call you much of a seaman yourself, Aubrey; but hitherto you have been uncommonly fortunate in picking the men who actually sail the ship. Now, I regret to say, your luck seems to be running out. If on returning to the *Bellona* you will take the trouble to glance aloft I think that even you will be startled by the number of Irish pennants everywhere to be seen, to say nothing of the great streaks of filth oozing from her head: though perhaps you prefer it that way.' A pause. 'I intend posting you to the inshore squadron. The navigation in the bay is extremely difficult and arduous; the innumerable reefs have not all been accurately charted – very far from it, indeed – and some months of beating to and fro, up and down, will teach you and your people more in the way of seamanship than countless lazy miles rolling down the trades with a flowing sheet. Furthermore, when the French in Brest see the kind of opposition that is waiting for them inshore, they may well be tempted to come out, and then the ships in better order may be able to deal with them.' The Admiral moved his lips for a few moments after this, but silently; then, visibly recovering himself, he said, 'I believe your surgeon is called Maturin, Dr Maturin. Be so good as to tell him that I should like to see him.'

'Dr Maturin,' said the Admiral as Stephen came in, much delayed by a visit to the sick-berth, 'I am very happy to see you again, sir. When I heard your name I hoped that you might be the same gentleman that I met in Bath, with Prince William, and now I find that I was right. How do you do, sir? Pray take a seat.'

'How do you do, my lord?' said Stephen in a noncommittal voice. 'I did not at once recall . . .'

'No, I am sure you did not,' said the Admiral. 'I was plain Koop in those days, Captain Hanbury Koop: I did not inherit until some years later. My name is now Stranraer.'

'So I have heard, my lord. May I offer my belated but hearty congratulations? Sure, it is a glorious thing to be a peer.'

'Well,' said Stranraer, laughing, 'it may not be quite what people expect, but it has its advantages. On occasion it gives one a certain amount of extra power, like a double-purchase block. But my purpose – one of my purposes, I may say – for troubling you is this: when we were sitting by his Highness' bed I was seized with a very violent very sudden pain here' – laying his hand on his waistcoat – 'and for a moment I thought it was the heart-pang, that I was going to die. But after a couple of words you whipped something out of your bag and in two minutes – no, not so much – the pain was gone. I was deeply impressed. So was the Duke, my old shipmate. He said, "There's Dr Maturin for you. He can cure anybody, so long as the tide is not on the ebb, and so long as he likes the patient."'

'I am afraid that is quite a widespread superstition,' said Stephen. 'In point of fact I can do nothing that any other ordinary medical man cannot do: the tide nor my liking is neither here nor there.'

Stranraer smiled, shaking a sceptical head. 'So my first purpose,' he went on, 'is to beg you will tell my surgeon Sherman the name of your elixir: the pain comes back from time to time, but the ignorant dog cannot find out the remedy.'

'No, my lord: there I must protest. Mr Sherman is a

very eminent physician. He has also made some surprising advances in surgery and the treatment of wounds; and no man knows more about the seafaring mind – or the minds of landsmen, for that matter. He was consulted in the King's malady.'

'Yes. I have heard that he was much cried up as a mad-doctor by land, and I wonder at his taking to the sea: but if he cannot cure an infernal burning *physical* pain, what good is he to me? My mind is as sound as a bell. I have no call for a mad-doctor, nor have my people. But I am wondering . . .' He rang for his steward. 'Light along some madeira, there; and bear a hand, bear a hand.'

'Now I understand it, sir,' he began when the wine was poured, 'you and Captain Aubrey have been shipmates for many a commission, and you often mess together. From this I believe it may be presumed that you are – how shall I put it? – well assorted, which does Aubrey much honour I am sure: but it must also be presumed that a man of your superior education and shining parts will have acquired a great influence over him.'

'There again, my lord, I must beg leave to disagree. Captain Aubrey's intelligence and learning are in many ways far superior to mine. He has read papers on nutation to the Royal Society, and upon Jovian satellites, that soared far beyond my reach, but which were much applauded by the mathematical and astronomical fellows.'

If Lord Stranraer was impressed by these words he did not show it but carried straight on, 'Another reason that I have for supposing this is my very clear recollection of what might properly be called your ascendancy over your illustrious patient – very much the sea-officer, in spite of everything – at your next visit, when you explained the Spartan system to him and he listened intently, never interrupting though his mouth often opened – explained it with such clarity and at some length: and when you left he said, "Now there's a head for you, Koop: there's a head, by God!" And this brings me, in a roundabout way, to my point: to the inclosure. I know that many people, including your friend, look upon as self-seeking hard-hearted wretches; and it is not impossible that my nephew Griffiths, who lacks the graces, and some of his associates may have strengthened this impression: but please allow me to assure you that there is another side to the question – an entirely different side, indeed. Mr Arthur Young cannot be described as anything but a benevolent and very knowledgeable writer on agriculture, and he is in favour of inclosures: the president of your eminently respectable Royal Society, Sir Joseph Banks, has inclosed thousands of acres, to the great benefit of his tenants and the country; and it must be added, himself. The produce from his estates has increased immensely, because rational cultivation is possible on a large scale: just how great the increase is I naturally cannot tell, but the yield in corn alone from my two manors in Essex has grown by twenty-seven per cent in less than three years since the miserable little scraps were thrown into large fields, properly hedged and ditched: while the harvest from my land in the Fens has increased no less than cent per cent, though to be sure it has taken ten years to do so and the drainage was a great burden, calling for a capital that the villagers could not possibly command. There is a legal expression where manors are concerned and I dare say you are acquainted with it: "the lord's waste"; and never was a truer description – hundreds, even thousands of acres that could be pasture or tillage under proper management but that in fact support no more than a few goats and an ass, a little game that is a standing temptation to poaching, rarely resisted – land that produces nothing but poverty, idleness and vice.'

Stephen felt Lord Stranraer's considering eye upon him. The Admiral had almost certainly lost the thread of his discourse and was now afraid of growing long-winded, boring, unconvincing: for his own part Stephen said nothing.

'However,' Stranraer went on, pouring more wine, 'may I first hark back to your Spartans, the Spartans of Thermopylae, and then suggest the comparison between a rabble, with arms of a sort but with neither leaders nor discipline, and these Spartans, or with a well-ordered regiment of today; or perhaps more appropriately between a parcel of fishing smacks with no clear organization – every skipper for himself – and a first-rate man-of-war, thoroughly worked up, well-manned and well-officered, the most formidable engine of war the world has ever seen. Doctor, I will not be troublesome with a wealth of details, but it seems to me that there is a fair analogy here between a well-inclosed estate, directed by men of education with capital, and the usual village of small-holdings and an immense, largely unproductive common. We are, after all, at war; and though this one may soon be over, above all if we can keep the French bottled up in Brest, there is sure to be another presently – foreigners are never to be trusted: look at Spain for example, with us, against us, and now with us again until it suits their purpose to turn cat-in-pan once more. And with the present system we simply do not grow enough corn: we do not produce enough meat to feed the navy, the army and the civilians. It seems to me and to many men of good will that just as it was the duty of the Spartans to bring up their young men to arms, so it is our duty to bring up farmers to feed the fighting-men, farmers with two or three hundred acres, often carved out of unproductive common. There is no room for sentiment in wartime: and after all your village Strephons with an oaten pipe were not very valuable creatures, if indeed they ever existed – I never came across any. There: forgive me, Doctor. I have explained myself very badly, I am afraid. But if you could put that point of view to your shipmate, particularly the image of a first-rate in capital order on the one hand and a straggling village, with pot-houses, small-holdings and more poachers, half of them on the parish, than farm-hands, I believe you would act as a friend. I cannot do it myself. Not only am I an interested party, but in my disappointment at his news I spoke – I used some unguarded terms: and Griffiths is quite incapable. Yet this is a time when sailors as well as neighbours should stand together. Victory – if it come' – he rapped the table-top – 'will be very welcome, but it will be a hard time for the service, with ships being paid off by the hundred, half-pay for almost everybody, and precious few commands: a time when a well-placed friend may prove . . .' He did not finish his sentence but coughed, and his commanding old face, unused to such an expression, took on a look of acute embarrassment. 'I am afraid I have been wearisome, Doctor, and I beg your pardon: but this is a point – a duty, as I see it – upon which I feel very strongly indeed. You will say that I am personally concerned, which is very true: yet I think I may place my hand on my heart and assert that I should be of the same opinion if neither I nor my nephew possessed an acre of land. Still, I know what assertions are worth, and I shall bore you no longer, except to observe that my secretary has some messages for you.' He rang a bell, told the servant to pass the word for Mr Craddock, and said, 'Doctor, thank you for listening to me so patiently: I shall leave you and Craddock together,' and with a slight bow he walked out of the cabin.

'Jack,' said Stephen when they were back in the *Bellona's* great cabin. 'I admire your fortitude in making no reply.'

'One of the first things one learns in the service is that any reply to a superior officer, any justification, protest and counter-accusation is absolutely useless: and if the superior wishes to destroy you, it is the best possible way of helping him to do so. No. It is a poor, shabby thing to blackguard a man who cannot answer; but I believe he was vexed to the very heart.'

'He was, too,' said Stephen, and they sat in silence for a while. It was a pleasant day, and the squadron, now well south of the Black Rocks, was standing across the bay under an easy sail, heading for the Saints, that deadly chain of reefs upon which so many ships had been wrecked.

'We are going to pass through the Raz de Sein,' said Jack, 'and then the Admiral will haul his wind and rejoin the offshore squadron west of Ushant, leaving us with the *Ramillies*, a couple of frigates and a cutter or so: he will look in from time to time, perhaps bringing reinforcements.

Presently I will show you Dead Man's Bay and the Pointe du Raz.'

Stephen gazed over the sea at the distant mainland; he felt the agreeable heave of the south-west swell, and he said, 'Here's space – here's air – the vast sweep of the ocean – this glorious room – servants and victuals a-plenty – no domestic worries of any kind – hundreds of miles from importunity – and as I understand it we simply go up and down in this spacious great bay – delightful sailing, sure. Perhaps after dinner we may have some music.'

'With all my heart,' said Jack. 'I have scarcely touched my fiddle this month and more. By the way, I have invited Harding and one of the new mids, a boy called Geoghegan, whose father was kind to us in Bantry. Poor fellow. He is quite clever with figures, and he plays a creditable oboe; but he cannot be taught to coil down a rope like a Christian.'

'Listen,' said Stephen, and once again it was apparent to Jack that his friend's mind was, and had been, elsewhere. 'Listen, will you now? The Admiral, in his artless approach, let fall some words having a certain misty reference to the future; and they seemed to me to chime with some of your indistinct deprecation to do with yellowing and your superstitious hatred of the colour itself, even. Be so good as to explain the matter in words adapted to the meanest understanding.'

'I was telling Sophie about it only the other day,' said Jack, 'so I hope I shall make it plain: though things one has taken for granted all one's life, like the flowing of the tide, are hard to explain to those who do not know the meaning of high tide or low, like the natives of Timbuktoo. Well now, formerly any man who was made a post-captain was sure of reaching flag-rank by seniority so long as he did nothing very wrong or refused service more than once or twice – by service I mean an offered command. When he reached the top of the captains' list he would become a rear-admiral of the blue squadron at the next promotion, and hoist his flag at the mizen. This was the absolute crown of a sea-officer's career, and he could die happy. If however he lived on, he would, still by seniority, climb through the various grades and eventually become admiral of the fleet. But this tradition was broke in 1787, when a very deserving officer, Captain Balfour, was passed over. Since then nothing has been the same. Now many people are placed on the Navy List as retired captains, or if this is too flagrantly unjust then as rear-admirals, but of no squadron whatsoever and of course no command. When this happens he is said to have been yellowed – to have been appointed to an imaginary yellow squadron. And if he has had the service at heart all his life he cannot but die unhappy. I am sure I should. It is an extremely public disgrace and your friends hardly know how to meet your eye.'

'But my dear you are quite far from the top of the list. Sure you must have served some years more before you need worry about your flag?'

'Certainly. But it is the running-up period that is so important, the time while the Admiralty are slowly making up their minds, the years when you must distinguish yourself if you possibly can and when above all you must not put a foot wrong; above all now, when there is a real danger of peace breaking out with countless officers thrown on the beach and commands as rare as needles in a haystack. I do not have to tell *you*, Stephen, how wholly I long to receive the order requesting and requiring me, as rear-admiral of the blue, to proceed to the smallest of commands, to His Majesty's sloop-of-war *Mosquito*, say, with two four-pounders and a swivel, and to hoist my flag at her mizen-mast. I should do anything for it. *Anything*.'

'Does Simmon's Lea come within the limits of anything?'

'No, of course not, Stephen; how can you be so strange?'

'It is an elastic term, you know. But, however, even if your fears are realized, that is not necessarily the end of your sea-going career. I made some very good friends in Chile, three of whom I met again in my recent travels across Spain, remarkably intelligent and well-informed men, who very clearly saw the inevitable end of this war and the independence of their country. They are also aware of the very strong likelihood of rivalry between the liberated provinces, of attempts at the domination of Chile on the part of Peru and the necessity for a Chilean navy, officered at least in part by very highly experienced men, victorious in almost all their encounters. What more suitable recruit than an admiral like you, even though he may have been yellowed by political jobbery?'

They sat in silence for some time, digesting this and the possibilities it contained. 'There is Dead Man's Bay,' said Jack. 'And we are now in the Raz de Sein, a devilish passage in heavy weather. By dinner-time – and I think I already hear Killick with the glasses – we should have the Pointe du Raz on our larboard quarter.'

Stephen nodded, and with a curiously knowing look, his head on one side, he asked, 'Can you foretell the dark of the moon with reasonable accuracy?'

'I believe so,' said Jack. 'Her motions are of some importance in navigation you know, and we learn them quite early.'

'Well, I am happy to hear you say so, for at the dark of the moon I must beg you to set me ashore, with a gentleman at present aboard the flagship, in a little cove just south of this same Pointe du Raz.'

Jack gazed over the sea. 'Just how serious are these people?' he asked after a while.

'Deeply serious,' said Stephen. 'They are closely associated with O'Higgins and his friends. They are men of great substance in those parts and they are wholly committed to independence. More serious you could not wish.'

Another silence. 'The dark of the moon will be in eight days,' said Jack.

Chapter Five

For five days, no less, they simply went up and down the fine spacious great bay, admiring the billows and fishing over the side – delightful sailing indeed – and in the evening they played music until supper-time or beyond. On the sixth day, misled by reports of a convoy coming up from Lorient, the inshore squadron sailed through the Passage du Raz once more and across the bay of Audierne to the farther point, where they lay to and sent the *Ringle* round to look into the harbour and inlets farther south.

Captain Aubrey had dined in the wardroom – a wardroom which on this occasion included the *Bellona*'s surgeon, a member of course by right – and now he was standing on the poop, drinking coffee with William Harding, the first lieutenant, Captain Temple of the Royal Marines, Mr Paisley the purser, a convivial soul, a great hand at whist, and always willing to play sentimental ballads on his viola while others sang, together with Stephen and a few others. 'There, Doctor,' said Jack, pointing to a truly dreadful reef half a mile on their larboard beam. 'There are the Penmarks.'

'I have often heard them mentioned,' said Stephen. 'Always with strong disapprobation and even loathing.'

'Scylla and Charybdis ain't in it, with a strong south-wester and a falling tide,' said Jack. 'Nor the Gorgonzola. And that's Penmark Head beyond. Lord, that must have been a rough wild night of it,' he added, to Harding.

'Indeed it was, sir,' said Harding. 'I never wish to see such another.'

'I do not suppose you do,' said Jack. 'Doctor, do you know about the *Droits de l'Homme*?'

'Few things are more familiar to me than that amiable

fiction. I my youth I wrote several versions, each more lib-eral than the last. In one I even included women, asserting that they were . . .'

The sailors smiled indulgently, and the purser said, 'He means the man-of-war, Doctor. A French seventy-four. It was in the days of high revolutionary fervour, in ninety-six or ninety-seven, when they gave ships names like that.'

'The time of Hoche's expedition to Ireland,' said Harding.

'That I remember,' said Stephen, with a chill about his heart: and then, feeling that something more was called for, 'Will you tell me about it, so?'

'Pray do,' said the Marine. 'I was in India at the time.'

'Well,' said Harding, collecting his thoughts, 'it began a little before Christmas of the year ninety-six, here in Brest. The French had gathered seventeen of the line, thirteen frigates, six brig-corvettes, seven transports and a powder-ship. We were aware of their motions, of course, although we could not tell where they were going, and Admiral Col-poys had a strong force off Ushant, while the inshore squad-ron was under Sir Edward Pellew in the *Indefatigable*, forty-four – you will remember, Doctor, that the *Indefati-gable* was cut down from a two-decker, and she was a heavy frigate, carrying twenty-four-pounders – I was a master's mate in her at the time. And under him he had three other frigates and a lugger. The Frenchmen came out one after-noon with a kindly east wind, forty-four sail of them with something like twenty thousand soldiers aboard; and they steered for the Passage du Raz, to avoid Admiral Colpoys. But one struck on the Grand Stevenet just at the opening of the passage and others went out by the Iroise, their admiral having changed his mind quite late in the day, when dusk was falling: there was a shocking confusion of signals and lights and guns. But although Sir Edward sent to the Admiral and to Falmouth they were never intercepted: no, they sailed on through fog and foul weather to Bantry Bay, where they had a perfectly appalling time of it – gale after gale, with ships driving from their anchors and being blown out to sea, frigates pitching fo'c'sle under, foundering, impossible to land troops, food running out; and eventually most of them straggled back to France. There was a second rendezvous off the mouth of the Shannon. A few looked in, but only one stayed any length of time before seeing it was hopeless, and having found nobody at Bantry either she steered not for Brest like most of the others but for some point south, probably Rochefort. She was commanded by Commodore La Crosse, a right seaman, and we – *Indefatigable* and *Amazon*, 36, first saw her in thick weather about half past three in the afternoon of January 13th, when we were in 47°30′N, Ushant bearing north-east fifty leagues, a strengthening squally wind from the westward and a heavy swell. She was some way to the north-east of us and far from distinct, but presently we made out that she was a two-decker with no poop, her lower-deck gunports closed, obviously *Les Droits de l'Homme*, known for swimming low in the water. And while everyone on the quarterdeck had her in their glasses, a squall hit her, carrying her maintopsail braces and then her fore and main topmasts, which fell over her lee-guns. They cleared away very quick, expecting us to attack on that side, but when we were within hail and under close reefed topsails, Sir Edward hauled up to rake her. Yet she hauled up too and we exchanged broadsides – prodigious musketry on her part, from all the soldiers aboard. Then Sir Edward tried to cross her bows and rake her fore and aft: she foiled him again and did all she could to run us aboard. In avoiding her we showed our stern, but with her lower-deck gunports so near the surface and the very heavy roll of the ship with so little to steady her – courses and mizen topsail was all she could spread – she did no great damage. Presently, when it was near full dark, *Amazon* came pelting up, fired her larboard broadside into the *Droits*'s quarters at pistol-shot and then steered to cross her stern and give her the other. Again the *Droits* clapped her helm over, which brought us both on her less damaged leeward side; and we all blazed away until half past seven, still running south-east, the wind having backed a point or two. Then we and the *Amazon* shot ahead to knot and splice and fill more powder – we had the legs of her, of course, with our topmasts standing. An hour later we were at it again, lying on her bows, one each side, and yawing to rake her by turns, while she did much the same – she still steered very quick – giving us some hard knocks and trying to board. About half past ten she cut away her wounded mizen, and rather later we hauled off to secure our masts, their rigging being much shattered; but apart from that the fire barely slackened until something after four in the morning, when the moon breaking through the clouds showed land close on board and all three ships hauled as near to the wind as ever they could to avoid it. Yet just before dawn there were breakers white on the lee bow. We wore ship, heading north-wards: and when day broke, there was the land again, very close ahead and on the weather bow, with breakers to lee-ward – wore ship to the southwards in twenty fathom water. And then, just after seven, there we saw her – there she lay, the *Droits de l'Homme*, right in with the land, broadside up with the tremendous surf beating clean over her. Just there,' he said, pointing, deeply moved by the strength of his recollections, 'just there, beyond that tall pointed rock ... At least six hundred dead, they say. I will not go into the horrors of war,' he said with an embarrassed smile, conscious of having talked too much. 'Anyhow, Doctor, you know much more about them than I do. The *Amazon* had gone ashore too, but farther along, farther in, and almost all her people were saved. The wind was right on the land, the tide was making, and there was nothing, nothing we could do for the *Droits de l'Homme*. We had four foot of water in the hold ... We just managed to claw off, though we shoaled water terribly at one point and though our people were so utterly exhausted they could scarcely haul the mainsheet aft. We lay off for a while, putting the ship into some sort of order, while the surgeon and his mates looked after our wounded and the cook got at least something for the hands to eat. And although the sea remained very high, the sky soon cleared over the Penmarks and the land inshore. It was that which made me think of the *Droits de l'Homme* in the first place, this same very curious greenish light over the reef and land, all along from the cape itself to St Guénolé, do you see? It is always taken to foretell heavy weather; and we certainly had a cruel time of it for the next week or ten days.'

'Mr Harding spoke of a week or ten days, did he not?' asked Stephen.

'I believe so,' said Jack. 'May I trouble you for the marmalade?'

'Oh, I beg pardon,' cried Stephen as the ship gave a furious lee-lurch and the jar flew from his hand.

'Killick. Killick, there. Swab and a damp cloth. And then another pot of marmalade.'

'Not again?' said Killick. 'Not a ... again? The same yesterday, the same on Thursday and that was with the poor bloody milk-jug too. All the forenoon watch on my poor bloody knees ... floor cloth never be itself again.' This in a mutter: in a louder voice from beneath the table, 'Which there ain't no more orange marmalade neither.'

When at last he had gone away, Jack said, 'Fortunately it was only a common old pot, not that splendid Irish cut-glass affair you so kindly gave us. Yes, he did mention ten days; but only in a manner of speaking, you know. These blows never go by the calendar.'

'When this present tempest slackens, perhaps we shall have a post. I quite long to hear from Woolcombe: and indeed from London and Ballinasloe. I had been led to believe that one of the very few advantages of the Brest blockade was that it allowed the sufferers frequent supplies of fresh food and mail.'

'To be sure it is better in that line than say the New Holland station, but only in summer. Your informant, the man who led you into this high state of indignation, must have been thinking of the *summer*, not the season of equinoctial gales or the even more dreadful turning winter storms. But do not despair. The glass is rising quite evenly: so is the humidity. Tomorrow night, or the next, which is the dark of the moon, we may have one of the fogs this bay is so famous for, particularly as the wind is sure to fall – indeed, it is less already. Steady rain, like this, often deadens both wind and sea. When you have finished breakfast, will you not put on a Magellan jacket and take a turn on deck?'

'I will not. In the first place because I dislike getting wet, and in the second because I must complete my account of our sick-berth, which Dr Rutherford wished to recommend for universal adoption: and of course there are my medical notes.'

'Yes, indeed. When you reach any height at all, you spend more time scratching paper than anything else. When I have done with the reefers, Mr Edwards and I must attend to the fair-writing of the log; and I have a score of returns to look over and sign. But after dinner if it calms enough for you to sit to your 'cello, let us work our way through the new Benda piece.'

'By all means. Is there any more coffee in that pot?' There was, and having poured it Stephen said, 'I was talking to that boy Geoghegan, and I find that I know some of his relations in the Spanish service – his grandmother was a FitzGerald. Will I tell you why he finds it so difficult to coil down a rope in a way that pleases his mentors?'

'Is it not just natural inborn vice?'

'It is not. Like many of his nation he is a ciotóg, a left-handed man; and left to himself he will always coil a rope against the way of the sun.'

'Then clearly he cannot be left to himself . . .' Jack prosed on about the need for exact uniformity in the service – for all ropes to run smooth – on the dreadful results, in an emergency, of the contrary practice – and when he paused for a piece of toast Stephen said, 'And there are degrees of left-handedness, some quite insuperable, others to be corrected if that is the right term, though usually at a cost, sometimes very great, to the soul. The harp of Brian of the Tributes, High King of Ireland and an unpersuadable man, carries the melody in the left hand; and this boy's oboe, made by his father, a skilful gentleman, from a length of bog-oak, is the mirror image of the usual instrument. Would it be improper, do you think, to ask him to play with us? He blows the purest note.'

'Indeed I love an oboe: it has nothing of the clarinet's cloying sweetness. But as for your boy . . . He seems a modest, well-bred young fellow, to be sure . . . Yet I knew a reefer in the West Indies who was amazingly good at chess – could beat anyone. The Admiral, a pretty good player, invited him, and was beat time and again. He laughed; but it did not end happy. The boy got above himself, talked too much, gave himself airs, made himself so unpopular in the cockpit and was kicked so very often that he had to be transferred. But I will take particular notice of young Geoghegan at nine o'clock; and if it can properly be done, we might try.'

At nine o'clock the *Bellona*'s young gentlemen who were not on duty attended in the Captain's fore-cabin washed pink, brushed smooth, and properly dressed, together with Mr Walkinshaw, the schoolmaster. 'Good morning, sir,' they cried, leaping up at the Captain's entrance, 'Good morning, sir,' some gruff, some still shrill, some wavering horribly a full octave. Jack desired them to sit down. Ordinarily, each by order of seniority, would have shown up his workings, that is to say his estimate of the ship's position, determined by observation of the sun's height at noon or by double altitudes, by dead reckoning, and on occasion by a certain amount of copying from their more gifted messmates. But the weather of the last days had been such that no observation was possible and Jack only required Mr Walkinshaw to lead them through Pythagoras once again, calling upon each in turn to rehearse the theorems upon which this most elegant, satisfying and wholly convincing argument was based. In his youth Jack had been wretchedly taught – mere rule of thumb at the best – and it was only quite late that the beauty of Pythagoras and Napier's Bones had been revealed to him, lighting a love of the mathematics that had burned steadily ever since; and he hoped that repeated exposure to them both might do the same for his youngsters. Generally speaking it had answered for one or two boys in each commission, which would probably not have happened if he had relied on ship's schoolmasters.

The man he had at present, Mr Walkinshaw, was better than most; he knew a fair amount about mathematics and navigation, and he was generally sober; but like most of his kind he had very little authority. He messed with the midshipmen in the cockpit, he was little better paid than they, the regulations gave him no status in the ship, and he would have had to be an exceptional man to acquire one by force of character. Mr Walkinshaw had not managed to do so, and his lessons were far quieter, more orderly and useful when the Almighty was present, listening most of the time, interposing on occasion, learning a great deal about the boys.

Today his eyes rested more often on Geoghegan than the others: again he noticed his awkward, cramped left-handed manner of writing, his modest way of answering a question, his smile when he was told that the answer was right – a smile that would have been enchanting if he had been a girl. 'He is too pretty for his own good, too pretty by far,' Jack reflected. 'He would be an odious little beast was he aware of it. Fortunately he ain't. Mr Dormer,' he said to a young gentleman whose attention seemed to be wandering, 'pray define a logarithm.'

Dormer blushed, straightened himself, and said, 'A logarithm, sir, is when you raise ten to the power that gives the number you first thought of.'

After a few more answers of this kind Jack desired Mr Walkinshaw to return to his remarks on the principles of spherical trigonometry and leafed through the rough copy of the *Bellona*'s logbook that his clerk was to write fair later in the day, when the diminished sea might make fair writing more nearly possible.

'Never say that I am no weather-prophet,' said Jack as he and Stephen sat down to dinner at a table that no longer required fiddles to keep the plates from one's lap. 'And I believe my fog is on its way.'

'God love you for your words, my dear. I should have been sorely vexed to miss my rendezvous.'

'Yet it must not be too thick, for although our Brittany pilot knows the bay like his own bed, he has to have a terminus a quo and a terminus ad quem.' He gave Stephen a satisfied look, and paused; but Stephen's face, civilly attentive, showed no change whatsoever; and Jack, never one to bear resentment, went on, 'He is marking *Ramillies*'s chart at present – by the way, I asked Ramillies to dinner today – we have an enormous great fat goose – but he begged to be excused. He is taking medicine.'

This meant that at seven bells in the morning watch the *Ramillies*'s captain had stuffed himself with rhubarb, brimstone, the inspissated juice of figs and any other cathartics that happened to be at hand, so that he would be confined to the seat of ease in his quarter-gallery, groaning and straining, for the greater part of the day, clearly unfit as a guest at a dinner-table.

'I wonder that a man of Captain Fanshawe's intelligence, education and taste should persist in that deleterious, superstitious self-torment,' said Stephen in a tone of real indignation. 'It is one of the unhappiest legacies of the dark ages – of mere barbarity.'

'Oh,' said Jack, 'but William Fanshawe has studied health, you know, and he understands more about it than most, I do assure you. He is a great reader, and he has a book by a man called Piggot who was all for the superiority of vegetables over bread, and who maintained that caps were far, far better for you than hats. His arguments, as I recall, were wonderfully convincing – to do with the humours.'

This was not the first time that Stephen had learnt about medicine from sea-officers: as usual, he merely bowed, and at much the same moment the enormous great fat goose came in, Killick bearing it against the swell with a very fixed expression indeed on his face and setting it down without a drop of the abundant grease astray.

When the massive remains of the bird, expertly carved by Stephen, had been sent down to the midshipmen's berth, according to the humane naval custom, and when the port was going to and fro, Jack said, 'I considered your young fellow this morning, and I think we might try. In these cases there is always the danger that if it don't answer it may do the boy or young man harm: I have known cases. Yet I think here we might try. Do you know the Mozart oboe quartet in F major?'

'Yes, sir.'

'Of course you do, of course you do,' cried Jack. 'I was only calling it to mind . . . no, what I mean is that I should love to hear it again: and Paisley is a respectable hand with a viola. We played it in Funchal with those cheerful Portuguese friars, and again – where?'

'I forget. But I do remember that the viola broke a string in its most important passage and we were all thrown into a sad confusion – a sudden loss of all cohesion – the ground dropping from beneath one's feet – anticlimax is far too weak an expression.'

'Naples. It was off Naples: the oboe was a castrato from the opera and John Hill of the *Leviathan* played the viola. At least as far as we went. I remember the grief of it – no spare strings. Stephen, may I beg you to ask Paisley whether he would like to study the score? Coming from me it would be so very like an order; and he is after all your messmate. And do you think you could find out whether the boy would be capable of bearing his part – whether he would like to try – and if so whether he too would choose to have the score. Do not take it amiss, Stephen, but these things would come so much better from a man who can clap leeches to their temples or rouse out their liver and lights – for their own good, of course – than from a fellow who cannot be contradicted and whose prime function is to command. No. I have put it very badly, I find. Do not be offended, Stephen – I do not really believe in all this gold lace: I do not really esteem myself another Pompous Pilate or Alexander the Great.'

'Never in life, my dear. As for young Geoghegan, I under-stand that chamber-music has been part of his family life since he was a little boy: and as for the purser, I know that he plays in his parish choir when he is ashore, and that although in the wardroom it is mostly Vauxhall and Ranelagh airs, he is perfectly capable of other things. Now' – pouring each another glass of wine – 'pray tell me about this Brittany pilot.'

'Oh, he is one of the fishermen *Calliope* picked up when she was rescuing people who were trying to escape after the Vendée fighting – royalists, of course.'

'Just so. I presume they have been carefully sieved?'

'Oh, I am sure of it. They have been with us, scattered about the fleet ever since; and I believe that during the peace they brought their families across to Market Jew in Cornwall. They have the same kind of language, as I am sure you know, and they get along famously with the country people and fishermen. This one is called Yann: the Admiral sent him over some little time ago to mark all our charts. He is marking *Ramillies*'s now, and he should be with us tomorrow.'

'So much the better,' Stephen finished his glass and said, 'I shall make my rounds now: and if the sea grows even a little more reasonable, I believe we may have some music after supper. And if the rounds do not take long I shall have made my inquiries well before that.'

'Well, my dear,' he said, coming in just before their toasted cheese – an invariable supper dish whenever they were within reach of the prime essentials – 'that was eminently satisfactory. I found the boy by mere chance, and he puzzling over a knot with his sea-daddy – are you acquainted with the expression?'

'Fairly well. My own sea-daddy, dear old William Parsons, was the best of men – endlessly patient.'

'So was this one. Again and again he said, "No, sir: right over left and then up through the bight" without any wounding emphasis. And when at last the knot was tied he said that Nelson could not have done it better – that Mr Geoghegan would make a seaman yet. He then walked off to stow the rope wherever ropes are stowed and I talked to the boy. Of course he knew the quartet – had played it repeatedly at home, his father with the 'cello, his uncle Kevin the fiddle and Cousin Patrick the viola – but should be very happy to look over the score again. Mr Paisley was almost as good. He did not absolutely assert that he had borne a part in this particular quartet but he let it be understood that he was intimately familiar with it: and even if he had not been he was, as the skipper himself would testify, so practised a sight-reader that he did not need to study the score before sitting down to it, so long as he had a good light on his music-stand.'

'Certainly, I have known him make his way through a sheaf of hand-written sheets seen for the very first time in a very creditable manner. What joy. Allow me to help you to some of this capital-smelling cheese.'

'If you would be so good. What do you tell me of tomorrow's weather? Is it likely to be suitable?'

'I will swear to nothing, but Harding and the master, who both know Ushant well, are of the same opinion: unless it grows so thick that we cannot see our music, why then, tomorrow' – touching wood – 'should be all that a reasonable being could ask.'

And indeed the four reasonable beings could hardly have been better served. There was still a heavy swell from the south-west, and urged on by the making tide it broke high, white and dreadful on the islands and reefs of the Saints and the mainland cliffs, but the wind had dropped to no more than a topgallant breeze, and although Jack's fog had made its infant appearance in the form of a veiling mist there was no question of its blurring even a hemidemisemiquaver. Yet when Jack and Stephen met for breakfast each looked at the other with a considering eye and Stephen said, 'Melancholy, brother? Hipped?'

'Somewhat,' said Jack. 'I do not much like the behaviour of the glass' – pointing to an elegant barometer in brass gimbals – 'Nor do I much care for poverty. I cannot afford to keep a table for my officers; I cannot afford to entertain my fellow-captains in the traditional service fashion; and what is more I cannot afford to buy extra powder to eke out our miserable allowance. Today, to the astonishment of one and all, we shall beat to quarters and carry out the great-gun exercise: but your only worthwhile exercise is with the true discharge, the furious recoil, the cloud of smoke; and even on this perfect day we can afford only two real broadsides for each battery. But Stephen, you are in much the same case, I believe? Haunted by the blue devils? Glum?'

'It is nothing that coffee and perhaps a very lightly boiled egg will not bear away,' said Stephen. 'Yet I *am* saddened by the reflection that although age has not yet seriously decayed my powers in other directions, or so I flatter myself, I have real difficulty in grasping the geography of this Behemoth of a vessel. The sick-bay I know perfectly well, the wardroom, and this series of booths and cabins; but when I walk about at haphazard, as I was doing when I chanced upon young Geoghegan, I grow strangely bemused, scarcely knowing front from back; whereas in the dear *Surprise* –'

'Bless her.'

'Bless her by all means – I knew every recess, however remote, and of course all the people. Here I am something of a stranger in a largely unknown city. I do not find my not inconsiderable maritime knowledge increases; and I am by no means sure that the bold figure of speech I heard directed by an aged quartermaster at a ship's boy, "Thou wilt never shit a seaman's turd" may not be applied to me.'

'Never in life,' cried Jack. 'You are the most seamanlike ship's surgeon I have ever known. Never in life. Killick. Killick, there. Light along that God-damned coffee, for Heaven's sake.'

'Which . . .' began Killick: but seeing the Captain's face he closed his mouth and the door.

'Not at all, Stephen. You are to consider, you have not been aboard very long, and for most of the last commission you were either looking after the sick or travelling about the

African wilderness collecting rarities, except when you were sick yourself, very sick, very nearly dead, or so weak as to be able to do no more than creep about the poop. Killick . . .'

'Which it's coming, ain't it?' cried Killick from behind his loaded tray, 'with a two-minute this morning's egg for his Honour.'

Breakfast did indeed sweep away a good deal of superficial melancholy, and after it they walked up the poop, watching the sun rise, round and orange, over France: what mist there was (and it was thickening) did not yet hide all the ships of the inshore squadron and Jack pointed them out in the stations where Fanshawe (his senior by six months and therefore in command) had placed them. 'There is *Ramillies*, right in the middle of the Iroise Passage,' he said, nodding towards a rosy haze of topsails almost due north. 'And if you were to jump up to the masthead and clear the haze away you would see one of the frigates, probably *Phoebe*, guarding the way out of the Passage du Four: a good many vessels try to get into Brest from the north that way. And between the frigate and *Ramillies* you can make out a cutter even now, *Fox*, I believe, lying there to pass on signals.' He ran through the meagre tale of ships posted off most of the important means of access, just as the *Bellona* was posted within gunshot of the Raz de Sein; and among other things he showed him the general position of the uncharted or badly charted rock upon which HMS *Magnificent* struck in the year four, on Lady Day in the year four – a total loss, 'but her people were all saved by the boats of the squadron, mostly from the *Impétueux*, as I recall . . . Mr Harding,' he said to his hovering first lieutenant, 'I believe you wish to speak to me?'

'Yes, sir,' said Harding, stepping forward and taking off his hat. 'I beg pardon for interrupting you, sir, but the *Nimble* is finding it hard to stem the tide, and if we want any effect of surprise among the people, perhaps we might call for the targets right away.'

'Make it so, Mr Harding, make it so.' And to Stephen, 'How I ramble on.'

He rambled no longer. The *Nimble* had been anxiously watching the *Bellona*'s upper rigging, and as soon as the signals broke out her boats shoved off, towing their targets. 'We will beat to quarters, Mr Harding, if you please,' said Jack, and almost instantly the drum volleyed and thundered. Some few of the newer, heavier Bellonas had not caught the signs of the coming exercise – the gunner's very particular attention to his charges, the captains of the gun-crews' sly checking of tackles, tackle-falls, trucks, ladles, rammers, sponges, worms, and their absent-minded easing of the tompions – and those few were properly amazed by the din. But by now all except the very, very stupid landsmen at least knew their action-stations, and they ran to them; while the very few exceptions were kindly guided by the bosun's mates.

Dr Maturin's station was of course the after-cockpit, and here he stood with his assistants, William Smith and Alexander Macaulay, together with a few unsatisfactory makeshift loblolly-boys – farrier's apprentices or out-of-work slaughterhouse hands – and in this space, bare except for instrument-racks and the chests of the midshipmen (its usual inhabitants) heaved together and lashed to form an operating-table, they stood silently listening.

The three foremost upper-deck starboard eighteen-pounders bore on the leading target almost at the same moment and fired with a triple crash that made the hanging lanterns tremble: they were instantly followed by the huge, much deeper voices of the gundeck thirty-two pounders, and for the next five minutes the entire hull was filled with a great bellowing din, so confused that no separate discharge other than those directly overhead could be distinguished: at the same time powder smoke came below, wafting its heady smell about them. Then all at once a deafened silence, followed by the rumble of guns being housed.

'Sir,' cried William Smith, much too loud, 'I saw a very curious thing: whenever there was a split second between the explosions just over us, each produced a different tremor in the smoke. You could distinctly see it against the lit edge of the lantern.' He spoke with something of the excitement of battle; and with much the same freedom Macaulay said that he did hope it had been a satisfactory exercise – there was such an agreeable feeling in the ship when they had done well. Before Stephen could reply the first of the casualties came down the after-hatch, carried by his team-mates, a young Marine who had been stationed at one of the after thirty-two-pounders to help run her up – she weighed about three tons – and who had misjudged the speed and force of the recoil.

'A very moderate tourniquet for twenty minutes, Mr Macaulay, if you please,' said Stephen, sewing up the gash, 'and a spica bandage; but by no means tight.'

Macaulay had been dresser to a famous London surgeon and his bandages were marvels of regularity, the admiration of all the seamen; but regularity was often cousin to constraint, itself close kin to gangrene.

In the early days of a commission, when many of the pressed men were still sad lobcocks, without discernment or sea-legs, it was usual for these exercises to cause a fair amount of damage – so much so that when Stephen returned to the quarterdeck Jack asked, 'What was the butcher's bill this time?'

'A few sprains and rope-burns,' said Stephen, 'and one flesh-wound – a strip of gastrocnemius – more spectacular than grave. As I sewed it up I reflected upon gangrene – always a possibility – and upon an interesting treatment that I discussed aboard the flag . . .' Yet as he spoke he remembered his friend's odd squeamishness about some aspects of medicine and even more of surgery and broke off to exclaim at the smoke-bank from their exercise, still remarkably solid and coherent there away to leeward. 'A satisfactory exercise, I trust?'

'Tolerably so, I thank you, for what very little it amounts to – scarcely more than two full broadsides. Still, with so many well-trained crews it was reasonably accurate and pretty brisk, roughly the equivalent of two and half minutes. And after all the *Royal George* sank the *Superbe* in Quiberon

Bay with only two broadsides – very heavy weather indeed and not one of her six hundred people saved.'

They fell silent, both thinking of an earlier command, the *Leopard*, which sank a Dutch man-of-war in the high southern latitudes, also with the loss of all hands. One or two messengers reached the Captain, who dealt with them in a firm, competent, official voice; then, turning to Stephen, he said in an undertone, 'I am so looking forward to our concert tomorrow.'

So was Stephen; but he was concerned for the prime performer, the oboe, the essence of their meeting. From the dispensary, far aft on the orlop deck, where he and William Smith spent some of the next forenoon grinding quicksilver, hog's lard and mutton suet together to make blue ointment, he could hear Geoghegan practising in the nearby midshipmen's berth, playing scales, changing his reeds, and venturing upon some of the more remarkable flights open to a well-tempered oboe. The *Bellona* had a reasonably good-natured set of midshipmen and master's mates, a dozen of them, mostly the sons of friends and former shipmates; certainly the younger members of the berth showed no obvious signs of oppression, and although Geoghegan was probably the youngest there, just old enough to be admitted to the berth rather than entrusted to the gunner with the youngsters, he clearly never hesitated to play serious, difficult music there. This was the more curious because of his somewhat anomalous position: he had been borne on the books of several ships commanded by his father's friends or relatives, in order to gain nominal sea-time without actually going afloat – a fairly common practice, but one that brought the young gentlemen aboard with so little knowledge of their profession that they were something of a burden to their shipmates, often unpopular, sometimes cruelly-treated butts. Yet this was not the case with Geoghegan. 'Of course, he is a very good-looking boy,' observed Stephen. 'Perhaps that has something to do with it. One has an innate, wholly disinterested kindness for beauty.'

The ointment was now made and Smith carried off a

suitable number of gallipots for their syphilitic patients: Stephen shut and double-locked the dispensary door (seamen were much given to dosing themselves) and hearing the main body of reefers leave their berth with a sound like that of a herd of mad cattle, he walked in.

'Good day, sir,' said Geoghegan, leaping up.

'And a very good day to you, Mr Geoghegan,' said Stephen. 'Please may I see your instrument again?'

It was a beautiful oboe, formed from the most elegant dark, dark wood; but neither praise of its appearance nor of its lovely tone seemed to give much pleasure, and Stephen returned to their earlier talk of Bantry Bay, the country round it, including the Reverend Mr Geoghegan's parish, and their common acquaintances. The boy was perfectly polite, perfectly well bred, but it was clear that he did not wish for any close contact at this moment nor any comfort for his evident anxiety. In the civilest way he was saying that he was not to be manipulated, nor to be made to be easy in his mind when he was not easy in his mind, however kind the intention.

'He is a respectable boy,' said Stephen, walking off, 'but I could wish he were not quite so tense. Were it not for some illogical and even perhaps superstitious reluctance – respect for innocence? – I should prescribe fifteen or even twenty drops of laudanum.' Laudanum, the alcoholic tincture of opium, a delightful tawny liquid that had floated Dr Maturin through many a bout of the most extreme anxiety and distress, though at a moral and spiritual cost that eventually became exorbitant: it was now replaced by moderate use of the Peruvian coca-leaf.

The boy was tenser still when he appeared at the door of the Captain's cabin, carrying his oboe in a green baize bag, as the last stroke of five bells in the afternoon watch was struck. The berth had done him proud. Not only was he as popular as a boy who was no seaman could very well be, but his appearance would reflect upon the credit of the after-cockpit as a whole, including Callaghan and three other master's mates and that almost god-like figure William

Reade, who had so often sailed with the Captain before, losing an arm in battle in the East Indies, and now his hair, having been very strongly brushed, was tied so tight behind that it stretched his features into a look of astonishment, while his face shone pink from an almost entirely superfluous shave; the brass buttons on his best blue coat outshone even those on his Captain's uniform, while the white patches on his collar, called by some quarterly accounts and by others the mark of Cain, would have put virgin snow to shame.

'There you are, Mr Geoghegan,' cried Jack. 'I am very happy to see you. Come and have a glass of sherry.'

After the sherry they sat down to a dish of codlings caught over the side that morning, to a pair of roast fowls with bacon and a great many sausages, to a noble apple pie and to the best part of a Cheddar cheese. The midshipmen's berth usually dined at noon, and Geoghegan, after a hesitant beginning, laid into his food with a wolfish concentration, replying 'If you please, sir,' to any suggestion of more. 'The young gent has ate eleven potatoes,' said Killick to his mate, passing the empty dish. 'Go and see if the wardroom left any.'

At last, when the cloth had been drawn and the King's health drunk in a glass of port suited to a very young head, they took their coffee and ratafia biscuits (the sea-going equivalent of petits fours) in the great cabin, where the 'cello, the viola and the fiddle leaned by their respective music-stands, well lit by the great stern-window – a suffused grey, near-brilliance, with the ship standing west-south-west under reefed topsails, making little more than steerage-way on a gently rolling sea.

'Another cup, Mr Paisley?' asked Jack. 'Mr Geoghegan? Then in that case perhaps we should set to.'

They spread their scores, and as they did so Stephen remembered with some concern that in the F major quartet the opening notes were played by the oboe alone: but when, after the necessary squeaking and grunting as the stringed instruments tuned themselves, Jack smiled at Geoghegan and nodded, these same crucial notes came out clear and pure, with no over-emphasis – a beautiful round tone in which the strings joined almost at once. And almost at once they were a quartet, playing happily along with as nearly perfect an understanding as was possible on so short an acquaintance.

With scarcely a pause they swam through the elegant melancholy of the adagio, Jack Aubrey particularly distinguishing himself and Stephen booming nobly; but it was in the rondo that the oboe came wholly into its own, singing away with an exquisite gay delicacy infinitely enjoyed by all four. And to all four, in spite of the music before them, it seemed to last for an indefinite space before coming to the perfect simplicity of its end.

'Well done, well done indeed,' cried Jack, leaning forward and shaking Geoghegan's hand. 'What a glorious pipe you blow, upon my word and honour. I have rarely enjoyed music more. If ever, indeed.'

Geoghegan blushed extremely; but before he could answer there was an imperative knock at the door and Mr Edwards, the Captain's clerk, came in with an untidy, disparate sheaf of papers in his hand. 'Sir,' he said, 'here are the memorandums we were to send to the flag, just your rough notes. You said you would read them for me to copy fair. The boat is here – has been this half glass – and is growing outrageous.'

'By God,' cried Jack. 'It clean slipped my mind. Gentlemen, forgive me, I beg. But had we gone on, we could not possibly have done better: I thank you all very heartily indeed.'

They filed out, with proper acknowledgements and in due order of rank, Geoghegan standing back to let Stephen pass, looked at him with open affection, all constraint and tension gone; and with Edwards settled at a desk Jack began from his informal and often cryptic notes: 'Purser: provisions for nine weeks full, of all species except wine: of that only thirty-nine days. Master: one hundred and thirteen tons of water, beef very good, pork sometimes shrinks in the boiling, the rest of the provisions very good. In cutting up provisions, master's mate, bosun's mate, captain forecastle, captain tops, and quartermaster. Pretty well supplied with stores; rigging and sails in good order; two pair of main shrouds cut in the eyes. Gunner: eighteen rounds of powder filled: plenty of wads, forty rounds. Carpenter: hull in good state. Knee of the head supported by two cheeks. Masts and yards in good state. Pretty well stored . . .'

'That was a very glorious piece, the glorious piece of the world, indeed,' said Stephen as he and Geoghegan separated outside the wardroom – the purser had already gone forward.

'So it was, too,' said Geoghegan. 'And how I admired the Captain's double-stopping – yours too, sir. But I am glad it did not go on. It was perfect like that; and I was afraid that if we started again it might take a great while, and I should miss the last dog.'

'A particularly amiable creature, I make no doubt.'

'Oh, sir,' said Geoghegan, with that delicate kindness the young sometimes reserve for the old, ignorant, and stupid. 'I should have said watch. The last dog *watch*, the second of those short ones at the end of the day, you know. When we are going along under a very moderate sail, and there is nothing much to do, no possibility of all hands being called, we reefers whose watch is not on deck often play about aloft. We call it skylarking.'

'I have heard of it: indeed, I have not infrequently seen the phenomenon. Yet it is not invariably confined to the young and light-built. Captain Aubrey and Admiral Mitchel once raced to the topmost point of a vessel whose name escapes me, for a dozen of champagne.'

'Heavens, sir! Pray who won?'

'Faith, the Admiral said he did: and who is to contradict an admiral, a senior? Superiores priores, you know.'

'Yes, indeed, sir. But if you will excuse me now, sir, I must go below and stow my pipe and change my clothes. Old Dormer and I are to see which can touch the maintopgallant truck first.'

Geoghegan ran down the ladder and in the lightness of his heart he kicked both his best silver-buckled shoes far into the cockpit. Callaghan was the only other person in the berth: he was writing a letter by the light of a purser's dip, writing with close concentration to his young woman; but he looked up and asked how dinner in the cabin had gone. 'Oh, very well indeed, once I got started: codlings, of course, then a pair of huge enormous great prodigious fowls, capons, I think, and the Doctor kept carving me glorious great bits and passing sausages. I could not in decency say no. And then there was an apple pie the bigness of a moderate wheel: and cheese, of course.'

'What did you drink?'

'Sherry-wine, claret, and then port.' During his discourse Geoghegan had taken off and folded away all his good clothes, and now he was in a striped Guernsey shirt and old sailcloth trousers.

'Well, I hope you did not eat too much. You must take it easy at first. Many a reefer have I known throw up his dinner merely from topping it the nimble ape among the royals and topgallants too soon after a meal.'

The ships that blockaded Brest off Ushant or nearer inshore in the bay itself were so very often blown and battered by strong south-westers, often bringing rain, or by north and north-east winds which might allow the enemy to come out, therefore calling for the closest attention, that the ship's boys and young gentlemen, to say nothing of the more athletic officers, had little chance of skylarking; and when it came they made the most of it. Stephen Maturin, though very much a spectator aboard, and very much given to standing on the poop or quarterdeck of a healthy ship (in a sickly one he spent most of his time below) and there watching the various manoeuvres or, in times of relative idleness, the dancing on the forecastle and the skylarking, had rarely seen so numerous a gathering. Right forward there was a fiddler and a man with a tabor playing hornpipes for a close-packed group on the forecastle, where the more expert dancers carried out some very elaborate steps indeed, to the delight of their friends, who clapped hands in time; but what caught his eye more immediately was the number of boys. The *Bellona* carried fifty or more, officers' servants, apprentices to the gunner, bo'sun, carpenter or the like, and plain ship's boys, and nearly all of them were gathered either along the larboard gangway leading from the quarterdeck to the forecastle or were already aloft, tearing about among the rigging and sometimes making great swings from one part to another like gibbons, high, high above the deck. Some were racing, some were merely having fun, moving with wonderful ease and certainty. The midshipmen on the other hand – using the term in its widest sense from master's mate right down to first class volunteer: the 'young gentlemen' as a whole – kept to the starboard side, either on the quarter-deck itself, which was their right, or along the starboard gangway; and they too were spending much of their time high in the air apparently weightless except when they slid with enormous speed down a stay, landing with a thump. While Stephen stood there, a fat midshipman called Dormer, the boy that Geoghegan was to race, came down the main-topgallant backstay into the mainchains with such force that his knees buckled under him. Stephen helped him over the hammock-netting on to the deck and asked whether the friction did not scorch his hands. 'Not much, sir,' he replied with a pleasant confidence, 'because now I am a really hard-ened old salt, and I check the rush with my feet.' He showed his palms, and although they were much stained with tar there was no trace of a burn. 'Now, sir,' he said, 'I am going to make the great traverse.'

'I shall watch you with close attention,' said Stephen; and he certainly meant to do so. But there were such numbers of boys and young men (the *Bellona* had about six hundred people aboard) moving in every direction, up, down, side-ways and diagonally, often very fast, that he soon lost sight of Dormer – all the sooner since an ambiguous tern came over, together with two gannets.

Having fixed the tern (an immature Sandwich in a sad state of moult) he returned to his contemplation of the sky-larkers, and after a while his earlier impression was con-firmed: although the ship's boys kept to the larboard and the young gentlemen to the starboard, and although there was virtually no direct communication between them, there was nevertheless a tacit rivalry. Some uncommonly agile boy, often the bo'sun's servant, would perform an exceptional – and exceedingly dangerous – feat; and with nothing but looks of intelligence between the more expert reefers, their champion would do the same or better. He watched this for some time and quite suddenly he recognized young Geoghegan in the striped-Guernsey-shirted boy who was obviously doing his utmost to outpace Dormer on his way up the main topmast rigging.

He was clearly less experienced than Dormer, but Dormer had already taken a great deal of exercise, he was fat, and he was tiring fast. They were on opposite sides of the main topmast shrouds, high up where they narrowed to pass through the topgallant crosstrees. Very near the top, where the main topgallant futtock-shrouds diverged, far from the vertical, Geoghegan leant backwards, one hand whipping out for the futtock, the other for the forward crosstrees; and here, both holds slipping in his haste, he fell: fell almost straight, just brushing the maintop in his fall and striking one of the starboard quarterdeck carronades, not a yard from the officer of the watch.

Stephen had been walking aft to meet Jack as he came from talking to the master by the wheel. At the general cry he turned, and calling out 'Do not move him' he ran to Geoghegan hoping that there might not be too much damage – that taken below with great care he might be recovered. After a moment's examination he could only report instant death.

Jack picked the boy up and carried him into the great cabin, tears running down his face. Later that evening they sewed him into his hammock with thirty-two-pound round-shot at his feet and buried him over the side according to the custom of the sea.

The fog increased that night, and Jack spent most of his time on deck, together with Woodbine and Harding, both of them experienced navigators with a fair knowledge of the waters off Brest. The *Bellona* had lain-to near the Ar Men rock for the brief ceremony and she had now to feel her way across some twenty miles of often dangerous water to a point a little west of St Matthews (most of the places had English names) where either the *Ramillies* or one of her boats would meet her, bringing the Brittany pilot and Stephen's colleague; for tomorrow was the dark of the moon, the time for the landing in Dog-Leg Cove.

Although the very slowly falling glass foretold dirty weather in the near future, Jack felt reasonably confident that he should be able to carry out his plan, which was to beat steadily up and down between the Black Rocks and the Saints by day, as usual, and at nightfall, after the turn of the tide, to double back and run through the Raz de Sein with the current, dropping Stephen as near to the cove as he dared and then to stand off and wait for the boat, anchored south of the Ile de Sein: twelve-fathom water and good holding ground. But first, of course, there was the essential rendezvous, and with the log heaved every glass or sometimes more often and the lead going steadily they sailed west by north with the wind one point free, the fog streaming across the binnacles and the storm lantern.

When by their very close and concordant reckoning they were well beyond the Iroise Passage the breeze strengthened, veering northwards, and presently it became obvious that even close-hauled they could not reach the channel through the islands they had hoped for: Jack therefore wore ship and set a necessary but most disagreeable course that would bring them close to the southern fringe of the Black Rocks and their outliers – not always accurately charted.

This held until four bells in the middle watch – low tide – when the infernal breeze wavered, grew uneasy, uttered some violent gusts and hauled a full point forward, with every sign of doing worse. Before it could come frankly into the north-east and head him, Jack Aubrey changed course yet again and stood right across the mouth of the Passage du Four, which had no more than seven fathoms in some places. The *Bellona* drew six. On and on, the three men

entirely closed upon their continually developing calcu-
lations, all based on the frequent reports of the ship's progress, their informed estimate of her leeway under this trim
and with this wind, the ebb and flow of the tide, the force of
local currents, the occasional dive into the master's sea-cabin
abaft the wheel where by a dim light a chart as accurate as
present knowledge would allow was spread out, and on their
own sense of the sea, intuitive, pragmatical, hardly to be
reduced to words.

'I wonder whether the others hear and feel that wicked
grind and crack as we strike a reef,' said Jack to himself.
'Probably.' He had felt it this last glass and more as they
drew nearer and nearer to St Matthews, now perhaps no
more than a few cables' length away in the north-east. Then
aloud, 'Mr Woodbine, do you smell anything?'

Pause. 'No, sir.'

Captain Aubrey, in a carrying voice: 'Back the main topsail: start the sheet right forward, there.' To the man at the
wheel, 'Down with the helm.'

The way came off the *Bellona*: she lay there, heaving in
the fog; and a voice some way on her starboard bow called,
'The ship ahoy. What ship is that?'

'*Bellona*,' replied Harding.

Relief, coupled with the intensity of Woodbine's unspoken
question, moved Jack to say, 'It is low tide, of course; and
I caught a waft of the rotting kelp.'

When the *Ramillies*'s boat had set both its passengers
aboard he left orders for the officer of the watch – the course
due south was safe for the next few hours – told Harding
and the master to get some sleep, and walked softly into the
cabin he was sharing with Stephen.

'Is all well?' asked Stephen.

'Yes. Your man is aboard, and I have put him in the
coach. The bosun is looking after the pilot. I am afraid I
woke you.'

'Not at all, at all. Will you not turn in?'

'It scarcely seems worth it; but perhaps I shall.'

For once his deep-founded habit of going to sleep at once

abandoned him. He lay awake for two bells and the first strokes of a third, working out the letters he was to send to Geoghegan's parents: as a captain he had had to do this several times. It was never easy, but this time the words would scarcely come at all.

The cleaning of the deck before sunrise no longer woke Stephen, but the piping up of hammocks and the sound of bare feet just overhead did so quite abruptly. He stared about, collecting himself, and without surprise he saw Jack come in, pink and obviously new-shaven, even in this dim light. 'Good morning to you, my dear,' he said. 'What of the day?'

'Good morning, Stephen. I trust you slept? It has cleared a little, but you still cannot see a hundred yards; and we have barely more than steerage-way. Do you choose to trim yourself? The sea is smooth, and I can put a famous edge on your razor if you would like it. And there is your . . . your guest. He will breakfast with us, no doubt.'

'Oh,' said Stephen, passing a hand over his jaw. 'I will do admirably for a day or two: until Sunday, indeed. In any case, I know Mr Bernard well.'

Mr Bernard, Inigo Bernard, came from Barcelona, where his family, considerable ship-builders and ship-owners, had been engaged in trade with English merchants for some generations: he had been educated in England and he spoke the language perfectly, yet like his family he remained deeply Catalan – Catalan to the extent of bitterly resenting the Spanish oppression of his country and of supporting the clandestine movement for autonomy if not downright independence; and it was this that had first brought him and Stephen Maturin together. Yet in much the same way as Stephen he had early decided that the French invasion – most particularly atrocious in Catalonia – required him to ally himself with any of the forces that opposed the enemy: in his case with the Spanish government. He had been more fortunate though by no means less enterprising than Maturin as an active member of his secret movement, and his name was to be found on no official lists of rebels or subversive elements; he was therefore able to join one of the Spanish intelligence services particularly concerned with naval matters. And when the Spaniards changed sides on the unfortunate advice of the Prince of Peace and became subservient to Buonaparte he was very well placed for passing information, above all naval information, to his friend. Even now that Spain was whole-heartedly at war with France once more, their collaboration had its advantages, and the two of them were now engaged on a joint mission; for the French side was by no means a united whole, but contained many people with divided loyalties, to say nothing of double agents.

He presented himself for breakfast in the great cabin as trim and properly dressed as his host, which made a good impression, and the meal passed off well, though in a rather formal manner: Jack, in these circumstances, was perfectly discreet and Bernard was far from expansive, confining himself to generalities and well-received observations about the beauty of the ship and above all of the truly splendid cabin.

After this Jack left them alone, except for dinner, spending much of his time with Harding and even more with the bosun, reinforcing the ship against the expected blow; though he reserved some hours for Yann, marking the *Bellona*'s charts according to his expert advice and listening to what he had to say about these waters.

'Soon, perhaps the day after Wednesday,' said Yann (he had difficulty with Thursday, though on the whole he was quite fluent), 'it will settle in the south-west and blow horrid. But I don't have to tell *you* about preventer-stays, sir,' he added, looking with pleasure at the *Bellona*'s rigging. And after a pause he said, 'I wonder them buggers' – nodding towards Brest – 'did not try for it when the wind was in the north-east: it was true north-east for a pair of hours after you picked us up. Plenty of time for a frigate to have come down the Goulet and away by the Iroise, ni vu ni connu. Or a fast ship of the line, for that matter: like their *Romulus*.'

'Tell me, Yann,' said Jack, 'if it stays as thick as this, will you undertake to carry the ship through the Raz? With no moonlight at all?'

'As thick as this, sir? I should be happier in a frigate or a sloop than in a heavy great seventy-four, as thick as this: I could do it, because the ebbing tide dashes up so white on the Vieille that I could barely miss it, knowing where to look, since I was a boy.' He held his hand, flattened, low down, to show his height when first he saw the Vieille. 'But never make yourself bad blood, sir: it will *not* stay as thick as this.'

How true. Towards sunset when they were lying off the Men Glas waiting for the tide the wind settled in the north-east again, and although there were patches of true fog still in the east and north-east, over the land, most of the bay to larboard was no more than misty. Indeed some fishing-boats could dimly be seen on the larboard beam half a mile away: larboard, because at this point Jack was some way along his northward run, the ordinary routine patrol. When darkness was almost complete he desired Harding to summon the officer of the watch, Whewell in this case, the master's mates and midshipmen: and when they were all there on the quarterdeck he said, 'Gentlemen, in fifteen minutes I shall put the ship about. I should like this manoeuvre to be executed as silently as possible, and with almost nothing in the way of light; and we shall proceed under reefed courses alone. There is no mad hurry: we are not running a race: but let there be no singing out. Each officer must pick his men. This is no caper for raw hands, however stout and willing. Mr Reade, you have checked the blue cutter, I believe?'

'Yes, sir,' said Reade, smiling in the dark. 'And I believe all is as you could wish.'

Against strong opposition from the more conservative, and from his own heart, Jack had rigged davits above the *Bellona*'s quarter-galleries, taking away somewhat from her beauty and committing an innovation; but now he rejoiced in the thought of that boat hanging there fully equipped, ready to be stepped into by the less expert and lowered down without danger, without anxiety on either part. He had put

Stephen ashore in many and many a place, generally by night; and the anguish, even in a dead-calm sea, of watching his unsteady, lurching journey down the side, though helped by gravity and devoted hands, had added years to his apparent age: any innovation, however barbarous, was worth the relief of seeing him sitting there with his hands folded, his baggage beside him, and the whole, container and contents, very gently descending until it touched the surface, with Bonden there to fend off and the cutter's crew leaping down like cats.

All this, however, was in the future. Once the ship had been put about – which was done with creditable speed, in near silence – and once she was heading south by east under reefed courses with the wind a little abaft the beam, as inconspicuous as a ship of the line could ever hope to be, her captain's station was in the foretop with the pilot, an attentive midshipman on deck to relay his orders.

For a long while there were no orders to relay. Jack and the pilot discussed the clearing of the mist, likely to be complete by the morning; the *Bellona*'s leeway, very slight; and her present position. 'On the starboard bow, sir, you can just make out the Bas Wenn. The course half a point to larboard, sir, if you please: thus, very well thus. And was it day you would see Dead Men's Bay to leeward.' A long silence, in which they heard the muted strokes of five bells in the first watch.

'Now, sir,' said Yann, 'we are well into the Raz, the tide running three knots and more; and in ten minutes, on the larboard bow, if God wishes you will see the white water on the Vieille. This westerly breeze across the strong ebb should throw it quite high.'

Jack stared, stared hard over the larboard bow. His eyes were perfectly accustomed to the darkness, yet they were not what they had been. One had been damaged in battle: 'My solitary point in common with Nelson', he had once said, when half-seas over, and had blushed for it afterwards. It was Yann who cried, 'There she is! Just a little more forward, sir.' And presently Jack caught it, a rhythmic whiteness that travelled from left to right in time with the moderate roll of the ship.

'Now, sir,' said Yann, when they had contemplated this for a while, 'if we steer south-east we should come as near as I dare take you to Dog-Leg Cove in half an hour.'

'Thank you, pilot,' said Jack. 'Lie to, if you please, when we are as close in as you think fit. I shall take my measures.'

He climbed out of the top with the nonchalant ease of one to whom shrouds and ratlines were as natural a path as a flight of stairs, and walked along the dark, silent gangway aft. In the cabin, its lamp hidden from without by deadlights, he found Stephen and Bernard playing chess. Stephen frowned, Bernard made as though to get up, but Jack begged him to remain seated and finish the game: there was perhaps half an hour left.

'Shall we call it a draw?' asked Bernard, after what seemed to Jack an endless pause of the most intense concentration.

'Never in life,' said Stephen. 'Let me record the position, and with the blessing we shall play it out another day.'

'Stephen,' said Jack, 'have you any messages, requests, letters you should like me to send?' Before action he and Stephen usually exchanged wills and the like.

'Not this time, my dear, I thank you very kindly. Lawrence holds all three farthings I possess, and dear Diana knows just what I should wish.'

'Then perhaps we should think of getting ready. The ship will heave to in a very little while; the sea is still and for the moment fairly smooth; and although you will be fifteen minutes before your time, I had sooner set you both ashore with dry coats upon your backs and . . . Come in.'

It was a midshipman: 'Mr Harding's duty, sir, and there is a light on shore, winking three times, then one.'

Stephen nodded and said, 'Let us go.'

Their meagre baggage was already in the boat: Jack led them across the darkened deck, absurdly hand in hand, helped them into the cutter, and leaning down grasped Stephen's shoulder with an iron grip by way of farewell. He heard the sheaves turn smoothly, 'Handsomely, handsomely,' murmured the bosun, saw the boat touch and bob: Bonden shoved off: Jack called 'Row dry, there,' and watched the cutter pull away towards the still-winking light. When at last it went out he turned from the rail, gave the orders that would carry the *Bellona* to her anchorage, and went below, deeply sad. He had seen Stephen off like this many and many a time, but his grief and anxiety never grew less.

As he went he noticed a dim star or two in the zenith; and by the time the boat rejoined, with Bonden's report 'that there was a parcel of gents on the beach, talking foreign, but right glad to see the Doctor – carried him and his mate ashore dryfoot', there was a fine sprinkling of them, with Saturn in the middle, and they so clear and sharp that their light showed him not only the now much greater surf breaking on the reef south of the Ile de Sein but the black, rugged outline of the island itself.

Chapter Six

The grief and anxiety did not die away, but of necessity they receded, and as the *Bellona* worked her way, tack upon tack, round the Saints to regain the bay at dawn, the top of his mind was taken up with the handling of the ship and with a very close watch to see just what harm the lax but harsh command of his jobbing captain had done. He had already looked through the recent gunnery records, which contained no account whatsoever of live firing, only of rattling the great guns in and out: the log, on the other hand, spoke of frequent flogging, more punishment than Jack would have inflicted in a quarter.

At one bell in the morning watch the *Bellona*'s tender, the *Ringle*, now commanded by that valuable young man Reade, a fast, weatherly, sweet-sailing schooner with much less draught than the great seventy-four, hailed to say that she was shoaling her water: ten fathoms, then nine. 'What do you say, Yann?' asked Jack – the pilot was standing at his side.

'What him bottom?'

'Arm your lead,' called Jack; and shortly after the reply came back across the calm, gently heaving sea, 'Hake's teeth and white sand, if you please, sir.'

'Carry on, sir,' said Yann. 'Next cast ten, eleven, twelve.'

A presence behind him, and a very agreeable smell. 'Which I thought you might like some coffee, sir,' said Killick, passing the mug. 'The Doctor said it preserved the frame from falling damps.'

'*Bellona*,' called the tender, 'nine fathoms, if you please.' A pause. 'Ten, and grey sludge.'

Yann nodded with satisfaction. 'If we carry on till come

two bells, and then wear ship and stand east-south-east and half east, we fine, we all right, sir.'

At two bells the idlers were called; the sentinels all round the ship cried 'All's well'; the mate of the watch, having heaved the log, reported to Miller, third lieutenant and officer of the watch, 'Four knots exactly, sir, if you please,' and this he wrote on the log-board, together with the *Bellona*'s present course of south-south-west; the hoarser of the carpenter's mates whispered, 'Four and half inches in the well, sir,' into Miller's ear; and Miller, turning to the Captain and taking off his hat, repeated all this to him in a voice calculated to be heard above the din of hand-pumps, buckets, swabs and holystones of various sizes that were preparing to clean the deck in the first half-lights of the coming day. But before they could begin Jack called, 'Belay, there,' and more gently, 'Mr Miller, we will wear ship, if you please, and stand east-south-east and a half east. The watch will suffice.'

Jack rarely tacked a line-of-battle ship when he had sea-room to wear her, letting her head fall off from the wind and come right round to the desired bearing: it was slower and less spectacular than coming up into the wind's eye, crossing through and steadying on the new course, but it called for fewer hands and it preserved both spars and rigging. He now watched the manoeuvre attentively. It was carried out smoothly; not very fast, but smoothly, with no bellowing or damning of eyes, and when the quartermaster at the con, seeing the compass dead on the true bearing, called to the helmsman 'Thus, thus: very well thus,' Jack went below, reasonably satisfied, but still low in his spirits: he hated to think of Stephen wandering about there on a hostile shore, among so many more or less trustworthy foreigners.

He sat there, reflecting, while the series of bells that had accompanied his life at sea for so many years continued their unchanging pace, bringing up hammocks with a fine rush of feet at the seventh set of strokes and news of breakfast at the eighth.

Almost the only advantage of being on the Brest blockade was that the victuals were usually fresh and plentiful; and breakfast, perhaps Jack's favourite meal apart from dinner, was fairly sure of being able to provide capital sausages and bacon, while the hens (and the *Bellona* was unusually well-found in poultry) being still in something like their native air, gave almost a superfluity of eggs.

Yet this was a lonely breakfast. Obviously, in the nature of things, the captain of a man-of-war, above all one who could not afford to keep a table (and this was Jack's case at present) must eat many and many a solitary meal; but for a great while Jack Aubrey had sailed with Stephen Maturin, and now he missed his companion quite severely – a wholly human and often contradictory companion, essentially different from the only other guests he could invite, lieutenants, master's mates or midshipmen, who were all debarred by custom, and by common prudence, from disagreeing with the skipper on any point whatsoever: and who in any case were not to speak until they had been spoken to.

'Come in,' he called.

'Sir,' said a midshipman, opening the cabin door, 'Mr Somers' compliments and duty, and the *Alexandria* is in sight.'

'Thank you, Mr Wetherby. Is she within signalling distance?'

'Oh, sir, I am sure I cannot tell,' said Wetherby, aghast – he was a first voyager – 'Shall I run up and ask?'

'Never trouble. I shall be on deck directly.'

'She might conceivably be bringing us our post,' reflected Jack. 'How I should love a fat parcel of letters – news of the girls – word of the village and that reptile Griffiths – and perhaps the *Proceedings* will be out.' He had combined his last visit to London but one to criticizing the naval estimates in the Commons as member for Milport and to reading a second paper on the precession of the equinoxes to the Royal Society as a fellow of that august and learned body: for he was a late-blooming but quite highly esteemed mathematician, specializing in the problems of celestial navigation. Uncommon mathematical and musical abilities are quite often to be found in men wholly ignorant of the laws of prosody and barely capable of assembling two score words of prose in a passably elegant, coherent and grammatical form. 'And there might even be an encouraging letter from Lawrence,' he went on: but the word letter reminded him of the shockingly painful one to the Reverend Mr Geoghegan that he must write out fair – he could scarcely ask his clerk to do so – in order that it should go to the flag as soon as possible: and to change the current of his mind he swallowed the last of his coffee and walked forward along the quarterdeck, all its inhabitants silently moving over to the larboard side as he appeared.

'Where away?' he asked.

'Two points on the starboard bow, sir,' said Somers, the officer of the watch, and two of the midshipmen exchanged a knowing look, for most of the people could see her perfectly well.

It was fully day now, though the sun was still hidden by cloud low over the distant land, and there was mist over the sea itself, and presently Jack, bringing his good eye to bear with a now habitual twist of his neck, made out the little frigate, her sails whiter than the whiteness between the two ships.

'She is heading for the Black Rocks,' said Jack. 'Has she uttered?'

'She dipped a topsail, sir,' said Somers. 'But that was probably just Captain Nasmyth's fun.'

'Give her a waft,' said Jack, who was much senior to Nasmyth, the frigate's commander, 'and throw out *Desire to speak you.*'

The signal midshipman, an oldster named Callow who had sailed with Jack before, and the yeoman were expecting this and the signal raced up, breaking out directly.

The *Alexandria* put before the wind, spread studdingsails and began throwing a bow-wave, most creditable in this moderate breeze.

143

'Say *Dyce: come no higher*,' called Jack. 'Then *Have you any news, any letters?*'

A short pause, in which all the telescopes on the *Bellona*'s quarterdeck focused earnestly upon the frigate: and even before Callow could read out the answer an audible sigh arose from the quicker-minded watchers. '*No news*, sir. *No letters. Regret. Repeat regret.*'

'Reply *Many thanks: the Lord will provide. Carry on.*'

The *Alexandria* carried on, vanishing entirely within half an hour as their courses diverged, Jack beating up for his usual station at this time of day off Dinant Point, where he might possibly fall in with the *Ramillies* coming down from St Matthews, or one of the cutters that plied between the squadrons.

But for the time being he was to attend to the young gentlemen. They were gathering there on the quarterdeck behind him, accompanied by the schoolmaster, and although some were furtively giggling, treading on one another's toes, most were decently apprehensive.

'Very well, gentlemen, let us begin,' said Jack in their direction, and he led the way into the fore-cabin. Here they showed up their day's workings, which, as there had been no noon observation the day before, were necessarily the product of dead reckoning, and they differed little, except in neatness.

Both Walkinshaw and Jack were perfectly at home with the mathematics of navigation and it was difficult for either to understand how very deeply ignorant it was possible for the young and feather-brained to be, particularly those young men who had spent most of their school-time ashore learning Latin and in some cases Greek and even a little Hebrew – possibly some French. This occurred to Jack with some force in the silence that followed his commendation of the neat and his giving back the workings; and out of this silence he said to a dwarfish twelve-year-old, the son of one of his former lieutenants, 'Mr Thomson, what is meant by a sine?'

He glanced round the general blankness and went on,

'Each of you take a piece of paper and write down what is meant by a sine. Mr Weller' – this to a boy who had been to a nautical academy at Wapping – 'you are whispering to your neighbour. Jump up to the masthead and stay there until you are told to come down. But before you go, gather the papers and show them to me.'

It was difficult to tell whether the schoolmaster or his pupils felt the more distressed as the Captain looked through the undeniable proof of such very complete ignorance of the first elements. 'Very well,' he said at last, 'we shall have to start again with the ABC. Pass the word for my joiner.' The joiner appeared, brushing chips from his apron. 'Hemmings,' said Jack, 'run me up a blackboard, will you? A flat dead paint that will take chalk handsomely, and let me have it by this time tomorrow.' To the youngsters he said, 'I shall write definitions and draw diagrams, and you will get them by heart.' He was not in the best of moods, and his absolute determination, together with his bulk and his immense authority on board, was singularly impressive. They filed out in silence, looking grave.

The next morning the blackboard was present, fixed by thumbscrews within easy reach of the Captain's hand, and from it the boys were taught, with words and diagrams, the nature of sine, cosine, tangent, cotangent, secant and cosecant, the relations between them, and their value in helping to find your position in a prodigious ocean, no shore, no landmark for ten thousand miles. All these things were to be found in Robinson's *Elements of Navigation* which, together with the *Requisite Tables* and *Nautical Almanac*, lay in their sea-chests, a necessary part of their equipment; and Mr Walkinshaw had tried to lead the youngsters through them. But nothing came anywhere near the concentrated forceful instructions of Jove himself; and after what seemed an anxious eternity to the midshipmen's berth but which in fact lasted no more than a few of the *Bellona*'s usual patrols from Douarnenez Bay to the Black Rocks in hazy, sometimes foggy weather in which they saw nothing at all and sometimes with such light airs that on occasion they lacked even steerage-way and the Captain had all the time in the world for trigonometry.

Yet Thursday came at last, a blessed Thursday, a make-and-mend day when the mist cleared, a decent breeze blew from the north-east and the youngsters sat in the sun on the forecastle with their sea-daddies showing them how to darn their stockings or mend torn clothes or tie the simple knots and learn the elements of splicing – a Thursday on which the lookout at the masthead hailed 'On deck, there. A ship's topsails right to leeward.'

Presently most of those who felt they could be spared below were aloft with telescopes and after a while it was found that she was the *Ramillies*, now lying to and presumably watching some suspect sail northwards along the Passage du Four, out of sight from the *Bellona*. No sooner was this agreed to by all than a second vessel was seen, a cutter coming from the direction of Ushant, beyond the Black Rocks; and then even a third, the heavy frigate *Doris*. After such loneliness the bay seemed positively crowded. The *Ramillies* was a right welcome sight to all hands and particularly to Jack: her captain, Billy Fanshawe, was an old friend of his. So indeed was the *Doris*; but what really delighted every man aboard, including those who could neither read nor write, was the identification of the cutter as one belonging to the flagship and employed for distribution of the mail throughout the squadron under Admiral Stranraer's command.

The *Doris*, out in the offing, had altered course to intercept the cutter well before the *Bellona* and she had her letters first, although Harding, who had left his wife expecting her first child, spread an unreasonable amount of canvas. Yet quite soon the Bellonas' grim, discontented looks gave way to tense and happy anticipation: the cutter came neatly alongside, seized the net dangling from a whip to the mainyard, put a fine round mailsack into it and sped off towards the distant *Ramillies*.

The sack was carried hotfoot to the great cabin, where Jack, the first lieutenant and the clerk sorted it: from the cabin it filtered down, first to the wardroom, then by way of the clerk to the warrant-officers and petty officers and then by way of the midshipmen to the ratings of their particular divisions.

Jack's mail obviously stayed where it was, and as soon as the cabin-door had closed behind Harding and the clerk he seized the first on the pile, a letter addressed, and badly addressed, in that most familiar of hands. They had parted on indifferent terms and he opened it with the liveliest expectation of all their affection being fully restored, smiling as he did so. The letter was dated from Woolcombe on the fourteenth: with these northerly winds it had taken no more than five days.

Mr Aubrey,
It is with a deepest, the *very deepest* concern, that I must tell you I have been shown unanswerable proof of your infidelity. In open contempt of your promise before God's altar you lay with a woman called Amanda Smith in Canada and got her with child. Deny it if you can. I have the proofs and I mean to take advice. In the mean time I shall give the Admiral notice to leave my house at Ashgrove and return there with the children.

Then came some tear-blotted and scratched-out lines. The obviously composed and recopied letter now abandoned its original and improvised, grew far less coherent, far less legible. He had just made out the words 'you left her bed and came into mine' when he was called on deck.

'Sir,' said Harding, 'you asked me to tell you if *Ramillies* gave any sign of life. This last minute she has thrown out our number and *Captain repair aboard*. I have acknowledged and given word to ready your barge.'

'Thank you, Mr Harding,' said Jack. 'Make all suitable sail, if you please.'

He returned to the cabin and having sat for a while he reached out for the other letter from Sophie and opened it with a hesitant, almost trembling hand.

The date was a week before that which he had just read, the writing more wholly familiar.

My dearest Jack,

How sorry I am to have sent you off so shabbily, and for a great while I have been meaning to beg pardon for my bad temper – trying to tell you how even a most loving heart – a female heart – can be affected by the ill-humoured Moon: but these things are very hard for a sadly ignorant creature to set down on paper so that the words give any real picture of her feelings, and before I had written anything but odd headings such as Love and Kisses and Forgiveness a letter came from Bath with the most frightful news.

You will certainly remember that Mama lived with a friend called Mrs Morris – the Honourable Mrs Morris – who helped her with the business, and that they had a manservant, a worthless fellow we all disliked when they lived here, particularly your seamen; but he was useful in the business because he understood horse-racing and the laying of odds.

Well, Mrs Morris has run off with him, apparently taking all the money and anything else they could carry and when Mama heard they were married, legally married in a church, she fell down senseless and had to be bled, and she has had fits ever since, laughing and crying. With dear Diana's help I brought her back here – she had almost destroyed their apartment in Pulteney Street and anyhow she was not fit to live there alone – the servants, apart from old Molly, had all left – and I am afraid she behaved dreadfully in the coach – and since the girls are back from school bringing friends with them, the little Nugent children, I have had to put her in your study, so near the necessary room: but do not fear – we have put a bed in the left-hand corner with a wardrobe and a chest of drawers behind it (I cannot tell you how kind dear Mrs Oakes has been) and she will never come near your precious ship-models or surveying instruments.

148

When you come on leave (and oh may it be soon, my love) and when the holiday girls and their friends are gone, we will move her upstairs; or possibly back to Bath, with a *much more suitable* companion. She says there is a clergyman who was on the brink of making her an offer.

Dear Jack, please do not worry about having money sent to me for housekeeping; we are very well with what comes from the farm, the dairy, the kitchen-garden and my poultry-yard, but even if it were not for them, Diana absolutely insists on giving us a very handsome rent for her wing of the house and the stabling – such stabling now! Such horses! With the help of the gentleman who lent her the coach she took you and Stephen down in – she has it yet – she pawned that enormous great blue diamond she brought back with her from America – 'Be damned to living on £200 a year,' she cried – and is launching into breeding Arabs again. And although that sad place at Barham is not yet sold, she has taken all Meares' pasture for them. She said it was absurd to keep the Blue Peter as they call it hidden away in a jeweller's case – she could not wear it at our Dorchester assemblies, only in London or Paris – and in any case she would soon have it again, once Stephen's affairs were in order. She looks forward extremely to a coach and six . . .

Jack laid the paper down, and in a dull, heavy way he wondered how he had come to be so deeply foolish as to leave Amanda's letters in a square cardboard box among his official and business correspondence; a certain liking, a certain gratitude had prevented him from balling them up and throwing them away. There would have been an in-decency in doing so, in spite of her extreme silliness. He felt no particular guilt except for this foolishness: by his code a man who was directly challenged must in honesty engage – anything else would be intolerably insulting. Yet had he known of this miserable old woman's prying and her malice he would certainly have played the scrub in Canada. He reflected on Sophie's general attitude towards these matters – her extreme disapproval of any irregularity, any levity in speaking of even a looseness that reached nowhere near as far as criminal conversation – for *her* looseness in conversation *was* criminal, almost in the lawyer's sense of the term.

'Sir,' said his first lieutenant, 'forgive me for bursting in on you, but your barge is lowering down. And sir, may I tell you Eleanor and I have a daughter, healthy, pink and cheerful?'

'Give you joy of her with all my heart, William,' said Jack, crushing his hand. 'And Mrs Harding too, of course. I am sure that she will turn out to be a good 'un.'

The ceremony of the side, and the Captain of the *Bellona*, preceded by a midshipman, stepped into the boat. Bonden shoved off: the bargemen gave way, pulling a fine even stroke across the fifty yards to the *Ramillies*. The ceremony of the side again, Captain Aubrey piped aboard and kindly greeted by Captain Fanshawe, his senior by a short neck, who led him into the cabin, placed a glass of brandy in his hand and with a curiously embarrassed air said, 'Well, Jack, I hope you had an agreeable post?'

'Not quite what I could have wished, as far as I have looked,' said Jack. 'But perhaps something better may appear. How was yours?'

'A charming letter from Dolly, and quite good news of the children: the rest was mostly bills. But Jack, I am truly sorry to say the cutter also brought me an order from the flag. I am required to acquaint you that on the night you received a pilot from *Ramillies* and shaped a course for the Raz de Sein two French frigates sailed from Brest with the wind at north-east and are now attacking British and allied merchantmen with great success. This cannot but be attributed to your negligence in not keeping a good lookout since from all appearance the Frenchmen must have crossed your wake. I am therefore to reprimand you severely: and you are hereby severely reprimanded.'

'Yes, sir,' said Jack, without expression. 'Is that all?'

'No,' replied Fanshawe with more expression than he intended and with his eyes on the paper in front of him. 'I am also under orders to require you to proceed off Ushant without the loss of a moment and to report to the flag: there you will be attached to the offshore squadron where it is hoped that other and perhaps sharper eyes will diminish the very grave consequences of such unseamanly negligence.'

A silence. Neither intended to comment on the Admiral's prose.

'Will you dine with me, Jack?' asked Fanshawe in an attempt at an ordinary conversational tone.

'Thank you very much, Billy,' said Jack, 'but *without the loss of a moment* stands in the way. And between ourselves, my post acquainted me that I have been taken in adultery without a goddamn leg to stand on and that there is the Devil to pay. It destroys a man's appetite, you know.'

'Oh, my dear Jack, I know, I know,' cried Fanshawe with great feeling. 'I know only too well. Come, drink up your brandy and I will see you over the side.'

Coming aboard the *Bellona* again Jack returned the many salutes, walked into his cabin, where the letters were still strewn over a medley of unopened covers, and sent for the master. 'Mr Woodbine,' he said, 'pray shape a course for Ushant, for wherever the offshore squadron is most likely to be lying at this state of the tide and in the particular wind. Or whatever wind we find out there.'

Indeed, the winds the offshore squadron experienced were generally very much harder than those that blew eastward of Ushant, especially the great south-westers, from whose full force and from whose prodigious seas the inshore ships were protected to some degree by the chain of the Saints, which acted as a not very efficient but still appreciable breakwater; and this was even more evident in the Chenal de la Helle, which Woodbine took that afternoon.

They made good progress, and although the topsails had to be double-reefed on reaching the wholly unprotected

Passage de Fromveur it was clear that the wind was diminishing. On the other hand, the monstrous sea it had worked up on the far side of the island was if anything greater still, in spite of the heavy rain, by the time they reached the squadron, lying-to off the Stiff Bay in the north-east; and when Jack, in response to the flagship's *Captain repair aboard*, made his way down into his wildly heaving barge he missed his footing for once and with his boat-cloak flying about his ears he fell plump into the water swirling about the boat's bottom. Much more water joined it on the way across, and it was a damp Jack Aubrey that stood waiting for his interview with the Admiral aboard the *Charlotte*. A long wait; and although Charles Morton, her captain, was civil enough Jack knew perfectly well that a man who was very much out of favour, who had just received a reprimand, a severe reprimand, was a dangerously infectious leper, above all in a ship governed by Stranraer; and he inflicted neither his remarks nor his presence on any of the officers about him.

When he was taken into the Admiral's cabin he found that the Captain of the Fleet was also present, sitting at Stranraer's side behind a long table set athwartship, with the Admiral's secretary and a clerk at the larboard end. 'Good evening, my lord,' he said. 'Good evening, sir.'

'Good evening, Captain Aubrey,' said the Admiral. 'Sit down. Now what have you to say about these French frigates you allowed to slip past you?'

'I have only to say that I very much regret any Frenchman should have got out of Brest.'

'Then you admit they went by?'

'I must have expressed myself badly, my lord. I expressed nothing but regret at what is said to have taken place: I acknowledged no sort of responsibility.'

'Where was your ship at sunset on the twenty-seventh?'

'Two cables north of the Men Glas, my lord, waiting for the tide.'

'Then how do you explain the fact that two frigates could leave the Goulet de Brest, run out by the Iroise and be seen a league north of the Ile de Sein three quarters of an hour later without they passed astern of you, almost within hail, certainly in sight?'

'I do not explain it at all, my lord. But I will assert that there was a lookout at each masthead and of course on the fo'c'sle, able seamen of known reliability.'

'So you deny the possibility of the Frenchman's getting past unseen?'

'I do not deny it. The weather was uncommon thick at times that afternoon and night – the pilot had to feel his way along past the Basse Vieille by the flash of surf – and it is not *impossible* that she passed unseen. What I do deny is the possibility of her doing so through the fault or negligence of any of my people.'

'So you blame it all on the weather, do you?'

'If blame there should be, I should certainly lay it on the fog, my lord.'

The Admiral looked at Calvert, the Captain of the Fleet and the officer principally concerned with discipline. 'What do you say?'

Calvert, a cold, withdrawn man, tall for a sailor and thin, looked dispassionately at Jack for a moment and said, 'In cases of this kind there is much to be said for gathering all the available *objective* evidence. Not only does the ship in question keep a logbook with remarks on the weather but there are also the officers' and midshipmen's journals. If this should ever become an important disciplinary matter – if there should be the least question of anyone asking for a court martial – they would certainly have to be looked at.'

Stranraer considered. The clerk mended his pen. 'Oh, I do not think it will come to that,' said the Admiral at last. 'If Captain Aubrey will solemnly declare that his ship was in a state of full preparedness on the twenty-seventh I shall rest content.'

Jack made the declaration. Stranraer stood up, saying, 'Then let us leave it at that.'

'Certainly, my lord. But if you will allow me, I have a request to make: a request for leave.'

'Leave?' cried Stranraer. 'Not more leave, for God's sake? Parliamentary leave again?'

'No, my lord, for urgent private affairs.'

'No. That really will not do. If every officer or seaman for that matter, were to go home every time there was an urgency in his private affairs we should never be able to man the fleet. It is not a sudden death, I trust?'

'No, my lord.'

'Then let us hear no more about it. Ours is a hard service, as you know very well; and this is wartime.'

Certainly it was a hard service, and neither Admiral Stranraer nor the autumnal gales had the least intention of making it any less so. The squadron was drilled, and most rigorously drilled, in all weathers short of a close-reefed topsail blow. Towards the end of the day boats would be seen carrying apprehensive captains across to the flag to hear the Admiral's candid opinion of their seamanship: his notion of drill was curious, rather like that of the army of an earlier age, when precision of button, pipeclay and movement counted for almost everything, together with evolutions such as counter-marches which had very little to do with war, an activity that might easily spoil a uniform. Lord Stranraer had little use for gunfire. He would certainly have grappled with the French had they come out, but during his very frequent drills the great guns generally lay idle, shining wherever polish was in any way appropriate and housed with perfect regularity. It was something like the West Indian discipline transported to the Channel, where it made even less sense than it had in the Caribbean.

Although he was constantly forming and reforming the line of battle, with the rear becoming the van and the van becoming the rear, combat itself did not really seem to interest the Admiral. He had in his youth been concerned in a certain number of actions, in which he had not behaved with discredit, but he pinned all his faith in the moral force of a large, intact fleet, impeccably expert in all possible manoeuvres and professionally far in advance of any possible rival, a body that would silently impose its will.

However, these drills did at least keep Jack Aubrey very fully occupied indeed. He was extremely unwilling to have his ship and by inference his ship's company picked out for harsh signals – *Bellona*'s number showing clear aboard the flag or the repeating frigate followed by *keep your station* or *make more sail* or some telegraphic remark such as *look alive* or *do you need assistance* – and since *Bellona*'s crew, though a very fair body for the purpose of fighting the ship, at present included more than a fair share of landmen, and (which was even more important) had never at any time been worked up to this kind of stop-watch performance in anything but gunnery, he and his officers had to do their very utmost to anticipate the next order, a wearing task and one in which they were not always successful. The *Bellona*'s barge therefore often joined those who were summoned aboard the flag at the end of the exercise to be told their faults by their rough-tongued admiral.

Jack did not enjoy these sessions but they did not touch him deeply even when the strictures were deserved, which with such a crew as his was sometimes inevitable, because his mind was in a very curious state of hurry, confusion and distress. Except when it was taken up with the day-long task of making his ship give as good an account of herself in a highly competitive series of operations, often in heavy weather, his mind ran on that letter and on the stranger who had written it. Innumerable possibilities came crowding, and an immense sadness alternated with a perhaps still greater frustration which took the form of a longing for battle.

This was clearly obvious to those that knew him well, and even the Captain of the Fleet, not an exceptionally percipient man, handled him with care aboard the *Charlotte*. On his own quarterdeck he awarded no punishment – there was little need – but occasionally he would clap his jaws shut on some intended rebuke; and this had an effect far more marked than any blasphemous roar.

'I hope to God he don't explode,' said anxious, unhappy Killick.

'God help the poor bugger he explodes upon,' said Bonden.

Solution or at all events relief through the very great and varied emotion of battle came in sight on a Monday. The day before, *Bellona* like all the other ships and vessels in the squadron, had rigged church: Jack Aubrey could hardly have been called a religious man, but as well as his many superstitions he also had his pieties. He revered the sound if not the full implication of the Book of Common Prayer, the Lessons and the usual psalms and readings: the other rituals such as the inspection of the entire ship and every soul aboard her, clean, shaved, sober and toeing a given line or rather seam, soothed his mind; and although today he did not feel up to reading a sermon he and all his people were perfectly satisfied with the even more usual Articles of War, which, through immemorial use, had acquired ecclesiastical qualities of their own. It is true that there were obvious and extremely painful associations with the parish church at Woolcombe, but the great heave of the sea, the creak of the rigging and the smell of tar put a great enough distance between the two and it was not until he had returned to his cabin that an unlucky shifting of some papers to make room for his prayer-book showed him Sophie's letter clear and the sense of desolation, fury and extreme distress returned with even greater force.

Jack Aubrey was on deck this Monday morning, having sent his breakfast away – four eggs untouched, congealing in their butter – and he saw the Admiral's signal. The *Charlotte* was a talkative ship, and although this was usually thought a tiresome characteristic it did give the signal-officers a great deal of practice, and now he heard Callow read off the hoists almost as they appeared, without referring to the book. The squadron was to proceed, in line abreast, on a west-south-westerly course under all plain sail, the *Bellona* at the southern tip: yet the glass was dropping; the southern sky, or as much of it as could be seen under the low cloud, was wanting in promise; and the sea of this ebbing tide had some curious pallid streaks, apparently rising from the depths. The first lieutenant and the master looked grave. Harding had dined with the *Charlotte*'s wardroom the day before and he had learnt that this sweep was being carried out primarily in order to find how fast and how accurately a signal could travel from one extremity of the line – the unusually wide-spread line – to the other and back again. Lord Stranraer had another admiral, an expert on signals, aboard as a guest.

Presently they were all under way and the line, after a great deal of nagging from the flag, was as straight on the surface of the ocean as the earth's curvature would allow. But this perfection did not last: a little before dinner the *Charlotte* made the signal for the squadron to tack together, emphasized by a gun; and as far as could be seen it was obeyed with tolerable regularity right across the broad front; though a second gun seemed to show that at least one ship on the far eastern end had been slow or had even missed the signal altogether – there was a good deal of murk over there. Another explanation was that the unknown ship, having already mixed its noon-day grog, was so infuriated by this untimely order that it delayed out of mere bloody-mindedness.

Having come about, the squadron made a fair board, quite time enough to eat their quarter of a pound of cheese (this was a banyan day), and then returned to the former course, though with a little more west in it.

Easy sailing: but presently the weather thickened, and the sound of the wind in the rigging rose steadily until it had traversed a full octave. Jack called for preventer-stays.

'We shall soon be going home,' said Harding to Miller, who now had the watch; and by home he meant that dismal stretch of sea off Keller's Island where the Admiral liked to shelter when the sea, wind and rain threatened to become more outrageous than usual.

'Reef topsails, Mr Miller, if you please,' said Jack. The topgallants had disappeared long since, and even the *Ringle*, as trim as a duck away there to leeward, showed little more than a handkerchief on each mast and a third right forward.

'Hands reef topsails' came the cry and the sharp cutting bosun's pipe: and as the men raced aloft Jack, gazing over the larboard bow, caught hints of whiteness away down in the troubled grey, the growing sea and its now much wilder crests.

'Port your helm,' he said quietly to Compton, the older of the two men at the wheel, a hand who knew him well, and the tone of his voice. Compton and his mate eased the great plunging ship a trifle to starboard, opening Jack a view as he stood there swaying to the sea, the telescope to his good eye.

A long pause, an electric tension on the quarterdeck and right along the waist of the ship, filled with men who knew or knew of him; then the first of a series of blinding squalls of mixed rain, sleet and snow; and when it had passed Callow said hesitantly, 'Sir, I believe I saw *Monmouth* repeat *Tack all together* just before she vanished.'

Jack and his officers stared briefly eastward. 'I see nothing,' he said. 'Did you make out any signal, Mr Harding?'

'None, sir.'

'Mr Callow: make *enemy in sight two leagues south-west by south heading north-west*. Mr Miller, shake out the reefs in the foretopsail: set fore topmast staysail half in.' He stepped over to the wheel and with his eye on those remote flecks in the infinity of other greys and whiteness, all shifting incessantly, he set a course to intercept the vessel, the enemy, the very probable enemy.

The ship's company, including those who had escaped from the sick-berth along with their attendants, lined the side. If there were any so morose as to disbelieve the Captain's implied declaration, they did not mention it. From his early days as an astonishingly successful frigate-captain, coming home with a tail of captured ships and a fortune in prize-money, Jack had acquired the status of a mythical being or something very like it, a being whose judgment in these matters could not be wrong; and any scepticism would have been most furiously resented.

The event confirmed the believers in their creed. Within half an hour the chase, raised high on a towering wave, was seen to be a frigate wearing French colours, herself pursuing a merchantman. She was not a national ship, however, but one of those powerful, fast-sailing privateers from Vannes or Lorient that were more deadly as commerce-raiders than the regular men-of-war and that were now making the most of what war was left to them, often running very extreme risks within miles of the Channel fleet.

She was called *Les Deux Frères* and so intent was she on her prey – already within long shot, but they far preferred boarding, in case a ball, causing a leak, should spoil the cargo – that she did not make out the *Bellona*, partly veiled in a squall for some minutes. On doing so she instantly bore up, bringing the wind not right aft but on her quarter, her best point of sailing; at the same time, out of mere spite, she fired at the merchantman and almost immediately set her flying jib. Little good did either do. The shot missed and the sail blew out of its boltrope.

Still, she fled along, throwing a splendid bow-wave, her heavy crew tending the sail with the utmost attention and risking long shots at the seventy-four in the hope of wounding her sails and cutting up her rigging, conceivably knocking away a yard or a topmast: after all, the *Deux Frères* carried a by no means contemptible armament, including some carronades. But even more than that every man and boy aboard knew that their last three captures in the chops of the Channel had made them the richest privateer afloat.

She fled with the utmost zeal therefore, almost as fast as the *Ringle* steadily there on her starboard bow, just out of shot. She fled with all the earnest desire to preserve wealth and freedom that can be imagined and with almost superhuman skill; but short of the *Bellona* being struck by lightning – a good deal was flashing above the low cloud-cover – she had no chance. For the sea was rising: minute by minute the crests were higher, the spume tearing away from their tops, and the hollows between them were deeper and wider; and in seas of this magnitude no frigate could outsail a well-handled ship of the line to windward of her, since in these deep valleys the frigate was becalmed, while the seventy-four (which in any case could spread more sail) was not, or not entirely, and she retained the momentum of her sixteen hundred tons. 'It is going to be a dirty night,' said Jack to the officer of the watch. 'Pray pass the word for the gunner. Master Gunner,' he went on, 'we will not touch the lower-deck port-lids, but it would be as well to ready the forward larboard eighteen-pounders. You drew them all yesterday, I believe?'

'So I did, sir.'

'And you are quite happy about your tompions, with all this wet about?'

'If any misses fire, sir,' said the gunner, his rain-soaked old face grinning with delighted anticipation, 'you may call me Jack Pudding.' Then the full horror of this remark striking home, he looked perfectly blank, his lips framing unspoken words. All conversation, all possible explanations, were cut off by a freakish sea flooding green over the quarter-deck rail and surging aft; and before it had cleared an even more freakish carronade ball from the *Deux Frères* struck and shattered the *Bellona*'s wheel, flinging the helmsmen right and left, unhurt. She put straight before the wind and offered to come up the other side, taken all aback; but she had right seamen aboard and they, brailing up the mizen-topsail and starting the main sheet, quickly brought her under control until the usual purchases to the tiller had been shipped, allowed the ship to be steered by orders called down to the hands on either side of the sweep.

In the few minutes that all this took the *Deux Frères* forged ahead; but when they saw the *Bellona* fill and square away with her upper-deck ports open and the guns run out, their hearts died within them. They abandoned the notion of crossing the *Bellona*'s bows and raking her with all they could throw: abandoned it entirely, came up into the wind, struck her colours and lay to.

Jack edged the *Bellona* over to make something of a lee,

sent the *Ringle* and the blue cutter with a well-armed prize-crew aboard under Miller, telling him to make for Falmouth and send the frigate's master back with his officers and papers. 'And be uncommon brisk, Mr Miller. It will be nip and tuck getting the boat aboard.'

Nip and tuck it was, with the wind increasing to such a shocking degree, and it took the whole of the afternoon to heave the cutter in. But at last it was done and the boat made triply fast. Well before that however the Frenchmen had been taken disconsolate below – Harding was tolerably fluent in French – and Jack, still on deck, said to the master, 'Mr Woodbine, it is time to steer for Keller's Island.'

'Yes, sir.'

'You do not seem happy, Mr Woodbine.'

'I am happy about the prize, and I give you joy, sir: but was I in command I should follow her into Falmouth. The bosun is just going to report that the mainyard is probably sprung in the slings: the mizen doubtful in the woulding: the beakhead bulkhead is stove. We have not had an observation these last three watches; and I do not believe the blow has reached its full strength, no sir, not by a very long chalk. It will be a great while before Chips and his mates can give us a right wheel and although steering with sheet and purchase is very well for a pleasant Saturday afternoon it is bloody awkward pardon me the expression all night long in a howling tempest bearing dead on Ushant and its cruel reefs – imagine trying to avoid a wreck with such a wind and with such a helm! And wrecks there will be by wholesale before daylight.'

Woodbine had obviously been drinking. 'We must do our best,' said Jack, not unkindly.

Their best they did, but it was not enough. Very late that night the blow turned out to be one of those notorious turning winds. It headed them when they were no great way from Ushant, and there was no beating into it even if the *Bellona* had had a full suit of storm canvas, intact masts, spars and rigging, and a fresh, full-fed crew. She had none of these things. The galley had been flooded in the graveyard watch. It had been All Hands right round the clock and not a man had eaten anything but wet ship's bread since yesterday's dinner: the people were utterly exhausted and the ship was making more water than the pumps could expel.

A certain lightening in the east, and it was first day at last. And they had their bearings, Vega some time before, through the tearing clouds, and old Saturn. The sea however was no less; the wind even more contrary. Jack bore up at last and sailed for Cawsand Bay.

As he had expected there were two other ships from the offshore squadron already there and one – with only a single lower mast still standing – from the inner: and they had taken up all the available places. 'I am sorry, Aubrey,' said the Commissioner, an old friend, 'but there it is. However, *Alexandria* won't take long – only a few ribs gone and an ugly hole plugged with a great piece of rock – wonderful how often that happens, ain't it? Almost makes you believe in guardian angels, ha, ha, ha! And as soon as she is done you shall have her place. But dear me *Bellona* does call for a lot of patching up. So do you yourself, Aubrey. You look dead beat. Believe me, what you want is a hot body bath. The whole body immersed in hot, hot water and kept there for five or even ten minutes. It opens the pores amazingly. They have one at the George, and will bring up boiling buckets in a trice. And after that a thundering good breakfast and sleep for twelve hours.'

'Certainly, sir,' said Jack. 'The moment I have written my necessary letter to the Admiral. Fortunately I have my tender to take it out to Ushant.'

'That pretty little Chesapeake schooner that came in with you? I have been admiring her: not a hair out of place. But of course, your letter to the Admiral must come first, as you say. And a note to dear Mrs Aubrey as well, I dare say. Pray remember me very kindly to her.' The Commissioner kissed his hand and walked off, chuckling.

Jack sat at his table:

Bellona,
Cawsand Bay
November 17th

My Lord,

I beg to acquaint you that his Majesty's ship *Bellona* suffered much in the severe gale of last night and this morning. The mizen mast received a violent wrench, and is sprung at the partners and elsewhere: the main-yard is also sprung. The mainsail, main topsail, the mizen and fore storm staysail were blown to pieces; one of the starboard main-chainplates drew; and the ship laboured so excessively in the trough of the sea, and shipped so much more water than the pumps could carry off, that it became absolutely necessary for her safety to bear away for this port, where I arrived in the forenoon.

I have the honour to inclose the ship's defects, and a copy of the log since receiving your last signal.

I have the honour to be, my Lord, &c.

Log of the *Bellona*

16th p.m. Strong breeze with heavy swell. Tacked ship as per signal. Lost sight of squadron in heavy and almost continuous squalls. Sighted strange sail in pursuit of British brig SW by S 2 leagues: pursued and took same, when she proved to be *Les Deux Frères* of Lorient, privateer frigate of 28 twelve-pounders and 2 39-pound carronades, 174 men: Dumanoir master. Sent her into Falmouth (a valuable prize, having taken two home-ward-bound Guineamen laden with gold-dust and ivory, and an outward-bound snow carrying ship's stores to Lisbon). At half-past ten strong gales with heavy squalls: carried away starboard main-brace and larboard main topsail sheet; sail blew to pieces; set a storm main and fore staysail.

17th a.m. At half-past six the storm mizen and fore

staysail blew from the yard: strong gales veering and backing irregularly. At eight obliged to scuttle lower deck; ship labouring very much, and gained six inches on the pumps. At quarter-past eight the carpenter reported the mizen-mast was sprung, in consequence of the vangs of the gaff giving way. At half-past eight was struck with a sea on the larboard quarter, stove in eleven of the main-deck ports, half filled the main-deck, and carried away the bulkheads of the wardroom.

At eight hard gales with violent squalls. Carried away the chain-plate of the foremost main shroud. Bore up under a reefed foresail. Saw a line-of-battle ship lying to, with her head to the southward, and her sails split and blowing from the yards.

Jno. Aubrey

Jack re-read his letter, realized that the two parts did not exactly coincide; but he was too stupid and heavy to deal with this, so he sanded, folded, addressed and sealed it. He and Harding had already seen to the transfer of the *Bellona*'s hands to receiving-ships and the few officers and midshipmen who did not cling to what was left of their cabins and berth where they could at least get some sleep had found themselves lodgings. All he had to do now was to carry this letter to Reade or Callow (they alternated aboard the *Ringle*) and ask for it to be taken out to Ushant. But no sooner was the seal well in place but he clapped his hand to his forehead and whipped the letter open again, adding

My Lord,

I am sending you this letter by my tender: but at the present moment I am so stupid after the night's blow that I forgot to beg that you would be so good as to send her back as soon as you may find convenient. I have, as your Lordship knows, a rendezvous at the dark of the moon; and if the repairs to *Bellona* cannot be carried out by then, I should wish to keep the engagement in *Ringle*: no other craft would serve the purpose.

He sealed the letter again, burnt his fingers on the wax, and a certain pettishness at last breaking through, he cried, 'Hell, death and damnation.'

'Is that you, sir?' asked Harding, looking through the door. 'I thought you was fast asleep at the George – gone ashore long ago.'

'No, I had to write to the Admiral first, and now I must take it to the *Ringle*, to carry across. But then I shall sleep, by God: sleep like a crew of hedgepigs in an ivy-tuft: then in the afternoon I shall go to Woolcombe for a few days – urgent family affairs. The yard will not start any important repairs till Monday: and even if they do, you know as much about the barky's needs as I do.'

'Give me the letter, sir: I will see to it. The sooner you are abed the better, if you are to make a journey. Sleep – God help us – nothing like it. I shall turn in myself in twenty minutes. Good-bye, sir; sleep very well, and you will wake a new man.'

Jack slept in his bath, slept in his bed at the George until noon, slept in the post-chaise that carried him towards Woolcombe at so handsome a pace that it would have been the fastest run he had ever made from Plymouth but for a linch-pin that slipped from its place, liberating the corresponding wheel, which bowled away at a great pace down the road, whilst the chaise plunged into a ditch, a harmless plunge into a soft, well-filled ditch. This took place just outside Alton, a village not five miles from home; but by the time wheel, horse, baggage and postillion were reassembled and the chaise hoisted upright it was dark and Jack decided to spend the night at the Cross Keys, an inn kept by a former bosun. Here he supped nobly and slept again, a deep, deep sleep, perfectly limp and relaxed until the first dawn woke him. He rose up, a new man indeed, not exactly cheerful but curiously sanguine. The chaise was not ready – the wheel needed a few more hours – but there was a respectable horse, and having snatched an early break- fast he mounted and set out, the sun just over Alton hill.

Quite what was in his mind as he rode into the stable-yard

he hardly recalled, but a first cold, cold shock was the sight of his daughter Charlotte, a leggier child than when last he saw her. She was in the kitchen doorway, staring: her face expressed no sort of pleasure: she shouted back into the house, presumably to her sister, 'It's Papa,' and vanished.

George came running out however, as Jack gave the horse over to Harding, and bade him a perfectly unaffected friendly 'Good morning, sir, how do you do?'

'And a very good morning to you too, George my dear. Where is your Mama?'

'They ain't down yet, sir. I believe they are drinking tea upstairs. But, sir, if only you had come five minutes earlier you would have seen Cousin Diana's new coach. Oh such a beauty! She is gone to Lyme with Mrs Oakes and Brigid. I love them much.'

Up the stairs, and they creaking with his weight and haste. The room opened to the east and the cool morning light fell full on Sophie and her mother as they sat side by side copying letters. Neither had dressed: Sophie had not yet done up her hair; she was wearing the sort of gown that women clutch about their throat. She was not looking at all her best; yet it was neither a lack of bloom nor of colour that struck him but rather the presence of some quality he had never seen in her at any time. Both women started, sitting upright from their papers as he came in. Mrs Williams continued the movement and clapping a hand to her head, rose up and ran out: she could no more be seen without a cap than without any upper garment at all.

'What are you doing here?' asked Sophie, and her voice, like her expression, might have been her mother's.

'*Bellona* is in dock for repairs,' said Jack, 'and I have come to spend a few days at home.'

'Not with my good will,' she replied.

'But above all I have come to ask your pardon, to say I am very sorry indeed, and to beg you will forgive me.'

The door behind Sophie opened a little. 'Not with my good will,' she repeated mechanically. 'I should not have been here, but the Admiral will not leave before his term.'

She put her hand to a falling swag of hair and speaking in a hurried voice she said, 'Here – look here – all these are her letters – your mistress's letters – and here is the ring you gave me before God's altar, before God's altar – and you come here to this house . . .'

'Oh, Sophie, my dear,' he said gently, coming a little nearer and looking her in the face.

Mrs Williams opened the door. He clapped it to and shot the bolt. She could be heard scrabbling the other side.

'Oh, come, Sophie,' he said again. But she cried out that he should never have come here – it was most improper, most indelicate – and that he must go away at once. Some of this was less than coherent, but there was no mistaking the vehemence of resentment.

He fell back and said, 'Is that indeed all you have to say to me, Sophie?'

'Yes it is,' she cried, 'and I never want to see you again.'

'Then be damned to you for a hard ill-natured and pitiless unforgiving shrew,' he said, anger rising at last, and he walked out, leaving her bowed over the miserable letters, utterly appalled by his words and by her own.

Chapter Seven

Two days after the dark of the moon Jack Aubrey, worn thin with his ceaseless efforts to make the dockyard work double tides, brought his ship with her sullen crew, bloated, blotch-faced, dissipated and bleary-eyed after so long in port, within sight of the offshore squadron.

He made his number and he was called aboard the flagship at once. The Captain of the Fleet received him with the words, 'Well, you have had a fine run ashore, Aubrey, upon my word: and I see the yard did you proud in the article of spars. But I am sorry to tell you that the Admiral is far from well, very far from well; and I understand you are to see his secretary.'

Mr Craddock, like most secretaries to admirals with an important command, was a discreet, capable, middle-aged man, thoroughly used to dealing with diplomatic and official correspondence and with matters to do with intelligence. He said that although Lord Stranraer had indeed received Captain Aubrey's letter and report sent by the *Ringle*, he had seen fit, because of confidential information received, to detain the tender for a certain period and to send her to the place of rendezvous some time earlier than the appointed date. The *Ringle* had not yet reported back to the squadron and it was not impossible that Dr Maturin, perhaps carrying important dispatches or information, might have directed Mr Reade to take advantage of the very favourable breeze to carry him to the Downs.

Captain Aubrey bowed, hoped that the Admiral was at least tolerably comfortable, and wondered whether he had made any observation on the *Bellona*'s parting company or on the taking of a prize.

'Those are matters quite outside my province,' said the secretary in an impersonal tone. 'But I am sure that Captain Calvert will have directions for your immediate proceedings.'

He had, of course, and although he too declined to be drawn about the *Bellona*'s inability to make out the signal to tack, he did say, 'As far as the prize is concerned – and I give you joy of her, I am sure: she sounds a genuine stunner – he is perhaps the only flag-officer in the service who would have been totally unmoved. He is not interested in money.'

Jack had heard this before: it formed part of the Admiral's reputation. Certainly he had an ample fortune, and at sea he lived very quietly, entertaining no more than was strictly necessary: yet this did not square with his passion for inclosing larger and larger tracts of common land, fens, and open pasture.

Pending Lord Stranraer's recovery – and as Craddock said, they longed for the return of Dr Maturin, in whom the Admiral had so much confidence – Jack was returned to the inshore squadron. Even at this late stage of the war, with Wellington well north of the Pyrenees, established on the Garonne and ready to push north, there was always the possibility of the French fleet, seizing the opportunity of a brisk north-east wind, breaking out of Brest, conceivably defeating Stranraer's divided force in two separate battles, and, if this coincided with one of Buonaparte's astonishing recoveries by land, reversing the whole course of the war: or at any rate of ending it for themselves in a blaze of glory.

In the meanwhile Captain Aubrey was to resume his patrolling under Captain Fanshawe's orders, but at the same time he was to pay particular attention to the surveying of stated parts of the coast and above all to the fixing of the position and depth of a number of submerged rocks, such as that upon which the *Magnificent* was lost, totally lost, in 1804.

A man could scarcely have been much lower in the spirits than Jack Aubrey: yet it was striking to see how he plunged back into life at sea, a hard life particularly at this season and in Brest Bay, but one with a set pattern he had known from boyhood, and one in which he had a task that gave him deep satisfaction. He had always liked surveying, and now he gave himself up to his submarine rocks with a conviction that settling their bearings was an absolute good. 'Perhaps Stranraer feels the same about inclosure,' he reflected, squaring himself in the boat and peering through the rain-misted sights of his azimuth compass at the buoys tossing five fathoms above the top of that cruel rock the Buffalo. 'Mr Mannering, note 137°E.'

In most commissions the midshipmen's berth yielded a boy or two who really liked navigation, sea-mathematics, and who began, with unconcealed delight, to seize the underlying principles: Mannering was the most recent, with the same zeal, earnestness and growing enthusiasm.

He was a comfort to Jack: so, on a very different scale, was the appearance of the *Ringle*, beating steadily into the usual sou'wester. Very soon a telescope made it apparent that Stephen was not on board – Jack had hardly expected him – but he did take pleasure in Reade's account of their splendid run up to the Downs: eight or nine knots most of the time, with points of an estimated fourteen when the tide was with them – never a dull moment – the Doctor in his highest form.

The splendid run had brought the Doctor ashore so soon, and the mail-coach had whirled him up to London at such a pace that there was time to leave a note for Sir Joseph at the Admiralty begging that they might sup together at their club that evening: and this a full two days and a half before he had thought it possible.

He took a room at the club, the only one available, a little cheese-shaped affair from which, if one chose to stand up very straight and peer over the parapet, one could look down into Mrs Abbott's well-known bawdy-house; but Stephen was really more concerned with coping with his shabby clothes as well as he could do with a nail-brush, while his dirty shirt was concealed by a black neckcloth carefully spread over all. A couple of stitches of surgical neatness fixed it in place and he went down into the hall, with its fine hospitable fire.

Sir Joseph hardly kept him waiting at all. 'How very glad I am to see you, Stephen,' he cried. 'By Warren's computation you were already a thousand miles from here, with the distance growing every day.'

'So I should have been, by our arrangements. But I learnt something of real consequence, and since I had no carrier pigeon at hand, I thought I should bring it myself. What a heavenly smell!'

'It is frying onions. The kitchen door is being repaired.'

'Frying onions, frying bacon, sardines grilling over vine-cuttings, the scent of coffee – these things oh how they stir my animal desires! I had no dinner.'

'Then let us sup at once – my dear Golding, how do you do?' – this to a passing member in court dress – 'What shall you eat?'

'Steak and kidney pudding, without the shadow of a doubt: I slaver at the very words. And you?'

'My usual boiled fowl and oyster-sauce, with a pint of claret: and I do not mind how soon I have it. The sight of your hunger has excited mine.'

They moved on to the already well-filled supper-room, and for some time they ate seriously, with few more words than 'How is your bird?' 'Capital, I thank you: and your pudding?' 'A fine honest piece of work,' said Stephen, taking a little wishbone from his mouth. The recipe for Black's steak and kidney pudding called for larks. 'And this, for example, is the true skylark, *Alauda arvensis*, not one of the miserable sparrows you find in certain establishments.'

When the cutting-edge of appetite was somewhat blunted, they talked of their most recent captures – moths, butterflies, beetles. Then pudding in the ordinary sense made its appearance: apple tart for Stephen, sillabub for Sir Joseph.

'I had a most gratifying journey,' said Stephen, lashing on the cream. 'Apart from the fact that a vessel which bounds, fairly *bounds*, over the main fills all aboard with joy,

I grudged every hour away from London. There are many things I must tell you, and I have real hopes of making your flesh creep.'

'Have you, though?' said Blaine, looking at him with a considering eye. 'Perhaps coffee at my house might be better.'

They walked up a foggy St James's Street and so to Shepherd's Market and the familiar book-lined room far from the sound of traffic.

'Have you ever met an amateur intelligence-agent?' asked Stephen, when they were installed with their coffee and petits fours.

'You would not mean Diego Diaz, would you?'

'Well, yes,' said Stephen, somewhat dashed.

'Oh, one sees him everywhere – Almack's, White's, the big dinners. He is very well with most of the women who entertain in London, and he knows a great many people. The embassy people fight rather shy of him, however, in spite of his grand connexions.'

'Yes, he is a little conspicuous. I will come back to him presently, if you will allow me. For the moment, may I talk about some Chileans I met in France?'

'Please do.'

'Met *again*, I should have said, since I was introduced to them first in Peru. They are warranted by O'Higgins, Mendoza, and Guzman; and with their friends they are interested in a renewal of our alliance, our understanding, with the Peruvians, but this time an alliance directed at *Chilean* independence. I have drawn up an account of our conversations, of their needs and their hopes, of their resources and of their undertaking with regard to slavery: and since, unlike the Peruvian enterprise, theirs depends to a considerable degree on a naval or quasi-naval presence, I think it proper to submit these papers to you in the first place, together with their credentials and letters from our friends in those parts, in the hope that you will talk the matter over.'

'I shall most certainly do so,' said Blaine, receiving the

packet; and looking intently at Stephen he added, 'How eager, how deeply committed do you think they are, compared with the Peruvians?'

'On the basis of my contacts with them in America and of my long, long interviews during the last week, I should say that our prospects of success are greater by perhaps a third. And as you will find when you read my pages they rely much more on attack and defence by sea – on the mobility conferred by even a froward ocean, as compared with the mountains and intolerable deserts of the lower western part of South America.'

'I look forward with the utmost eagerness to reading your account: many of the people here who supported us last time will be enchanted.'

'Dear Joseph, how kind of you to say so. You will put it into the proper Whitehall prose, scabrous, flat-footed, with much use of the passive, will you not? I may have allowed something approaching enthusiasm to creep in.'

Sir Joseph poured them out some remarkably smooth full-bodied old brown brandy and when each had thoughtfully drunk about half his glass he said, 'There are only two things to be said against your otherwise Heaven-sent coca-leaves: they do diminish one's acuity of taste, and they do prevent one from sleeping. Happily I have taken none today, though I shall do so tonight in order to digest your papers – that was a mere parenthesis, and I go on. But how very much their advantages outweigh them – the vivid intensity of reflection, the vividness of life itself, the reduction of commonplace distresses, cares and even griefs to their proper status. And I have recently found that they enhance one's appreciation of music, particularly of *difficult* music, to a very high degree.'

They talked for a while of their sources of supply, of the difference between the leaves from various regions, possibly from different sub-species of the same shrub, and each showed the other the contents of his pouch.

Then Stephen said, 'May I turn to my particular friend Jack Aubrey?'

'Do, by all means,' said Sir Joseph.

'Like most officers of his rank and seniority he is of course deeply concerned about the likelihood of his being yellowed at a future flag-promotion. Can you properly tell me anything about his prospects?'

Blaine poured more brandy, and said, 'Yes, I can. I wish I could say that they were better than they are; and I am not at all sure that he would not be well advised to retire as a post-captain rather than risk the humiliation of being passed over. He is of course a brilliant sailor, as most people would admit. But to some degree he is his own most active and efficient enemy, as I have often told you, Stephen, begging you to keep him at sea or down in the country. He so often addresses the House, speaking with authority as a successful officer; but very rarely does he say anything in favour of the ministry. And his vote is by no means sure. As an aside I will also say, with regard to his present difficulties in the law-courts, that the legal people at the Admiralty might take a different view of defending him were he more reliable: were he a cast-iron, heart-of-oak supporter of Government.'

'I cannot but admit that when he gets up and speaks of corruption in the dockyards and improper material being used on men-of-war he is sometimes regrettably intemperate.'

'What a gift you have for understatement, Stephen. And then again he makes powerful enemies outside the Commons. Lord Stranraer's recent dispatches have done your friend – and mine too, if I may say so – the utmost harm. Neglect of duty: leaving manoeuvres in order to chase a prize ... A prize that is likely to cost him dear, splendid though I hear it was – fairly ballasted with gold-dust in little leather bags.'

'You know how this ill-will arose, sure?'

'I know that the Admiral, a most zealous incloser of land, advised his heir and nephew, Captain Griffiths, to inclose a common bordering on his estate and Aubrey's; that at the last stage Aubrey opposed the petition before the committee; and that it was thrown out. He is also said to have set the country-people against Griffiths, whose stacks have been burnt, his game and deer massacred and himself and his servants pelted in the village, so that his life there is no longer worth living. Stranraer sees this unnatural insubordination of the villagers in exactly the same light as naval mutiny, and of course abhors it. Stranraer's word against a serving officer carries great weight with Government.'

'I know little about the gentleman.'

'He is very able, of that there is no doubt, and a great political economist. To be sure he has made no particular name in the Navy, but that may well have been from lack of opportunity. In his youth he was unusually good-looking and he made a brilliant marriage – a widowed lady with very large estates in her own right – far, far more important than his. It is true that they go to a son by her first marriage or rather to his guardian, since he is an idiot, but while she lives he controls at least nine seats in the Commons, quite apart from the considerable number he guides by his personal influence. He speaks, and speaks very well, for the moneyed landed interest and his support is very much valued by the Ministry – his support in the Commons, I mean, since in the Lords the government majority is so great that his vote there hardly signifies.'

'Has he the reputation of an honest man? A scrupulous man?'

'He is generally much respected: I know nothing against him: but I should not put my hand in the fire for any man as powerful as he has been these many years, so concerned with politics, and so passionate in his religion of inclosures, the country's one salvation.'

'I ask because there was some appearance of orders coming from the Brest squadron that in the ordinary course of events would have prevented Aubrey from appearing before the committee.'

Blaine raised his hands. 'Oh, as for that, I cannot express an opinion, of course; but I do not think any hardened politician would think such a caper anything but venial, if that. Yet scrupulous or something less than scrupulous, Admiral

Stranraer does not love Captain Jack: and his word counts.'

'Nor does Captain Griffiths, who votes with his uncle, and who inherits.'

'Just so. But on inheriting, Captain Griffiths loses his parliamentary value entirely, and he can do no harm. His vote in the Lords is neither here nor there, and he does not influence a single voice in the lower house. The Stranraer estate controls no seat, no borough, and all Lady Stranraer's patronage goes elsewhere. Griffiths becomes a cipher with a coronet; and he is even more likely than Aubrey to be yellowed.'

'I should hate to see Aubrey yellowed.'

'So should I. I have a very real liking for him, as you know. It may not come to that.' Sir Joseph walked up and down the room. 'Melville has a kindness for him, too. So has your friend Clarence. Conceivably a shore appointment could be arranged – commissioner, say, even something civilian, which would put him out of the running for a flag, and then there could be no question of his being yellowed. Conceivably something hydrographical, with the possibility of recall: I know he is a famous surveyor . . .'

Blaine sat down, and for quite a long time they stared into the glowing fire like a pair of cats, saying nothing, each lost in his own reflections. At last Sir Joseph took the poker and delicately prised a splitting lump of coal in two: the halves fell apart with a gratifying blaze, and sitting back he said, 'You were in hopes of making my flesh creep, I believe?'

'So I was too. They are somewhat diminished by your recognizing my villain right away, yet even so you may still fall senseless to the ground. Don Diego does not sound a really formidable villain, does he?'

'I cannot say he does. My impression is that of a very expensive young or youngish man, much given to high play, uncommon high play, at Crockford's and Brooks's, eager to make political acquaintance and to ask indiscreet questions, apt to suggest deep knowledge and private sources of information. He is remarkably well-introduced and although you might think he was merely showing away when he names half a dozen dukes and cabinet-ministers, in fact they are perfectly genuine. Some may perhaps indulge him with odd-ments of more or less confidential information, which he retails, also in confidence, with an important air: they would do so because many people think him amiable, though foolish, and perhaps because he entertains so well. A busy creature, but not, I should have thought, of any consequence except to women with a train of daughters to marry and an appetite for high-sounding titles and a great fortune. Am I mistaken? Pray tell me what you know about him.'

'The titles, the fortune and no doubt the amiability are as genuine as his important friends in this country; but I think this appearance of harmless foolishness is assumed: though it may have been genuine enough some years ago, before let us say 1805. He is the only surviving son, begotten with enormous difficulty, after endless pilgrimages and offerings to countless altars, of a grandee, as wealthy as only a Spanish grandee and former viceroy can be, and devoted to him. His elder brother was killed at Trafalgar: Diego became the heir and I am told that he matured to an extraordinary extent. As far as service was concerned he preferred foreign affairs; but being extremely impatient of superior authority or restraint he induced his father to arrange for the creation of yet another branch of Spanish intelligence, with himself at the head. He is chiefly concerned with the naval side, his people having been traditionally sea-borne rather than horse-borne; but almost from the start he has been obsessed by the problem of double-agents . . .'

'Who is not?' asked Blaine, who had been listening with the closest possible attention.

'Who indeed? Early in his career he was given my friend Bernard as one of his chief assistants . . .' Sir Joseph nodded with intense satisfaction '. . . and between them they seized a good many people in French pay, who, in the usual fashion, were persuaded to name others, so that the French connection was virtually abolished. Of our men Diaz only caught Waller – the result of a very gross indiscretion – and Waller would not talk: nor, obviously, did Bernard produce any others. He speaks of don Diego as a man with remarkable intuitive powers, naturally secretive but singularly winning when he chooses, persevering, hard-working and dogged to the last degree in his pursuit, but apt to launch into spectacular adventures without always weighing the possible cost. Though even the cautious Bernard admits that the burglaries he organized in Paris yielded astonishing results.'

'Oh, oh,' murmured Blaine, aware that the crisis was at hand.

'Will you look at these names?' asked Stephen, handing him a slip of paper.

Blaine ran through the list, muttering 'Matthews, Foreign Office; Harper, Treasury; Wooton . . .' Then quite loud, 'But Carrington, Edmunds and Harris – these are our people.'

'They are all men of standing?'

'Yes. Some of high standing.'

'They have all been unwise enough to play cards or billiards with don Diego. They all owe him more money, sometimes much more money, than they can easily repay. They all tell him what ministers, what important officials, like you, carry papers home. Don Diego's respectable lawyers in London, like his respectable lawyers in Paris, gave him the names of people, of concerns, dealing with private inquiries, with the collection – sometimes the forcible collection – of debts, and with the gathering of evidence, usually of marital infidelity. These people, if not directly criminal, are in touch with criminals who, if told what to look for, and if guaranteed their price, will nearly always bring the required objects or documents. On occasion don Diego goes with them: he justifies it by saying that only he can choose the essential papers. Perhaps so, but Bernard says it excites him, and he has known him to put on quite extravagant disguises.'

'So did poor Cummings,' said Blaine.

'He may do so on Friday, when they mean to visit you,' said Stephen.

'What joy! Oh what joy!' cried Blaine. 'Let us instantly

put the names of half the Spanish cabinet and all their top intelligence people on our pay-roll.'

Stephen uttered his rare discordant creaking laugh and said, 'It is tempting, sure: but think of the possibilities of holding him, caught in the act, seen by undeniable witnesses, in possession of stolen property obtained by breaking and entering a dwelling-house by night. It is capital, without benefit of clergy: and he has no diplomatic immunity whatsoever. Tyburn tree, with perhaps the indulgence of a silken halter, is all he can expect. From the extreme embarrassment of his government, from his family's anguish – to say nothing of his own uneasiness – what concessions may we not expect?'

'My heart beats so that I can hardly speak,' said Sir Joseph, whose face had flushed from deep red to purple. 'Tell me, my most valued friend and colleague, how this is to be accomplished?'

'Why, by means of your good Pratt the thief-taker – the excellent intelligent Pratt who did so much for us when poor Aubrey was taken up for rigging the Stock Exchange, the best of allies. He quite certainly knows these "private inquirers" and their even less presentable associates – he was born and bred in Newgate, you recall – and once he is clear on the moral side and his own immunity he will arrange matters according to local custom and local rates, which he knows to the last half-crown. This may cost an elegant penny.'

'It could not possibly cost too much,' said Blaine, and laying his hand on Stephen's knee, 'Of course you are perfectly right about Pratt. Why did I not think of him before?'

Sir Joseph Blaine's library, where he worked at night on official papers and where he kept those he often referred to in an elegant mahogany cupboard, with files arranged alphabetically, had two looking-glasses at the far end: rather long looking-glasses in black frames; and the bottom inch or so of their back was unsilvered. They did not really suit the room, being rather modern and even flash, but this did not worry the bearded man busy with the lock on the mahogany cupboard, by the desk. He had never been in the room before – he had never seen the mirrors, nor the specimen-cases with their wealth of beetles, nor the perfectly enormous bear that stood against the wall with one paw out to receive a hat or an umbrella, under a stuffed platypus, to the left of the desk.

'Oh do get on with it,' muttered Stephen Maturin, watching through a hole in the wall exactly behind the unsilvered glass as the man gently, silently tried skeleton keys by the discreet light of his dark lantern. Sir Joseph, also standing in the darkened passage behind the corresponding hole to the other glass, felt the rising strength of a sneeze and to master it he contorted his purple face, pressed his upper lip and closed his eyes. When he opened them again the man had opened his dark lantern a little and from the files he drew a fat document.

At this the bear flung off its head, drew a crowned truncheon from its bosom, and in a shrill, squeaking voice said, 'In the King's name I arrest you.'

The room was filled with light, with people running: Dark Lantern was pinned, handcuffed, and in the struggle his foolish beard fell off.

'I will not appear,' said Stephen, shaking Sir Joseph's hand. 'May I inflict myself on you for breakfast?'

'Do, do, my dearest fellow,' cried Blaine, laughing for joy. 'What a coup, what a coup, oh dear Lord, what a coup!'

Chapter Eight

It was indeed the most glorious coup, the completest thing: the other intelligence service gazed at Sir Joseph with admiration, respect, unspeakable envy, and did their very utmost to gather any scraps of credit that might be lying neglected – a vain attempt if ever there was one, for Sir Joseph, though a mild and even a benevolent man in ordinary life, and charitable, was perfectly ruthless in the undeclared civil war that is so usually fought, with all the outward form of politeness, between agencies of this kind, and he gathered every last crumb for his own concerns, his own colleagues and advisers.

But so glorious a coup could not be exploited to the full without a grave expense of time, and it was long before Dr Maturin was called before the Committee to be told that the Chilean proposals, as they were put forward in his minute of the seventeenth, had been read with considerable interest, and the preliminary discussions and even the first material preparations could go forward so long as it was clearly understood that at this stage His Majesty's Government was in no way committed to any agreement, that the whole undertaking was to be conducted privately, in a vessel that did not form part of the Royal Navy but only in craft hired for hydrographical purposes by the appropriate authority or authorities, and that any contribution should not exceed seventy-five per centum of the very, very considerable sum left by Dr Maturin in South America at the end of his last journey. It was agreed on both sides that this was a merely tentative understanding, one that could be put in motion at the time thought proper by both sides or that could be relinquished by either on reasonable notice.

During this period he was staying at the Grapes, an agreeable old-fashioned inn, a quiet place in the Liberties of the Savoy, where he had a room of his own the whole year round, and where his two god-daughters, Sarah and Emily, lived with his old friend Mrs Broad. They were as black as black could be – he had brought them from a small Melanesian island, all of whose other inhabitants had died of the smallpox brought by a whaler – and their hair was naturally frizzled; but they gave no sign of being foreign, uneasy or ill at ease as they ran about the lane or fetched a hackney-coach from the Strand. They had picked up English with extraordinary ease and very early in their voyage from the Pacific (a long, long voyage with a long, long pause in New South Wales and Peru) they had perceived that it possessed two dialects, one of which (the racier) they spoke on the fo'c'sle and the other on the quarterdeck. Now they added variations on a third, the right Cockney as it was spoken from rather above Charing Cross down the river past Billingsgate to the Tower Hamlets, Wapping and beyond. This they picked up mostly in the streets and at their primitive little school in High Timber Street, kept by an ancient, ancient priest, a Lancashire Catholic who called them thee and thou and taught reading, writing (in a beautiful hand) and arithmetic, and attended by children of every colour, as Mrs Broad observed, except bright blue. Theirs was a busy life for they not only learned cooking (particularly pastry), shopping in the City markets with Mrs Broad, and turning out rooms with almost naval thoroughness with Lucy, but fine sewing too, from Mrs Broad's widowed sister Martha. Furthermore they often ran errands for the gentlemen who stayed at the Grapes, or fetched a coach; these services were rewarded, and when the rewards reached three and fourpence, the sum exactly calculated for the expedition, they treated Stephen to a pair-oared wherry from their own Savoy steps to the Tower, where they showed him the lions and the other moderately wild beasts kept there time out of mind, and then fed him raspberry tarts from a little booth outside.

'If you had seen Emily thank the keeper for his explanations and beg him to accept this sixpence, I believe it would have touched your heart,' said Stephen, by the hall fire at Black's.

'Perhaps,' said Sir Joseph. 'I have heard that there is good in children. But even a greater example of affectionate attention would not tempt me into the wild adventure of begetting any. I do wish, my dear Stephen, that now you are as rich as a Jew again you would take a post-chaise like a Christian, rather than this vile coach: you will be huddled in with all and sundry, bumped about in an odious promiscuity, pushed, snored upon all night, suffocated, and then put out at your destination a little before dawn, for God's sake!'

'It is quicker than the mail-coach. *And I have paid for my ticket.*'

'I see you are set upon it. Well, God be with you. We must be away. Charles, a coach for the Doctor, if you please. How I wish these bags may all arrive at Dorchester' – pushing one crossly with his foot – 'At least I shall go to the Golden Cross with you, and make sure they are taken aboard.'

Through Sir Joseph's care the bags did reach Dorchester and the King's Arms in the thin grey light, the faintly drizzling Saturday morning. The guard put them down, thanked Stephen for his tip, and bawled into the courtyard, 'Hey, Joe: show the gent into the coffee-room. Three small trunks and a brown-paper parcel.'

The other inside passengers had been much as Blaine had described them, and one had an unfortunate way of jerking out his legs in his sleep. However, the King's Arms gave Stephen a famous breakfast, smoked trout, eggs and bacon, a delicate small lamb chop: the coffee was more than passable, and humanity returned like a slowly rising tide. 'I should like a chaise, if you please, to take me to Woolcombe as soon as I have finished,' he said to the waiter. 'And I could wish to be shaved.'

'Directly, sir,' said the waiter. 'I will tell the barber to step in. And I believe you will have a pleasant ride. The day is clearing from the east.'

So it was, and before the chaise was half-way to Wool-combe the sun heaved up his brilliant rim above Morley Down. This was very familiar country now and presently they were running along the side of Simmon's Lea: far over he could make out three riders and a man running with them, far down towards the mere, a woman and two children, one of whom he could have sworn was his daughter if the little figure had not been riding astride: but the runner was certainly Padeen.

'The next on your right,' he called to the post-boy.

'I know it, sir,' said the post-boy, smiling back at him. 'Our Maggie is in service there.' He swung the chaise into the forecourt.

'The farther wing,' said Stephen, since that was where Diana, Clarissa and Brigid lived: he would pay his respects to Sophie later; and to Mrs Williams, in the west wing, later still.

'Just put these inside the door,' he said as he paid the post-boy. 'The brown-paper parcel I shall carry myself.'

He walked up the stairs and opened the door gently. As he had expected, Diana was still in bed, pink and sleepy. 'Oh Stephen,' she cried, sitting up and opening her arms. 'What joy to see you – I was thinking of you not five seconds ago.' They embraced: she looked at him tenderly. 'You are surprisingly well,' she said. 'Have you had breakfast?' Stephen nodded. 'Then take off your clothes and come into my bed. I have countless things to tell you.'

'Dear me, Stephen,' she said, lying back, her hair, her black hair wildly astray on the pillow and her blue eyes filled with a splendid light. 'I have a thousand things to tell you, but you have driven them all out of my mind.' She stroked the limp arm lying over her bosom for a while and then said, 'Tell me, have you just come from the fleet? Are you on leave? Is Jack with you?'

'I am not. I am just come down from London. I have not

seen Jack these many weeks: he is still with the blockading squadron.'

'Then you don't know that my Aunt Williams came to live here after her friend Mrs Morris ran off with that odious manservant they had – Briggs. Just then the west wing was being done up and oh such quantities of other things, so she was put into Jack's room and there, poking and prying everywhere, she found a box of letters that silly goose Amanda Smith wrote him from Canada, telling him he had got her with child: and certainly she begged him to go through the motions, you know. These Aunt Williams seized and ran to Sophie as fast as ever she could and poured out all her bile and Methody cant about fornication and so on, working the poor girl up into a frenzy of self-righteousness and jealousy. It had always astonished me that a woman with as much sense as Sophie – and she is no fool, you know – can be so influenced by her mother, who *is* a fool, a downright great God-damned fool, even where money is concerned, which is saying a great deal. But there it is. Sophie wrote him a letter with all kinds of high-flown Drury-Lane stuff: and when the poor fellow came posting up from Plymouth to say he was sorry and should never do it again she turned him away, clean away. So away he went, with a parting shot about goddam ill-natured unforgiving shrews that went home. And she has been crying her eyes out ever since.'

'Poor soul, poor soul. But it was an ill-fated marriage. She has never taken pleasure in the act itself: she has always dreaded pregnancies: and her deliveries have been extremely painful. It has long seemed to me that jealousy and frigidity or at least tepidness are in direct proportion to one another. And Jack is what is ordinarily called a very full-blooded man.'

'I dare say you are right about frigidity and jealousy. But I believe you are wrong in calling Sophie frigid. Certainly, when her mother is by, I think she would be a poor companion for a lively, eager man – indeed, Jack would never have got her into his bed at all if she had not run away in a ship, far from her mother's eye. And then again I have it on the best authority that Jack is no artist in these matters. He can board and carry an enemy frigate with guns roaring and drums beating in a couple of minutes; but that is no way to give a girl much pleasure. In better hands she would, I am sure, have been a very likely young woman; and oh so much happier.'

'Clearly, you know more about these things than I.'

'She has a lovely body still, in spite of these children,' said Diana. 'But what is the use of a lovely body if neither you nor anyone else enjoys it?'

'Sure it is a great waste: the great shame of the world.'

'Clarissa, who knows a great deal about the subject, and I – but Lord, I have left out a most important part. I never told you that Aunt Williams is gone back to Bath. Mrs Morris's fellow turned out to have several wives already and he has been taken up for bigamy, false pretences, person-ation, forgery, theft and God knows what, a right wrong 'un. And Aunt Williams is to be the prime witness for the prosecution. She is so proud and important – swears she will never leave till the man is hanged and she and her friend will end their days together – I bought them a little place just off the Paragon.'

'Barham Down is sold then? How clever of you.'

'No, no. That is another thing I was forgetting. After you had been gone a while I began to think it was just God-damned silly to squalor along on two hundred a year when you have an enormous great diamond like the Blue Peter. I happened to mention it to Cholmondeley – I still had his coach until a little while ago – and he agreed it was great nonsense: why did I not borrow fifty thousand or so until our affairs were settled? He could easily arrange it in the City. So I said yes, and now I am absolutely swimming in money. Do let me give you some money, Stephen dear.'

'Sweetheart, honey, you are kindness itself, but our affairs *are* already settled. They are just as they were, or even some-what better; my loss of the receipt did not signify, and I shall unpawn your bauble tomorrow. Now I come to think of it,' he went on, stalking like Adam across the room to his brown-paper parcel, 'here is a present to go with the jewel.' He unwrapped a swathe of Lyons silk velvet, blacker than the darkest night.

After several shrieks of rapture she thanked him very prettily, congratulated him on his brilliant conduct in putting their affairs in order – she had always been sure that *he* could do it, however complicated, wrapped a fold or so about her pure white torso, and having collected her thoughts she went on, 'You would not believe the difference in Sophie with her mother gone. For some time Clarissa and I had been trying to comfort her, trying to make her understand that men and most women see these things quite differently, that for a man to leap into a welcoming bed does not mean treason, felony or real, serious *unfaithfulness* at all. She scarcely minded what we said. But once it was known that Aunt Williams was settled in Bath with Mrs Morris, busy buying chintz and swearing affidavits, Sophie listened much, much more attentively.'

'How I wish I had heard you.'

'You would have learned a good deal, I believe.'

'That is what I mean. Little notion, very little notion do I possess of the way women talk among themselves, above all on such matters.'

'And we went on about the very intense delight there is or ought to be in love-making – I said it was an absolute duty to enjoy it and to give as much pleasure in return as ever one could – that the pleasure was infectious. Clarissa spoke, and spoke very much more delicately than I did, quoting some Latin author about the way men like their partners to behave and poor Sophie looked absolutely blank, muttering she thought you just lay there and let it happen. Oh, we said so many things. I made one rather good remark, or so it seemed to me at the time: *a man does like some mark of appreciation of his efforts, you know.* Then I said, but in a tone I thought she would understand, that what she most urgently needed was a really kind, gentle and considerate lover to put her in tune and show her what all the talk and poetry and music and fine clothes were really about, and how it justified them all. A man like Captain Adeane, who danced with her at all the last Dorchester assemblies and who was so discreetly particular. Do you know him, my dear?'

'I believe not.'

'He is a soldier, and he has a big place behind Colton, kept for him by a rather young and skittish aunt. Being so absurdly handsome, he is usually called Captain Apollo. He will have nothing whatsoever to do with girls, but the young married women of the neighbourhood – well, I will not say that they actually stand there in lines, but I believe he is a fairly general consolation. He gave a splendid ball last week.'

'I should like to meet the gentleman.'

'Oh, and another thing we told her, perhaps the most important of all, we both insisted upon it much, was that there was nothing, *nothing* so bad for you, or for your looks, as self-righteousness. Nothing so wholly unamiable and souring as that habitual put-upon expression of discontent and implied reproach. The only thing to do, if you knew your lover or husband or whatever was being unfaithful, was to pay him back in his own coin, not out of wantonness or revenge but to avoid worse: to avoid self-righteousness. For having *done that* you could never be a martyr again or put on a martyr's horrid face. She cried shame on us for saying such dreadful things: we were really quite immoral and she was ashamed for us. But she did not sound very convincing – she did not hurry away, either – and presently she said, yes, that was very well, but what about babies? People really could not keep having babies right and left. Of course not, we said: did she really think that babies were inevitable? Yes, said she: that was what she had always understood. So we told her, and I must say Clarissa was amazingly well-informed; though she did say that trusting to the moon – to the calendar – alone was not *absolutely* safe.'

'Dear Clarissa. I believe I saw her riding this morning, a great way off.'

'Yes. She is a very tolerable horsewoman now. She took the children out at break of day: they have little Connemara ponies, very sweet mannered. Oh, Stephen, I must show you my Arabs . . . but there is one thing that worries me . . . Throw me my drawers, will you? Sophie breakfasts at nine, and she is sure to ask us. And it is that we might just possibly have overdone things – that she might have taken me literally, Sophie does tend to take things literally. But anyhow he joins his regiment in Madras next week, so . . .'

'Stephen, dear, how very splendid you look!' cried Sophie, embracing him.

'Ain't I the beauty of the world?' said he, spreading the arms of his fine new coat and advancing one leg of his satin breeches. 'Lewd seamen belonging to other ships took to calling "Old clo' Any old clo'?" like rag-pickers when I was rowed by, and it did so grieve the poor Bellonas, from the captain to the humblest ship's boy, not a week from the Marine Society's depot. So I have turned myself out like a peacock in all his glory or like a whole band or screeching of peacocks.' While he was talking in this airy, somewhat disconcerted manner, his grave eye told him that the beauty of the world in fact stood there before him, tall, straight, and in the very height of her charming bloom.

A hand plucked his coat: turning and looking down he saw pink Brigid beaming up, with the promise of as much beauty and even more. 'Dear, dear Papa,' she said, 'how very, very happy I am to see you. I have breeches for riding, do you see, and I would not lose a minute changing them. May I sit next to you?'

Charlotte and Fanny came and made their bobs, looking stupid and awkward. George bade him welcome with an open happy smile very like his father's. Stephen kissed his old friend Clarissa and with Brigid on his other side he sat down by Sophie. 'You have not just come back from *Bellona*?' she asked.

'Not at all. I have been in London and elsewhere this age.'

'When did you last see Jack?'

'No memory for dates have I, but it was a great while since.'

'He had not had any letters from me?'

'He had not. We all complained most bitterly of the want of post. Yet apart from that he was looking well and cheerful – extremely busy with his patrolling and working up the ship's company. I hope to see him even better in a day or two's time, when I rejoin. I hear he has taken a splendid prize.'

'We had so hoped you would stay for Christmas,' she cried.

'No, my dear honey. I only paused in my flight to see you all. At eleven o'clock a post-chaise from Dorchester is coming to take me to Torbay by way of a village whose name escapes me.'

'Nonsense,' said Diana. 'I shall drive you down as I drove you down before, but this time in our own coach. Sophie, forgive me: I must have the horses readied and put on some decent clothes.' She vanished.

'Oh I shall come, I shall come, I shall come on the box!' cried Brigid, bouncing as she sat.

'No you shall not, my dear,' said Stephen. 'Never in life.'

'Certainly not,' said Sophie. 'There is the dancing-master and Miss Hay.'

'I shall ask Mama,' said Brigid: and at the door, 'I shall certainly go.'

Never in life, he had said, and no gentle wheedling in Irish, no tears would move him: added to this there was the monstrous injustice that Padeen, the great traitor, *was* going, standing up behind in a fine livery coat. And with Diana gone Sophie was obliged to say, 'Dear Brigid, how sad it would be if your father's last sight of you was tears and an angry, slobbered face. Run away and put yourself in order, brush your hair and find a new handkerchief. Stephen, I am just going to scribble a couple of lines to Jack. Please will you give them to him, with my dear, dear love?'

She hurried away to her desk, a little satinwood bonheur du jour that had belonged to Jack's mother, and after some hesitation she wrote, 'Dear Jack – may I beg for forgiveness? Oh how I hope you are a better-natured creature than I was. Love S.' She sealed it, not without misgivings about its want of style, dignity, possibly of correctness, and ran back to the steps where everyone was already gazing at the fine dark-green coach with Diana on the box, Stephen beside her, Padeen up behind, and grooms holding the horses' heads.

Sophie handed up the note; Stephen leaned down and kissed her. 'Let go,' cried Diana, gathering the reins. With the coach in motion Stephen looked back, and indeed his last sight of his daughter was a rain-washed but fairly cheer-ful face and a clean white handkerchief waving frantically.

They were silent for a while, with Diana addressing the horses from time to time, individually or as a team: they were Cleveland bays, well matched, usually well-mannered but now a trifle apt to caper, particularly in the village, where people called out greetings, sometimes running alongside to send their duty and dear love and respects to the Captain, and some waving sheets or the like from upper windows. Presently however they were on the high road, climbing to the top of the down that overlooked Woolcombe valley, pull-ing well and all together: just enough frost to whiten the grass – now on the road itself – and the horses' breath a glorious cloud.

'How wonderfully smooth it is, this fine green machine,' said Stephen.

'Yes,' said Diana. 'Handley's made it, and they told me about the new kind of springs they put in: long strips of the best Swedish steel overlapping and sliding upon one another and cased in leather, and fastened to the body by pivoting brass . . .' When she had finished a pretty detailed account of the coach's building, which she had followed with the closest interest, and of the innumerable coats of paint and then of varnish that had been laid on, together with the history of her visit, guided by the invaluable Mr Thomas Handley, to the wheelwright's shop, where among other wonders she saw the shrinking-on of a tyre, she said, 'You would have loved it.'

'I am very certain that I should,' he replied; and after a decent pause, 'Please may I beg you to relieve my mind?'

'Of course you may, dear Stephen,' she said, with an affectionate sideways glance: and much, much louder, 'Norman, you God-damned bastard, bear out, bear out d'ye hear me?' Norman heard both her emphatic voice and the crack of her whip not six inches from his ear, and at once ceased boring into his neighbour, an irritating trick he often displayed early in a run.

'I say this because Brigid is a shatter-brained little creature, as quick as a trout: she was once off my saddle-bow and into a pile of filth one day on the common – soft filth – although I had a hand on her shoulder: she had seen a baby rabbit. So in pure compliment to me, swear and promise and pledge yourself never to let her on to the box of a coach, so tall and the road so hard; purely and simply in compliment to me and my superstitions.'

'Very well, my dear,' she said in the kindest way, 'and here is my hand upon it' – patting him quickly.

Now they were on the flat, a broad road with woodland on the left and not a soul upon it: the horses were suppled and warm, eager to run. She encouraged them, leaning forward, calling them by name, whistling, wheeoo, wheeoo, wheeoo, and the smooth coach fairly raced along for two blissful miles before she reined in, laughing, at the foot of the next hill with a series of turns and a high-perched village.

'This is what coaching should be,' he said, when they were through and on the open, uncrowded road again. 'The weather is perfect, and you, my dear, are the delicate whip of the world.'

On and on, the hedges flying past, and they baiting where they had baited before, navigating the devilish bridge and its corner at Maiden Oscott with an almost insolent ease; and they slept at the comfortable inn where they had slept last time.

Here, as the horses were being walked up and down, Stephen talked at length to Padeen about the small farm in the County Clare that had so enraptured him when Stephen promised it as a reward for looking after Brigid and Clarissa in Spain, a rapture that had waxed and waned; it still retained a theoretical existence, but perhaps little more. From this conversation in the twilight, the longest they had had for a great while – a conversation full of the turns and evasions of an Irish person who wishes to say something delicately defined but who would like to do so without giving any hint of offence – Stephen came away with a variety of notions. Did Padeen feel that a wife was an absolutely necessary part of a farm, and did he dread marriage? Was he afraid of being unable to run the holding, having been so long away from the land? Had so many years of servitude done away with his independence? As he sat on an ancient cane-bottomed chair in their chamber, mechanically arranging the horse-hair curls of his wig, a wilder fancy came into his mind: was the poor soul consumed by a hopeless passion for Clarissa Oakes? Although it was not very, very much more remote from possibility than his own for Diana he shook his head and determined to say no more, other than suggesting a tenant to keep the land clean and in heart.

'Are you never coming to bed?' she called. 'The candle is guttering dreadfully.'

The next day was a much shorter run and they did it in splendid time, the weather more perfectly late autumn than ever, the horses obviously enjoying themselves, except when Mangold cast a shoe and all hands stood in or about the nearest smithy, surrounded by smoke, the wheeze of the bellows, the flying sparks and the scent of his well-pared hoof.

Before noon they were on the Torquay strand, gazing out over the bay at the men-of-war: but this time there was no tedious to-and-froing, no mounting anxiety. They had not been there five minutes before Stephen, hearing the cry 'Dr Maturin!' looked round straight into the smiling face of Philip Aubrey, Jack's much younger half-brother, now in charge of a boat belonging to the *Swallow*, an aviso bound for the offshore squadron, from which Stephen could easily reach the *Bellona*.

The offer could not be refused, but they parted reluctantly, like lovers, unwilling, forced and constrained, regretting the fair breeze that carried the boat out, out and away.

Philip and Stephen could not speak freely until the boat reached the aviso, but there Philip commanded a private, roughly triangular space with just room for two, and here, while they regaled on fresh bread and cheese, Philip said, 'I do not like to sound holier than thou nor to speak disrespectfully of my elders, but I must say that poor Jack's mother-in-law does come it pretty high. George – he is my nephew, you know, though I can't make either him or the girls call me uncle – has just started going to that mouldy little school between Folly and Plush run by our parson's brother. Well, the first day he went there the other boys asked him what his father was. "My father is a sea-officer," said George: then, drawing himself up, he went on, "and an adulterer." "How do you know?" they asked. "My grandmama told me and the girls," said George. I laughed at first – you know how George swells when he is proud – but then I thought it was a miserable God-damned thing to tell children: don't you agree, sir?'

'Mrs Williams is no blood-relation of yours, I believe?'

'No, sir. My grandfather, the General, married again after Jack's mother died: she was called Stanhope. And I come from the second marriage; so when Jack married Sophie Williams, that didn't make her mother any relation of mine.'

'Then in that case I will tell you that in my considered opinion she is a perfectly odious woman.'

As though struck down by a judgment the moment he had finished these words, he pitched forward out of his chair on to what little deck was free. Philip plucked him up and raced on to the deck which had been left in charge of an even younger midshipman who in the pride of his heart had committed the vessel to a manoeuvre that, the guys being untimely cast off, resulted in a truly monumental gybe. The aviso did not quite overturn, but the tangle of parted cordage, the sprung boom and the horrid condition of the bowsprit and its gammoning kept the captain (a master's mate), Philip and his companions – happily there were some prime seamen among them – busy most of the rest of the day and of the fine moonlit night.

The aviso was at least presentable when she raised the topsails of the offshore squadron a little after breakfast – a much enlarged offshore squadron, with at least three more ships of the line as well as frigates, sloops and gun-brigs – and Philip, though pale and drawn, could have passed a not very rigorous muster when he went aboard the *Queen Charlotte* with Stephen. His last words, in a whisper rendered hoarse by extreme fatigue, were 'You won't tell Jack, sir, I beg.'

On seeing Dr Maturin the officer of the watch sent word to the first lieutenant, who asked Stephen to come and see Sherman, the flagship's surgeon, in his cabin.

'Dr Maturin, sir, how good of you to come,' said Mr Sherman. 'My assistants and I are deeply concerned about the Admiral, who has often mentioned you, hoping for your return to the squadron, and I should be very much obliged for your opinion. He is now so weak that I do not think he could stand going home aboard a small vessel in the gales we are certain to have at this season of the year, and he absolutely refuses to detach a capital ship.'

'I should be happy to see him,' said Stephen.

'Dr Maturin, how happy I am to see you,' said Lord Stranraer, half rising in his cot. 'Many is the day I have hoped you might return to the squadron.'

Stephen looked at him with a keen, wholly objective eye, and saw a hag-ridden old man, sick, and like so many patients, dreading the immediate future; a dropsical tendency in spite of some degree of physical collapse; a very, very rapid and irregular pulse, as Sherman had said – though it was clear that the Admiral had no opinion of what Sherman had said and probably an exaggerated notion of Maturin's powers.

'Pray take off your shirt, my lord,' he said, and helped him to do so. To Mr Sherman, 'Be so good as to ask the officer of the watch to stop any running about on deck: let there be no thumps.' A relative silence ensued and Stephen set about an intensive auscultation of Stranraer's chest, tapping like a woodpecker, watched by Sherman with barely concealed astonishment. Straightening up at last and covering the Admiral with the bedclothes he said, 'This is grave, of course, as you know very well: but I think it looks, and feels, worse than in fact it is. I shall consult with Mr Sherman and his colleagues, and look over the ship's dispensary; and I believe we shall agree upon a course of physic, of natural forms of physic, that will give you relief.'

The Admiral took his hand and with a look of affectionate regard on a face not accustomed to show affection, thanked him for his care.

'Clearly,' said Stephen, when he and the surgeons were in the captain's cabin and drinking the captain's madeira, 'the trouble lies essentially with the heart – there is a not inconsiderable hydropericardium – and of course with the mind, as is almost invariably the case where anything but wounds or infections are concerned. First we must reduce this frantic pulse and recall the heart to its duty. What does he take at present?'

Sherman mentioned a low diet and a few harmless substances and went on, 'But I am sorry to say that we do not enjoy the patient's full confidence, and I have reason to believe that most of our draughts end in the close-stool. It is difficult to discipline an admiral who is also a peer. May I ask you about the oedema that you speak of? It is not at all apparent, or at least not to me.'

'Auscultation shows it clearly enough, once I had grown accustomed to his particular bodily sounds. It is a very valuable diagnostic tool, little known in England, I believe.'

'I have never seen it done.'

'A friend of mine in France called Corvisart has made great progress with the immediate percussion that I was using – post-mortems have provided a most gratifying confirmation of many of his diagnoses. And another French friend with whom I studied, Laënnec, is carrying the method still further.'

'I heard him lecture in Paris during the peace,' said one of the assistant surgeons, speaking for the first time. 'But since he used the continental pronunciation I could not follow his Latin very well.'

'For the pulse I should advise digitalis purpurea,' said Stephen. 'Does your chest contain either the tincture or the infusion?'

'Neither,' replied Sherman. 'After two most unfortunate experiences I declined the use of digitalis altogether as too dangerous by far. My predecessor however left a sealed jar of the dried leaves.'

'They will answer very well. In the Admiral's case I should exhibit one grain and a quarter, inclosed in a wafer; and if you think fit I will administer it myself, together with twenty-five minims of laudanum. You will not find the pulse diminish sensibly before Thursday evening, but the laudanum will quickly produce a better frame of mind, a readier compliance with medical direction or perhaps in the case of an admiral I should say *advice*. If the first dose of powdered leaves is well tolerated – if there is no severe vomiting or seeing everything blue (which I do not expect at all) it may be repeated, together with the laudanum, at two-day intervals and if it is at all possible I should like to be informed of his progress. Now, if you agree, I will ask the young gentlemen to put up the doses so that I may administer them directly, for I have patients of my own waiting for me aboard the *Bellona*.'

'Sir,' said the other assistant-surgeon with an evident satisfaction that the powerful drug was now to be used and he a witness to its effects, 'I have read Dr Withering on digitalis, and I shall take great pleasure in powdering the leaves exactly to his direction.'

The flagship's cutter came upon the *Bellona* off the Black Rocks, lying to with her foretopsail to the mast and her driver just drawing while her captain made a final check of a wreck's depth and bearings. His grim mathematical face broke into a smile; as soon as the boats were in hail he called, 'Welcome home, Doctor. You will be just in time for dinner.'

And when they were aboard, with Stephen's sea-chest and small baggage below and proper greetings made – 'Which you look prime, sir,' said Killick, looking really quite agreeable, 'almost as if you had been to the Lord Mayor's show,' while Bonden told him that his head was quite healed, 'could be hit with a top-maul and never a word' and himself lively as a parcel of grigs (and this with no hint of that somewhat slurred familiarity that had grieved Stephen earlier, with its suspicion of mental damage) – Jack told him that Captain Fanshawe was coming to dinner, so that he, Stephen, was in great luck, since he could have his share of the last shoulder of mutton in the ship, probably in the whole inshore squadron. 'I am so glad you are here to carve it,' he went on, sitting down and pouring them some sherry. 'There is no worse joint to tackle in public. But tell me, Stephen, how do you do? And how is Diana, if you have seen her again? You look extremely fine, by the way.' They had both changed for the ceremony.

'Why, I am extremely rich again, and the two tend to go together, you know. I believe I told you that I had mislaid my fortune, but apparently my negligence did not signify: all is well now, and vast wealth improves a man's looks amazingly. So does an eminent London tailor. She is uncommonly well, I thank you; and so is Brigid. They both send their love. And I am charged with this' – drawing a letter from his pocket – 'with Sophie's dear love as well.'

Jack's face changed. 'Did she say that?' he asked sternly.

'I believe those were her very words: or perhaps *dear, dear love.*'

Jack took the letter, muttered 'Forgive me', and retired.

He came back after a while, taller, straighter, his face glistening. 'Dear Lord, Stephen,' he cried, 'that was the best letter I have ever received. Thank you very, very much.' He shook Stephen's hand, looking down on him with infinite benevolence. 'And admirably well wrote, too – such a delicate hand.' He gazed about, in a confusion of happiness; then plucked his fiddle from its case, tuned it more or less – it had laid long untouched – and dashed off a truly astonishing trill, interrupted by the bosun's calls as Captain Fanshawe was piped aboard.

'I do beg your pardon, Jack,' he cried, making his entrance. 'I am abominably late. The current set north-east like a goddam millrace, and we had to pull against the tide as well.'

'Never mind, Billy, never mind. Even I miscalculate at times. Drink some sherry and recover your breath. You know Dr Maturin, I believe?'

'Of course I do: we are old friends. How do you do, sir? It is a great while since I have had the pleasure of seeing you.'

Harding came in at this point, and Killick just behind him, to ask, with half a disapproving eye on Captain Fanshawe, 'whether his honour would choose to have the soup *held back still longer*, or whether it might be set on table now?'

It was set on table, a lobster bisque (the one delight of these bleak rock-strewn waters) with the guests gathered round it; and presently Fanshawe, pushing his third plate away from him, said, 'Well, Jack, you and your people look wonderfully rich and happy and comfortable; I don't wonder at it, with such a prize under your belt, and a kindly Commissioner at Dock. But tell me, did the Yard serve out any slops?'

'Not so much as a tarpaulin jacket,' said Jack. 'I had no money by me, the prize not having been condemned, so there was no question of the customary presents here and there; then again I was much engaged in the country at the time; and although the Commissioner was wonderfully good to me where cordage and spars were concerned, and the powder-hoy, the bloody-minded victuallers were shocking remiss. And since I was in such a tearing hurry to get to sea, I did not stir them up but relied on their coming out to the squadron.'

'Then you may wait until we ground on our own beef-bones,' said Fanshawe. 'In *Ramillies* we are down to a few casks of bread, some weavilly oatmeal and what we can catch over the side. No poultry left – pigs a remote dream – precious few rats to be had under fourpence apiece – and as for slops . . . why, the purser told me but yesterday with tears in his eyes, that we had no jackets, no blankets and no slop shoes at all – this with winter coming on . . . The last store-ship was beaten back into Cawsand Bay, so nothing till next month. Can you spare us any? Even a couple of blankets for the sick-berth would be welcome.'

'I shall ask my purser,' said Jack, looking eagerly at the mutton, just coming in with a certain pomp-mutton, welcome, very welcome, in itself and because it might change the course of Fanshawe's dreary conversation.

The shoulder, though succulent and expertly carved, did not do so at first. 'No stores and no news,' said Fanshawe. 'The last we had was a great while ago, when Austria declared on our side. But Boney had thrashed the Austrians again and again, and he will certainly beat them this time too. Wellington sits there on the Garonne – the Land of Goshen, no doubt – instead of marching north; so the French ships of the line in Rochefort, La Rochelle and even Lorient can lure the offshore squadron westwards and combine with those here in Brest to cut us to pieces. Not that a battle would be much out of the way with the Admiral so far out of sight of Ushant it is impossible for us to prevent the French getting in with a west wind by either of the two main entrances. We take great pains, as you know damn well, and an anxious time we have of it, what with tides and rocks – more danger in this station than a battle once a week.'

'Allow me to carve you a slice of mutton, sir,' said Stephen.

'Well, if I must, I must. Thank you: it is truly capital mutton, perfectly hung. Now I will just quote you a piece from a letter I wrote to my poor wife, and then finish my dirge – apart from throwing out the remark that we do not possess a single second topsail among us all. Here is my piece. "I therefore bid adieu to snug beds and comfortable naps at night, never lying down but in my clothes. We hear no news here, and cannot be in more seclusion from the world, and with one object in view – that of preventing the French from doing harm." There. I have done.'

'A glass of wine with you, Billy,' said Jack, and the decanter went round, and round again; then the claret was replaced by port and after the first glass Stephen rose, begged Jack's pardon, but he had promised to see his patients at six bells, and he had just heard them strike.

'Mr Smith and Mr Macaulay,' he asked, far below, 'how do you do, the both of you? I am happy to see you so apparently well.'

They were well, they admitted, though hungry – the berth had eaten all their private stock and now they were down to ship's provisions – but they were afraid he would not be so pleased with the sick-berth nor with the medicine-chest. The run ashore at Dock had produced such a number of cases of pox that the berth was over-filled and the chest almost bare of venereal medicines. They had also to add that in the last storm but one three men had been washed bodily off the fo'c'sle, and that in the effort to get some sail on the ship to prevent her rolling her masts out, they had four broken limbs and some ugly dislocations, mostly reduced by now, but some with disquieting sequelae.

Before beginning his rounds Stephen asked, 'How is Bonden, the Captain's coxswain?'

'The man with the wig? Oh, quite well, sir, though I believe he asked for a purge some time ago. Yes, I gave him rhubarb, ounce a half: and it answered.'

'Please let him know I should like to see him, when it is his watch below.'

Eight bells, and with the usual sound of a great wooden hollow rumbling some hundreds of men hurried to and from their appointed places. Bonden was pinned and led to the dispensary, looking anxious. 'Oh, it's you again, sir,' he cried, smiling as he saw Stephen. 'I did not have time, just now, to ask after the ladies: I hope you left them well?'

'Very well indeed, thank you, Bonden: and they send their kindest wishes. Now I should just like to look at your head.'

The head, now covered with stubble, was indeed fit to be struck with a top-maul. The scars could be made out, but there was nothing of that yielding either side of the sagittal suture and a little above the lambdoid that had worried Dr Maturin. 'There,' he said, replacing the seamanlike wig, 'in my opinion you are as good as new. I shall tell the Captain: he was much concerned for you.'

'I know he was, sir – kept me from work as much as ever he could. But you know, sir, Killick and me, we are much concerned for him, if I may be so bold.'

Stephen nodded and said, 'You may find him better presently.'

In point of fact he was better already, very much better, recovered from his first almost painful ebullience and sitting there in the evening cabin with deadlights shipped and the *Bellona* snugged down, a moderate roll and a south-west breeze with a fine steady glass for once, he was perfectly ready to listen with close attention to Stephen's account of Woolcombe.

'I am heartily glad that Mrs Williams is gone back to Bath to live there with her friend,' he said. 'Sophie was never the same with her in the place. And I must say it was amazingly handsome in Diana to give them the little house.'

'Dear Diana: she is in funds again. So am I, as I told you.'

'And for my part I am not quite the abject, bankrupt pauper I was. The lawyers sent me some reports that would have sent me to the masthead if Sophie's letter had not arrived just before them: two of our appeals have succeeded, and Lawrence, that dear good man, says he is virtually certain of winning the third and last. And my share of this last prize should just about set me afloat again, in a very modest fashion.'

'From all I hear it was a splendid prize. I give you joy of her, brother, with all my heart.'

'Thank you, Stephen. She was, indeed. Rather in the style of the Frenchman we took off the Dry Tortugas, *Hebe*, formerly our *Hyaena*, you remember. She had taken an English Guineaman and her lovely cargo of gold-dust and ivory. Except that the *Deux Frères*, this most recent prize, had taken *two* Guineamen, each of them larger and richer than that dear old *Intrepid Fox*.'

Stephen nodded gravely. 'I am sure you pursued her with all the zeal in the world.'

'So I did, by God. But with no real thought of prize-money – certainly not prize-money to that staggering extent. No. I saw her chasing one of our merchantmen, already within long shot. I was fairly spoiling for a fight: it was the fight I was after and it was the fight I cracked on for. And the plain call of duty too, of course.'

'It has been reported that you broke away from manoeuvres and chased from a desire for gain.'

'That was an untrue report. The weather was thick and growing thicker; signals were barely visible. I had to act quickly or not at all, and I may not have been strictly correct in acknowledging, but I certainly did say I was chasing north-west, before the rest of the squadron disappeared from sight. And in fact I did take a dangerous enemy privateer and I preserved a British merchantman: that was my aim. The money, though uncommon welcome to all hands, had nothing whatsoever to do with it – was neither here nor there.' A pause. 'No,' Jack went on. 'I was brought up to think that making money was a very proper thing to do: the proper ... something ... of mankind. Pursuit, perhaps: the proper pursuit. My father did not have a great deal of time to improve my morals, but now and then he used to urge me to take notice of various precepts of a religious nature. He was at Eton, you know ...'

'That large school near Windsor?'

'Just so.'

'A sad place, I fear. I was there with a friend – we had

meant to view the castle – but on reaching a place called Salt Hill we were beset, surrounded by a host of boys and youths dressed as Jack Puddings and merry-andrews in antic garments who insisted upon alms, sturdy threatening beggars: we had little between us, and they gave us very ill language indeed before going on to some unfortunate newcomers in a gig. Yet it is true that I have heard they possess a store of Greek between them.'

'I dare say they have: but it is almost the only Latin that my father learnt, and the text he always quoted to me was

> Rem facias, rem
> si possis, recte, si non, quocumque modo, rem.

Just where it was in the Bible I am not sure. My father thought it was one of the minor prophets. It often occurs to me when I am shaving or when church is being rigged, but it was not in my mind at all, not for a moment when I was chasing the *Deux Frères*, though it would have been appropriate in a way, and perhaps even lucky. Sometimes I think I ought to hand it on to George. When all is said and done, a Latin text is something for a boy to possess.'

'Dear Jack, I am sorry to contradict your father – probably some wicked school-fellow made game of him – but it is Horace, not the Bible; and Mr Pope renders it very well

> Get place and wealth, if possible, with grace;
> If not, by any means get wealth and place.

and you would never wish that upon your good open-faced little fat boy as ancestral wisdom, sure. But this brings me to my conversation with Sir Joseph Blaine. I conceived that you would not take it amiss if I were to talk to him about you?'

'Never in life, never in life, upon my word. I have the greatest possible respect and esteem for Sir Joseph. He has been very much my friend – I owe my reinstatement largely to him. Of course you could talk to Sir Joseph Blaine.'

'I talked to him about your prospects of a flag. He told me that they were not what he and your other friends could wish. He said that your repeated and vehement criticism of the ministry in Parliament, together with your frequent abstentions had done you much harm in Government's opinion; and reports of negligence on the Brest station together with abandoning manoeuvres to indulge in very highly profitable chasing had done the same in that of the Admiralty. He explained the capital importance of Lord Stranraer's friends and dependants in the Commons . . .' Stephen recapitulated Blaine's analysis and went on, 'Sir Joseph felt that your friends might be well advised to urge you to retire as a post-captain rather than expose yourself to the affront of being passed over at a forthcoming flag-promotion. He is, as you say, very much your friend and he did throw out some confused remarks about the possibility of a commissionership or even some civilian employment, conceivably to do with hydrography . . .'

A silence fell: a silence of voices. The steady heave of the sea carried on, barely perceptible unless one paid attention, and the countless sounds of masts, yards, rigging and the current round the rudder: but then an impact, curiously prolonged.

'That would be a whale, scraping his side,' observed Jack.

Stephen nodded, and went on. 'I then raised another point. As you know, I was in France; and there I met some of the men I had known in South America when we were concerned with Peruvian independence: but these gentlemen were from Valparaiso, in Chile. They are as ambitious of independence from Spain as were the Peruvians, and in my opinion they are more reliable; and the Chileans are much more concerned with the naval side of the matter than the Peruvians. Sir Joseph put all this to the proper authorities and in their guarded way they express themselves as willing to give unacknowledged, unofficial support and comfort to the movement.'

'You are very much in favour of independence,' said Jack. 'I have often noticed it.'

'You too might think more highly of the state, had you been dependent.'

'I am sure I should. I beg pardon. Please go on.'

'What I have to say now is very much up in the air, quite hypothetical. But there is a possibility that this war may come to an end quite soon. It is likely to be followed by a period of confusion, possibly a change of ministry, certainly a vast paying-off of ships and very widespread unemployment in the Navy.'

'Alas, it is but too true.'

'Now, suppose that during this period you were withdrawn from the list and from the competition, being employed in Chilean waters, ostensibly and no doubt actually surveying, distinguishing yourself in various ways, behaving much as you did aboard the *Surprise* not so long since, in a temporary, nominally retired condition, reinstatement being promised, together with the *probability* of a blue flag in due course – a rear-admiral's flag, how would that suit you? Sir Joseph and Lord Melville think that from the service point of view it could be arranged.'

'Lord, Stephen: it is a most prodigious attractive prospect.' He considered for some minutes. '. . . to be out of the hurly-burly for a while . . .' he muttered; and then, 'You did say Stranraer's influence was the strongest thing against me, and that if he died his influence would no longer be there – would not pass to Griffiths?' Stephen nodded. 'They say he is very poorly indeed. Is he likely to live, do you think?'

'Jesus, Mary and Joseph,' cried Stephen, starting up. 'Do you ask me to discuss a patient, sir? Be damned to your impertinence. You will be desiring me to give him a quietus next.'

'Oh pray do not be angry, Stephen – I did not mean to ask you as a medico – I only threw it out like that – talking in my sleep, as it were – sit down again, I beg – it was a most scrub-like thing to say even silently, and I do apologize without the least reserve. Yours is a beautiful idea: I like it of all things, and am infinitely obliged to you and Sir Joseph. Pray let me fill your glass.'

They sat reflecting; and when Jack had filled their glasses

yet again he said timidly, 'It would be the most beautiful idea in the world, but for that wretched *probability* – the *probability* of a flag.'

Chapter Nine

Christmas, and a dismal time they would have had of it too, but for a singularly fortunate encounter in the first dim light of December 24th, when the fo'c'sle lookout reported two fishing-boats directly to leeward.

Fishing in the bay was a dangerous pursuit, for quite apart from storms, rocks and tide-races, the French authorities punished contact with any ship of the blockading squadron very severely indeed, sometimes with death; and whenever there was even tolerable visibility watchers with telescopes kept the fishermen in view, while both setting out from port and return were registered. The two boats in question therefore did their best to get away; but they were horribly embarrassed by their catch – a vast net not only crammed with mackerel but also with the porpoises that had been pursuing them and that were now hopelessly entangled in fold upon fold of twisted mesh.

Happily the fishermen were on the *Bellona*'s seaward side: they could not have been seen from the shore even if the light had been far better. Harding quickly had the quarter-boat lowered, and in a brisk exchange bought net, mackerel and porpoises for two guineas. They were hoisted aboard with infinite good will and almost all the mackerel, as fresh as ever fish could be, were eaten for breakfast, while the porpoises, rather strangely jointed by the ship's butcher, were served out for Christmas dinner and declared better, far better, than roast pork.

They were, however, but the faintest, most wistful of memories a month or so later – a month still quite bare of store-ships, post or news, other than vague rumours of French reverses in Leipzig and of more convincing recoveries in other places far away – when according to their custom the *Bellona*'s captain and her surgeon met for breakfast.

'Good morning, Stephen,' said Jack. 'Have you been on deck?'

'I have not – a good morning to you, however – what little air came down from the hatches as I walked along was so very disagreeable that I chose rather to make my morning rounds before breakfast, close, fetid and nasty though it was down there, in spite of my ventilators.'

'And I am afraid it is but a fetid, nasty and goddam meagre breakfast that is waiting for you now, very far from the delights of Black's or even Woolcombe. Yet at least the coffee, though precious thin, is liquid and still reasonably hot. Allow me to pour you a cup.' Having done so, he went on, 'If you had not gone below, you would have seen a prodigious curious sky. With the glass rising and falling so often, I really do not know what to make of it: nor does the master. I wish Yann were still aboard. In these waters it is a joy to have a pilot who has fished the whole bay since he was a youngster. I may well be wrong, but I am fairly sure of that odd mixture of strong wind and fog that we met with – that we suffered from – off Patagonia.'

They spoke of Patagonia, that uncomfortable shore made glorious only by the presence of a gigantic sloth, a ground sloth, unseen it is true by literate man but certainly skinned by his earlier, illiterate cousins: Stephen possessed eighteen square inches of hide, and part of a knuckle-bone.

'I was called with the other idlers this morning,' said Jack, 'but unlike them, I lay for a while, and I reflected upon the extraordinary and I am afraid very ungrateful way I jibbed at the word *probability* when we were talking about your beautiful scheme some time ago. You may have forgotten it – I hope so – but I spoke as though I could conceivably have the *certainty* of a flag, a flag promised years ahead, which is great nonsense. Apart from anything else I still have a great many years to serve: there are quantities of people ahead of me on the list who must die or disgrace themselves before I can really hope for anything – and praying for a bloody war and a sickly season don't seem to answer nearly as quickly as one could wish. Nevertheless, it would make the probability much more probable it, as you so kindly put it, I were to distinguish myself in the meantime, and wipe out some of the uncivil reports that have been made about me. So, do you see, I quite withdraw any implied fling at the word *probability*: though on the other hand I do cling, cling with all my might, to reinstatement. You did use the word reinstatement, did you not?'

'I did. And as I recall it was quite unqualified.'

'There is no more beautiful word in the English language, which, I am told, is richer than the Hebrew, Chaldee or Greek. How I honour that dear Sir Joseph. What is it, Killick?'

Preserved Killick walked in with a look of surly triumph on his disagreeable shrewish face and said, jerking his head in Stephen's direction, 'Which I only wanted to ask his honour where this little green parcel was to go. In the dispensary? Down the head?'

'Jesus, M . . .' Stephen checked himself and went on, 'It had flown out of my head entirely, with the anxieties of the journey and the tumult of the waves. It is a Troy pound of Jackson's best mocha. He sells it by Troy weight as a precious substance, which indeed it is. Good Killick, honest Killick, pray grind it as fast as human power allows and make up a noble great pot.'

Killick had never been called honest before and he was not at all sure how he liked it now. He sidled out, with suspicious glances back into the cabin.

'Another point I reflected upon as I lay there this morning,' said Jack, 'was your notion that this war might be over quite soon. As for the political side of things I am sure you know much more than I do; but there is also the naval side, and all other things being equal it is weight of metal that decides a battle at sea. A twelve-pounder frigate cannot take on a ship of the line.'

'There have been exceptions,' said Stephen, smiling.

'Oh, surely not,' said Jack: then, catching the allusion (his fourteen-gun sloop *Sophie* had captured the thirty-two-gun frigate *Cacafuego*), he went on, 'Well, yes, there are exceptions, but broadly speaking it is true; and the French are now building ships at a great pace in Venice, along the Adriatic, where they have much more oak than we have now, and better, Genoa, Toulon, La Rochelle; and here in Brest there is immense activity as well as down the coast. I cannot state it as a fact that we are outnumbered, but I am very sure that we soon shall be.'

'My dear, you said *all other things being equal*: but surely it is generally admitted that they are *not* equal – that our seamanship is very much better than theirs?'

'On land it is generally admitted that we are the very pink of perfection and that heart-of-oak tars cannot put a foot wrong. But the Americans showed us that we were not quite infallible, and showed us in fair fight too. And as for the French, they have always built better ships than our people could do: our seventy-fours and most of our frigates are modelled on their lines – your own dear *Surprise* was built at Havre. We certainly were better seamen at the beginning of these wars, when their absurd revolutionary ideas practically wiped out their old seasoned officers. But although that Napoleon is, as you say, a mumping great villain, he has at least knocked all these pernicious democratic and republican notions on the head, and by now there is a new race of French sea-officers, certainly not to be under-estimated. The Admiralty don't under-estimate them, I can tell you. We have been reinforced to a remarkable extent . . .' Jack was called away at this point, and Stephen, having emptied the pot, made his way below, where an unhappy patient awaited his knife, already held down by leather-padded chains, already calmed, to a certain degree, by thirty drops of laudanum, his belly already washed and shaved, with his particular friend and tie-mate already standing by to comfort him. The operation was a suprapubic cystotomy and it was one that Stephen had often carried out, almost always with success: he approached this particular case with an unstudied calm that soothed the poor rigid sweating seaman more than the laudanum, more than his friend's 'All over very soon, mate – just a twinge or so and Bob's your uncle', cast his eye over the range of instruments that his assistant had laid out, took off his coat, reached for the alcohol, and said, 'Now, Bowden, I am going to pour spirits of wine over your belly to take away the pain: but at first you may feel a little stab. Do not fling away, or I may not be able to come to the trouble.'

'Carry on, sir, if you please,' said Bowden. 'I shall not sing out.'

His mate nevertheless tightened the chain a full link: and indeed the first incision drew a shuddering gasp from the patient. Shuddering gasps had no effect of any kind on the surgeons, however, and they worked steadily on, passing needles, passing forceps, until the last suture was looped, pulled firm, cut short, and the trembling but infinitely relieved patient dismissed to the sick-berth, carried by Graves, the senior loblolly-boy (once a horse knacker) and Butcher, then and now his assistant, and followed by Bowden's messmate, the paler of the two, but crammed with matter for conversation on the mess-deck.

'Pray, sir,' asked Macaulay, 'why do you use the spirits of wine? Have they a particular virtue?'

'The sudden chilling from evaporation has some slight effect: the knowledge that the surgeon wishes to avoid giving pain probably has more: but upon the whole I use it empirically, no more. Duranton, who taught me at the Hôtel Dieu, always used it, above all when he opened an abdomen; and he was a remarkably successful surgeon. So I do the same, perhaps out of a superstitious reverence for my master.'

'I shall certainly imitate you,' said Macaulay, 'cost what it may.'

Stephen wiped his hands, put on his coat, climbed the ladder and reached the quarterdeck. 'Good morning, sir,' said Harding. 'Have you come up for a breath of air?'

'I have, if you have any to spare.'

'Oh, I assure you there is enough for all hands – but

should you not like a tarpaulin jacket with a hood, at least? Mr Wetherby, jump down to my cabin and fetch the Doctor a grego: there is one hanging against the bulkhead.'

It came in time to protect Stephen from a stinging gust of rain, and Harding said, 'I am afraid this is really very disagreeable weather. I had hoped you would see our new reinforcements all spread out on the azure main. *Grampus* is somewhere over there' – nodding into the greyness on the starboard beam. 'She will certainly not be far off: Faithorne has her, and he don't know the bay, so naturally enough he keeps very close.' Naturally indeed, since the *Bellona* was on her usual southern patrol, heading for the Pointe du Raz and its horrible reef, rocks, tide-races, things abhorrent to a blue-water sailor.

'What is the *Grampus*?' asked Stephen.

'She is that unhappy thing a fifty-gun ship,' said Harding. 'A fourth rate, with fifty guns on two decks. She is incapable of fighting a seventy-four, a ship of the line, of course, and her two decks makes frigates run. Even if she does catch and take one, there is no glory in it, while if she is beat (as well she may be) by one of the heavy American or even French frigates, it is total disgrace. The wind is backing northerly,' he observed in passing. 'Then we have another seventy-four, the *Scipion*, taken in Strachan's action, and a couple of frigates, *Eurotas*, I am very sure – and *Penelope*, as pretty as her name. And sometimes the *Charlotte* looks in, to see how we are getting along, while never a week goes by without a cutter or two from the offshore squadron. We used to cheer them, sure of letters, news, slops, or at least something to eat: but no such thing – they only come for reports from the craft that have looked into Brest and for the usual returns: numbers in the sick-list, quantity of water remaining, powder, round-shot ... mind out, sir.' The making tide threw a freakish wave curling over the starboard hammock-nettings, knocking Stephen down and, in spite of the tarpaulin jacket, soaking him with a quite extraordinary thoroughness, so that water ran from every part of his person, every garment that covered him.

Harding picked him up and dabbed ineffectually with a handkerchief, apologizing as he did so. He seemed to feel that it was all his fault; and this opinion was shared, strongly shared, by the two elderly seamen to whom Stephen was delivered – Joe Plaice and Amos Dray, the Doctor's shipmates this many a year and now members of the afterguard, who propped him aft to the warm, dry cabin with many an indignant glance at their first lieutenant.

Killick changed and dried him – nothing more fatal than damp feet – and seeing that dinner would be up very soon, urged him (since he practically qualified as a patient) to eat very sparingly – only two glasses of wine and water – pudding could not be recommended: it was apt to weigh on the vital spirits.

Jack came in, as wet as Neptune, from the maintop, where he had been surveying the weather and all the bay that was visible, with keen attention. 'I do ask pardon for being so late,' he called from his sleeping-cabin, where he was towelling himself with great force. 'I shall not be a moment.' Nor was he. Clean, dry shirt and breeches had he found at once, but the only coat immediately at hand was that of the rear-admiral's uniform which he had necessarily worn in his last commission, a voyage to West Africa that he had made as a commodore commanding a squadron – a commodore of the first class, no less.

'This was the only dry coat I could lay my hands on without being later still,' he said, looking at the broad expanse of gold lace on the sleeve with some complacency. 'I quite like to wear it, now and then, though the Dear knows whether I shall ever appear in it publicly again.' Killick muttered something and set a blaze of silver down before him. 'This liquid is technically known as soup,' Jack went on, having taken off the cover. 'May I ladle you out a measure?'

'It is pleasant enough to see the remnants of peas so aged and worn that even the weevils scorned them and died at their side, so that now we have both predator and prey to nourish us: and what is pleasanter still, is to see the infamous brew spooned from that gleaming great tureen, the gift of the grateful West India merchants.'

'We tried to sell the whole service, you know; but happily the silversmiths turned up their noses. I am very glad of it now, because however poor you are – and nobody could be much poorer in reality than sailors in a ship without any stores – what crusts you may scrape together eat with more relish in handsome silver.'

Next came a truly villainous piece of salt beef that had travelled to the North American station and back in its time, growing steadily more horny and wooden as years went by. Jack ate it without concern – he had grown and thrived on worse – and as he ate he said, 'I was telling you about the French navy's seamanship at breakfast and I was on the very point of giving you a splendid example when I was interrupted. I did tell you that we had been reinforced, did I not?' Stephen bowed. 'Well, one of our new frigates is *Eurotas*, my splendid example in person. But I dare say you heard all about *Eurotas* in London?'

Stephen shook his head. 'I know the Eurotas only as a Spartan stream, and Sparta made no part of our conversation in London at any time.'

'Well, early in the year two frigates got out of Brest: they parted company somewhere about the Cape Verdes after a fairly successful cruise, and when she was homeward-bound, one of them, the *Clorinde*, which carried twenty-eight eighteen-pounders, two eight-pounders and fourteen twenty-four-pounder carronades, fell in with *Eurotas*, Captain John Phillimore, a thirty-eight-gun twenty-four-pounder frigate, a very powerful vessel, throwing a broadside of six hundred and one pounds as opposed to *Clorinde*'s four hundred and sixty-three: in size and number of crew they were about equal ... *Eurotas* saw *Clorinde* first at two o'clock in the afternoon in 47° 40'N, the wind south-west by south, the *Clorinde* close-hauled for home on the starboard tack. *Eurotas* at once bore up in chase, having no doubt of the *Clorinde*'s nationality: half an hour later the *Clorinde* bore up too, packing on sail. By four o'clock the wind had veered north-west, slackening; yet still the *Eurotas* gained. When the *Clorinde* was rather less than four miles ahead she suddenly shortened sail and made as though to cross *Eurota*'s hawse. This brought the two ships much closer, and at 4.45 *Eurotas* bore up' – Jack moved one of the two pieces of biscuit with which he was making the manoeuvre clear, 'and passed under *Clorinde*'s stern, firing her starboard broadside: but then, as she luffed up under the enemy's quarters, the Frenchman fired so fast and straight that by the time the *Eurotas* reached *Clorinde*'s larboard bow they brought her mizenmast down. It fell over her starboard quarter; and at much the same time *Clorinde*'s foretopmast carried away. This did not prevent her from shooting ahead, however, and she tried to cross *Eurotas*' bows and rake her fore and aft.' Stephen shook his head: he had seen the results of a full broadside tearing right down the whole length of a crowded ship. 'But, however, Phillimore clapped his helm hard a-port and luffed up, meaning to board her. Yet the wreckage of the mizen made that impossible and all he could do was to fire his larboard broadside into her stern. This brought them side by side again and they blazed away until 6.20, when the *Eurotas* had her mainmast shot away – can you imagine that, Stephen, a mast two foot three across? – but luckily it fell to starboard, her unengaged side, so the gunfire was not interrupted. Then the *Clorinde*'s mizenmast came down, while at 6.50, the ships still being in much the same posture, *Eurotas*' foremast fell over her starboard bow and a minute or so later *Clorinde* too lost her mainmast. *Eurotas*, mastless, was unmanageable: *Clorinde* almost so, though a little after 7, when she was on the *Eurotas*' larboard bow, she managed to set what was left of her foresail – for you remember she had lost only her fore *top* mast – and a forestaysail and moved away south-east, out of gunshot. Captain Phillimore had been wounded early in the fight – fainted three times from loss of blood – and now he went below. By 5 the next morning his people, under the first lieutenant, had sent up a spare maintopmast as a jury main: by 6.15 a foretopmast for a jury foremast, and a rough spar for the mizen. The *Clorinde* was now six miles ahead. By noon, with jury-courses, top-sails, staysails and spanker set, *Eurotas* was making six and a half knots and obviously gaining. Then of course, what heaved up? Why, *Dryad*, of course, a thirty-six-gun eighteen-pounder frigate you know quite well, and *Achates*, a sixteen-gun sloop. But that is not the point, nor how the prize-money, gun-money, head-money and the like was shared out: no, my point is that now, at present, a Frenchman, inferior in metal and in sailing qualities, is so well manned, and so well officered, that she can fight like ten bulldogs and reduce one of our heaviest and best frigates to a dismasted hulk. That is why it makes me uneasy to hear of them building at such a rate. In spite of poor *Eurotas*, I should still feel confident of engaging any French seventy-four we might have the good fortune to meet: but I should certainly not engage *two* of them; and that is what it may come to if we are outnumbered: while as for the soldiers . . .' He broke off, his head raised and intent, like a hound trying to catch an elusive scent. 'Did you hear anything?' he asked.

Both sat, silent, concentrated, trying to pierce through the countless voices of the ship and the sea. 'If it is not distant thunder, would it be gunfire, at all?' asked Stephen. Jack nodded, ran on deck, sent the second lieutenant down into the hold (a capital place for catching the tremor of a broadside a great way off) and listened himself from the master's day-cabin, together with Harding.

'Either *Ramillies* and *Aboukir* are engaging the St Matthews batteries or the French are coming out with this north-easter,' said Jack. The second lieutenant joined them. 'I believe it is a sea-fight, sir,' he said, panting with haste and emotion. 'I clearly heard broadside for broadside, never the irregular fire of a battery.'

'Thank you, Mr Somers,' said Jack, who was of the same opinion. 'Mr Harding, a lee-gun if you please; and when *Ringle* is within hail, tell Mr Reade to make the best of his way to *Ramillies* and say we shall be there as soon as possible. *Grampus* is to join us and observe our motions.'

Returning to the cabin he darted an accusing eye at the

coffee-pot. But Killick, during the few moments he could spare from eavesdropping near the master's day-cabin, had for his part observed the Doctor's motions – as unscrupulous as ever where coffee and certain sweetmeats were concerned – and another pot was already on its way.

'As I had hoped,' said Jack with great satisfaction, 'the French have taken advantage of this blessed north-east wind to attempt a sortie, and we . . .' He raised his voice very much indeed to carry above the bosun's, 'All hands, all hands, there' and the subsequent thunder of feet, emphatic orders, and the huge variety of sounds caused when a ship of the line, sailing large under courses and reefed topsails, is suddenly required to change course from almost due south to west-north-west and spread all the canvas she can bear. '. . . and we are pelting up to join *Ramillies* and *Aboukir*, who seem to be engaging them. It will take some time, since we have to bear up; but I have hopes that the wind will back westerly. Now, when I have finished this glorious cup and changed my good coat, I shall go and urge the ship on by force of mind. I shall also keep my fingers crossed,' he added privately.

He might indeed have indulged in even grosser forms of superstition; for this dreadful bay, thickly sown with rocks, isolated or in reefs, largely invisible through low cloud, sheets of rain and even downright fog, called for a mind that could retain some hundreds of bearings and shift the internal chart according to the ship's speed and directions, never forgetting the local current and the all-important ebb and flow of the tide. Fortunately Jack possessed this sort of mind, if not to perfection then at least to a high degree: furthermore, he had been up and down this great stretch of water, patrolling all of it and surveying much, for what seemed eternity; and above all he was on terms of good understanding – friendship might be the better word, with the *Bellona* and her people.

Reade in the tender had almost equal knowledge of the bay, since he had accompanied his captain on most of his movements and surveys, and since the *Ringle* could lie so much closer to the wind he was soon out of sight even when the murk parted; but the unhappy *Grampus* was perfectly new to Brest, and she kept so perilously close to the *Bellona*'s stern that Jack stationed a hand with a speaking-trumpet to warn her where he was about to tack, a fairly frequent exercise in these waters, though somewhat less so as the wind continued to veer westerly.

From time to time, Stephen, resuming the tarpaulin jacket, stood in out-of-the-way places on the leeward side of the quarterdeck: the ship might have been sailing, perhaps at a very great speed (with everything – sea, foam, squalls, fog – in furious, apparently random motion it was impossible to judge) through a nightmare lit only by battle-lanterns and through one of the noisier, unrecorded, circles of the Inferno: and it was both wonderful and comforting to see the wet, cheerful, unconcerned faces around him, perfectly willing to tally aft and belay or leap into the rigging and vanish upwards at a pipe or the word of command – competent, at home, eagerly expectant.

Space might scarcely exist, having lost all boundaries, but time was still with them, measured by bells; and at six bells in the middle watch Stephen made his way cautiously down and down (the size of this ship still surprised him) to the sick-berth, which, in comparison, was a gently lamplit haven of peace: so much so that his cystotomy and all the other patients and their attendants were fast asleep. He sat listening to the cystotomy's even breathing for a while, and then, noticing a change in the *Bellona*'s motion, he returned to the quarterdeck, feeling that in this wild rush through the obscurity his presence (though useless) was called for, by decency, if by nothing else.

'There you are, Stephen,' said Jack. 'We have just reached the western end of the Black Rocks and we are starting our run in for the Goulet. Do you hear them banging away? They are well to the east of St Matthews: right in the Goulet. Dear Lord, what a prodigious great deal of weather! Not a fit night out for man or beast, as the Centaur observed, ha, ha, ha!'

With this western tendency in the turning wind the *Bellona* now received it where she liked it best, and at four bells in the morning watch the midshipman in charge of the log reported, 'Nine knots and one fathom, sir, if you please.'

Killick came out, shielding a jug of coffee, and as Jack came aft to share it with Stephen he nodded towards a wicked swirl of white water a quarter of a mile on the starboard beam and said, 'That is the Basse Royale, a death-trap for a ship of our draught in a hollow sea, near the bottom of the ebb: and over there,' nodding to larboard, 'you would see the Basse Large, was you on the poop, which is worse by far but more obvious. Mr Whewell' – raising his voice – 'I believe we may shake out the reef in the foretopsail.'

The mingled cloud and fog lifted a little about this time, just before the first hint of day in the east, and its grey lower surface showed crimson with the stabbing gunfire ahead. 'Yes, they are right in the Goulet, by the Basse Beuzec,' said Jack. 'Happily the St Matthews battery cannot see a thing, perched up there: we shall have to pass right under their guns.'

'Sail on the starboard bow,' bawled a lookout, adding confidentially, 'Tender, I do believe.'

'The ship, ahoy,' called a voice from that direction. 'What ship is that?'

'*Bellona*, Mr Reade,' said Jack. 'Come aboard.' And directing his voice forward, 'Pass a line there.'

'Stand by to fend off,' cried Harding, careful for his paintwork.

'What is the position?' asked Jack as Reade came over the side.

'They are two French seventy-fours, sir,' said Reade, 'and they have battered *Aboukir* and *Ramillies* pretty badly. *Aboukir* is stuck on the near Basse Beuzec and the Frenchmen would have boarded her, but *Naiad* came up and kept peppering them, while *Ramillies* hit one of them very hard – there was an explosion amidships.'

'Very good. Just how does *Aboukir* lie?' Reade explained. 'Then cut back and do what you can to lay out a kedge

east-north-east. With any luck the tide should lift her in –'
He looked at his watch by the light of the binnacle – 'twenty
minutes. Master gunner,' he called, and after a short, largely
formal exchange with Mr Meares he said to his first lieutenant, 'Mr Harding, let us beat to quarters. Stephen,' he added
in an aside, smiling as he spoke, 'away below with you, out
of the falling damps.'

The *Bellona*'s surgeon and his assistants sat there in the
cockpit, listening intently: the midshipmen's sea-chests,
lashed together under the lantern, covered with tarpaulins,
then sailcloth and then a fine white sheet made fast all round,
stood in the middle: the instruments, shining clean and,
where an edge was called for, shaving-sharp, stood in their
accustomed order, saws to the larboard.

They listened, and even down here the rumbling grumble
of the French seventy-fours, the *Ramillies* and the *Naiad*
made the bottles tremble; while a little later the poor hard-hit
Aboukir, lifting to the tide, brought her broadside to bear
and returned the enemy fire with all the pent-up fury of a
ship that has been punished without being able to reply.

But their own battle, the *Bellona*'s rippling broadsides
they had heard so often during the great-gun exercise, did
not begin, and tense expectation was drooping even to the
point of discontent when, with a wholly different and immediate sharpness, her bow-chasers fired, followed by the
foremost guns of her starboard broadside, deep-voiced guns,
loud and clear, firing well-spaced, carefully-aimed deliberate
long shots.

'It has started,' cried Smith, who had seen no action; and
as if in reply a spent, harmless round-shot hit the *Bellona*'s
side. Smith gazed at his colleagues with a wild enthusiasm.

'What is it, Mr Wetherby?' asked Stephen, seeing the boy
come in.

'Captain's compliments, sir, if you please, and *Aboukir*'s
surgeon would be most grateful for a hand with his casualties. There is a cutter alongside, if you please to come with
me.'

'We are to expect no more action, I collect?' asked Stephen: he began filling a basket with instruments, bandages, pledgets, tourniquets, splints, laudanum.

'Not at present, sir, I am afraid. The Frenchmen are running for home.'

It would have been temerity carried to a criminal pitch if the Frenchmen had not done so, when they were confronted with a resuscitated *Aboukir*, a largely intact *Ramillies*, a thirty-eight-gun frigate, and now two perfectly fresh and untouched two-deckers, particularly as one of the French ships of the line had had seven ports beaten into one and several guns dismounted by the explosion. Yet it was disappointing. 'Call that an action?' asked Mr Meares, addressing his mates. 'I call it a fart in a blind alley. A genteel fart in a blind alley, is what I call it. And after all our hurry and preparation – all hands day and night, then cartridges filled without so much as a hot dinner, screens shipped, decks sanded and wetted and who for God's sake needed any more water on a God-damned day like this?'

'It was disappointing,' said Jack, as Stephen joined him for what had to pass for breakfast. 'But there was no help . . .'

'Come, sir, if you please,' said Killick, with a bucket of hot water, soap, towel, dressing-gown. He guided Stephen into the quarter-gallery, leaving him with the words, 'You know the Captain can't bear the sight of blood, and there you are soaked, fair soaked, from head to foot and what poor Grimble and I shall do to the floorcloth with all them nasty footprints, I don't know. Now take off everything, sir, shirt, drawers, stockings and all and throw them into that there bucket. I will keep your coffee hot: his honour will not mind waiting.'

Neither Captain Aubrey nor Dr Maturin was an outstandingly meek or patient man, yet such was Killick's total conviction, his moral superiority, that the one waited for his longed-for coffee without complaint and the other not only washed obediently but would have shown both hands, front and back, if required.

*　　*　　*

'Yes, it was disappointing,' said Jack. 'But there was no help for it. The Frenchmen were hopelessly outnumbered, so of course as soon as they made out our full force and as soon as *Aboukir* had lifted they spread all the sail they could – unhappily they lost no more than a mizen topmast between them in the action; and that don't signify, since now they have a leading wind.'

'They could not be pursued, with this same leading wind, I presume?'

'Certainly they could be pursued, and by steady fire, yawing now and then for a broadside, we might well knock away a few spars and even conceivably take them, right up in the Goulet, before they reach their friends in the inner bay. But how do you propose to bring them out with the wind in the west, the powerful tide against us too, and the fog lifting with the sun so that we are exposed to the batteries?'

They heard a boat alongside reply '*Ramillies*' to the sentinel's hail and Jack hurried on deck to receive Captain Fanshawe. 'Come and have a cup of coffee,' he said, and brought him into the cabin. 'You know Dr Maturin, I believe?'

'Of course, of course: long since. How do you do, sir? And so you have real coffee? We have been down to grains of barley, roasted and ground, these many weeks. How I should love a single draught of right Arabian mocha. Heavens, Jack, you were a welcome sight, you and poor old *Grampus*, heaving up out of the murk. I had a horrible feeling it was more Frenchmen coming to join their friends – a rendezvous – and we were in a wretched posture to receive them, with *Aboukir* hard and fast . . . but, however, now the tables are turned, ha, ha ha – What glorious coffee – Turned as pretty as you could wish.'

'Turned indeed: and the Doctor wants us to bring them out in triumph.'

'If we had some of those vessels that are said to sail against wind and tide, we might do so,' said Fanshawe, looking affectionately at Stephen. 'But as we are only simple ships of the line I believe we must return to our dreary blockade, sending word to the Admiral that *Aboukir* will probably have to go into Cawsand Bay.'

This they did, patching up the *Aboukir* as well as the assembled carpenters and sailmakers could manage, although eastwards they heard remote but quite unmistakable and heavy gunfire, borne on the still westerly breeze.

'No,' said Fanshawe, 'our orders are to patrol the bay, which implies preventing the enemy from coming out or getting in and above all from joining forces. If you like I will send *Naiad* and your tender to see if either of them can find the flag and ask for orders, but that is as far as I can go. Our clear duty, as I see it, is to go up and down this vile bay until we are told to stop.'

'You always was a pig-headed brute, Billy,' said Jack; but this was a totally unofficial aside (they were alone in the cabin) and it was taken as such: in point of fact Captain Aubrey and all the rest continued to go up and down that vile bay, blockading the port of Brest and growing steadily hungrier – up and down until a little before two bells in the afternoon watch of Friday, a brisk topsail breeze at south-west, the weather clear, a moderate southern swell, when the *Bellona*'s masthead and every other masthead belonging to the inshore squadron reported a sail four points on the larboard bow. As they were then heading for St Matthews, the sail was clearly from Ushant: and since she was travelling fast, with a favourable breeze, further details came down at quite short intervals. 'On deck, there: a three-decker, sir.' 'On deck, there: a brig and a ship in her wake – store-ship, I believe.' 'On deck there: the *Charlotte*, sir.'

Well before that awe-inspiring (but scarcely unexpected) name, the captains' servants began titivating their masters' best uniform against the almost inevitable signal *Captains repair aboard the flag* and the first lieutenants hurried about anxiously looking for imperfections that might bring discredit on the ship. Unhappily there was no time for blacking the yards, but at least everything that should be taut was tautened with tackles, Spanish burtons or just plain heaving staves, while the dirtier midshipmen were sent below to wash, while all were desired to brush their hair, change their shirts and put on gloves.

Aboard the *Bellona* every urgent measure had been taken and they were beginning the fine-work, such as whitening lanyards, when with real concern they saw the flagship round to and at once begin to lower down her barge. Captain Fanshawe was the senior captain present and his ship, the Admiral's natural victim, was seized with a renewed frenzy of zeal, her people hurrying about like ants in an overturned ant-hill: but they were mistaken. Very soon it became apparent that the barge was heading for *Bellona*, whose Royal Marine officers now conducted the most rapid and thorough-paced review of their 120-odd men in the history of the corps, finishing only when the barge, in answer to the wholly superfluous hail, replied 'Flag', and hooked on.

Lord Stranraer came nimbly up the side, followed by his flag-lieutenant and a much duller figure in a blue coat with no gold lace, the *Queen Charlotte*'s surgeon, Mr Sherman. The Admiral saluted the quarterdeck, and acknowledged the Marines' flashing presentation of arms and Jack's salute by touching his hat, and saying 'Captain Aubrey, I hope you and all the other captains of the inshore squadron, will dine with me this afternoon: but for the moment Mr Sherman and I should like to see Dr Maturin.'

'Certainly, my lord,' said Jack. 'If you choose to walk into the cabin, I will desire him to join you. In the meantime, may I offer you a glass of madeira?'

Jack, Harding and all those who had any pride in the ship's beauty and her seamanlike appearance had done virtually everything in human power to make it impossible for any candid eye, however severe, to find fault with her: they knew that the Admiral could not honestly say that her yards were not exactly squared, nor could he complain that the hens had flung their litter about the deck (a not unusual grievance when there was nothing else to blame) because no poultry whatsoever had survived the dearth. But they had never thought of Stephen. No one had washed, brushed or dusted

Dr Maturin, and he came up in more than his usual squalor, unshaved, fresh – if such a word can be used – from his greasy, malodorous task of dissecting the inedible parts of yet another porpoise.

None of this disturbed the Admiral, stickler though he was for precision in uniform. 'My dear Dr Maturin,' he cried, leaping, *leaping* from his chair and coming forward with outstretched hand. 'I could not miss this opportunity of coming across to express my sense of your – of your great goodness in prescribing for me. I knew it would answer, your physic, but I had no idea it would answer so prodigious well – I was in the maintop this morning, sir: I ran up to the top! I had hoped to be allowed to consult you, but Mr Sherman here assured me it would never do – would be quite impossible – that he had a lien upon me – and that no physical gentleman of your eminence would consent to examine one of *his* patients without he was there.'

'Sure, Mr Sherman was in the right of it entirely,' said Stephen. 'In the medical world we too have our conventions, perhaps as rigid as those of the service. Some of them are puzzling to patients who in the wild licentiousness of their imaginations supposed that they can wander from physician to surgeon to quacksalver and back again just as the whim bites; and some are, on occasion, thought offensive, such as our rule of using Latin when we discuss the sufferer's case in his presence. This has its advantages, such as extreme accuracy of definition and from the nature of the language an admirable concision. But if my colleague agrees, I should be perfectly happy if we were both to examine you.'

Bows all round, and Captain Aubrey withdrew. The examination was thorough and although Killick, on the other side of the door, was of a contrary opinion ('Once they start talking foreign, mate, it is all up: you can send for the sexton as soon as you like – here lieth Arthur Grimble, died of the marthambles, Brest bearing west by north ten leagues 1814') profoundly satisfactory. Stephen's only advice was extreme caution with the digitalis – dose to be steadily diminished – patient not to be told the name of the drug, still less allowed access to it. 'More men, particularly sailors, have died from self-administered doses than ever the enemy killed in action,' he observed; and turning to the Admiral, 'My lord, you are the most gratifying of patients. The anomalies that we noticed before have virtually disappeared, and if you will run up to the maintop every morning, half an hour after a *light* breakfast, and observe Mr Sherman's precepts, I see no reason why you should not rival Methusalem, and succeed officers as yet unborn as Admiral of the Fleet.'

'Ha, ha, ha! How well you speak, dear Doctor,' said the Admiral. 'I am infinitely obliged to you – to you both (a bow to Sherman) – for your advice and care.' He put on his clothes, and with a certain embarrassment asked Stephen to dine aboard the *Charlotte* with Aubrey and the other captains.

Lord Stranraer's dinner was as splendid, as far as the food was concerned, as anyone would expect from a flagship; but for the captains of the inshore squadron, deprived of almost everything for so long, it was far, far beyond even the most fervent expectations and they ate with a steady intensity of greed from the first course to the last. There was almost no conversation apart from 'Just another leg, if you please,' or 'Well, perhaps another couple of slices,' or 'May I trouble you for the bread-barge?'

The Captain of the Fleet, however, who sat next to Stephen at the foot of the table, entertained him in a low confidential voice to a very highly-detailed account of his digestive processes – his very complicated and prolonged digestive processes – and a catalogue of the substances he could not eat: on the subject his usually pale, phlegmatic face grew pink and assumed a look almost of enthusiasm. He was dealing with the effect of cardamon in all its varieties when he became aware of a silence all along the table and of the Admiral at its head, clearly poised to make an announcement.

'Gentlemen,' he said, 'before we drink the loyal toast, I think I should give you some news that may perhaps incline you to drink it with even greater fervour. But first, since contrary winds and foul weather have cut most of you off from the world for so long – not for nothing do we call certain parts of this station Siberia – I may be allowed to give you a short account of recent events on the Continent. It may well be imperfect: there are many land-borne officials who do not always understand the seaman's hunger for news. But in the main I think it accurate enough. I dare say you are all aware that Napoleon suffered a severe defeat before Leipzig some months ago, but that even so he beat the Germans and Austrians again and again – he was doing so even a week or two ago. But that was his undoing. His forces are all away in the north-east, his left flank is open and the Allies are marching upon an almost undefended Paris. Wellington, as you know, has taken Toulouse. He has now crossed the Adour and he is moving north at a great pace. At present there is some kind of a congress meeting at Châtillon; but since Napoleon was offered reasonable terms three times even after Leipzig and refused them all, he will gain nothing from this congress, now that he has no organized army at all. The ships that sailed from Brest and those we met with west of Ushant had intended to join by way of a final fling; but they never met; the gallant Captain Fanshawe here, and Beveridge offshore put an end to their capers.' Many hands beat discreetly on the table, many officers raised their glasses, bowing to Fanshawe and Beveridge; and the Admiral went on, 'It is usually considered unlucky to predict a fortunate outcome of anything whatsoever: but on this occasion I shall be so bold as to foretell a sensible end to this congress at Châtillon, the downfall of Napoleon, the end of this war, and our return to England, home and beauty. Gentleman, the King.'

Something of this speech reached the ships of the inshore squadron, but without much force. The end of the war had been foretold so very often, and as Killick (who stood behind Jack's chair) had found Lord Stranraer's manner of speaking difficult to follow, all that the lower deck gathered at first was that there was to be a new king of France called Châtillon, or something like that, probably related to Wellington. And in any case all public and private attention was taken up by the store-ship, crammed with food, drinks, slops, spars, cordage, sailcloth, everything they had been lacking for so long: and even more, there was an abundant post. In the dog watches very little of the ship's ordinary work was done, and once the precious stores were stowed, little groups formed round the more literate, and while his friends stood at a discreet distance, a man would listen while his letter was read out.

For once no cruel tidings reached the *Bellona*, which for a ship's company of more than six hundred men and boys, nearly all with close and mortal relatives, and a long absence of mail, was very far from common.

The mild domestic news from Woolcombe was charmingly uneventful, though Sophie's bantam had brought off a clutch of minute chicks. Diana and Clarissa were settling into their wing, furnishing the dining-room with walnut objects of the last age, which they found at auctions, sometimes travelling up to fifty miles for a handsome piece. And it was rumoured that Captain Griffiths meant to sell and move to London.

Yet in spite of this deep and abiding contentment Jack was low in his spirits. 'Do you think the Admiral's account was reasonably sound?' he asked.

'It certainly coincides with what I have heard,' said Stephen.

'A sad booby I must have looked, prating away to you about the French navy and my fear of a long war, with them building away at a great pace.'

'I thought it perfectly reasonable from a naval point of view; and you could not tell that on land Buonaparte had completely lost his wits: it was almost unbelievable how he threw away his chances, and countless lives, in these last few months.'

Jack shook his head; and after a while he said, 'I do not mean to say a single syllable against William Fanshawe, but upon my word I think the Admiral might have mentioned

Bellona. He will not do so in his dispatch, either. Yet our people worked like demons – all hands watch upon watch – to get her up there in time, and it would have been a bloody disaster if she had not arrived . . . From a purely selfish point of view, I am so glad you told me about your scheme for Chile. There is to be no distinction for me, this side of the ocean. I do not mean to top it the tragedy queen, Stephen, and I should not say this to anyone else, but I feel the yellow rising about my gills. Come in,' he cried.

Harding came in, bringing the sun with him. 'Forgive me for bursting upon you like this, sir, but I have had such a pleasing letter – my wife has just inherited a little estate in Dorset from a distant cousin: it lies between Plush and Folly. I am to be squire of Plush!'

'Give you joy with all my heart,' said Jack, shaking his hand. 'We shall be neighbours – my son is at school there, Mr Randall's school. How happy my wife and I will be. But I am afraid that I must warn you that Plush often leads to Folly.'

'Why, yes, sir . . .' began Harding, somewhat staggered: but then he caught the nature of Captain Aubrey's witticism (perhaps the best thing Jack had ever said) which depended on a knowledge of the fact that when grog was served out the ordinary members of each mess of seamen received slightly less than the regular measure: by ancient custom, the amount of grog left, which was called plush, belonged to the cook of the mess; and unless he had a good head for rum, this often led him to commit a foolish action.

Jack's gravity had not lasted quite as long as Harding's, and his whole-hearted mirth continued for some moments after Harding had recovered himself: but he received the wardroom's invitation with a decent complaisance.

'That is certainly the best thing I have ever heard, in the naval line,' said Harding, 'and I shall write it down – how Eleanor will roar. But my errand is really to beg for the honour of your company to dinner in the wardroom tomorrow. We have been shocking remiss these many, many weeks, but now that the store-ship has found out where we lie at last, we hope to make up at least some of our leeway.'

When he was speaking to Stephen about the Admiral Jack
had not made a good many of the unkind reflections that
had naturally occurred to him: he had not, to take a very
small example, said that Lord Stranraer's claret was meagre
in quantity and execrable in quality (his lordship had no taste
whatsoever for wine – never drank it for pleasure himself –
was convinced that others judged only by label and price
and that if they saw neither they would never know the
difference) because he had seen the Admiral's evident esteem
for Stephen and he did not know whether the liking might
be returned.

In any event, the wardroom's dinner to their Captain
could not possibly have led to such a reproach, uttered or
suppressed. Dr Maturin was of course a wardroom officer:
he usually looked after the wine, and for occasions such as
this, when the claret brought out by the store-ship in casks
had neither been bottled nor given a moment of rest after a
violent tossing about, he had provided a fine old very full
bodied Priorato.

It went down extremely well, but it was of course con-
siderably stronger than most Bordeaux, and the conversation
up and down the table was somewhat louder, more general
and less restrained than usual. The table itself was a fine
sight, with a dozen officers sitting there, mostly blue and
gold, with the Marines' scarlet coats setting them off pleasantly, and their servants standing behind their chairs: but
the general mood was one of anxious uncertainty, repressed
out of consideration for their guest, but evident enough for
one who had been so long at sea. He looked down the table,
considering the many faces he knew: and in a momentary
silence he heard a hand on deck call out 'Mark of the fore-
brace down, sir,' and the officer of the watch reply 'Belay,
oh.'

'Belay, oh,' said Jack to the table in general. 'From all I
see in the papers *Queen Charlotte* brought us, and from what
I heard aboard the flag, it seems to me that all of us will

have to belay very soon. Tie up, belay and pay off.' A pause while he finished his glass of wine. 'War of course is a bad thing,' he went on. 'But it is our way of life – has been these twenty years and more – and for most of us it is our only hope of a ship, let alone of promotion: and I well remember how my heart sank in the year two, the year of the peace of Amiens. But let me offer this reflection by way of comfort: in the year two my spirits were so low that if I could have afforded a piece of rope I should have hanged myself. Well, as everyone knows *that* peace did not last, and in the year four I was made post, jobbing captain of *Lively*, and a lively time we had of it too. I throw this out, because if one peace with an untrustworthy enemy can be broke, another peace with the same fellow can be broke too; and our country will certainly need defending, above all by sea. So' – filling his glass again – 'let us drink to the paying-off, and may it be a peaceful, orderly and cheerful occasion, followed by a short, I repeat very *short* run ashore.'

Chapter Ten

The paying-off was over and that was the best thing that could be said about it. Even before Napoleon's abdication the ships of the blockading squadron had been sent home in ones and twos, the *Bellona* being almost the last; and during all this time those of the crew who had been pressed from merchantmen had grown more and more discontented. Throughout the war, or rather wars, the merchant service had been short of hands and wages were correspondingly high; and now here were these ugly, unscrupulous dogs in *Grampus*, *Dryad* and *Achates* going into port to pick up the gold and silver before anyone else, although they had not been on the blockade half as long as the *Bellona*, had not had a quarter of the hard lying and short commons. There were also some who wanted to see their wives and children; but this did not have quite the same urgency, nor the same effect of intense frustration.

They told their divisional officers of it and the officers told the Captain; he acknowledged the hardship, but there was nothing, absolutely nothing, that he could do about it. His few attempts led to a most disagreeable rebuff or to total silence; and the last weeks were thoroughly uncomfortable aboard. For example, there was little inclination to bring decks to a very high pitch of cleanliness when it was known that they would soon be desecrated by dockyard maties in hob-nailed boots, stripping and unrigging the barky and laying her up in ordinary: this and a thousand other things led to short answers, ill-will, and sullen looks, though to no deliberate insolence or failure to obey orders – not even the first smell of mutiny. Apart from anything else, these 'awkward buggers' as they were technically known, scarcely amounted to a dozen messes out of fifty-odd, many of the rest of *Bellona*'s people being old man-of-war's men, some of them indeed Captain Aubrey's shipmates for many a commission, and they would not give the slightest countenance to capers of that kind, or anything like them.

Yet even so the awkward buggers made the last days unpleasant, and they prolonged the necessarily painful end: they included all the *Bellona*'s sea-lawyers, and when the Commissioner and his clerks came aboard, together with the ship's pay-books and some heavily-guarded sacks of money, they produced such a series of quibbles about dates of entry, first rating, dates of being turned over, deductions for slops, venereal medicines and the like that the process had to be carried over to the first hours of another morning.

'Even so, it ended happy,' said Stephen.

'I suppose so, if you call this happiness,' said Jack, turning his eyes from the dock where the *Bellona* lay waiting to go into ordinary, deserted and looking doubly so, since some facetious hands had loosened lifts and braces, causing her yards to hang all ahoo, like a sea-scarecrow – turning them to the left-hand side of the carriage, where a gang of local women had gathered to receive those Bellonas who were still capable of walking as they emerged from the doors of the Old Cock and Bull, where the prize-agent's clerk had met them.

'I do love a jolly sailor,' sang the women.

'Blithe and merry might he be . . .' A brewer's dray interrupted them and stopped the carriage, but when they had done with screaming and making gestures at the brewer's men, they sang on

> 'Sailors they get all the money,
> Soldiers they get none but brass.
> I do love a jolly sailor,
> Soldiers they may kiss my arse.
> Oh my little rolling sailor,
> Oh my little rolling he,

I do love a jolly sailor,
Soldiers may be damned for me.'

Most of the women might have looked tolerable by lamp-
light, though there were many old hacks fit only for darkness;
but the strong unforgiving sun on their raddled faces, dyed
hair, flimsy, tawdry and dirty clothes, was a melancholy
sight. Jack had taken leave of many old companions as they
left the ship, and just now he had given his officers a farewell
dinner, officers who did their best to disguise their extreme
anxiety about another ship: it was a superficially cheerful
occasion that left deep sadness behind it; and now Jack found
the whores' antics more depressing than he might have done
at another time. They drove on in silence.

Yet presently they were out of the town, into the country
and the spring, with rare white clouds sailing very slowly
across a pure blue sky on a breeze just strong enough to stir
the bright new leaves, and this had a soothing effect on
bosoms that had been blockading Brest through one of the
roughest winters ever known, particularly as the post-chaise,
at Stephen's request, had taken side-roads through charming
cultivated country – springing crops on either hand – a
stretch of country much favoured by migrants. Stephen
knew that Jack did not feel passionate about birds that did
not offer a legitimate shot, so he did not trouble him with
a rare warbler near Dartford, nor with a probable Montagu's
harrier, a cock bird, away on the right; but when they were
walking up and down outside the half-way inn while the
horses were being changed he said, 'While you were
attending to ship-affairs and the people's pay, the Commissioner's secretary gave me some letters that had come
down from London. They confirm my arrangements. Will
I tell you about then?'

'If you please.'

'I thought we should take a holiday for a couple of days
at Black's, doing nothing whatsoever apart from attending
the Royal Society on the second day. Then on the third you
will have to meet the Chileans, and I think that would be

better done in my room at the Grapes – we could hardly talk about such matters at Black's, and in any case it would be more discreet. On Saturday and Sunday we can take our ease again – we might listen to some music. And then, always providing that you and the Chileans do not dislike one another, we must go and be interviewed by the Committee; and if that goes well, to the Admiralty for the necessary formalities.'

'That will remove me from the List?'

'*Suspend* might be the better word. An essential step to allow you to command a hired ship: a private vessel with a private person as her master.'

'Well: I am glad it is not to be on a Friday.'

'Jack, it does not require great discernment to see that the idea of being removed from the List scarcely fills you with delight.'

'No. It don't.'

'My dear, if you have any reluctance at all, let us forget the scheme entirely.'

'No, no. Of course not. Forgive me, Stephen. I am foolishly hipped ... these last days, seeing the ship and her company falling to pieces, herself for the knacker's yard, all my mids thrown on the world, aghast, without a penny – no half-pay for them, you know – and with very, very little chance of a ship ... it makes one low and I am afraid damned ungratefully inclined to cling to having one's name on the List, any kind of List. But it is great nonsense – with half or even more of the Navy being laid up, and with Stranraer's dispatches and his influence against me I have not the faintest chance of a command. And without a command now I have scarcely the faintest chance of *not* being passed over when the time comes. To avoid that I should happily take a duck-punt to Spitzbergen, let alone dear *Surprise* round the Horn again. No, no, my dear Stephen. Please forgive me: it was only a weak, foolish burst of superstition ... lycanthropy might be a better word, perhaps.'

'Perhaps it would ... but tell me, Jack, you have not forgot the promise of reinstatement, have you?'

'Oh dear me, no. I cling to it day and night, like a bull in a china-shop. But promises are made of pie-crust, you know. First Lords can die and be replaced by wicked God-damned Whigs – oh, I beg pardon, brother – and by people belonging to another party, who know not Abraham: whereas one's name, printed in that beautiful List, is as solid as anything can be in this shifting world – here today, gone tomorrow.'

'That is one of the things I like about this place,' said Jack, the post-chaise having brought them to the open, welcoming door of Black's. 'There are no wild, *enthusiastic* changes here. Good evening, Joe.'

'Good evening, Captain Aubrey, sir,' said the porter. 'Good evening, Doctor. I have given you seventeen and eighteen: Killick took your bags up this afternoon.'

Jack nodded with pleasure, and waving towards the cheerful fire at the far end of the hall he cried, 'There. I will lay a guinea that fire was burning in just the same way when my grandfather used to arrive from Woolcombe; and I hope it will be burning when George walks in as a member.'

They hurried upstairs, put on the town clothes that Killick (always efficient in the abstract, and even kind) had laid out for them, and met again on the landing.

'I am going straight to the library to read the history of our missing weeks. Nay *months*, for all love,' said Stephen.

'So shall I,' said Jack. 'But perhaps a bite first would be a clever idea. Then one could sit reading one's *Morning Post* or *Naval Chronicle* without one's belly rumbling and distracting one's mind. I had almost no dinner, you understand – could not relish my victuals.'

'If men did not vanquish the brute within, there would be no learning,' said Stephen. 'Besides, it is too early for supper: you would only get the broken meats from dinner, faintly warmed. Come, James will bring you a sandwich, I dare say, and a can of beer.'

For some time they read silently, avidly; and with an extraordinary degree of self-command they started at about the equinoctial gales of last autumn which cut them off from anything like regular communication, so that only isolated, almost meaningless victories or defeats, almost all by land, came through the cloud of unknowing. But presently Jack, forging ahead in the concentrated sea-water of the *Naval Chronicle* rather than the turgid pages of *The Times*, which paid far too much attention to campaigns in Silesia and such places, as well as home politics, cried out, 'So they have given Boney Elba, the island of Elba: ain't you amazed? And he is gone aboard *Undaunted*, 38, young Tom Ussher's ship. Do you know him at all? He is an Irishman.'

'Sure, I know several Usshers: there were two or three at Trinity. They swarm in the eastern parts; and they have a family habit of being Archbishops of Armagh – Protestant archbishops, of course.'

'So I suppose they are important people?'

'At the Castle they are, without a doubt.'

'The Castle?'

'Dublin Castle, where the Lord-Lieutenant lives, when he is not elsewhere.'

'Tom never spoke of grand connections, but that would account for it. He was made post in the year eight, before he was thirty. Not that I mean to say anything whatsoever against him – we were shipmates once or twice, and although he was a gentle, quiet young fellow aboard – not one of your Hectors at all: no bawling out or quarrelling – he was the very devil in cutting-out expeditions, extraordinarily gallant and dashing. But there are other extraordinarily gallant young men – young men who have no interest – who are not made post before they are thirty. Indeed, who are not even made commanders, but die as mere lieutenants – even as elderly master's mates. Promotion in the Navy is a very rum go. Think of Admiral Pye.' He sighed, and with scarcely a pause went on, 'Do you think we could have supper now?'

'Just let me finish Talleyrand's infamous speech, and I am with you,' said Stephen.

The club was rather full – not only was this the beginning of the London season, but all those members who were sea-officers and free to move had hurried up to besiege the Admiralty and all their influential friends in the hope of one of the few commands available or at least of an appointment of some kind. They saw Sir Joseph Blaine, supping with a friend in his usual place: he rose to greet them, hoped they should see one another again on Thursday, and returned to his guest. They sat at the large round members' table, where Heneage Dundas had been waving his napkin since first they appeared.

'It is long since I had the pleasure of seeing you,' said Stephen's neighbour on the left. 'Are you in town for some time?'

'At the Academy of Ancient Music, so it was,' replied Stephen. 'No: for a few days only, I think.'

'Still, you will be here tomorrow and I trust disengaged? They are singing a great deal of Tallis.'

There indeed he was, with Jack, and they took a deep pleasure in the music, deriving a sense of inward peace that certainly did Jack Aubrey a great deal of good, wound up as he was by the complicated miseries of relinquishing his command at the worst possible moment, paying off, passing his accounts, doing what very little he could do for those at least morally dependent on him – two of his younger midshipmen were the sons of officers who had been killed as lieutenants, leaving their widows fifty pounds a year by way of pension, while others were almost as helpless: and then there were elderly seamen, not eligible for Greenwich, who had no one else to look to.

The next day and most of the day after they did nothing whatsoever but take their ease in the library, talk to their many acquaintances in the bar or the front morning-room, walk along Bond Street to try fiddles and bows at Hill's, or play, not very seriously, at billiards. Stephen delighted in the smooth progress of the balls, their exact lines and the satisfying angles that resulted from their contact – that is to say, when they made contact, which was rarely the case when he impelled them from any distance, he being far more a theoretical player than Jack, who frequently made breaks of twelve or more, taking the liveliest pleasure in the winning hazard. When he had brought off this stroke three times in succession he put down his cue and said, with infinite satisfaction, 'There: a man cannot ask much better. I shall rest my laurels on that. Come, Stephen, we must shift our clothes and hurry along.'

They hurried along to the tavern where many Fellows of the Royal Society gathered to dine before the formal proceedings at Somerset House, in what was generally called the Royal Philosophers' Club. Here they arrived with naval promptness shortly before the president, Sir Joseph Banks, who greeted them very kindly, gave them joy of the victory, and hoped that Dr Maturin would now at last have time for some serious botanizing, perhaps in Kamschatka, a very promising region, almost unknown – 'But I was forgetting,' he said. 'You are married now. So am I, you know: a very comfortable and blessed state,' and moved on to speak to other Fellows, now hurrying into the long low room by the score.

Before they sat down they both saw many friends: the Hydrographer to the Admiralty gave Jack a significant look, but said no more than 'I do hope you will soon give us another paper on nutation,' while the Surveyor to the Navy, Robert Seppings, the famous architect who had strengthened the *Bellona* with diagonal bracing and trussing, pushed through the press to ask Captain Aubrey how the ship had stood up to the huge seas and south-westerly gales off Brest. 'Admirably, sir, admirably, I thank you,' said Jack. 'Rarely more than six inches in the well, and as stiff as a man could wish.' 'I am delighted to hear it,' cried the Surveyor, and he went on to speak of his son Thomas, who was incorporating the same principles in the smaller ships and vessels that he was intending to build or repair in his new yard at Poole. '. . . full of hope, just married, eager to work double tides, and now this peace . . .' After a few more words on the same subject they were parted by the call to take their seats.

The Philosophers were not a particularly ascetic body of

men: few of them had ever allowed philosophy to spoil their appetites – their president weighed over fifteen stone – and they now set about their dinner with the earnestness it deserved.

'I do wish I could persuade you to drink some of this porter,' said Jack, holding up his tankard. 'It goes admirably well with roast beef.'

'If you will forgive me,' said Stephen, 'I believe I shall wait for the wine.'

He did not have to wait long. When the beef, admirably carved and gratefully eaten with horseradish, mustard, turnips, potatoes and cabbage, had all disappeared, the cloth was drawn and the wine appeared together with warden pie, treacle tart and every kind of cheese known in the three kingdoms. Stephen seized upon a variety as they trundled by, Stilton, Cheddar and Double Gloucester, a decanter of claret (probably a Latour, he thought) and some crusty bread: he drank to all those who called out 'A glass of wine with you, sir,' bowing to him, but he raised his glass only to Sir Joseph and once again to a new member, a mathematical duke from Scotland. He came away therefore perfectly steady on his feet, which was more than could be said for all the Fellows and their guests, particularly Jack Aubrey, who had kept steadily to port, never leaving a single acquaintance out of his toasts. However, it was quite a walk from the Mitre to Somerset House: virtually all the Fellows were reasonably philosophic by the time they got there, and the hard benches, and the arid nature of the paper read to them, dealing with the history of the integral calculus and a new approach to certain aspects of it, sobered them entirely.

Jack and Stephen walked back to St James's, passing by the Grapes: it was late, and both the bar and snug were full, so they went up to Stephen's room to make the arrangements for the Chileans' dinner tomorrow – fish, preferably John Dory from the nearby Billingsgate – and while they were about it the little girls burst in, wearing their night-gowns, to ask the Doctor how he did. They stopped dead on seeing the Captain too, and Stephen had to lead them in by hand to pay their faltering duty: Jack had been a very dreadful figure aboard, at least to those of Sarah's and Emily's age.

'Well, sir,' said Mrs Broad, when they had padded barefoot upstairs, back to bed, 'I never thought to have seen them so abashed. In the street or in the bar they will answer, and very sharp too, if anyone is at all what you might call jocular. But I warrant you, you will have the finest John Dorys in Billingsgate: they are the best market hands you can imagine, kind and civil and well-liked, but not to be put upon for a moment, no, not if it is ever so. But tell me, sir' – this to Stephen – 'do your foreign gentlemen speak English?'

'Sure, two of them are fairly fluent; and although the third can barely ask his way, the others can keep up a conversation.'

They could indeed, if the conversation were not too demanding; and when they were seated at a table in Stephen's private room they were particularly civil to Jack, whose sea-going reputation they knew well and whose words they followed with close attention; but their knowledge of the language did not enable them to discuss the fine points of the scheme (they were there in fact to assess Captain Aubrey's size and moral capacity) and this they left to García and Stephen, they begging Jack's pardon for their Spanish. All three guests were very well-bred men, somewhat dark but rather good-looking than otherwise; and although their complaisance slightly exceeded that usual in England, they had strong faces. They were clearly not men to be trifled with; and although they could not be induced to drink more than one glass of the excellent Meursault, nor eat more than a trifle of the good honest suet pudding, Jack found them pleasant company, and when they parted they shook hands in the friendliest way, García saying, with an earnest look, 'Very happy.'

'I hope you got along as well with your man as I did with my two,' he said, when the Chileans had been put into a hackney-coach. 'I found them very decent creatures.'

'Yes: García and I were in complete agreement – we had

discussed it in some detail long before, in Santiago, you know. We shall have to put something in writing for the sake of our masters but in essence it is what I outlined to you earlier on: you will survey and chart their coasts in *Surprise*, sailing early next year – there is to be a six months grace on either side and of course you are free at any time if England should go to war. You will help them to build up and train a small navy; and if the Peruvians, having declared their independence, attack Chile, you will defend the country. You will however be absolved from all duty towards them in the event of a war that involves England with any foreign power. Just exactly what your status will be with respect to the Admiralty I am not yet quite certain: we shall not know that until we have appeared before the Committee, but I am reasonably certain that you will be given indefinite leave in your present rank and that you will be lent to the Hydrographic Department. When your survey is complete or whether you consider your task is done, you may return, to be reinstated with no loss of seniority. You will perceive that this gives you an opportunity for service and distinction when all other captains, candidates for flag-rank, are sitting idly on shore or, at the most, drilling their ships in the peaceful inglorious Mediterranean.'

'Stephen,' said Jack, stopping in the street outside St James's Palace, 'I am infinitely obliged to you. I could not ask more – no, not half as much.' He walked on, almost under the wheels of a carriage and pair that swore most horribly, the whip crackled about his ears. 'But *Surprise* will certainly need strengthening for the Horn. How glad I am to know about Seppings' son. And oh how I hope the Committee and the Admiralty will look as though they love me, in spite of everything.'

'At the Committee you will have mostly friends or at least well-inclined neutrals: it is not a body in which Lord Stranraer has much influence if any at all. You might be well advised, on Monday, to dress very soberly and well, to say nothing unless you are directly addressed and then to keep your answers clear and short, *short*; and at all times to look both intelligent and attentive, but never cynical or amused.'

This was a Friday evening and they found Black's almost empty; after a trifling supper of Welsh rabbit and a distracted game of backgammon or two they went early to bed, Jack saying as they parted, 'If you are a tenth part as anxious as I am about the Committee and the Admiralty, I cannot tell how we shall pass Saturday and Sunday.'

They spent Saturday in fact at Greenwich, at the great naval hospital, calling on former shipmates, ancient or crippled or both, dining with the officers and returning to London with the tide for yet another concert; while on Sunday, Stephen having attended Mass with the little girls and Jack having walked down to the Queen's Chapel, they hired two mild old grey mares (sisters) and rode up to Hampstead, exploring the Heath and revisiting their old haunts.

On Monday morning Jack's anxiety cut his appetite, and he ate nothing but a piece of toast. 'I wonder at your insensibility,' he said, watching sausages, bacon, fried egg disappearing from Stephen's plate, the yolks being wiped up with bread.

'It is strength of mind rather than insensibility,' said Stephen. 'I am perfectly aware that this interview may make the essential difference between your being either blued or yellowed in the fullness of time; but I bear the trial with a manly fortitude.'

'I hesitate to correct so heroic a creature – such prodigious constancy of mind – but you will allow me to observe the "blued", in the sense of being made a flag-officer of the *blue* squadron, though plausible, is not used in the service. "Yellowed", I am sorry to say, is employed only too often.'

'I cannot recommend more than one cup of coffee,' said Stephen. 'Two, in a subject of a nervous temperament, may well bring about an untimely sense of urgency, a need that cannot be satisfied, or relieved, however imperative.'

They walked silently along Whitehall: Jack was not at ease in his civilian clothes; nor, indeed, in his mind.

'Listen, brother,' said Stephen, laying his hand on Jack's

sleeve as they turned the decisive corner. 'In this meeting, five of the members are my friends. They are benevolently inclined towards you, as I have said. Of the others none to my knowledge is in any way hostile; and all are aware of your reputation as a sailor. This is really not going to be a serried interrogation: the important people there already know all they need know; and this official meeting, like so many other official meetings, is very largely to endow what has already been decided with unanimous official approval.'

So it appeared. The discussion was directed by Sir Joseph Blaine and an intelligent man from the Foreign Office, and as the talk moved from one end of the table to the other, some members having to be told the same thing twice in slightly different forms, so Jack's mind relaxed. He continued to look as intelligent as was convenient, and attentive; but it was clear to him that the three or four men who really understood were in favour of the scheme and that although the Treasury dragged his feet, he would soon be drawn along with the current. The few questions Jack was asked by any but the Hydrographer (who was clearly on his side) could be answered very easily and clearly: this he did, but much of the confused talk between departments escaped him. He did not much regret the loss.

'And Captain Aubrey thoroughly understands the position?' asked the chairman, who did not seem to have total confidence in Jack's political sense by land.

'He does, sir,' said Sir Joseph. 'Dr Maturin has explained it all, at proper length.'

'Then in that case, gentlemen,' said the chairman, 'since we are all in agreement I believe we may terminate the session, leaving the rest to the Treasury, the Hydrographer, and the procurements officer. And for my part let me wish Captain Aubrey a calm, prosperous voyage and a happy return.'

The Admiralty, the next day, did not at first promise to be nearly so grave a trial, partly because the building was so very familiar and partly because Jack was in naval uniform in the most naval of all surroundings. He was to ask for Sir Joseph Blaine, and as soon as he uttered the name the porter's stony face, worn to inhumanity by perpetually denying the First Lord to the countless officers who wanted to see him, almost smiled and he said, 'Certainly, sir. Job, show the Captain into the farther waiting-room.'

Here Sir Joseph joined him directly – asked after the Doctor – congratulated Jack on the Committee's unanimous approval – and led him along unknown corridors to a particularly dismal, ill-lit, low-ceilinged office with an aged official sitting at a desk, his feet on a carpet eight feet by three, a mark of very great seniority. Even so, the aged official rose, waved them to dimly-seen chairs, and said, 'Sir Joseph, I believe that you will be pleased with me. I have all the necessary papers signed and in two instances sealed here on my desk. If Captain Aubrey will be so obliging as to draw his chair a little nearer, so that he can put his name to this acknowledgement of each item – but stay, Sir Joseph, would you have the great kindness to pass them, one by one, so that there can be no mistake in number or content? I will first snuff the candle: some are wrote very small. '

One by one Jack acknowledged their receipt; and one by one he put them into his bosom. After the last, which contained the formal condition 'I clearly understand that the suspension hereby granted is at once cancelled in the event of war between England and any other power', the ancient gentleman sanded the signatures, stood up, and said, 'There, Sir Joseph: as expeditious a piece of work as ever I have seen. Such comfort to an orderly mind.' With this he bowed.

'It was a wonderful display of exactly-regulated celerity,' said Sir Joseph.

'Very like a well-ordered broadside,' said Jack. 'I am deeply obliged to you, sir.'

The official gave a wintry smile, bowed again, and opened the door for them.

'Now I must take you to the Hydrographer's quarters,' said Blaine, leading Jack through still other corridors. 'Let us hope that Mr Dalhousie will be equally brisk.'

He was not, nor anything like it: but Mr Dalhousie had spent much of his life at sea – he was a marine animal – and Jack was very much at home with the surveyors and surveying. Theirs was a pleasant, friendly interview; yet even so, when Jack reached Whitehall, the broad and open street, he was still in something of a daze from that earlier series of orders, instructions, dockets and other papers that he had received and signed for, and by which he was now bound.

'I was perfectly amazed,' he told Stephen. 'I had expected pretty long discussions, explanations, directions and so on, probably with the Fourth Sea Lord and some other grandees, with a possibility of putting in some humble requests of my own: but nothing of the sort – I was packed up like a parcel, and here I am, changed in a little over five minutes from a person fairly high on the post-captains' list to a man removed from it, lent to the Hydrographic Department and told to proceed to Chile in the hired vessel *Surprise* within seven calendar months from the present day, there to survey the coast and islands, my proceedings being at all times subordinate to the requirements of the political adviser. My full pay however will continue until the end of this lunar month, after which only half can be claimed or expected. So here I am' – tapping his swollen bosom – 'as free as the air and strangely uneasy.'

'I too have had an almost equally disturbing experience. The person responsible for hiring vessels on behalf of His Majesty received me, instantly agreed to the sum I proposed, gave me a bill at ninety days for the first quarter's hire, and bade me good day. He even wished me a pleasant voyage.'

'There is an ale-house somewhere near Dunmow that I used to pass when I was shooting in those parts called The World Turned Upside Down,' said Jack. He stared out of the window; then, smiling as he turned he said, 'What do you say to being dogs for once and treating ourselves to a chaise all the way down to Woolcombe? I can see my prize-agent this afternoon, buy some presents for the family, pack

Killick off with our chests by the coach, and set out tomorrow after breakfast.'

Stephen considered for a moment, and returning the smile he said, 'With all my heart.'

When a sailor, a sailor of Jack Aubrey's kind, a man-of-war's man through and through, has sunk the land for a week or two he insensibly parts his ties with the shore (in its wider sense) and returns to his ordered, exactly regulated, deeply traditional seaman's life, the solid world being bounded by the ship's bows and stern, the liquid by the unbroken rim of the horizon; this, together with time measured out by bells, being the natural form of existence.

The same applies in reverse: the sailor, kept long enough at home, particularly in a county far from the sea, will in time revert to the ways and even the looks of the majority; and few people, seeing Captain Aubrey on his stout, stolid grey mare, riding back to Woolcombe, would have taken him for anything but an ordinary cheerful pink-faced country gentleman, like so many of his neighbours. And this was the more remarkable in that he had not really been cut off from the sea, but from the first week after coming home, had been much engaged with the *Surprise*, carrying her round with a scratch crew from Shelmerston to young Seppings' yard at Poole, and then going over on most Wednesdays to see how they were getting on – a practice interrupted only by his horse playing the fool and coming down with him on a slippery piece of road near Gromwell, a foolish caper that resulted in a broken collar-bone and the replacement of the sprightly gelding by the serious-minded grey mare.

It was rather his companion, Dr Maturin, that the indifferent observer might have taken for a seaman: this however would not have been caused by anything about him nor by his seat on a horse (in this case the prettiest little Arab filly imaginable) but by a disreputable old blue coat that could still just be recognized as part of a naval surgeon's uniform and that, according to its owner, still had a great deal of wear in it.

They reined in at the top of the hill and looked down at Woolcombe, the village, the house, the farms and outlying cottages, the great stretch of Simmon's unviolated Lea. 'Lord,' said Jack, 'how well I remember our coming home . . . all the women in the blue drawing-room, together with the parson's wife and Lady Butler, talking away twenty to the dozen and drinking tea. *Amazed* to see us – taken all aback – glad, in course: kind words and kisses: but George and Brigid were the only ones that did not seem out of countenance. I felt like an intruder. I had no idea women would get on so well together, just women alone: perhaps nunneries are like that.'

'Perhaps they are,' said Stephen, who had seen a good many. 'I hope so, indeed.'

'Then they all called out that it was peace now, huzzay, huzzay: we should be home for ever and the children would not grow up so rude and wild. Then there was the awkward business of saying, between cups of their vile tea, that no, not at all, we were off to Chile as soon as the barky could be patched up – what a hullaballoo!'

'I take great credit to myself for saying that we were engaged only for six months or perhaps a year; and that Government was being extraordinarily liberal.'

'That *was* pretty well, it is true. But the real turning-point came at supper, when *I* said they should all come, with the children, seeing us on our way as far as Madeira, admiring the island with us for a week or two and then going home in the packet. A cruise may not mean much to Diana or Clarissa, but Sophie has never been abroad at all and she is wild to go. So are the children.'

'They often ask me Portuguese words, and chant them by the hour. But, my dear, are you not being unjust to Sophie? She is as strongly opposed to your being yellowed as ever you are, and she very clearly sees that further service and the possibility – probability – of distinction are the very best insurance against it.'

'Yes, of course she does *now*, because day after day I have told her that however childish it may seem to her, hoisting my flag is the only thing that would make me happy – make me feel that my career had been a success. But I do believe that those brilliant words about the cruise were the beginning of the light – might also have been influenced by her.'

'They certainly did no harm.' Stephen might have added Sophie's conviction that a husband busy in the South Pacific could not be doing himself harm in the House of Commons; but that would have been to betray her confidence; and as they rode on he reflected that Diana's attitude, though less solicitous, was more comfortable. She was a soldier's daughter, and for her, martial engagements, the prospect of advancement and distinction, took precedence over every other consideration. On being told that Stephen was bound for the Horn, she reflected and said, 'I shall set some of the fishermen's wives to work at once, knitting you really thick under-shirts and drawers of *unbleached* wool.'

They rode into the courtyard, and George and Brigid came running out to meet them, both telling Stephen that there was a dead bat in the farther stable; they had covered it with hay; and please, *please* would he stuff it for them?

Jack walked in alone, Padeen taking care of the horses. Sophie was in the hall, looking pretty; they kissed, and she asked him how the ship was coming on. 'What they have done is very, very good,' said Jack, 'and when the ship is ready she will be as strong as a Greenland whaler, and as tight: perfect for the southern ice. But they have still not advanced beyond the midship riders – I will show you on the model – and now they are at a stand for some knees that were promised last month; while their foreman Essex has given his foot a shocking great gash with an adze. Poor young Seppings confounds himself in apologies and I am sure he does all he can; but when we shall sail, the dear Lord alone can tell. Next time, sweetheart, you must come with me, and see what female charm can do. Diana will drive us over, if you don't choose to ride.'

Yet the charm of even three women together – for Clarissa had come too – all dressed for the occasion, could not advance the work at a pace that would allow delivery before the end of the year; and since the Woolcombe estate was almost entirely made up of holdings let to tenant farmers, with only enough pasture for the horses and cows kept in hand, and since there was little fishing within reach and no shooting at this season, Jack was deprived of the usual country gentleman's pursuits; and he might have run melancholy mad had it not been for his duty as justice of the peace, the company of his wife, his friends, his children, a large inherited acquaintance, and his old love astronomy. Somewhat richer now (though not at all indecently) he caused a really efficient little observatory to be built and installed his telescopes.

The big, spreading old house lived at the steady pace it had been accustomed to for so many generations, a mild but continuous activity. Stephen, with the help of Padeen and old Harding's grandson Will, established a pretty exhaustive census of the nesting birds, particularly of the waders round the mere; Sophie, and often Diana, paid or received the necessary calls; while at all times Diana trained, exercised and took care of her Arabs; Clarissa taught George and Brigid Latin verbally, as well as French, and read enormously, disturbing the dust of ages; and always there were familiar faces at hand, in the house, in the stables, in the village and all over the countryside. And at home, if anyone should forget his duty, there was always Killick to tell him of it; while the very frequent disagreements between Bonden and Mnason on the boundaries between a coxswain's rights and those of a butler prevented domestic harmony from becoming monotonous or cloying.

Then – Jack still attending at Poole each week – after a kindly harvest, autumn came round, and Jack and Stephen shot a fair number of Woolcombe partridges, some pheasants almost certainly from Captain Griffiths' stock (the house was shut up and the keepers dismissed), wood-pigeons, rabbits, hares and the odd quail.

In November Mr Colvin's hounds met a large field at Woolcombe House, including Diana, Jack and Stephen; and from this time until the hard frosts came all three went out at least once a week, rarely having a blank day, and on occasion some glorious runs. And when the hard frosts did come they brought remarkable quantities of wigeon and pintail and even three great northern divers to glorify the mere. Yet all these delights – very intense for those whose taste lay that way and whose frames could stand the strain – never kept Jack long from Seppings' yard. Occasionally Stephen, *Surprise*'s nominal owner, went with him to be shown the progress, however slow; but once the divers were on the mere and an almost certain snowy owl, there was no tearing him from his carefully-constructed hides.

Yet one day a little after Christmas, the northern birds' innate sense having told them that they might now return to their dreary wastes and the snowy owl having proved a myth, Stephen rode out to meet his returning friend, finding him on the road he always took, just this side of Southam. This he did with the greater zeal as Jack had been away since Monday, seeing friends in Portsmouth who might help him to some copper, still in absurdly short supply.

'Well met,' he cried from a few yards off; and then, quite close, 'Why Jack, art sick? Art mad?'

'No,' said Jack. 'Only cold, and low in my spirits. I passed through Portsmouth, as I told you I should, and there on Common Hard, just by the Ship, I saw Lord Keith going down to his barge. I stood aside, of course, pulled off my hat and stood there, smiling like a simpleton. He looked right past me: no change of expression whatsoever. It was the coldest, cruellest cut – a man I so admired. By God, that shows how the wind is blowing: no wonder I look yellower still.'

'Was Lady Keith there?'

'Queenie? Yes: an even older friend. She was leaning on her woman's arm, all wrapped up in a fur pelisse and picking her way: though it is true she might have been watching her step, on that surface. I like to think so, anyhow: an even older friend – she almost brought me up, as I think I told you. I dared not call out.'

'The Admiral is for the Mediterranean, I believe?'

'Yes. In *Royal Sovereign*.

'What a load of responsibility – what details – things to remember! Lord Keith must be close on seventy.'

'Yes. I see what you mean and I hope you are right. However, let me tell you something more cheerful: Seppings finishes the hull – as pretty as cabinet-work – next week. And the copper is in hand, two thousand odd sheets of it and seventeen hundredweight of countersunk nails, together with ten reams of paper to go under the plates. He thinks he can promise delivery in the first or second week in February.'

'I am glad of that,' said Stephen, 'because I have heard from our Chilean friends. They will be in Funchal by the end of the month, or in the first days of March.'

'It can be very delightful in Madeira by March. I long to show the children oranges and lemons.'

'Custard apples.'

'Pineapples and bananas.'

'And Madeira has a wren of its own, which I have never seen; far less its eggs.'

'If we are to sail in the second week of February,' said Jack, 'I must go to Shelmerston again quite soon and recruit some of the best old Surprises. Even though we cannot offer them much in the way of prizes, with this American peace, I still think we can have our choice, so many ships having been paid off, and the merchantmen not wanting to take any more fresh hands until trade has revived.'

The second week in February took on an enormous importance. George and Brigid studied the calendar and neglected their lessons to such a degree that Clarissa, who very rarely used a harsh word where they were concerned, said that they were a couple of shatter-brained ninnies, only fit for the stable-bucket. All Sophie's and much of Diana's energy was taken up with preparations – clothes for the cool part of the voyage and for the warmth expected in Madeira, the proper regulations of the house and the poultry-yard in their absence, a thousand things without a name. Happily Sophie now had a housekeeper, an old acquaintance from the village called Mrs Flower; she was a widow, and before her marriage she had been in service, having started in the still-room at Woolcombe House itself, in Jack's mother's time; but even so, such a hurry of mind once the date of departure was set! And then such indescribable confusion, near-panic, when Captain Aubrey returned from Poole, said cheerfully, 'Well, there we are: Harding, Somers and Whewell would be very happy to come. The last coat of blacking on the yards is dry, the shrouds are rattled down, stores and water are aboard, we have a leading wind, with a steady glass; and we can go aboard tomorrow.'

They did not go aboard quite tomorrow, but very nearly; and it was a pale, nervously exhausted Sophie who sat nodding in the coach opposite Clarissa as they approached Poole. Indeed, she was positively asleep, with her mouth open, when they came in sight of the *Surprise*. George and Brigid were good, kind children, on the whole, and seeing that she had dropped off they kept quiet; but at the view of the *Surprise* Brigid put her hand gently on her knee and whispered, 'There she is.'

Sophie woke instantly and saw the little frigate whole, full on, newly painted, her yards exactly square, her sails furled in the bunt. She might have been waiting for the King (or now alas the Prince Regent) to come aboard with a covey of admirals, holding her breath as she did so; and of course her people had been watching for the fine green coach driven by a lady.

A splendid lady she was, too, and they would have received her, the Captain, the Doctor and his wife with all the restrained formality allowable in a private vessel – in effect a yacht, an ocean-going yacht. But Brigid, that intrepid sailor (she had crossed the Channel in the *Ringle*), burst free from all control and darted over the brow to greet and even embrace her former shipmates, ruining what modest ceremony they had proposed.

She delighted in small-craft, ships and the sea; she had picked up and retained an extraordinary number of sailor's words from her first voyage and her second, in an English

254

packet that brought her back from Valencia, and all these she explained to George in a high clear voice, hurrying him fore and aft.

'Welcome aboard, sir,' said Harding. 'What a lovely vessel. Is she as weatherly as she looks?'

'She will lie almost as close as the dear *Ringle* over there,' replied Jack, nodding towards the tender, laid up over the water. 'And she too despises leeway. I am sorry to have to leave the schooner.' Harding looked at him; but questioning one's superior officers was not encouraged in the Navy, not even in so marginally naval a vessel as this, with women and children all over the deck, and no Marines.

By way of acknowledging his first lieutenant's restraint Jack said, 'But the blue cutter has been coppered, and if we step her mast six inches forward I think she will do very well.'

With his fortune restored, Stephen had passed the word to give the ship all she could wish; and Jack, easier now with his most recent prize, had filled those gaps that only a seaman could perceive, adding among other things Manilla cordage, blocks of the very first quality, full suits of sails for all weathers, cut by an artist in excellent canvas.

Their leading wind was still with them and the glass beautifully steady as they cast off, took in fresh milk and vegetables, warped out into the harbour, spread their snowy wings and swept out on the ebbing tide.

'That's the main-brace,' cried Brigid, as they trimmed the sails for a perfect departure. 'No, booby – at the end of the yard.' She was hoarse with explanation and George, though he admitted her superiority, had been growing a little sullen; but now, as the *Surprise* met the heave and roll of the sea and her bow-wave built up and up, tearing down her side with the most exhilarating sound in the world, all his sweetness and candour returned and he swore he should go up to the masthead as soon as the hands were not so busy.

In fact his father, knowing that George was afflicted neither with giddiness nor seasickness, took him up shortly after; up, if not to the very head of the mast itself then at least to the topmast crosstrees, going by way of the maintop and placing his feet from below: from this height, the day being fine and clear, George could see for about fifteen miles, a vast expanse of glittering sea to larboard, with some shipping, and the English coast stretching away and away to starboard. 'If you look aft you will see the Wight,' said Jack, moving about with the ease of a spider – an enormous spider, truly, but benevolent. George's look of ecstasy touched his heart: and presently he said, 'Some people don't quite like being up here, just at first.'

'Oh sir,' cried George, 'I don't mind it: and if I may I shall go right up to the very top.'

'God love you,' said Jack laughing. 'You shall quite soon, but not until you are perfectly at home up to the crosstrees. There is St Alban's Head, and Lulworth beyond. We are making about eight knots and steering south-south-west, so about dinner-time you may see Alderney and perhaps the tip of Cape La Hague in France.'

George laughed with joy, and repeated, 'Cape La Hague, in France.'

When at last he could be prised off the crosstrees and so down through the maintop and by way of the ladder-like shrouds, he slid the last few feet to the deck by the topmast breast-backstay like his father. Dusting his hands he looked up at Jack with a glowing face and said, 'Oh sir, I shall be a sailor too. There is no better life.'

There was nothing in the rest of this not inconsiderable voyage to change his opinion. The almost unvarying topgallant breeze from the north-east carried them along at between seven and ten knots day after day, and although they handed topgallants by night and sometimes took a reef in the topsails, it often looked as though they should reach the island in a week. Yet once or twice the wind hauled forward and the children had the pleasure of watching the frigate beat up tack upon tack, which she did with wonderful ease and fluency, for not only was she as handy as a ship could well be, but her people were right seaman who had known her for years and years, often in very furious seas indeed.

Only once did the wind fail them entirely, and that was a barely disguised blessing, for all hands were able to watch a school of dolphins feeding eagerly upon a school of green-boned garfish, a school that dwindled as they watched. Then, George and his father having swum from the jolly-boat, they all gazed at a turtle, apparently asleep, just under the stern.

'It cannot be eaten. Oh, it cannot be eaten, sure,' said Brigid, looking very earnestly at Stephen: she loved the turtle, and she had heard of turtle soup.

'Never in life,' said Stephen. 'Never in life, my dear: he is a hawksbill.'

That evening hands sang and danced upon the forecastle until the watch was set, ending a day that might have been designed to steal a boy's heart away. George had been twice to the maintop crosstrees with Bonden; and the only thing wanting for perfection was a whale.

Yet an island stretching broad this side of the horizon next morning was a reasonable compensation for a whale: an island with tall mountains in the middle, tipped with snow, although down here it was shirt-sleeves weather, even at breakfast. On the larboard quarter there was another island, perhaps fifteen miles away, and on the bow some others, long rocky thin affairs that the hands told them were the Desertas. Yet though the name had its charm, they had eyes for nothing but Madeira itself, which came nearer and nearer, the coast, often sheer cliff, moved steadily from left to right. 'Oh how I wish Padeen was here,' said Brigid. 'He dearly loves a cliff.'

'Somebody has to guard the house, with all the men away,' said George. 'Padeen is strong enough to tear a lion in two. And someone had to take the coach home with the groom.'

The *Surprise* passed through a squadron of Portuguese men-of-war, those jellyfish with a kind of crest well above the surface, by which they are said to sail along, directing their course by the frightfully poisonous stinging tentacles that dangle a great way below. 'Was you to swim among those creatures, Master George,' said Joe Plaice, who had sailed with Jack all over the world, 'you would have died in screaming agony, being brought aboard maimed something horrible, though dead.' He laughed, and added, 'Worse nor sharks, seeing it lasts longer,' and laughed again at the reflection, which he repeated.

But this damped no spirits: Funchal harbour was opening, a bay full of shipping with a small fort on an island rock, and then the town sweeping up behind it, white-washed houses one above another to a great height, with palm-trees bursting green among them, then vineyards and fields of sugar-cane rising higher still, and mountains beyond them.

Stephen came and stood on the forecastle too – the women were busy packing below in their usual rather disappointing way – and with his glass he showed the children not only oranges and lemons, but also quantities of bananas among the sugar-canes, and the inhabitants of the island, dressed in the Madeiran manner, wonderfully strange and gratifying to an untravelled eye.

Over to starboard Jack and Harding gazed at the ships and vessels in the harbour. A fair number of merchantmen and many, many fishing-boats, but what really interested them were the British men-of-war. '*Pomone*, thirty-eight,' said Jack with absolute certainty, he having captured her in the Mauritius campaign. 'Wrangham has her now, I believe.'

'Yes, sir: I think so. And behind her *Dover*, thirty-two; but she is only a troop-ship at present. I am sure you have noticed the union flag over the little fort, sir?'

'Yes. And over the castle above the town. It seems that we are looking after the place for the Portuguese – left over from when we and they were both at war with Spain. Then beyond the brig there are two corvettes, *Rainbow* and *Ganymede*. We had better anchor just inshore of *Ganymede*: there is something of a sea running and she will shelter us. The ladies would not like being wetted. They would not object to a bosun's chair to reach the boat, either.'

*   *   *

They made no objection, but sat quietly in the stern-sheets of the launch with Jack and Stephen, the children wedged in where they would fit, forbidden to trail their hands in the water, talk, or play the goddam fool; and they made their way through the many boats plying to and fro between the strand and the ships, carrying water and stores in one direction and liberty-men from the naval vessels in the other, all looking pleased, all dressed in their shore-going rig.

When the launch was two or three cables' lengths from the landing-place Stephen murmured to Jack, 'Among the people there, I believe I see our Chilean friends.'

He was quite right. With a spurt the launch ran up the fine grinding shingle and the bow-men heaved her high. The Chileans handed the ladies out with infinite courtesy and told Stephen that the whole party were their guests: and they had provided a conveyance to take them to an English hotel. This was a curtained sledge for four, with broad wooden runners that slid, more or less, up the brisk, uneven slope, drawn by oxen. The children, though fairly well disciplined and biddable in ordinary life, absolutely refused to get in, but ran by the side or in circles round it.

The hotel might have been an English inn of the better sort in a country town, except for the wild burst of tropical plants in the courtyard; and here, while the women were unpacking, Jack, Harding and Stephen met several naval acquaintances. Stephen's was the surgeon of *Pomone*, who came over and asked him how he did; they talked for a long while, Jack and the Chileans having moved off to show Sophie, Clarissa and the children the wonders of Funchal. Stephen was fond of this Mr Glover, a most respectable, conscientious medical man; and when, with a certain hesitation, Glover asked, 'Would you think it improper if I were to speak of one of your patients?'

'I would not, in your case,' said Stephen.

'Well, now, I was aboard the *Queen Charlotte* a little while ago and Sherman asked me to look at the Admiral. I thought him in a *very* declining way. Sherman agreed: said you had prescribed digitalis . . . that he and the Admiral had noticed a marked improvement after two or three days: that the patient had increased the dose, and when Sherman protested had said you were a physician and therefore knew more than a mere surgeon. Indeed, he appears either to have confiscated the bottle or to have obtained the substance from another source – here poor Sherman's account was rather confused, though I should say that he at no time criticized your prescription – but at all events the unhappy Admiral must by now have absorbed great quantities. When I saw him and told him that there was grave and very dangerous excess, he was barely lucid.'

'Thank you, dear colleague,' said Stephen. 'I shall write to Lord Stranraer at once, this very hour itself, dissuading him in the strongest possible terms. And I shall send Sherman a note suggesting the tincture of laudanum, to allay the constant anxiety that accompanies such a condition: then shore-leave as soon as possible.'

'Or the grave,' said Glover in a low voice. 'Now will you come and look at my poor captain? He is a straightforward broken leg – tib and fib falling down a hatchway – in the dear nuns' hospital just up the way. It would comfort him, I am sure. And then I must admit it has been going on too long – will not knit. I should value your opinion.'

The Chileans were kind, hospitable, civilized creatures: they knew – it was obvious – that Captain Aubrey and Dr Maturin wished their families to see the island before the packet left for England in a fortnight's time, but they did want to get Jack away to South America as soon as ever they could and they conducted the visit at a speed that reduced even the children to an exhausted silence: two vineyards and an extensive plantation of sugar-cane one morning, the cathedral and the charnel house in the afternoon. The mountains, on mule-back, the next day, with a pause to see the curious buildings in which madeira was matured in a vast barrel at a temperature that would have been considered excessive in the calidarium of a Turkish bath. A mysterious further delight was promised for the next day, and the victims were discussing various schemes of escape as they sat on the hotel terrace, eating a splendid English breakfast and gazing out over the harbour when Jack saw a xebec with an extraordinary press of sail come tearing in, weave through the moored shipping and race up to the landing-place. A young naval lieutenant in formal uniform leapt out, ran up the strand and vanished in the narrow streets below.

'By God, that fellow was in a hurry,' said Jack, relaxing. 'I was sure he must foul a cable. My dear, pray be so good as to pour me another cup of coffee. I am quite exhausted.'

The coffee crossed the table, gratefully received, but not half of it was drunk before the young lieutenant appeared, gazed about, saw Jack, advanced, whipped off his hat, begged pardon for interrupting Captain Aubrey, but here was a letter from the Admiral.

'Thank you, Mr Adams,' said Jack, who had last seen him as a midshipman. 'Sit down and drink something long and cool while I read this in my room. Forgive me, my dears,' taking the letter and bowing all round.

The letter was from Lord Keith: it was dated *Royal Sovereign, at sea 28 February 1815* and it ran

My dear Aubrey,

Tom coxswain tells me that I walked straight past you on Common Hard the other day. I am heartily sorry for it, because it might have looked intentional – might have led to a misunderstanding.

However, a *particular friend* of yours and of Dr Maturin's at the Admiralty told me where to reach you, so I trust I can put that inadvertence and *some other things* right: for this is a moment when we have need of good officers.

Napoleon escaped from Elba the day before yesterday. You are to take all His Majesty's ships and vessels at present in Funchal under your command, hoisting your broad pennant in *Pomone*, and as soon as *Briseis* joins you will proceed without the loss of a moment to Gibraltar, there to block all exits from the Straits by any craft soever until further notice. And for so doing the enclosed order shall be your warrant.

   With our very best wishes to you and Mrs Aubrey,
   Most sincerely yours,
                              Keith

At the bottom a familiar hand had written Dearest Jack – I am *so* happy for you – love – Queenie.